I0561653

DAWN

OF THE

PACK

Dawn of the Pack

A NEW ADULT PARANORMAL ROMANCE

MIDNIGHT WOLVES OF SMOKY FALLS
BOOK THREE

LAUREL NIGHT

Chapter One

LILLIANA

~

"We can't make a move until we know exactly what's going on over in Montrose." Uncle Dom's voice is deep and decisive. "We have no idea why Nielsen suddenly decided to claim him, for starters."

Roxanne's tone is more measured. "I have a hunch it's Derrek suddenly coming into his abilities, and using them to help our alpha. That could mean he's in very real danger, and we should act sooner rather than later."

I've long since grown tired of this conversation, and instead my eyes have glazed over while I stare at the fire from my favorite seat in the library. I should be making all the decisions, calling all the shots; but I'm more than a little terrified of making the wrong choice, and incredibly distracted by my own thoughts.

Besides, I'm lacking my support system. Jared and Landon had to help one of their dads with... something. I didn't really pay attention to their exhaustive explanation, to be honest. Milo's in the house, but he went to change and fetch something from the kitchen.

"The alpha won't do anything to his only heir. Especially not one who can cast spells." Sarcasm heavily laces Dom's dismissive reply.

"You can't know that. He already has a witch. He doesn't need Derrek for his magic. In fact, he has a vested interest in making sure *we* don't have access to a similarly powerful person." Roxanne is beginning to sound exasperated. "Lily already told us Derrek didn't know who his father was, even being part of the pack for all those years. Is it so hard to believe that Nielsen didn't know, either?"

"So what?" He counters.

Milo slips into the room and hands me a steaming mug—a latte, from the scent of it—then sits beside me and nudges me with his elbow. "Sure you don't want to get in on this?" He thrusts his chin in their direction. "It sounds like they're trying to make plans without you, and you're supposed to be the one telling them what to do."

He's freshly cleaned up—his cedar scent sweet and mingling nicely with the steaming mug of coffee in his long fingers—and sporting a black button-down shirt rolled to the elbows with faded jeans. The warm, familiar vibration of physical contact with my fated washes over my skin.

His arrival jolts me out of my haze, and I turn to smile at him ruefully. "They haven't gotten anywhere in the last two hours, and I really don't feel up to arguing anymore." No need to explain how distraught I am that Derrek is being held captive; he already knows. Even if he didn't like him before, Milo appreciates Derrek is important to me, and the warlock's dramatic rescue last night tipped all of my fated to a more favorable opinion of their former rival.

I shift my weight away from the arm of the couch and press myself against his body, taking comfort in the solid warmth of him.

"You could always give them an alpha command to stop," he suggests with a very subtle note of teasing.

My belly contracts and pushes out a hint of a snort. "It's an entertaining idea, but I think it would be disrespectful to the former alpha, not to mention the beta who's literally taught me everything I know about being a wolf. Besides, their hearts are in the right place. They want all the same things I want. And it's a terrible leader who doesn't listen to the people around her."

Milo considers for a moment. "Weeeeell, you could just command them to take a break and go find another way to work out all that sexual tension," he lowers his voice suggestively.

This time, my snort is more of a giggle than a sarcastic dismissal. "This is hardly the time, Milo."

He shrugs. "Hey, I'm just saying, I think they have

some stuff to work out and maybe it'll take the edge off."

Roxanne's tone rises an octave. "You can't be afraid to make a move, Dom."

Milo and I exchange a glance; he raises an eyebrow and I pinch my lip between my teeth.

Dom's voice rises. "There's absolutely no excuse to go in half-cocked."

"I didn't say anything about half-cocked, but if we wait too long, it may never happen."

A steady gurgle of noise rumbles in Milo's chest, and his cheeks turn pink with the effort to hold in his laughter. I can appreciate the humor, but I'm hardly in the mood for dirty jokes.

Heaving a sigh, I push to my feet and feel Milo rise behind me in solidarity while I reenter the conversation. "We need to get Derrek, and soon. There's plenty of reasons that Nielsen might hurt him, and plenty of reasons we need him on our side, on our territory."

Dom waves a hand dismissively. "Your teenage impulses are getting the better of you. As someone who had decades of experience as alpha, you need to remember I have the perspective here."

Roxanne glances my way with worried eyes.

Fury bubbles up in my stomach, my skin heating all over with rage as my wolf tries and fails to claw her way out. "That's a bold statement from the man who disappeared the *second* I became alpha and left me to take over this curse at eighteen. The man who kept *all* of this," I wave my hand around, indicating far more than the lush library, "a secret from me for over a year. A year I could have been preparing, could have used to learn and maybe even tried to work on finding the cure. We haven't even addressed that deception — obviously you wanted to wait until I was trapped before you told me the truth.

"But now you're back and just think you're running the show again? Have you forgotten who I am?" Even though I'm not giving a command, the double-timbre of the alpha voice reverberates in my chest.

Now that it's unleashed, my anger swells to fill me from top to bottom. "I've listened to you two bicker for the last two hours about what you think *you* should do with *my* pack. Every time Roxanne speaks, you dismiss her as if she reports to you. She's my beta, and you have apparently failed to realize that you fall below her now.

"When I tried to inject a word into the conversation, it was like the two of you didn't even hear me. I thought I'd wait out your little argument and then we could start doing something actually useful, but I'm tired of it. You both need to sort out your issues so you can actually contribute something useful."

Roxanne and Dom exchange a glance, and my uncle lowers himself back to his seat with a red face.

"I'm sorry, Lily," Roxanne is the first to speak. "You're right, of course. We spent so many years making decisions together, I guess it was easy to fall into old ways."

"Apologies, Lilliana," Dom adds stiffly.

"Milo and I are going to get some lunch and leave

you guys to hash it out. When we come back, we'll refocus on Derrek."

Milo and I grab a quick lunch from the kitchen and retreat to my room. But even though I'm mentally exhausted and snuggled up next to him, I can't seem to sit still.

"What about this one?" Milo is clicking through my Netflix list, just pulling up shows I've earmarked to watch and trying to tempt me with some distraction.

"Sure, whatever you want to watch," I respond vaguely, my eyes gazing, unfocused, out the windows. It's a beautiful, bright fall afternoon. I imagine the air is crisp and the breeze sharp. A restless energy zips up and down my legs, despite Milo's calming presence.

"But what do *you* want to watch, Lily?" A gentle finger tips my chin up and toward Milo, whose intense eyes claim my own.

My head shakes back and forth, shoulders rising as I struggle to pull together a thought. Frustration builds within me, and I sigh heavily. "If I'm honest, I don't really want to watch tv." My gaze drifts back to the bright sunlight pouring in through the window. "I think I want to go for a walk." I know immediately that's the right choice, and my heart lightens just a smidge. Standing, I move toward my room to find some shoes.

"Okay, a walk sounds great," Milo replies, also rising.

I freeze in my tracks. I don't want to hurt his feelings, but I realize that I'm internally screaming for space, for a moment alone.

Turning slowly, I face him. "I'm sorry, would you mind staying back? I think I just want a little time to myself. I haven't really gotten time to process everything."

A muscle flexing in his jaw is Milo's only reaction, and it's a moment before he responds. "Are you sure that's wise? After so many people got on pack lands last night, we don't know who may have access to this property right now."

"It's alright, Dom showed me how to lock down the territory last night. For the time being, no one who is not pack can cross into town, even with the invitation of someone from the pack. They caught most of Jean-Yves' friends last night, and I kicked the others from the pack so they won't be able to reenter. It'll be fine."

He looks as if he wants to argue, but something, some tell on my face or in my expression, stops him.

I always thought Landon was the one who could read my emotions the most clearly, but perhaps I haven't given Milo enough credit.

"Okay, if that's what you want," he concedes with a small smile. "I'll touch base with Landon and Jared while you're out. Is there anything else you want me to do?"

I dive for his chest and hug him tightly, breathing in his comforting fragrance. "No, that's perfect," I murmur into his shirt. "I won't be long, promise. I just... need some air."

Warm arms wrap around my shoulders, and his lips press lightly to the top of my head. "I understand. Just please take your phone with you, just in case."

Stepping back with a grin, I hold the device up. "Never leave home without it!"

It only takes me a few minutes to get appropriately dressed for the weather and slip outside. The icy breeze is refreshing, biting at my cheeks and carrying a fragrance of fresh pine and burning leaves. My feet steer toward the path that leads back to the greenhouses, and my spirits lift immediately. I draw in a deep lungful of the chilly air, wrapping my scarf closer around my neck, and try to breathe out the stress one exhale at a time. Finally free of prying eyes and concerned gazes, the tears begin to trickle down my cheeks.

Walking gets my blood pumping and shakes out the stiff feeling of being cooped up and frustrated, but it doesn't entirely solve my problem.

Derrek. The pain I've felt since Nielsen took him away has changed from a sharp, stabbing sensation to a deep throbbing wound in my heart that feels as though it keeps bleeding. I've ignored it for a few moments at a time, only to be surprised by a searing pang shortly thereafter. It's been all but impossible to focus on making plans when I'm actively working to suppress the agony of my mate being ripped from my fingers.

I haven't told anyone what he truly means to me. How would I even begin to explain that this man, who is half warlock and half wolf from our enemy pack, is apparently my fated mate? For generations of Harridan alphas, there have been three fated mates from the same families. Ever since the split. And the biases of these people—*my* people—run so deeply, I don't even know if they'd accept it coming from me, the alpha.

Not to mention my other three fated. They grew up together, practically brothers, for their entire lives. And they've never liked Derrek. Their inherent mistrust was seemingly vindicated when he turned out to be part of the Montrose pack. His rescue last night earned him grudging acceptance, but something told me they were a long way from calling him brother.

A guilty feeling temporarily replaces the ache in my chest. At least I understand now why I was so impossibly attracted to Derrek despite having my three fated. It's hard to wrap my head around why I didn't recognize it for what it was; there could be many reasons to explain why my connection to him had felt so different from the others. Probably a whole ton of mystical wolf crap I will never understand. But my mind churns over what Mr. Carson told me, and everything I learned from Roxanne.

Prior to the split, the Harridan alphas would take several mates from the existing eight key families, as many as they felt the connection to. It was only after the split that it was just three mates, because the bulk of the other four families splintered off. There has to be some connection with them still; this group of families had been together for centuries as a pack.

And since they never interacted again after my great great aunt—or was it three greats?—died because of the curse, there was no way of knowing if the subsequent alphas would have claimed anyone from Montrose as a mate.

So it's not surprising this has never come up before, but I'm still uncertain about what to do with it, or what it means.

My feet follow the path to the midnight gathering place, seemingly of their own volition, while my brain works over thornier problems.

I'm fairly certain that if Dom and Roxanne knew Derrek is my fated mate, there would be much less deliberation and much more action in the rescue mission. But I'm not ready to tell the rest of my fated, and I'm uncertain how the pack would react if they found out. As annoying as it is, Dom's insistence on caution makes sense. Even though my heart is bleeding for him and my wolf would like nothing more than to tear out a few throats to get him back, I know I can't put my pack at risk without first considering all the information carefully.

I have no way to be certain, but it sure feels like the Montrose alpha knew what he was doing when he ripped Derrek from my hands. I don't know what exactly is tipping me off, but I can't shake the feeling that lingered when he left: a deep, malignant hatred, the intent to injure so intensely that it goes well beyond simply acknowledging his own child.

Something is telling me knew it would hurt me, and he did it expressly for that purpose.

But the question remains: How did he know before I even knew myself?

It's like every answer I get in Smoky Falls just leads to five more questions. A heavy feeling of despair wars with my innate need to keep moving forward for the protection of the pack. Now that I've connected with it, it's become second nature to tap into the energy of the people across my pack territory. Scanning their collective emotional color map for problems is almost a calming activity for me now, reassuring me that my people are mostly safe, content, and happy.

If only I felt the same way.

I don't know how long I can keep the truth of what Derrek means to me from my family, and particularly Milo, Jared, and Landon. It seems impossible to feel content and relaxed in their presence now, knowing that I'm still not *whole*. Never mind that now the tables have turned and I'm the one keeping secrets from all of them.

I finally reach the clearing, and march straight to the center where a pile of browning leaves is bathed in sunlight. I sit with crossed legs and release another deep sigh, letting the warm glow heat my cheeks.

Despite knowing how they've wronged me, I can almost sympathize with Peter Jean-Yves and my mother's other rejected mate. This feeling could almost drive me mad, if I let it. And I didn't grow up knowing Derrek was meant to be my mate, then face the aftermath of him leaving by choice. At least in my case, he had no say in the matter.

If my situation were different, I could imagine the bitterness settling in; hardening like a shell around the hurt, trying to protect me from this deep wound so I might find a way to keep on living.

Would I grow to resent the rejection so much I projected that hatred onto his offspring? There's no way of knowing. My eyes continue to leak, and I've done nothing to wipe the tracks from my face as they make their way down to my chin and soak into my scarf.

I'll sit here as long as it takes for the pressure to dissipate and my eyes to dry. Then I'll head back into the house and start again on finding a solution to this mess.

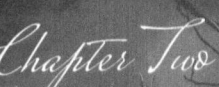

Chapter Two

DERREK

"So, this is what a freak in a cage looks like. I always wondered what it was like to go to one of those traveling shows. You know what I'm talking about? The dog-faced boy, the bearded lady?" Azalea drawls from the exterior of my magically fortified prison.

I ignore her attempts to goad me. I may be locked up, but at least I have some freedom—namely to pretend she doesn't exist. It beats my previous circumstances, when I lay on the cold cement floor for hours last night, hog-tied with my mouth taped shut, while she worked the spell. I don't honestly know how long it was. I dozed off at some point.

It's maddening to know that I finally tapped into my power and could do nothing to stop her. By preventing me from using my hands or my voice, a simple roll of duct tape effectively cut off my magic. I hadn't yet learned to work spells without them, and even if I could, there were limits on that kind of power.

So, even though I now find myself stuck in a ten-by-ten cell with nothing but four walls, a drain, and an empty bucket, I'm not tied up; it's an improvement on my position from before. I have my back to the corner, arms crossed, while I wait for whatever comes next.

As soon as they pushed me through the opening in the bars and Azalea finished the spell, I tried to test my strength against hers. Turns out she's really been doing her homework. When I recovered from the breathtaking agony of the invisible shield, she treated me to a one-hour lecture on how to combine a variety of spells in order to create such an impenetrable prison.

Truly fascinating.

However, it did nothing to help my situation. Now I have no recourse but to listen to her ramble on and on like a cartoon villain explaining how she got the better of me. After she tired of throwing her advanced magical skill in my face, she switched to school-yard insults, and that's where we've been for quite a while. I continue to stare blankly ahead, watching her through my peripheral vision just in case she tries something; as she already explained, just because nothing can go *out* of my cell doesn't mean something can't go *in*. And I wouldn't put anything past her at this point.

"I mean, I've just never heard of a *hybrid* before. Didn't they used to kill them? I'll have to ask Granny if she remembers. I suppose it's not something that comes up often, is it?" She lounges casually on the seat she had the wolves drag in for her. It's a wheeled office chair, padded, the type that has a hydraulic handle on the base to go up and down. She eventually tired of playing with it and has draped herself across the armrests like the queen of Sheeba.

My eyes track the silver knife that hasn't left her hands since I arrived. It's not the same one I had; obviously, since that one is locked up somewhere in Smoky Falls territory. But it's similar, with a wickedly curved blade featuring runes etched into the metal on both sides.

Currently, Azalea is using it to clean her fingernails, her leather-clad legs swinging off the armrest like a bored five-year-old while she babbles on. "Or maybe you never hear of them because they're like mules. You know what I mean, right? Since mules are a cross between a donkey and a horse, they're sterile, so they can't breed. So maybe there have been some in the past, but they were considered freaks of nature, and since they couldn't reproduce anyway, people just didn't talk about them." She says it all conversationally, but I know she's trying to get under my skin.

Finding out that my actual father was none other than the Montrose alpha was definitely a shock to me. I'd heard the rumors that my dad was a wolf, of course. But my mom never confirmed it. She just told me he wasn't a good man, and she wanted nothing to do with him.

So she gave me her own last name and left the father's name on my birth certificate blank.

Nielsen has yet to even speak to me. He tied me up and dragged me from Smoky Falls, then stuck me in the back of a truck with a handful of his minions. Apparently he isn't entirely sure about how resistant I might be to the alpha command, given my half-breed status, so the gag made sure I wasn't a threat either way.

I haven't seen him since.

I'm not sure if Azalea is here keeping an eye on me or just reveling in her victory, to be honest. I can hear people in the hallway just outside the door, which separates me, Azalea, and a second cell from the rest of the world. That one also has steel bars, but I'm fairly certain mine is the only one that's spelled.

Azalea yawns, stretching leisurely, then makes a show of checking her watch. "I'm bored to tears, cousin. Why don't you regale me with your stories of life as a runaway teen on the streets of LA?"

Despite having my eyes trained stonily ahead, I can see the exaggerated smirk on her face. Even if I couldn't see it, it's audible in her tone.

"I just find it fascinating that you pretended to be a teenager for *years*, just to hook up with a *Harridan*. First, like, don't you have any shame? And, not that I'd judge family, but it's kind of gross, isn't it? A grown man trying to get with a little girl?"

I grind my teeth together and resist the bait, but it's getting more difficult. Instead, I focus harder on tuning her out.

Implying I had anything but a familial attachment to Lilliana when she was a kid is disgusting. Yes, I became more attracted to her as she grew closer to adulthood, and I may have had a few racy thoughts on certain occasions when I felt—*something*—between us those last few months, but I never acted on it.

It wasn't until I arrived in Smoky Falls that my hormones went into overdrive. The second I laid eyes on her, it was like I'd found a new drug and I was constantly chasing the high. Just being around her made my skin tingle like it was crawling with electricity. I've never felt even a tenth of that kind of chemistry with another woman.

Granted, I had my fun in college, right until I gave up everything to live on the streets so I could protect her. Then it was like my sexuality went dormant, waiting until a few weeks ago.

And even then I knew it was stupid; I know very well how the packs work, and that she already has her three fated mates. I am keenly, *painfully* aware of that.

But there has to be something drawing us together, too. Otherwise, she never would have kissed me.

Kissed me back, I amend mentally. I pressed her up against the door and practically forced myself on her.

My stomach turns at the thought, but then a quick flash of memory drops a warm stone in my gut that calms it.

I may have initiated it, but there's no doubt in my mind it's what she wanted. She attacked me right back, wrapping her legs around me and thrusting her hands into my clothes. The memory is all too easy to relive, and I allow my mind to run over each delicious second until it occurs to me this is neither the time nor place.

I have to pivot from this train of thought; the last thing I need right now is to get myself all worked up and then be pitching a tent when they come to get me from my cell.

This new, apparently evil Azalea would find that highly amusing. She's certainly not the girl I remember from before I left. That Azalea was a sullen teenager who just wanted to live as if she was human, and pretend this entire world of magic and wolves didn't exist. She was even more of a disappointment to the family than I was, and that's saying something. Of course, it turns out I had the abilities after all, but I doubt her mom blocked her magic for her own good like mine did. If I remember correctly, she treated Azalea pretty harshly for being a dud.

Since I don't actually know much about what happened after I left, I decide to change the focus of this conversation. She's still rambling on about my apparent attraction to little girls, so I clear my throat and glance in her direction. Azalea pauses gleefully, assuming she's drawn a reaction from me.

"Hey Azalea," I begin casually, pulling one knee to my chest and draping an arm over it. "Where's your mom, anyway? I haven't seen Aunt Hyacinth in ages."

Azalea laughs scornfully. "That witch? She's long dead. Finally got what was coming to her."

"And I suppose you had something to do with that."

She snorts scornfully. "Of course I did. She never did anything except berate and deride me for my entire life. Wasn't my fault I was born unable to connect to the earth's magic. If anything, I'd say it was hers."

"So what happened, exactly?" I lean in and make my tone curious, hoping she'll be pleased to brag about how clever she is.

And she takes the bait. "Well, since you asked…" Azalea sits up in her seat and does a full spin before wheeling herself closer to my cell. "After you left, everything with my mom got way worse. She kept saying it was my opportunity to seize control while you were gone, claim our birthright. She tried to force me to call on the magic, kept saying I was just 'blocked' and needed proper motivation."

An uneasy feeling swirls in my stomach. "She was always awful to you," I comment in a low voice. It doesn't really cover the physical and psychological abuse I know Azalea received, but I'm not sure if that's the best subject to touch on, either.

A brief twitch of surprise crosses her face, but she recovers quickly and replies with a sneer. "Yeah, well, she only acted that way because your mom got all the glory and she was basically shunned. Even though she was just as talented, my mom never got a chance to shine when she was relegated to the role of pack seer."

That's not exactly true, but I have a hunch that right now is not the time to argue with my cousin.

Instead, I keep pressing. "So what happened?"

Azalea sighs dramatically and continues. "I started

hiding out at Granny's even more, and I think she pitied me for my lack of natural ability, so she let me have the run of the place. I knew there had to be something she'd squirreled away that would help me—the woman is practically a hoarder—so I just kept digging until I found something."

"What was it?"

"A spell. You know, at first it was completely useless. There was no way I could pull it off, since I couldn't even work simple spells. So I put the book away and pushed the thought to the back of my mind. I was honestly considering pulling a Harridan and running away. And then you sent the knife back."

The uneasy feeling in my stomach turns into a decidedly sick one. "What does the knife have to do with anything?"

Azalea grins like the Cheshire Cat, the expression enhanced by her electrically pink and purple hair. I'm fairly certain it was still blonde last night, so she must have gotten bored at some point and changed it with magic. "Well, the first thing that happened was the pack kicked your mom out completely."

I force myself to remain neutral; the way she says it so gleefully turns my sick stomach to stone. My mom was run out of town with nothing, completely cut off from everyone and everything she knew. "And?"

"After that, my mom finally showed them what she could do, and let me tell you, they were impressed."

"I don't see what this has to do with the knife."

"I'm getting to it, patience little Leaf. Anyway, after

that my mom put even more pressure on me. She promised the alpha she'd send me to complete the job you shirked on, and she was determined to make me into the witch she expected. If I'd had any doubts about my plan before that, they were long gone at that point. So I told her I wanted to do a dry run, and I needed the knife to practice." Azalea snorts derisively. "She was so desperate to see any improvement, she fell for it. She thought I was going to do a moon sacrifice, which I guess I did in a way. But she didn't realize *she'd* be the sacrifice."

"So why-"

"The spell required the *knife*. It had to be a runed blade with certain properties, one of which was being imbued with the power of thirteen witches."

This was the first I'd heard of the knife having such powers. "I thought it was an ordinary ritual knife. How did it have the power of so many witches?"

"You really need to do some reading, Leaf. When a blade is used by a witch to perform a ritual, the blade becomes an extension of that witch. Therefore, a trace amount of her magic remains *in* the knife. That one had been handed down in our family for so many generations there were probably far more than a dozen."

"Why do you say 'were'?"

Azalea shrugs. "Because the spell used that power to transfer my mother's magic to me when I slit her throat. I was a complete and utter dud; not a drop of magic in my blood. Which is why the blade was necessary—I needed other witch's powers to make it work.

Now, of course, I've used it up. Hence why I had no problem returning it to you. Thought you might like the keepsake." She grins evilly.

"I guess in the end, I'm glad you got revenge on your mom. She deserved it."

"Thank you." Azalea fakes a bow from her seated position with a flourish of her new knife.

Since we're on these friendly terms, I decide to push my luck. "I mean it, Azalea, that woman was evil. I'm sorry she treated you the way she did. You didn't deserve it."

Her chin wobbles, eyes softening for just a moment, before the sarcastic mask returns. "I guess what they say is true after all: If you can't beat 'em, join 'em. Or in my case, if you can't beat 'em, take their place with a blood sacrifice."

"But you don't have to *become* her, Az," I press in my gentlest tone. "I consider your payback fair and square, but that doesn't mean you can't use those powers to be better than your mom ever was."

"I rather like being a badass witch, thank you very much. At least now no one fucks with me. They respect me."

"And I'm happy for you, truly. But I don't see what that has to do with keeping me in a prison cell. I was never mean to you."

Azalea's eyes flash and she stands abruptly, power crackling around her like an oncoming storm. "No, but you never *helped* me, did you? You were my big cousin, the closest thing I had to a brother, or really any family at all. You and your mother just abandoned me to the wolves… literally." Her expression shifts, and she affects a carefree demeanor. "But no matter, I have all the power I could ask for now."

She settles back in her seat and flips the knife in the air, deftly catching it by the handle. "And it turns out the alpha is *very* grateful for my help. He's quite generous, in fact. Compared to having some random human off the street or weak-ass wolf as a daddy, you could certainly do much worse."

"Is that what he wants me for, then? To be his son?"

The wicked grin returns to her face. "Wouldn't you like to know?"

Chapter Three

LILLIANA

~

Eventually the cold from the ground seeps into my bones, complimented by the biting wind, and I have no choice but to get up and make my way back to Harridan House. Even though I still feel Derrek's absence, my emotions have settled enough for me to start strategizing again. It's still early afternoon, and incredibly difficult to accept that twenty-four hours ago I was getting a make-over from Roxanne for the big homecoming dance that never was.

Passing through the kitchen door without drawing attention from the staff, I slip upstairs and into my suite.

The tv is on but muted, and Milo is on the couch,

staring anxiously down at his phone. Surprise crosses his face when he sees me, followed by a relieved smile.

"Hey Lily, did you get what you were after?" He taps a few words into his phone before setting it on the table and crossing the room to greet me.

"Yeah, I feel better. That's definitely what I needed. Is… everything okay?" I glance pointedly at his phone, now facedown on the coffee table.

"Of course." Milo grips my jacket at the collar to help me slip out. "We were just worried about you being on your own. I promised Landon and Jared I'd let them know you made it back safe."

"Sheesh, and here I thought becoming alpha would mean I got to be a grownup now." It's only a little sarcastic; their concern for me is part of our bond, and I know it's not a reflection of how capable they think I am.

Milo opens his mouth, but I press a finger to his lips before the apology could cross them. "I'm just teasing. I know you don't mean anything by it." I replace the finger with my lips, hoping a kiss will completely erase the sting from my comment.

It works. He's thoroughly distracted. One warm hand cups my cheek and the other wraps around my waist, pulling my body closer while our kisses deepen. My arms twine around his shoulders and I toy mindlessly with his satiny hair. Tension builds in my belly, and I let myself drift into the delicious warmth of our physical connection. I don't know if it's a fated mates thing or a hormonal teenager thing, but nothing can shut off my anxious brain like intimacy with one of my guys.

Milo's fingers trail along my jaw and thread into my wind-blown mass of hair, curling to pull gently at the strands. Electricity courses over my skin; it feels good, but it's not the same as Derrek's forceful tug that curled my toes and clenched my belly.

And just like that, I'm hit with a stabbing pain in my chest, remembering Derrek is somewhere I can't reach him.

With a gentle hand to keep him in place, I pull away from Milo and break our kiss. Instead of breaking contact completely, I tuck my face into his chest and wind my arms around his waist, and he obliges my need for comfort by wrapping warm arms around my shoulders and squeezing me tightly.

We stay there in silence for a few long moments before I speak, murmuring into his shirt.

"I have to get Dom and Roxanne to help me come up with an actual plan to rescue Derrek."

"Mmm," is Milo's reply. He rests his cheek on the top of my head and squeezes.

"I don't want to force them to comply. But I don't have a lot of experience in coercing people to agree with me, either."

"Mmm-hmm." His chest is warm against my cheek, and the rumbling vibration of his voice blends with the natural vibrations close contact with his body always gives me.

"I know nothing about Pack Montrose, or where

they would put Derrek, or honestly, what they really want him for."

One of Milo's hands starts rubbing circles on my back, and my eyes close in contentment, despite the increasingly fast beat of my heart.

"I'm afraid I'll make the wrong decision and more people will get hurt." It's easier to admit my fears in this warm, safe space with my eyes closed. I still can't bring myself to admit my biggest concern to him, but this is close.

Milo continues rubbing my back wordlessly, his body supporting me as I sag against him.

"I don't know what to do." My voice is barely above a whisper, and I'm not even sure he can hear me.

"Trust your instincts, Lily," Milo finally replies. "You were born to do this, and we're all here on your side. Whatever you decide, the pack will follow you."

"Will they?" I question in a tremulous voice. "Or will I have to force them to do what I say? And if I make a mistake after that, how can I call myself a leader?"

"I don't believe there is any such thing as a perfect leader. There are good people with good intentions who do the best they can. Perhaps these people are smart, and they make informed decisions. Perhaps they consider the advice of those around them. But everyone makes mistakes, and leaders are no exception. Even the world's greatest leaders have slipped more than once in their careers."

It feels rather on the nose, but it makes me feel a tiny

bit better. "I'm afraid that I'll do what I think is right and I'll be dead wrong."

"I know. But I believe that if you stay true to what you think and feel and believe is right, there's no way it can be wrong."

I'm torn between dismissing him as someone who has to tell me what he thinks I need to hear because he's my fated mate, and grasping onto his words like a drowning woman would clutch a life raft.

"How do you have so much faith in me when I have so little in myself?"

"Maybe that's why Landon, Jared and I exist, Lily. To bolster you when you doubt yourself. Did you ever consider that?"

I pause, considering. "No," I answer honestly. "I just assumed it was a politics and mating thing."

"Well, don't forget that—assuming you choose to accept us all—we become a team of alphas. Once we complete that ceremony, it's not all on your shoulders anymore."

"So then, it's like... an oligarchy?" I'm pleased to dredge up the political term from my GED cramming over the last year. Apparently, more is still rattling around in there than I realized.

"I'm not sure, exactly. There hasn't been a mated alpha in my lifetime. But from my studies I assumed it was something like we, as your mates, have alpha authority, and sort of serve as your council. You'd still be the 'top' alpha, but the three of us function as a team to help make decisions and run the pack."

A guilty feeling accompanies my immediate thoughts of Derrek. "And how does the mate-claiming thing work again?"

Milo gives me a reassuring squeeze. "It's not as big of a deal as you think. Basically, it's like the first ceremony where you shifted, except instead of being on the full moon, it's on the lunar eclipse. The whole pack gathers, you make your declaration to claim us as your mates, and then we all four shift and run together to seal the bond, with the pack following."

"And what if…" I lick my lips, searching for the right words. "What if one of you can't make it? Like you're sick or something?"

"You don't have to worry about us, Lily. Even if we were at death's door, we'd be there."

"I know, but if you couldn't?" I press, grateful he can't see my expression when I ask; he'd know immediately I wasn't talking about the three of them. "Could I just claim you in name?"

"From what I remember of Pack History classes, that has never been an issue. So I really can't give you an answer, but maybe Mr. Carson would know? He's the pack historian, after all. Or maybe the pack seer, since it's more about how the magic works than anything. But I always assumed it was the act of running together with the pack as witnesses that seals the deal." He squeezes me again, pressing a kiss to the top of my head. "Regardless, it's not something you need to worry your pretty head about. We would never fail to be there for you. Again, assuming you choose to claim us."

Milo's efforts to avoid pressuring me are sweet, but even I can hear the conviction in his tone when he talks about the three of them being my mates. It's such a foregone conclusion for him; he talks about our future status as mates in the same casual way he describes the color of the sky, as if it's obvious to anyone who can see it.

My ache for Derrek has a new sense of urgency. Not only do I need to get him back, to have him here with me where he's safe; I need him to bond, somehow, with Milo, Jared, and Landon before the next lunar eclipse, which is a little over a month away. Of course, that includes me explaining the entire mess to all four of them.

Which brings me back to the matter at hand: Rescuing Derrek.

I pull away from Milo and claim his hand, tugging him toward the door. "I suppose we should see how far Dom and Roxanne have gotten in the rescue planning."

As it turns out, not very far. The leftovers from a lunch tray are congealing on plates they've piled on a nearby cart, and they're both clutching coffee cups despite the mid-afternoon hour.

Dom is still stubbornly insisting on working slowly

and quietly behind the scenes to reconnect with his Pack Montrose contacts, and planning the wolf pack equivalent of a hostage exchange.

Roxanne has apparently convinced him that Derrek is valuable for us to bring in, but not that he could be in imminent danger.

"I'm telling you, Nielsen will not hurt his only heir. We have time to do this the right way."

"How do you know Derrek is his only heir?" Roxanne counters. "He could have claimed him for a number of reasons, not just out of necessity. And most of those reasons are not anything that'll be good for us, I guarantee it."

Dom sighs heavily. "It's widely known in Pack Montrose that Nielsen's mate died during the birth of their first child. He hasn't taken another mate, which only leaves the boy."

"Clearly he sowed some wild oats despite having a mate, given Derrek's existence in the first place. It's not too much of a stretch to believe that he may have other children we don't know about."

I join them at the table, and Milo fixes us both a mug of coffee from a nearby carafe before he settles in beside me.

"Did you get some fresh air?" Roxanne smiles warmly in my direction, even though her eyes are tired. Clearly, arguing with my uncle wears on her.

"Yes, getting outside was a good reset. Perhaps you both should take a break?"

"No need to worry about us. We're both committed to being here and figuring out a plan," Dom answers. "We can keep the coffee coming all night if we need to."

Drawing on Milo's supportive presence, I state, "Good, because I want him out of Montrose territory by the end of this week."

A worried expression crosses Roxanne's face as she glances between me and Dom.

"No way," my uncle answers decisively. "We don't want to go in there half-cocked and start a war with them over someone who isn't even part of our pack. I know he's your friend, and I know you're worried about him. But we're not Seal Team Seven, and he's not a high-value pack member. I'm still not convinced this is even something we should focus on right now."

Fury rises like a wave in my ears, dulling every sound but the powerful beating of my heart. It takes everything I have not to scream at him. Derrek is as important to me as one of my own limbs, which I'd happily sacrifice to get him back.

I take a moment to choose my words, then speak in the most respectful tone I can manage. "I appreciate your input, Dom, but I disagree. Derrek is our connection to the family that cast the curse, and he may be our best shot at undoing it. You yourself believed the answers lay with Pack Montrose, and I can't think of a single benevolent reason for Avery Nielsen to sneak into our territory to claim him. If it was for an innocent reason, he would have gone about it differently. That he forced Derrek to go with him tells me Derrek is in danger; he's obviously being held against his will or we'd have heard from him by now."

Dom waves me off dismissively. "Have you considered that he made that move to test our defenses? We've shored up the weakness for now, but don't believe for a single second that Nielsen isn't looking for a way to get one over on us. We don't know how many of our pack members may be compromised. Before we even think about attacking another pack, we have to get our own house in order."

Rage simmers under my skin. "I know I still have a lot to learn about being alpha, but it is *my* job to protect *my* pack. I'm confident in the current status of the Smoky Falls wolves.

"Derrek was taking care of me when none of you knew I existed. To me, he's pack, and he's in danger. His witch of a cousin is definitely planning something, and I don't intend to sit around and find out what it is when we're too late to do anything about it."

My uncle's voice rises, his tone both snide and condescending. "You're practically still a kid, Lily, and you have no idea what it means to have people's lives in your hands—being alpha isn't just power, it's responsibility. And that responsibility is the safety of the *pack*, not some guy you lived with as a teenage runaway."

Milo bristles beside me. "Now wait a minute-"

Roxanne speaks at the same time in a gentler tone. "Dom, I think you ought to-"

But I've had enough of his holier-than-though attitude. My wolf demands that I put him in his place and remind him who the alpha is. Standing, I slam my hands on the table to get everyone's attention.

My gaze is laser-focused on my uncle's incredulous expression. "You may have been alpha in my absence, but you no longer hold that responsibility." The alpha voice is so strong it almost feels as if it reverberates through the room. "I am the alpha, and *I* am the one who makes all decisions for the Smoky Falls Pack. I respect your opinion, but don't presume to give me orders. I give the orders, and I am saying we will rescue Derrek by the end of this week, if not sooner. Every day he's in Montrose is a day he's in danger. I've heard your thoughts on what should be done, and I have chosen a different course. Now your job is to help me create a plan and execute it. I don't want to force my will onto anyone, but the alpha has that power for a reason. Don't make me use it."

If my statement surprised him, he doesn't show it. "How typical, for a teenage girl to throw a fit when things aren't going her way. Just because you have alpha blood, it doesn't mean you are in any way prepared to lead a pack. My sister trained to take over as alpha until the day she disappeared, and she clearly was incapable of leading anyone. You don't know how things work here. If I had any choice, I would not have allowed you to take over as alpha until I was certain you were ready, but magic doesn't care about the practical, in the end.

"So, being unable to lead anyone, you're just going to resort to using the alpha command and forcing everyone to do what you say? That sure seems like a terrible way to run a pack. But what do I know? I only did it for twenty years."

"Enough." My voice is a deep, simmering growl, laden with the alpha command, and it silences Dom immediately. "You dealt with constant disquiet during your tenure because you were a poor excuse for an alpha. Your criticism of *my* use of the alpha command to force compliance is a joke, given everything I know about how you operated. Don't get me started on keeping me under Roxanne's compulsion for a year just to keep me under your thumb.

"Since I'm more generous than you, I'm going to give you a choice between two options: either stay and assist me, showing the deference I'm due as your alpha, or leave Smoky Falls. If you stay, you can consult and offer your opinions when asked for, but otherwise, you will completely *cease* challenging my decisions. If you leave, you are no longer a member of this pack.

"I'm leaving. When I come back, you'll either be here and prepared to be an asset to my team, or you'll be nothing more than a memory."

I stride away from the table, my back stiff as I march across the room and out the door. Milo follows close behind me, and I hear nothing but deafening silence in my wake.

MILO

Despite crowing internally with pride for my mate, I can't help worrying about how she's feeling. I follow as she storms out of the library, heading directly for the stairs. Fury rolls off of her in palpable waves so thick I can practically see them.

"Are we-" I try to ask about her plans, but she cuts me off.

"I need to get out of here." Lily's tone is clipped, as if she's afraid of speaking more than is absolutely necessary and unleashing her rage upon me.

"Sure, let's go for another walk. I can grab our coats-"

"No, I mean *out* of here. This house. This property. I would leave Smoky Falls if I could." She starts trotting down the stairs. "You have your car, right?"

A wave of discomfort rolls through my gut. "I do."

"Great. You're driving."

"Of course. Where are we going?"

"It doesn't matter, just away from *here*."

Despite her much shorter legs, I'm practically sprinting to keep up with her. It turns out she can really hustle when she wants to.

I expect her to wait in the entry while I bring the car around like normal, but apparently it's not in the cards. Lily marches straight out the door and hangs a left toward the former stables that now houses an impressive garage, where my car is parked outside. I slip my hand into hers and thread our fingers together, hoping it'll comfort her. It seems to help, but not by much. She's too agitated to be comforted.

The temperature seems to have dropped overnight, making the brisk air feel more like winter than the pleasant fall afternoon I was expecting. Lily doesn't react to the weather, either. Her movements are almost mechanical, like she's on some sort of autopilot.

I wait until we're in the car, seats warming as we're zipping down the driveway, before I speak.

"That was impressive, Lily. You did the right thing, you know. He deserved to be put in his place."

She stares out the window wordlessly, watching the bare trees speed by.

"I was almost expecting Dom to get on his hands and knees and beg for forgiveness. Honestly, he should have. Whether or not he agrees with you, his job is to do what you tell him to do, period. He shouldn't have spoken to you that way."

Lily's chest rises and falls dramatically under her crossed arms, and she turns to face me with sad eyes and a trembling lip. "I shouldn't have lost my temper like that. He was right. I don't know what I'm doing."

Hot indignation rises in my chest. "What? No, the hell he was *not* right. You're the alpha. That's all he should care about."

"But he has way more experience being alpha than I do."

"I'll admit the situation is unusual—typically someone doesn't become alpha until the previous alpha dies—but nothing about this pack has been 'usual' for decades. That doesn't change the fact that he owes you his respect, not to mention his loyalty. If he was meant to be alpha, your manifestation wouldn't have made *you* alpha. That alone is proof that you're more worthy of the position than he ever was."

My eyes dart back and forth between the road and her face like a pair of ping-pong balls. Her emotions are overwhelming, a big mess of grief, fury, frustration, helplessness, and something a lot like heartache. The need to comfort her sets my blood racing through my veins.

"What's going on in your head, Lily? Despite our heightened connection, I still can't read your mind, you know."

That elicits a ghost of a smile. "Too much," she admits. "Too much to put words to. It's like a crowded room and all my thoughts are different people trying to speak over everyone else. It's just a jumble of noise."

"How can I help?"

"Just... drive, if you don't mind? Maybe there's somewhere we can go? Right now I just want quiet, and distance from that house and everyone in it."

"Anything for you, my darling." I tug at one of her crossed arms and she loosens her posture, allowing me to thread my fingers through hers. I lift her hand to my mouth for a kiss, then settle our joined hands into her lap and focus on the road.

If she wants to drive in silence to sort her thoughts, then I'm happy to oblige. After a quick mental inventory of options, I decide on somewhere to hide out; somewhere private, and somewhere that no one will come looking for her.

Chapter Four

JARED

~

"I really don't like this, man. We should have talked to Lay- I mean, Lily, first. Since she's the alpha and all." Landon can't seem to stop twitching in the passenger seat, and it's getting on my nerves. He's flipping a guitar pick back and forth across his knuckles like a mobster in an old movie, and for some reason, seeing it in my peripheral vision is fucking annoying.

"Yeah, well, the point was to show her we can think for ourselves and not stress her out any more than she already is. We plan to be her mates, also alphas for the pack. Maybe she needs to know we can help her without having to be told." I keep my hands on the wheel and my eyes focused on the road. As much as I'd like to pretend otherwise, I'm just as nervous as he is. But *one* of us has to be calm.

"And you really think this is the way to show her how mature we are?"

"Look, I know we're taking a risk, but I think it's worth it. Even though we're her fated, we're still not officially mated to her, so we can still get on their territory without being noticed. Besides, no one really looked at us last night; all of their focus was on her and *Leaf*." His name comes out as a snort, despite my honest attempt to be civil. "Even though I don't like the guy, he means a lot to her. He's basically all she's got from home—or whatever used to be home for her—and like it or not, she cares about him. So if he matters to her, he matters to me."

"Yeah, I know," Landon grumbles. "He's *okay*. And it could be useful to have a wizard around. Or a warlock, or whatever the male equivalent of a witch is. I just can't get over that he feels... off."

He hit the nail on the head with that one. "Right? Like, I can't explain it, but he's something different. It's weird."

"It's probably just because he's a wolf *and* a wizard."

"They're just called witches, Landon. Male or female. But I'm not so sure that's it."

"No, witches are definitely women. And if it's not the hybrid thing, what do you think it is?"

"Haven't you paid attention in pack history? Or are you just getting your information from novels? He's a witch. Regardless, he's never shifted before, right? I mean, as far as we know. He sure didn't seem to pretend *not* to be a wolf. And he seemed pretty shocked to find out he was the Montrose alpha's heir."

"Yeah, but that could just be the heir part. We don't know for sure he's never shifted."

"Just call it a hunch, then. All I know is, he doesn't feel like anyone else, and until I know why, I don't trust him." I ease down on the brake and roll up to the stop sign, checking carefully around the empty intersection as if a pack of wolves could come charging from any direction at any time.

Which, honestly, they could.

We cruise past the 'Welcome to Montrose' sign on high alert. It takes several seconds to realize we're both holding our breath and bracing for attack, Landon scanning the right side of the road and me the left.

If some kind of 'rival pack' alarm has gone off, the people on the street don't know. There aren't many; it's blustery and cold out despite the blue sky and sunshine. But they appear to just be going about their day, shopping and grabbing coffee like normal people.

I force myself to breathe out slowly and drive well within the speed limit. The last thing I need is for their local authorities to pull us over and see Smoky Falls on my driver's license.

"So... we're in. Now what?" Landon's knee is shaking, his hands playing drums on his lap to release the nervous energy.

"I guess we explore a bit? I hadn't really got past the point where we drive into town. We're just trying to find out where they took him."

"I mean, it could be anywhere. Do you think they have a peace officer building like we do, for tourists?"

"Why don't you try google?" I thrust my chin at the phone he tossed on the dashboard of my truck.

"Oh, good idea." He swipes the phone and taps on the screen while I continue our slow roll through town.

Honestly, it's a lot like Smoky Falls. Coffee shops, local restaurants, and gift shops with fall stuff in the windows, colorful fall wreaths on the lampposts. Growing up hearing how monstrous these people are, it's hard to make that idea fit with the reality of this average little town.

"Montrose, North Carolina, has a population of 1,873. Established in 1923, this small mountain town is nestled in the Blue Ridge Mountain range-"

"Nestled?" I interrupt scornfully. "What the hell are you reading? We're supposed to be casing the joint, not learning fun facts."

"I was on their Wikipedia page." Landon rolls his eyes as if it were obvious.

"You know those aren't factual, right? Anyone could put whatever they want on there, including Pack Montrose. They can write *whatever* they want. How about some useful information? Where's the alpha's house? How big is the territory? Are there any old mines or factories they might keep someone prisoner in?" We've reached the end of the main street, so I turn left and rumble slowly down a residential street. My truck takes up far more than half of this road; I hope I don't come across another car before I can find a better place to blend in. Even though I know my truck is normal, it feels like I've got a neon sign over my head flashing 'ENEMY!' for everyone to see. It's making me edgy.

Apparently, it's Landon's turn to be an asshole. "This isn't a detective novel, Jared. For all we know, they aren't even holding him prisoner. You know, he could be perfectly happy, reunited with his long-lost family." He goes back to his phone, scrolling for more info.

"You saw what he did when they took him away. I don't know everything, but I know that man didn't want to leave with them." His expression still haunts me, and I don't even like the guy.

"Well, they don't have a residence like Harridan House-"

"Who does? It's ridiculous."

Landon ignores my comment. "But there is a 'Mayor's House' that's a historical landmark built in 1926. Apparently, the 'mayor' still lives there to this day." His voice takes on a smug tone.

Know-it-all.

"That sounds like a place worth checking out. Is it in town?"

"Sort of. It's more on the outskirts, up on a hill that overlooks the town." Landon pinches and spreads his

49

fingers over the screen. "There's only one road, like Harridan House. But it looks like there are some trails nearby. Fancy a hike?"

LANDON

After I guide Jared to the entrance of a convenient public trail system, we hop out of the truck and prepare to take a hike in hopes we'll get close to the 'mayor's house' (aka alpha's house) of Montrose. The satellite images definitely make it look like the trails run close enough for us to slip into the woods and approach the grounds, but you never know.

Jared's antsy, moving around and shaking his hands out like he always does before a game. "Let's go already!" He grumbles.

I know him well enough that when he's nervous, he's kind of an ass, so I let it slide. I'm tucking away the stuff he left lying around in the truck that might give us away. "Give me your wallet."

He looks at me like I'm insane. "Why, are you internet shopping right now? What the hell, man?"

Pulling my own from my pocket, I show my intent by dropping it into the glove box. "If they catch us, our best bet is to pretend to be tourists who got lost on the trails. Smoky Falls ID will kind of ruin that effect, don't you think?"

"Oh. Yeah, that makes sense." He pulls the wallet from the pocket of his sweats and hands it over. We've purposefully worn clothes with no ties to Smoky Falls, not even Jared's ubiquitous SFC hat. I've replaced it with a University of Tennessee hat, the signature orange 'T' a clear signal of where we're pretending to be from. Neither of us is exactly dressed for hiking, but general athletic gear is good enough.

With the branches bare, the dense forest is actually pretty bright right now. Sunlight streams in between the trees, and we crunch along over a blanket of fallen leaves. There's a small brook that follows along the winding trail, and regular markers to keep visitors headed in the right direction. Even though it's like Tennessee, it just feels like a different forest from home.

"So, do we have an actual plan?" Jared falls in step with me as I head down the trail, attempting to follow the route I noted in the photo.

"For now, we're hiking. We've parked at a public trailhead so that shouldn't draw any suspicion, and our story is just that we're UT students who came to town for the weekend to meet some girls we talked to online. They ghosted us, so we're exploring. Planning to head back to school tomorrow, staying at the Horsehead Inn in Bishop, that town we passed about twenty minutes back."

Jared's face is unreadable under the brim of his hat,

but he sounds impressed. "You just came up with all of that in the last five minutes?"

"I was thinking on the drive here that we should have some kind of story. It's a small town, and we're not exactly your typical tourists. I assumed we'd stand out, so I came up with something to explain us being in town."

"That's smart, man. So what should our names be? We need to have a good cover story. Like James Bond." He rubs his hands together as if this suddenly became an exciting adventure.

"Okay, first of all, James Bond never had a cover story. Everyone knew who he was, and he told them if they asked. But we should keep it simple; you're Jared, I'm Landon. The more stuff you lie about, the harder it is to keep it all straight. We should change our last names, though, since they probably know the families from our pack."

"Right, right. What about Smith and Wesson?"

"What are we, the heirs to a gun manufacturer?" I snort. "Really subtle."

"Fine, Smith and Wes-*ton*, then. We're trying to keep it easy, after all."

I mull it over. "Landon Smith and Jared Weston. Works for me." We follow the left branch of the trail and start up a moderate hill. "If I'm reading it right, we'll meet another fork in about a half mile and the right branch will take us close to the house. It's hard to tell from the photo if there's a difference in elevation or not, but this area doesn't seem too mountainous, so maybe it won't be much."

"And what do we do if they have security or something?"

"It's a town of 1800, Jared. I doubt they have security."

"Harridan House has security," he counters.

"Yeah, because a couple of generations back, a witch cast a curse on our alpha. Plus, it's a much bigger property. It'd be weird if it didn't have security."

"Now that you mention it, isn't it weird that this town is so small? Smoky Falls is like four times the size."

I shrug. "I don't think so. We all have to stay on pack lands, and they don't remember. I guess the benefit of not being cursed is you get to live where you want."

"Oh yeah, you're right. Bastards."

He's silent for a few beats, and I split my focus between the screen in my hand and potential hazards on the trail.

"All jokes aside, do you think they'll recognize us?" Despite his bluster in the truck, I knew Jared was just as nervous as me.

Surprisingly, having a task to focus on has helped and I'm suddenly the calmer one. "There's no reason to assume the guys who came with the Montrose alpha are anywhere near this house right now. We don't even know if this is the place they took Derrek. So there's no point psyching ourselves out."

"Yeah, you're right. But what if they recognize our scent?"

"I thought about that. They may be able to tell that we're from a pack, but I don't think they'll know which pack. If it comes to it, we can say we're from a pack on the other side of Tennessee. I heard there's one south of Nashville. Franklin Pack. They won't know the difference."

"But what if-"

I stop walking and turn to face him. "Jared, you're over-thinking this. All we're doing right now is familiarizing ourselves with Montrose territory and—if we can—locating Derrek. Okay? We're not trying to confront anyone, or rescue Derrek right now. We're just here to get some information, see what we can find out, and leave."

He sighs. "I know, but I feel like we're going in unprepared. I'm used to having a list of plays, like plans for what to do."

I snort a laugh. "Bro, this was your idea. If you didn't have a plan at the beginning, how did you expect it to go?"

"You're right, it was stupid to just decide to drive out here on a whim. I just needed to feel like I was doing something. I'm not the type to sit around and talk, you know? I just get out and *do*. I'm a *do*er. And something needed to be done."

"I agree, and that's why we're here. So let's do something. Our plan is absolutely to not get caught, period. If something happens, we break and run directly for the truck; your phone will lead you back to it. It's better if we don't split up, but if we have to, we can meet there. Okay?"

He nods in agreement. "Okay. No getting caught. No splitting up. Back to home base."

I clap him on the back. "You good?"

"Yeah, I'm good. Let's go."

We reach the next fork in a few minutes and continue toward the mayor's house. As we get closer, I'm suddenly more aware of every sound we make, my ears searching for something to indicate people nearby as well. The leaves crunching under our feet are too loud, echoing in the suddenly quiet forest. My heart rate picks up.

"Jared," I say in a low voice, stopping.

He turns to me with a confused expression. "Yeah?"

"I think it's right there." I point to my left, where a hill rises from the trail and prevents us from seeing beyond it.

"Are you sure?" His head tilts to the side. "It doesn't look like anything's up there besides more trees."

In response, I show him my phone, the map indicating a structure immediately to the left of the blue dot marking our location.

We both pause, listening for any sign of someone other than us. Besides the thudding of my heart, there's a light breeze stirring leaves and some distant animal sounds. No voices, cars—nothing.

Jared and I turn to each other, eyes locking. My hand trembles as I tuck my phone back in my pocket.

"Well, I guess this is it. Are you ready?" A steely determination crosses his face, the same look when he's about to head onto the field.

I nod, swallowing. "Yeah."

"Let's go."

And without another word, we turn and start picking our way up the hill.

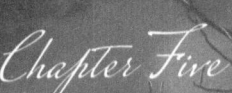

Chapter Five

MILO

My gaze darts to Lily when we pull into my drive, but she doesn't react to the surroundings. I'm not even certain she recognizes it, since our last time here was at night. A quick flash of memory short circuits my brain —the way she looked under the warm lights, her creamy skin bare, head thrown back in pleasure as I feasted on her. My body reacts viscerally to that mental image, blood rushing with immediate lust. It doesn't help that the scent of her fills my senses in the cozy luxury of my car.

I force myself to breathe slowly and press back the rush of desire; that's not why we're here today. Her needs right now clearly lay along the emotional line, not the physical. Lily was quiet for the entire ride, arms crossed, her usually bright emerald eyes thunderous with frustration. I don't need the ability to sense her emotions to understand what she's feeling.

This time, we head for the large front door instead of around the back. She already had plenty of time outside today, and it's growing colder; I don't think more fresh air is what she wants. A sudden bout of nerves rushes through me, and I realize I'm about to show her into my sanctuary for the first time.

Not that I have anything to hide, or don't want her to see it; she's my mate, and although she hasn't officially accepted me, I already belong to her body and soul. But for some reason, this feels like a tremendous moment, like it's the last part of me she has yet to touch. I'm suddenly, inexplicably apprehensive that she won't like it.

We pass through the cold modern space that is my parents' house, and I try to speed her along without making her hurry. She doesn't seem interested in looking around at the steel and concrete decor, following me instinctually while her thoughts clearly wander somewhere else. Once downstairs, I hold the door open for her, guiding her into my room with my heart in my throat. I get another whiff of her cherry vanilla scent as she passes, but at this moment, my need for her acceptance is even stronger than my desire.

I wish I could read her thoughts; her silence as she examines my room with crossed arms is deafening. Fortunately, I'm always neat, so there are no embarrassing piles of soiled underwear or half-eaten pizza crusts on display like a certain football player I know.

However, there are things in this room that reveal a lot more about me than I've even told her. It didn't seem pertinent at the time; all I wanted was to get to know her and what she needed. But now I realize she might feel like I've been keeping secrets.

She spins slowly in the center of my room, her tiny feet sinking into the plush area rug. My gaze trails hers, taking in the rich wood accents that run up the wall, my platform bed neatly made with the thick forest green duvet, a gas fireplace that I flicked on as soon as we entered the room, the side table with my grandfather's record player, and finally the desk with my sketchbook on top. Her head tilts back as she takes in the frames lining the far wall, forming a grid nearly floor to ceiling, and I swallow thickly, my hands tucked into my back pockets to affect a posture of complete ease despite my racing heart.

Without a word, she crosses to the desk for a closer look, inspecting the drawings at her eye level. My heart is beating a mile a minute; surely she doesn't hate me for not saying anything? Her silence has become very difficult to interpret. I'm not sure if I should try to distract her with a drink and offer her a seat on the low couch by the fireplace, or continue standing here, awkwardly, waiting for her to say something.

"Did you draw all of these?" She asks softly without turning toward me, almost as if she's asking the pictures themselves.

"Yeah." I don't know what else to say.

"Why didn't you tell me?" She steps to her right, following the line of pen and ink studies closer to the fireplace.

"I…" I clear my throat, searching for an explanation. "I don't know, honestly. I wasn't trying to keep it a secret. There just didn't seem to be a time to talk about it." She's getting closer to my most recent work, and my nerves kick it up a notch.

I have little rhyme or reason for where I put each drawing. I've been switching them out for years; when I finish one and am happy with it, I just pick a frame and replace the older piece with the newer. They're all sorts of subjects: landscapes, portraits, buildings, animals, still lives. Lately, however, one particular subject has occupied my mind, and she's about to discover it.

It's obvious when she realizes; she was walking slowly, examining the detailed drawings casually, and her entire body freezes. My body is radiating so much heat I question if turning on the fireplace was a good idea. Lily's gaze is traveling up the wall, taking in each miniature recreation of her in black and white.

I hadn't done it with any actual intent; my hands just seem to shape a subject and it flows from brain to fingers with very little input from me. That's actually one reason I stopped taking art classes, since I was terrible at completing assignments and was really not interested in any other medium. I just wanted to sketch whatever popped into my head at the moment, and I've always been content with pen and ink.

I'm braced for some sort of outburst, or question, or accusation of being a liar or a psychopath, but none of those happen.

She turns toward me, drops her arms to her sides, and bites down on her bottom lip. My breath catches; there's something in her gaze that I've never seen before, a well of vulnerability and emotion, blended with unmistakable lust. Prickling energy crawls across my skin, sinking beneath my flesh to electrify my insides.

With a barely audible growl, she launches herself at me, looping her arms around my neck and straddling my hips. My palms instinctively grab her lush bottom, holding her against my body, as her mouth crushes against mine in a desperate kiss.

Momentarily startled, I freeze for a second as my brain struggles to catch up. Lily is impatient, and her tongue slides along the seam of my lips, begging for entry. In seconds my earlier lust resurfaces, and I'm kissing her back.

Our tongues tangle, vying for dominance. Her sudden attack is surprising but certainly not unwelcome; I'm even more turned on by her overt demonstration of attraction for me. I squeeze her perfect ass with both hands, turning to press her against the door without breaking the kiss. A primal, possessive growl rumbles deep within my chest, shocking in its intensity. Her answering moan sends more heat rushing through me, hips grinding my erection against the answering heat between her legs.

This is nothing like I imagined. Our previous intimacy has been so gentle, so measured and calculated. My plans to delicately and respectfully woo her are completely out the window, and instinct has taken over. Her hands skim across my chest until she finds my shirt buttons. Frantically, she pops them open one by one, working her way down until she's undone them all and runs her hands across my bare flesh. We continue kissing without coming up for air, and she presses herself against me, breasts pinned between us while her nails rake down my back. The sharp sensation isn't painful, but it seems to energize my inner beast even more. I wrap my arms around her firmly and pull away from the door, carrying her across the room before I lower her onto the bed.

One press of her hand to my chest has me immediately standing back up. "I'm sorry, I got carried away," I apologize automatically, panting.

Lily stands as well. Her chest rises and falls rapidly, but she doesn't look upset—the only thought that comes to my mind is that her eyes look *hungry*.

Without a single word, she grabs my face and kisses me deeply, then pushes my shirt off my shoulders and drops it to the floor. Her fingers hook in my belt loops and she tugs me toward her as she sits on my bed, gaze dropping to my waist.

At this point, I have no words, so I follow her silent instructions. Her fingers swiftly unbuckle my belt, letting it hang open while she unfastens the button and slides down the zipper. I can barely breathe, and not being in charge means I don't know what to do with my hands. They hang limply by my sides while she dips her fingers through the opening of my boxers, her fingers grazing my sensitive, swollen head. A shudder of pleasure zips up my spine, but I force myself to put together a rational thought.

"Lily." I tip her chin up with one finger, forcing her to meet my gaze. I'm trying to understand this sudden change. "What are we doing?"

Her eyes glimmer in the low light. "I don't know, exactly. I just know that I want you, Milo. Isn't that enough?" She stands, claiming my mouth again and sliding a hand down my belly, under my waistband. Her fingers trail down my length before she palms me and squeezes gently.

I suck in a sharp breath, willing myself not to lose control. Her every touch is like lightning on my flesh, and I'm struggling to hold back the instincts telling me to tear her clothes off and claim her. I've never been this close to the edge before, and it's maddening and intoxicating all wrapped up in one delicious, curly-haired package.

Lily scrapes her teeth along my neck, planting kisses under my jaw. Suddenly, she nips my earlobe with her teeth and sucks it into her hot mouth. She's everywhere, her touch all over my body as if she had a thousand hands, a million fingers. My eyelids flutter shut and another animal-like groan escapes my lips.

My well-thought-out plans for our first time mean nothing; all that matters is what my mate wants, what she needs. If this is her desire, then I'm more than willing to give it to her… but I need to be sure.

It takes a herculean effort, but I summon the willpower to interrupt again. My voice is rough when I ask, "Are you sure this is what you want? If you're just trying to work out the frustration, I'm happy to give you release. No return required." I'm actually quite proud of myself for getting the words out, considering the stroke of her hand has made me so painfully hard I'll need to take care of it, with or without her help.

"It's not frustration, Milo. I just want… you close to me." She breathes the words into my ear, sending shivers down my spine. The difference between her forceful actions and hesitant words still leaves doubt in my mind.

I wish my tone was more commanding, but it comes out almost like a plea. "What do you want? Tell me, Lily." I can't help it. I need to hear her say it. To be absolutely sure.

She pulls back, emerald gaze locking on mine. "I want you. All of you. In the way an alpha claims her mate."

A shiver of anticipation runs through me, my last vestiges of self control melting like ice cream in the summer sun. *Yes*. I've waited for her my entire life, thought about this moment more times than I could possibly count.

My fingers tangle in her wild hair, and I gaze into her eyes with a lump in my throat. "Lily, I-"

She presses a finger to my lips, cutting off my

words. A faint blush appears on her pale skin and she says, "Let me."

Lily pulls free of my grasp, drawing her fingers from my erection and immediately hooking both hands into the waistband of my boxers while lowering herself to the edge of my bed. When she pushes my jeans down my legs, my rigid length bobs in front of her face, begging for attention. The cool air is delicious against the inferno of my skin, and I'm practically shaking with anticipation of her next move. She wraps one hand around me, blowing lightly across the tip already glistening with liquid, then drags her tongue up and around my head before wrapping her perfect lips around it.

A groan rumbles in my chest; I've never allowed another woman to touch me. I've only done what I thought was necessary for me to learn to please my future mate. The sensation of her hot, wet mouth is more than I was prepared for. My hand instinctively fists in her hair as I struggle to remain still. "You don't have to…" I hear myself muttering, fighting the instinct to thrust myself forward. I nearly lose all control as she takes me deeper between those wickedly soft lips. My other hand rises, tugging gently on her hair as my hips rock, seeking more of her heat.

The action must encourage her because she wraps a hand around my shaft and sucks me deeply into her mouth until I hit the back of her throat. The sensation is unreal, and I release a string of curse-laden praises for my perfect mate. A gagging sound nearly stops me completely, but she pulls away and slides her hands up and down, spreading her saliva to coat me and enhance the incredible feeling of her skin on mine. I'm perfectly happy to enjoy her strokes, but she determinedly swallows me down again and again, figuring out her tolerance and rhythm quickly. It's tempting to lose myself to the pleasure, but if she keeps this up, I'm going to explode in her throat. Which is absolutely not how I want this to end.

Not this time, anyway.

Summoning every scrap of my remaining willpower, I cup her face and pull free from her sweet mouth. She protests, but I pull her up gently and claim her lips with mine. The intensity of this kiss is like a simmering inferno. We've shared sweet and sultry kisses, even kisses filled with lust and desire. But now there's no more frantic energy, just a deep, burning certainty that this is absolutely right.

Pausing our kisses, I step out of my shoes, followed by my jeans—and end up standing absolutely naked before my fully clothed mate. Her gaze travels up and down my body, emerald eyes glimmering with desire as she takes in every inch of me, exposed and waiting for her. Her tongue slips over her lower lip, drawing it between her teeth as her gaze finally lands on mine.

Now that she feasted her eyes, I close the distance between us and inhale her intoxicating scent. Even fully clothed, I can smell her desire, and I restrain myself from shoving my hand in her jeans to sink my fingers in the wetness waiting for me. I'll get there soon enough.

I duck my hands under the hem of her shirt and slowly, sensually run them up her sides, peeling the garment from her body. She's already tugging down her own jeans, kicking them off in much the same manner as I did. All that's left between us is few little scraps of light purple lace.

I bite down on my lip to suppress a growl. Those little matching sets are so infernally sexy, especially on Lily. My hand slips between us as I pull her in for another deep, earth-shattering kiss. The heat between her legs is heavenly, and my fingers scrape against the fabric to find it completely soaked with her desire for me. She moans against my lips, pressing herself against my hand, silently begging me for more.

Happy to oblige, I press more firmly, then slip my fingers under the lace so there's no barrier between her hot flesh and mine. Lily's head tips back, and the shuddering gasp she releases almost sends me over the edge. But I fight to keep my control, withdrawing the fingers coated with her desire and sliding them into my mouth with my eyes locked on hers.

Lily wastes no more time, and her lingerie swiftly falls to the floor, leaving her beautiful, flushed body on full display. Her eyes are deep pools of emerald, chest rising and falling beneath her tangle of dark curls. Molten desire floods through me like I've never experienced before. I've never admired another woman like my fated mate; she's the pinnacle of every need, perfectly suited for me just as I'm made for her. The surety of it fills me; the surety of her, of us, and of this moment.

If things had followed my plans, I'd have laid out the perfect scene, chosen the perfect moment, managed every detail down to the last flickering candle. But ironically enough, it didn't come down to my plans at all. Lily chose *this* moment, and that makes it even more perfect.

Cupping her cheeks with trembling fingers, I utter, "You are everything I've ever wanted. You are my queen, my goddess. Now it's time for me to worship you the way you deserve." I plant a kiss against her parted lips before lifting her onto the bed and covering her body with mine.

Peppering her smooth skin with open-mouthed kisses along her neck, I nip at her shoulder, gradually working my way down to her soft curves. Her nails dig into my back when I draw a pert pink nipple between my lips, teeth grazing the firm pebble. Her back arches off the bed, silently demanding more. My hand rises to replace my lips, pinching lightly as I continue my perusal down her silky stomach, over her hipbone, until I reach the part of her body I've been desperate to taste since we arrived.

Her fingers tangle in my hair, her eyes soft, breathing shallow as she parts her legs before me. With grateful release, I dive in like a starving man attacks his favorite meal.

LILLIANA

A gasp bursts past my lips as Milo buries his face between my thighs. His talented tongue sends immediate waves of pleasure through my body, causing my legs to quake. Even though I've enjoyed his particular form of worship before, something about this time feels different. Perhaps it's knowing another piece of the puzzle that is Milo Vernice, or perhaps it's knowing that we won't stop here. I've spent far too long waiting for things to happen to me, not sure how to choose what I wanted and when. Tonight, I choose to claim Milo as my own, cementing our bond as firmly as an oath sworn before a priest.

I have no experience to draw on; just some general knowledge about how certain things work that I've compiled from health class, secrets whispered between teenage girls, and lewd comments shouted by men on the street. Things that had never quite been intriguing enough to attempt until tonight. Kissing Milo, touching his skin and feeling his erection pressed between my legs, fed a wild instinct that quickly took over. It had never interested me before, but I was struck with a sudden desire to run my tongue over the silky flesh of him, taste his desire the way he'd tasted mine. And the more he reacted to my actions, the further I craved to go. My fingers practically had a mind of their own. A deep, throbbing need for him rose within me like the tide, a desire to open myself to him, to welcome him into my body, into my flesh. To be as close to him as one person can be to another.

Tingling spreads across my skin as Milo increases his efforts, forcing my wandering mind back to the present. His arms wrap around my legs, hands pulling me firmly to the experienced lips of my mate. Slowly, he pulls back, gazing up at me with adoring, lustful eyes as he releases my left hip.

I barely raise a questioning brow before I'm treated to a firm stroke at my entrance. His left hand pressing on my belly, Milo slides a finger inside me. The sensation is novel and exhilarating but somehow not enough, which he immediately fixes by adding a second. Now my heart races in earnest, my body adapting to the strange and wonderful pressure of a part of him inside my most intimate place. His eyes are glassy and half-open, lips parted as if he's enjoying this almost as much as I am. His fingers move gently, in and out, for just a moment. Then he presses them deeply inside me and keeps them there, moving in such a way that a new heat builds in my belly.

But just when I think I've figured out what's going on, he lowers his head and adds his mouth into the mix again, teasing my sensitive bundle of nerves until my body bucks and grinds with no conscious effort of my own. Milo's hand presses more firmly against my belly, holding me in place while everything else continues to move and drive a rapid wave of pressure deep in my core. My hands travel south and pull his head closer to me, fingers tightening in his silky hair.

Milo hums in response, and I fall right over the precipice with his name on my lips.

My body continues bucking, legs trembling as wave after wave of shudders wrack my body and starbursts flash behind my eyelids. I find myself completely unable to move, not even the fingers fisted in Milo's hair. He takes a few lazy laps with his tongue that send aftershock jolts across my body, then gently disengages himself from me. My fingers release him, but my hands don't move, dropping to my hips. My legs remain splayed, the air cold on my sensitive flesh without Milo pressed against it.

When I finally land back on earth and open my eyes, it's to find Milo hovering above me, his eyes sparkling with adoration.

I lift my heavy arms and pull him close for a languid kiss. Somehow, that simple act stokes the embers of my earlier fire, rekindling the deep burning need for him. My hands drift between us and I find my target: the silk-covered rod of his desire for me. Some instinct drives me to stroke it against myself where his lips have so recently been, and I'm suddenly not as sensitive as I was.

I'm already ready for more.

I drag his head through the slippery evidence of my desire for him, and Milo's eyes flutter closed, a groan escaping his lips that only encourages me further. I angle him at my entrance, my hips lifting of their own accord, seeking... more. Milo pulls back slightly and gazes down at me with utter devotion.

My eyes lock on his, and I have no more thoughts. I'm lost in the infinite depth of connection between us.

"Lily." His breath is warm and sweet on my face. "I love you. Not just because some witch declared you were my fated mate. I love you, Lilliana Harridan, for the incredible woman you are."

A single tear leaks from my eye, emotion rising in my throat. I didn't know how that would affect me, how badly I needed to hear it, until just now.

"I love you too, Milo. I didn't grow up knowing about fated mates, but since the first time we met, I've felt like I've always known you. The love I feel for you, and Landon and Jared, is all equal, but so incredibly different. What you and I have is special in a way I can't quite describe."

Milo's eyes turn glassy, an emotional smile curling his swollen lips. My brain and my heart are completely focused, hanging on the power of this moment.

My body, it seems, has no need for instruction from either. At the same time Milo presses gently forward, my hips rise to meet him, and he sheaths himself inside me completely.

A gasp rips from my lips at the same time as a moan slips from Milo's. My tight muscles flex and relax, trying to adjust to the way his presence is stretching me. The sensation's foreign and slightly uncomfortable, but I don't want him to withdraw.

With our eyes locked, he begins to rock his hips,

slowly emptying and refilling me over and over again. I'd frozen in place but now my body comes alive again, instinctually matching his rhythm, enjoying the novel sensation of being completely connected to him.

"Is this okay?" He murmurs with concern, watching my expression.

His body is hard against mine, and I realize I'm grimacing and still incredibly tense, which is probably why he's asking.

I draw a deep breath and nod, relaxing beneath him and allowing myself to open more. His pace increases, and soon my stomach flutters with that familiar pressure building low in my abdomen. I wrap my legs around his hips, urging him on, then pull him down for another kiss.

Soon we're lost in each other, our bodies speaking a language all their own. Heat builds between us and instinct takes over. I nip at his bottom lip with impatience. My fingernails carve into his back until he releases a rumbling growl and quickens his pace.

This is what I was seeking when I didn't know how to put it in words. This closeness, this intimacy, the two of us becoming one entity physically that somehow binds us for eternity. All this time I was afraid of sex, afraid of ending up a pregnant teen on the street or being taken advantage of. Finding out I had fated mates made the concept even more confusing, the expectation of intimacy with three men I'd never met before I arrived in Smoky Falls a few short months ago.

Now I understand the difference between sex and

making love, and what it means to have a mate. The primal part of me, the part with instincts and burning desire, knows how sex works, how it connects us. But it's also tied to the intangible connection between me and my mate. The physical pleasure is incredible, but something within me knows the deep emotional satisfaction I feel is more than just the physical act.

Milo slips his hand between our bodies, his thumb caressing my sensitive nub with a single stroke that pulls me firmly away from ruminating on our connection and drives my focus to the here and now. I'm aware of nothing but his continued motion, our bodies moving together and apart as if two pieces of one machine. The pressure of his thumb circling is enough to send me spiraling into oblivion, my body clenching around him as he continues to move within me. I shatter into a million pieces of ecstasy, clinging to him as he follows me over the edge, a low moan vibrating in his chest. He braces himself on his arms, but I pull him to my chest, both our bodies slick with sweat, and my tender, swollen lips seek his for a few more gentle kisses.

We lay for an indeterminate moment, our breath slowing and bodies cooling, enjoying the cocoon of intimacy that surrounds us.

My body feels boneless, every muscle heavy and relaxed. I don't have a care in the world. A haze coats the edges of my mind and I float within it, completely content to just be in the moment.

Eventually, he rolls to his side and scoops my body

against his, curling around me. Our forms mold together like they were made for this, and I nestle into the utter peace, wrapped in his warmth, inhaling his woodsy cedar scent.

"I should have shown you my drawings sooner," he quips in a whisper, pressing a kiss to the sensitive skin behind my ear.

A smile curls my lips; I feel home, in a way I had been seeking all my life. The ironic thought that at the very least I was no longer in danger of being a pregnant homeless girl flits through my mind like a leaf on the wind, and I snuggle tighter against Milo's chest.

Only for my eyelids to fly open a second later. Stiffening, I sit upright. *Oh no.*

"What's wrong?" Milo rises, worry etched into his handsome face.

I swallow hard. "We didn't use a condom. After all the lectures I've heard my entire life, the first time I have sex and I completely forget to use protection. I'm like a Lifetime special. What if I get pregnant?"

Milo rubs a palm across his face and smiles, releasing a relieved sigh. "Don't worry about it, you can't."

"What do you mean? Are you, I mean... can you not..." I don't know how to ask, since I've heard men are super sensitive about that subject.

He barks a laugh. "No, that's not it. You can't get pregnant until you accept all of your mates at the lunar eclipse; it's part of the weird and wonderful pack biology. Once we're officially mated, the pack witch will brew you a potion to prevent pregnancy… until you're ready to be a mom."

"Oh." How did I not know that? That definitely feels like something someone should have told me.

"Everything's fine, Lily. Come here." He lays back down and opens his arms. Taking the offer, I nuzzle into his chest and let him pull me close. Finally, I can relax; I breathe in his comforting scent, and allow myself to accept that he's truly mine.

Chapter Six

JARED

It feels as if every living thing within five miles of this place should know we're coming; that's how much noise Landon makes while we're *attempting* to sneak up on our enemy's stronghold.

"Can you be any louder?" I hiss for the third time.

Landon just glares back at me. "Everything is covered in leaves, genius. What do you want me to do? You're not exactly Mission Impossible over there, either."

I think I'm a great deal quieter than he is, but it won't get any better if we keep bickering. Instead, I ignore him and veer further away, hoping it'll be less obvious if we split up the noise.

When I reach the top, I'm relieved to discover tall

green hedges blocking me from view of the windows. It's also a lot windier up here, so the blowing leaves and creaking branches provide a fair amount of covering noise.

Rising above the hedge, a pristine white building sits rather close, clearly old but maintained. I run up and crouch next to the green wall, and Landon joins me a moment later. We both listen intently, but there's no sound aside from nature.

Landon's eyes meet mine. "Now what?" He asks in a low voice.

"I guess… we could walk around and see if there's a way to get through the hedge?"

He shrugs and nods, and we start our route along the back side.

It isn't a hedge so much as tall skinny evergreen trees planted so close together they grew into each other. The tips are about eight feet high, and the bushy branches end inches above the ground. In a pinch, we might be able to shimmy under, but I'd rather not.

Unfortunately, it's a solid green wall all the way around to the other side. We follow it quite a way down what we assume is the driveway, only for it to end at a low stone wall. Peeking around, I note that the other side is exactly the same, and there's no gate between them.

We duck back to the safe side to regroup. I glance over at Landon. "Any ideas?"

His expression is thoughtful, obviously already

trying to come up with a plan. "We can't go up the drive. It's like fifty yards with zero cover."

"Agreed."

"There's a couple cars parked in front, but I didn't see any activity, and the windows are dark. Not that it means anything, it's still daytime."

"Okay…"

"I don't think there's much else we can do aside from hang out a bit and hope we get lucky. Why don't we go back to the house and see if we can, like, peek through the trees or something?"

I shrug my acceptance of his idea and follow him back the way we came. His plan reminds me of a cartoon villain, but I don't really have any better suggestions, so it's worth a shot. We've just gotten close to the front of the house when the unmistakable sound of an approaching car reaches my ears.

We both drop to the ground, as if someone could spot us through the thick foliage.

Fearless super spies we are not.

The car rumbles up—some kind of sports car, or at least something with a souped-up engine—and comes to a stop just feet from our hiding place.

My heart is practically in my throat. Landon and I stare at each other with wide eyes, and I completely stop breathing when the car doors open.

"I can't believe he called us back here this soon," a reedy male voice grumbles. "I didn't get home until dawn." As if to emphasize his point, he yawns audibly. "Why can't someone else do guard duty tonight?"

A deeper, gruffer voice answers. "Because he doesn't want everyone to know what's going on yet, dimwit. Consider yourself lucky that Alpha trusts you enough to be involved."

The doors slam. "But why does he need guards? The witch built him an impenetrable *magic* prison. That freak's not getting out of there, period."

Footsteps crunching across leaf-strewn pavement move away from us. "He doesn't trust that witch any further than he can throw her. Did you know she killed her own mother for more power? That's cold, man."

"Yeah, she gives me the creeps. I mean, she's hot, but something about her screams crazy. I wouldn't touch that with a ten-foot pole."

The deeper voice laughs. "You're full of shit. If you got the chance, you'd hit it."

"Hell no," reedy voice insists. "I've made that mistake before, and I learned my lesson. You don't touch crazy. Not even for a hookup. *Especially* for a hookup. It's never worth it."

Their conversation stops right before a knock sounds, and a few moments later a door opens, then closes again. After that, it's just us and the wind in the trees.

I push out a heavy breath and breathe in again deeply. "I don't think I'm cut out to be a spy," I admit with a sheepish grin.

"Same," Landon agrees, his face flushed. "I have many talents and spying isn't one of them. Let's get out of here."

"I'm right behind you."

It's not until we're safely back on the trail with a fair amount of distance between us and the house that I dare to talk.

"So, I guess your instincts on that were dead on."

"Which ones?"

"This being the right place, first off. And he's definitely being held against his will. I'd say you were right all around."

"Yeah, I guess I was." Even though I just admitted he was right, Landon doesn't seem cheered by the thought.

"Everything all right?" I nudge him with my elbow.

"Not really. We know where he is, but we also know he's being guarded, and they've got him in some kind of magical prison. We have no way of getting him out of that, and Azalea is clearly still working with them. So I'm not sure how much it helps."

We clear the trees and find ourselves back at the trailhead, where my truck waits. I hit unlock on the remote and we clamber inside.

"That's true, but… she's not the only witch around." I start the engine and flash Landon a grin, then turn my tires toward home.

Chapter Seven

LILLIANA

~

I fell asleep in the comfort of Milo's arms, and when I wake up, it's a little disorienting. His room has no windows so it's impossible to guess what time it is, and he's still asleep judging by the even breaths tickling my ear.

As warm and relaxed as I feel, something is bothering me. Something drew me from sleep, insisting I get moving again.

It takes a moment for me to realize that I no longer feel that humming across my skin that signified I was touching one of my fated. A quick assessment of my body confirms it; our naked skin is touching in more places than I've ever had contact with another human, and I don't feel a single ripple.

Milo's arms tighten, and he radiates contentment that washes over me like a soothing fog. His lower body presses against mine and I feel him harden, drawing a flush to my cheeks at the memory of what we did earlier. It also immediately stokes the embers of my desire again.

Milo's lips press lightly along the back of my neck. "I have to say," he murmurs in a silky voice, "that this is definitely the best way I've ever woken up in my life. Hands down, no contest." His hips roll, pressing his erection into the convenient space between my cheeks.

The offer is tempting; it'd be easy to roll over and wrap my legs around him, getting lost in the physical and emotional connection that pushes anything else from my mind.

But I remembered what was bothering me, and even though it's not as painful as it has been, it's not going away.

I also realize I can't keep it a secret any longer.

As soon as I start moving Milo's arms loosen, allowing me to turn and face him. His dark hair is adorably mussed, flat on one side from sleeping on it. When I don't pull away completely, he gives me a sleepy version of his one-sided smile and my heart stutters.

"Do you know what time it is?"

I think he's going to ignore my question in favor of running a lazy finger along my shoulder, but he turns and asks for the time from his phone's AI.

I should have thought of that.

She answers that it's only a few hours since we left Harridan House, still evening. Milo moves on to tracing patterns across my chest and down to my breasts, and while it'd be very easy to let him continue, I know I need to cut this off.

"Milo," I start as he moves in to kiss my jaw.

"Mmm?" His tongue flicks out and taps my earlobe.

"Milo, I need to tell you something."

"Mmm-hmm?" His kisses have moved to my neck.

"Milo!" I can't help a giggle; it's like he's drunk on me. To regain control of the situation, I press both hands on his chest and he reluctantly moves a few inches back, his blue eyes promising mischief.

"I need to tell you something," I repeat, trying to get him to take me seriously. "And I don't think you're going to like it."

That did it. His playful expression changes to cautious curiosity. "Okay, I'm listening."

Now I'm nervous. What if it really upsets him? I don't know what kind of bomb I'm about to set off.

"Well… you know how we're fated mates…" I begin.

His sexy smile returns. "Yes?"

"And how Landon and Jared are also my mates?"

"Of course."

"And how none of us had a choice in the matter, it just… is?"

His smile drops. "Are you having second thoughts?"

The emotional hitch in his voice could break my

heart. "Of course not! Of course not. I love you." I lean forward and kiss him tenderly, and he accepts the reassurance. Sighing, I pull back. "There's just... something else we have to discuss about this whole mate thing."

His fingers are back to skimming across my skin. "What's that?"

I force the words out in a rush. "I think Derrek is my other mate. My *fourth* mate."

Milo's hand stills immediately, the lovey-dovey expression freezing on his face and turning into a neutral mask. "He can't be." His voice is clear, certain.

"Why not?" Despite my own feelings on the matter, I'd love for him to have an irrefutable reason Derrek can't be my mate. It would make things so much easier.

I can see the wheels turning behind his suddenly stormy blue eyes. "Because... he's not from our pack."

"Montrose split with us, so originally we were all one pack. They have the same family lines we do, so it's not impossible."

"The seer said *we* were your mates."

"The seer told each of your families that *you'd* mate the Harridan heir. I didn't have a seer present when I was born. So there was no one saying that *only* you three would be my mates."

Emotion floods his voice, and his expression turns concerned. "But why would this change now? It doesn't make any sense."

"Just... think about it for a minute with me. Before the split, the alpha took as many mates from the other seven families as she connected to. It wasn't unheard of for her to mate the others, but they defected because she most *often* mated the three. What if… what if there were other alphas after the split that would have mated wolves from Montrose, if only they'd had the chance? But the curse kept them apart?"

"It's impossible," he whispers, but the certainty he had a moment ago is gone.

I cup his cheeks with my hands, kissing him again. "Milo, it changes nothing between us. I love you, and Jared, and Landon. I'm claiming all of you at the ceremony. But I know in my gut, in my *heart*, that Derrek is also meant to be my mate."

"How do you know?" His sorrowful eyes search my face for answers.

"I feel… the same way about him that I felt about you three. As soon as he came to Smoky Falls, I realized there was something more to our connection than just our history. It kept calling me to him, and I think it was driving us both crazy because we couldn't figure it out."

"But you kicked him off of pack lands. You wouldn't do that to one of your fated."

"Wouldn't I? I thought he had betrayed me, and he wasn't even a wolf. Then he came back and saved me from Azalea, and I felt it again, like a… like a cord between us. And then we found out he's the Montrose alpha's heir. And that's when it all clicked into place. I was so hung up on knowing that you three were my mates, I didn't recognize the feeling for what it was. I didn't even consider it." Emotion wells in my throat and creeps into my voice. "But now my heart *aches* for him. It's killing me he's not here with us, safe, where he belongs. The way I feel… it's more than just concern for a friend. It's been ripping me apart since they took him away," I admit, my voice breaking. The emotion I've held back spills from my eyes in a trickle of hot tears that run across my nose and soak into the pillow.

Milo pulls me against his chest and tightens his arms around me. "It's okay, I'm sorry, Lily. It'll be okay." His murmured reassurances are peppered with kisses to my forehead. "If he's your fourth mate, that makes him part of our family. We'll get him back. You know better than any of us. I'm sorry I questioned you."

He waits until my sobs quiet, then gently pulls me away from the safety of his chest. His eyes lock on mine. "I'm sorry I reacted so poorly. For some reason, it felt like him being your mate meant that we weren't good enough… that *I* wasn't good enough. I know that's not how it works. But I'm over it, I promise. Okay?" He ducks his face to gaze up at me from beneath his lashes.

"Of course it doesn't mean you're not good enough, silly. All of you are probably far more than I deserve. I-"

"Well, now you're just being ridiculous," Milo growls, pushing his fingers under my arm and tickling my side. His other hand joins in and elicits peals of laughter from me as I try to fight him off and regain my dignity.

Once he's certain my mood is lifted, he stops tickling, and leaves me breathless with a goofy smile on my face.

"Come on, princess." He sits up and tugs at my hand. "We'd better get you back to Harridan House and figure out how we're going to rescue my new brother."

MILO

After the epic highs and spectacular lows of the last few hours, I'm not sure I can take another confrontation between Lily and Dom. Connected as we are now, I could easily lose my shit the second he so much as looks at her wrong. I'm half in a rage just imagining it before I realize what's going on. Focusing on the calm I feel from her touch, I bring myself back down to earth.

We dress quickly and get back in the car. The scent of her clings to me, my senses filled with it, and I realize I don't need to hold her hand to feel connected anymore. The sky is darkening, the sun already behind the mountains, but I can't help stealing glances at my gorgeous mate while I drive. Lily's dark hair is absolutely wild, her lips swollen and glossy from so much kissing.

As if she feels me watching, her gaze drifts from the road ahead to my face. A smile curls her lips, adoration clear in her emerald eyes. I return the grin and refocus on the road, filled to the brim with satisfaction.

"So, do you think Dom will still be there, or do you think he'll be gone?"

She's quiet for a moment, thinking. "I hope he's still there. I don't think he'll leave; he obviously cares about the pack. If what he said was true, he only left in the first place to search for a way to break the curse, and he came back."

"What if he only came back for Roxanne?" I suggest gently.

"Then… they have to do what's best for them."

"You could order her to stay."

"I couldn't do that to her. I know how much she cares about him, and I think it'd be pretty shitty of me to force her to choose. Besides, they haven't even worked through all of their issues yet."

"That's certainly true."

"So, I think he'll be there. I hope the ultimatum knocked some sense into him, or if not, that Roxanne knocked some sense into him."

A chuckle rumbles in my chest. "That's my alpha. Not concerned about him being right anymore?"

Her tone turns flirtatious. "Well, I seem to remember *someone* telling me he deserved to be put in his place."

A smile curls the corner of my lips. "Sounds like a wise person."

"I agree. I think I'll keep him around."

"I think that's an excellent idea."

Abruptly, the playful tone drops. "Regardless, I

can't be constantly worrying I'm making the wrong decision at every turn. I have to consider my options, listen to input from the people around me, and choose. If I choose wrong, I have to deal with the consequences."

"When did my adorable mate become so wise?"

"Maybe I just needed a nap."

"Maybe you did."

We ride in silence for a while. It's comfortable, not tense. I presume Lily is considering what to do in both scenarios, with Dom either there when we arrive or gone. Despite her casual response, I know she'll be upset if he left instead of staying and following her. It will feel like a strong rebuke on her ability to lead the pack. An incredibly unfair and selfish rebuke, for which I may have to hunt him down and use my fists to explain the error of his ways.

I suddenly realize my jaw is clenched so hard my teeth feel as if they could shatter, and my knuckles are white from gripping the steering wheel so hard. I force myself to draw in slow breaths and relax.

What the hell is going on? I feel as if I've been on an emotional rollercoaster in the last couple of hours. The only thing that's changed is...

"Hey, question: after... everything tonight, does anything feel different to you?"

I have no idea why I can't say what I mean, but hopefully she can read between the lines.

"Different how?"

"I dunno, just different."

"Well, I realized I don't feel the same when I touch you anymore."

That's not what I expected. "Is that a good thing or a bad thing?"

"I don't know. I don't think it's bad. When I first met you all, it was like... electric tingles on my skin when you touched me. Then when we got closer, it was kind of like a vibration. And now," she reaches over and claims my hand, "nothing. It feels the same whether or not I touch you."

"That's a bummer," I tease. "So I don't do it for you anymore. Is that what you're saying?"

"No," she laughs. "I'm saying that the comforting feeling I got from touching you is just... all the time now. Like you're always with me. Is that what you mean?"

I allow myself to preen internally while I consider what she said. "Not exactly, but now that you mention it, something does feel... different between us. I mean, aside from the obvious."

"Were you asking for a reason?"

"No, just curious."

"Hmm." Something tells me she doesn't believe me, but she won't push the issue.

Which is good, because I don't even know what the issue is yet.

"Lily?"

"Yes?"

"I... I'm really happy. Is that weird to say, with everything going on?"

"I don't think it's weird. Despite everything, I'm happy we made love, too."

My heart rate picks up. "No, not that. I mean, yes, that makes me happy, too. But I mean just… in general. I'm happy we're together, and I'm happy you figured out that Derrek is one of your mates and it makes you happy. I mean, I assume it makes you happy. You were kind of sad about it, but that's because he's at Montrose…" I trail off when I realize I sound like a lunatic.

What the hell is going on with me? I've never suffered from this kind of verbal diarrhea before. It's like I have absolutely zero control over myself right now. Like I'm freaking Landon.

Fortunately, Lily laughs it off. "That's a lot of happy. But I think I know what you're trying to say, and I feel the same." She gives my hand a squeeze and my heart slows again.

Deciding it's safer to stop talking, I focus on the road until we arrive safely at Harridan House. When we climb out of the car, I walk around to Lily and claim her hand. Whatever we're about to face, we're going to face it together.

Chapter Eight

DERREK

~

Apparently, it *is* possible for Azalea to tire of taunting me. After another couple hours of her droning, she stands up suddenly and announces she'll be back later.

I stopped really paying attention ages ago and have been trying to sleep, so the silence is quite welcome. When I hear the door shut I crack an eyelid open to peek, and sure enough there's no sign of her anywhere.

With a sigh, I stretch out on the cement floor, figuring laying on my back will be the most comfortable option. Even on the street I had blankets and something to use for a pillow. But I know the peace can't last forever, so I'd best make do.

Voices outside the door wake me from my nap, but

I'm still far too tired to care, and try my best to go back to sleep.

Unfortunately, it appears I have another visitor.

The door opens and Avery Nielsen's deep voice sounds remarkably jolly. "Well, I'd say you look pretty comfortable. Who says concrete doesn't make a good bed?"

I ignore him, uninterested in his taunting.

That was apparently not the desired response.

The light tone disappears from his voice. "I'm talking to you, son. The least you can do is answer."

"My apologies. It didn't sound like you were expecting a response. I thought it was a rhetorical question." I don't bother sitting up, preferring to answer without opening my eyes.

"A smart alec, I see. Well, I'm glad that the money our pack spent on your education wasn't completely wasted. Even if you did run off to live on the street like some mongrel."

"Indeed."

"I'm here to talk to you, boy."

"I'm listening."

His tone shifts from annoyed to thunderous in an instant. "You'll sit up and call me sir. Do you understand me?"

The reverberation in his voice rips through my body, squeezing my guts and making me gasp. I have no choice but to push myself into a sitting position, but I can still glare at him with every ounce of loathing I can muster. "Yes, *sir*."

"Now, that's better."

Ah, suddenly jolly again. So he's the kind of man who's nice as long as he's getting his way.

"How was your night, son?"

My jaw clenches. "Long, *sir*. Didn't get much sleep with my cousin hanging around. Finally managed to doze off when you arrived."

"Well, I apologize for that. You know how women are. She needed you to know how proud of herself she was. But I don't expect she'll be back for a while."

"Good to know, *sir*."

The malicious compliance is testing his patience, but it's not enough to piss him off yet.

"Have you had anything to eat? I'm sure you must be hungry. Maybe something to drink?"

"Can't say I've had either since I got here, *sir*."

"Well now, that won't do. Billy!" He shouts the name, and a man immediately appears in the doorway. "Fetch my son some food, will you? And bring him some water. Don't be stingy."

"Yes, Alpha." Billy hastens out the door to carry out Nielsen's bidding.

"There, Billy'll get you set up. My apologies you've gone this long. Usually, our hospitality is better than that."

"Thank you, *sir*."

His eye twitches, but he continues on. "I bet you're wondering why I came and got you like that last night."

The thought had crossed my mind, *sir*."

"Yes, well, you should know I didn't know you were

my son until a coupla nights ago. Your cousin was doing a... well, she did some spell, and she figured it out somehow. Can't say I understand how it works, magic and all. But then I remembered your mom and I had a bit of a fling, back in the day, and realized it was possible."

"I see, *sir*."

"'Course you understand once I knew I had a son, I had to find you right away. My mate passed before we had any children, and it was such a blessing to find out I've had a son this whole time."

"I imagine it was, *sir*. Bit odd you *forced* me to leave with you."

"Well, I hope you don't take that to heart. Since you didn't know who I was, I figured I ought to make it easier on everybody until we could have a chat. I didn't mean to upset you."

"Since I've never been under alpha compulsion before, *sir*, I'd say it was pretty upsetting."

"And I apologize for that. When it's just part of your everyday life, you don't quite remember what it was like without it."

Billy chose that moment to make his reappearance, carrying a tray laden with food and several bottles of water.

"Wonderful, thank you, Billy. Azalea said you can just pass that right through the barrier, it'll allow stuff to go in but not come back out. Just push it through the slot there. Why don't you grab hold of that when it comes through, Leaf?"

"Yes, *sir*." I accept the tray as it slides through the slot in the metal bars. A faint line of energy crackles around it, but otherwise it arrives safely in my hands.

Even though the food—and especially the water—is tempting, I glance up at Nielsen suspiciously.

"Go on and eat, son. No tricks, I promise. I have no reason to want to hurt you."

I consider for a long minute, but eventually decide the wise move is to accept what I'm given for now. It won't do me much good to die of dehydration in a few days, and I need to keep up my strength in case I get a chance to run.

I crack the top on one bottle and swallow down half of it before coming up for air.

"There you go, you enjoy. I think I'll head out for now. Let you get some rest. Billy! Get him some blankets and a pillow, will you?"

Billy's head ducks through the doorway, bobs, and disappears in a matter of seconds.

"If you're really interested in having a relationship with me, it'd probably be a good move to let me out of this prison."

Nielsen turns and smiles down at me. "Well, until I know I can trust you, I'm afraid I can't do that. We need to make sure we'agree about a few things first. But don't you worry, we'll have another chat. I'll see you soon, son. Real soon."

Chapter Nine

LILLIANA

~

When we walk into Harridan House, Mr. Carson rushes to welcome us.

"Dinner has just been served, Miss Lilliana. Everyone's already in the breakfast room." With a grave face, he motions for us to walk ahead.

My gaze darts to Milo, but he just shrugs. What exactly does he mean by 'everyone'?

As we get closer, some familiar voices reach my ears, and my heart gives an involuntary leap in response. Laughter from several people echoes down the hall. The anticipation makes my steps quicken, and I lengthen the distance between myself and Mr. Carson a good deal by the time we pass through the doors.

"...you know, I've never been a fan of facial hair,"

Jared pauses in the middle of his joke. He has a captive audience, the knowing grin on his face a telltale sign that he's having a good run. "But it's growing on me!"

Another round of appreciative laughter from the staff milling by the kitchen door and the group seated at the table.

"You really should get some new material," Milo teases loudly. "You told me that one last week."

"Yeah, and you laughed last week," Jared fires back, hopping out of his seat and crossing to greet us. He's handsome as ever with his warm brown skin and dark, shining eyes—even wearing a slightly muddy sweat suit.

"Woah, woah, hold on just a minute," I press a hand to his chest to stop the oncoming hug and affect a serious air. "What on earth is on your head? Is there something you need to tell me, Jared?"

He's confused for just a second until he reaches up and snatches the bright orange cap off his head. "There's a reason for it, and it's not that I'm transferring to UT, promise." His thick lips split into a pearly grin, and he holds his arms wide for me, waiting patiently.

I duck into his chest and enjoy the warm vibration that flutters across my skin when his lips touch my forehead.

"I missed you today, gorgeous."

"We missed you too. And you too, Landon," I add, peeking around Jared's muscular shoulder to grin at my other mate who's waiting his turn.

Landon grabs my hand with long, delicate fingers

and tugs me away from Jared. "Not as much as I missed you, I guarantee it." His light brown eyes sparkle with joy, the sexy dimples appearing on his cheeks as he leans in for a kiss.

My heart does a little pitter-pat when his fingers caress my jaw and his lips touch mine. I still maintain that if he had the inclination, he could easily become the lead singer of a band and break a million girls' hearts. However, he is extremely shy about his music and vehemently uninterested in any girl but me.

I pull back, slightly breathless, and gaze up at him dreamily. It takes me a minute to notice he's in a hoodie and track pants, also coated with a fair amount of dirt.

"What did your dad have you guys doing, rolling around in the mud?" My gaze sweeps between them, and their sheepish expressions ping my instinct that something's up.

Eyes narrowing, I cross my arms and take a step back. "Obviously, you guys aren't telling me something. Out with it."

Jared pipes up. "We'll tell you everything, but why don't we sit down and have dinner before it gets cold? We can talk and eat." He doesn't sound worried; in fact, he sounds rather pleased with himself.

I raise a brow in disbelief. "Mrs. Dowling is fine with you two sitting at the table like that?"

They both glance down in unison, as if only now realizing how dirty they are.

My uncle's stern voice calls out from behind my mates, silencing the room completely. "Mrs. Dowling is off tonight; I told them it's okay, so if she wants to lay into someone she can talk to me."

The boys split apart, so I have a direct line of sight with Dom. He's got an odd sequence of expressions crossing his dark features, as if he can't decide whether he's amused, embarrassed, or annoyed. Roxanne is beside him, and after a moment elbows him subtly in the ribs.

"I mean," he adds gruffly, "if that's okay with you, of course. It's your house."

My gaze darts to Roxanne, who nods slightly and shoots me a small smile. When I refocus on Dom, his expression is now solidly uncomfortable.

I decide to let him off the hook. "Alright, they might as well eat since the food's ready. Just... put a napkin on the chair or something, guys. You know Dowling will notice a solitary *speck* on those embroidered cushions."

Dom's face relaxes, and the four of us head to the table to claim our seats. Dishes of tender beef, whipped potatoes with thick gravy, fragrant, fresh-baked rolls and brown sugar carrots make their way around the table.

My stomach rumbles loudly, and Milo glances my way with that sexy smirk. "Hungry, are you? You must have really worked up an appetite earlier."

I almost snort water straight out my nose, but manage to swallow the mouthful and set the glass down before I injure myself. Milo reaches over and pats me gently on the back as if he hadn't just made a comment laden with innuendo. A few small coughs and my windpipe clears, so I shoot him a warning glare. "I can't say I did. It was a pretty dull afternoon." Even though my tone is sharp enough to cut through stone, Milo continues grinning.

"My mistake."

If anyone else is curious about our brief exchange, they don't act like it. I'd been slightly apprehensive about returning, and not just because of Dom. Since I arrived in Smoky Falls, it's seemed as if everyone could tell exactly what was going on between me and my mates without a word from any of us. This occasion— which to me feels huge, even outside of the every-girl experience of losing my V-card—seems like a non-event as far as they all can tell. I thought for sure my other mates would notice something different, but they sure aren't acting like it.

I decide to tuck into my dinner since that's occupying everyone else currently at the table. The staff have long since retreated to the kitchen to eat.

Knowing that my mates are bottomless pits when it comes to food, I'm not really surprised that they're far too busy stuffing their faces to talk right now. However, I am surprised that Dom and Roxanne haven't spoken a word, particularly since they normally consider meals the best time to catch up.

It occurs to me that things aren't all sewn up between them following Dom's sudden arrival last night. Also that they might be hesitant to talk in the wake of my outburst earlier.

Everyone continues eating silently, and the scrape of

knives and forks on porcelain grows unbearably loud in the uncomfortable silence.

"So, let's hear it, you two." Everyone glances up from their plates, and Jared and Landon realize my gaze is focused on them. "What were you up to today? I'm getting the feeling you weren't 'doing something for your dad', as I was told."

They glance at each other, volumes being spoken between their eyes. I can practically hear the silent conversation, each of them trying to convince the other to answer.

Finally, Jared returns my gaze. "You're right, that was just an excuse so you wouldn't ask what we were doing."

"You realize I'm asking now, right?"

"Yeah, we just didn't want you to know until we got back."

Landon swings a backwards fist at Jared's arm and lands a solid blow, making Jared wince and rub the afflicted spot. "It's not that we didn't want you to *know*; it's that we didn't want you to worry."

"That's fine, but somebody needs to tell me what you did and why I would be worried if I knew."

"We went to Montrose territory," Landon forces out at double his normal pace.

"You *what*?" My incredulous question is echoed across the table in my uncle's disapproving voice.

Jared takes over. "We thought—since we're not officially mated yet—it would be easy for us to slip into town and just see if we could figure out where they're holding Derrek. We knew you were worried about him, and we also knew it would be a long, drawn-out process to come up with a plan. So we just went for it. And we found him!" He adds in a rush, noting the furious expression on my face.

His last-minute comment completely derails me. "You did?!"

"Yeah," Landon nods, grinning. "Turns out Montrose has a 'mayor's house' that's kinda set back in the woods, and there are some hiking trails nearby. So we found our way to the house and just kind of snooped around outside, hoping to hear or see something. And these two guys showed up whining about having to do guard duty."

My fingers clutch Milo's under the table. "That's... that's great! So he's at this 'mayor's house,' you're sure? Did you hear anything else?"

A wide grin spreads across Jared's cheeks. "Sure did. They said Derrek is in a magical prison cell that Azalea made, and that their alpha doesn't want the entire pack to know what's going on, so he's keeping his circle tiny."

Landon pipes up. "And that Azalea killed her own mom to take her powers."

"She *what*?" This time, the interruption comes from Roxanne. "That's impossible."

Landon shrugs, refocusing on his food. "I dunno. That's what they said. They also said she's crazy."

Well, that tracks.

My eyes seek Dom's across the table. "I guess we know where he is now."

My uncle nods slowly. "Sounds like it. It's definitely a good starting off point." He turns his focus to the guys. "What else can you tell me about this house?"

"We didn't get inside, and we don't know exactly where Derrek is. But the house itself is on top of like a little hill, there's one driveway up to it, and about fifty yards out from the house a giant hedge lines the drive and surrounds the entire thing. Short of bringing a chainsaw, you won't get through it. The only options are going over somehow—it's over eight feet and impossible to climb—or going up the main drive where you'll be completely exposed to everyone in that house. Easy pickings for anyone with a rifle."

Dom's eyes cloud as he considers their assessment. I poke at my food, appetite suddenly gone.

It's not like I'm some kind of battle strategist, but that doesn't sound good. Milo squeezes my hand in encouragement and lobs a question of his own.

"You guys never told us why you look like you fell out the back of a truck."

Jared's chin ducks, his expression distinctly embarrassed. "We got kind of freaked out when we heard those guys pull up and we dropped to the ground. I guess it was kind of muddy there. We didn't really think about it until we were almost here and didn't want to turn around and go home first. We have some stuff here, after all. And then they said dinner was ready right when we walked in the door, so we figured, might as well shower after."

"I'd say that's a solid plan. Why don't you two get cleaned up and then we'll all convene in the library to go over this new information." Dom winces as if in pain, then adds, "If that is alright with you, Lilliana?"

Once again my eyes dart to Roxanne, who's stroking her bundle of neat black braids with downcast eyes and an unmistakable smirk.

"I think that's a great idea, thank you," I answer with a benevolent smile. "But dessert first."

LANDON

Even though I know we're going to be her mates soon and involved in these decisions, it still feels weird to be sitting at a table with the alpha, the beta, and a former alpha, discussing plans of this magnitude. Milo's been glued to Lily's side since we arrived, and Jared and I sit on either side of them. Even though it's meant to be a team working together, the thick tension in the air makes me wonder if Jared and I didn't miss something major during our outing today. Lily and her uncle are clearly doing their best to behave civilly, and only achieving it half the time.

"We know where he is now, for certain. We should at least try to get onto Montrose lands and see if it works. You don't know that he's banned me from the territory. It's just speculation." Lily's voice is razor sharp.

"Just as it's speculation that we'll be able to march up to that house and find him," Dom retorts. "We don't know what's laying in wait inside; there could be any number of guards, hazards, or traps."

"But Landon and Jared said-"

"I *know* what they said, but we have to try to verify more before we plan an attack."

Milo slams his hands on the table, standing to his full height and leaning forward with a sneer. "Don't forget who you're talking to, *Dominic*. You're lucky Lily is still including you in this conversation at all. If you want to continue to be a part of this discussion, I suggest you apologize to my mate for interrupting and listen to your alpha." His voice is a throaty growl, and I'm shocked; I've never seen Milo lose his cool like that before.

Jared and I exchange a wide-eyed glance, and even Lily looks up at him in surprise.

"Thank you, Milo," she soothes, placing a light hand on his forearm to coax him back in his seat. "I'm sure Dom didn't mean any disrespect."

Dom's face has turned a deep shade of red, as if he wants to shout but knows better, so he's holding it in.

Roxanne decides this is the opportune time to speak up. "I know we all want the same thing: to rescue

Derrek as quickly as possible, in the safest way we can. The information Jared and Landon provided is extremely helpful, but I do agree with Dom that it's not enough to launch a full-on attack and just hope for the best."

Dom blows out a breath, and the color in his face gradually returns to normal. "Yes, thank you. That's what I meant. I apologize for interrupting, Lilliana. I think we've accurately covered the information we know, but we need to figure out what information we still need, and how we're going to get it. That should be decision number one."

Lily's eyes close for a few seconds and she draws in a deep breath, then releases it. "Okay." There's another handful of heartbeats before her eyes open and she speaks again, her gaze laser-focused on her uncle as she runs down her thoughts like a list. "We need to know if we can cross the boundary into Pack Montrose. We need to know how many people are in the house at any given time. We need to know where Derrek is exactly, the properties of this magical prison they said Azalea has him in, *and* what it takes to get him out."

Dom nods in agreement. "Yes, to all of that. We also need to know how many of Nielsen's pack are actually involved or know what's going on, and why he's suddenly so keen to have Derrek under lock and key."

"Agreed. So now that we have our list, how do you propose we get these answers?"

At this, the former alpha's lips curl into a grin that

looks distinctly devious when combined with his dark beard and flashing eyes. "From the enemy themselves, of course."

Chapter Ten

DERREK

The first thing I notice when I wake up is that I'm warm and reasonably comfortable, which is a surprise given that I'm sleeping on a concrete floor. But the thick blanket and pillow that Billy brought in did the trick, and I actually feel rather well-rested.

Then the feeling of being watched registers, raising the hairs on my neck, and I know I'm not alone.

They must have been staring at me, just waiting for me to wake up, because the second I move, they begin speaking.

"Ah, there's my boy. Sleep well, son?"

An unpleasant voice answers, "Sure sounded like it to me. I didn't know someone could snore that loud."

Well, this is bound to be interesting.

I sit up slowly, taking my time to meet the two unwelcome faces staring at me through the metal bars and the invisible shield of my cell.

"Sorry, didn't realize we were doing the family reunion today. I'm not exactly dressed for the occasion." I gesture to my shirtless, unwashed state. Given the lack of bathroom facilities, I'd had to avail myself of the bucket. So I sacrificed my shirt to cover it to reduce the foul smell and discourage associated insect life.

"Always that sharp sense of humor, just like me." Nielsen grins as if he's truly a proud father.

Azalea rolls her eyes and shifts her weight from one one black platform boot to the other. "Hilarious. Shall we get on with this? The smell is disgusting."

Nielsen waves her forward, and Billy steps out of the doorway with a set of keys. When I spot something made of black leather in Azalea's hand, I jump to my feet on high alert. I don't know what's going on here just yet, but my every instinct is telling me it isn't good.

Billy inserts the key into the lock and turns, then carefully grips the iron bars of the door and swings it open. The magical wall flickers, his proximity enough to make the spell react.

Azalea struts through the opening and eyes me up and down with a nasty smirk on her face. I might be able to use magic against her since she's within the force field, but something tells me she's already considered that possibility and I wouldn't change my circumstances by trying.

She strides slowly around me, as if assessing my

sorry state. "The last twenty-four hours haven't done you any favors, cousin. You look terrible, and you smell like a *dog*."

I should have seen it coming, or at least suspected something. But my focus is torn between her and Nielsen, and I thought if there were any surprises, they'd come from him.

Just as she whispers the last word in my ear, something black flies past my eyes and tightens around my neck. The second it touches my skin, it shocks me like waves of open electricity. I gasp for breath and the searing bolts shoot down my throat, inflicting such agony I can't even breathe. My fingers scrabble at the thick leather, trying to find purchase to rip the thing off. Doubled over in pain, I drop to my knees and struggle vainly to draw in air.

Azalea snickers and exits my cell, passing through the magical field as if it were nothing more than light.

My hands slide to the back of my neck as I search for some sort of buckle, but there's none; the collar is as smooth as the front, and equally adhered to my skin. The only difference is some kind of metal loop attached to the leather, but there's no break in the circle around my neck.

"It's not going to kill him, is it?" Nielsen asks mildly. "He's kinda purple."

"Nah, just give it a minute for the spell to settle. He'll be fine."

"Good, 'cuz he's no good to me dead."

"Same."

Nielsen glances aside at Azalea, his eyes narrowing in response to her words. If she notices she doesn't react, just settles herself onto the wheeled office chair she used yesterday and leans back, waiting.

After an unimaginably long, torturous moment, the pain subsides and my throat opens, allowing me to draw in ragged breaths. The alpha seems somewhat relieved, and Azalea is clearly smug.

"See? He's just fine. In another minute or two, he'll be right as rain."

"And you're sure this will work?"

"Oh yeah. I tested it on some kid's dog. Lassie didn't have any way to tell mister Rogers that Timmy was in the well with that thing on."

I spare a second's hope that she was just referring to the show and hadn't actually hurt a child before considering my own plight. Glaring daggers at them both, I focus on filling my lungs and wait for the next nasty surprise.

"I think you ought to prove it before we go any further here."

Whatever is going on, Nielsen clearly doesn't trust Azalea. I file that away for later. It could be useful.

Sighing theatrically, Azalea answers, "Fine. Leaf, what do you think of your new accessory?"

I choose not to answer that comment, and after a few beats, she sighs again. "This really isn't fun, Leaf. We're dying to get your thoughts on the matter. Would you tell me for a cookie?"

I stand up, planning to tell her where she can shove

that cookie, but when I try to speak the blinding pain erupts in my throat, leaving me gasping for breath and madly clawing at my neck like a raccoon on a leash.

The second I think about it, the blood drains from my face in realization. Azalea's taunting about smelling like a dog wasn't just bluster; she literally put a collar on me.

"There, you see?" she states in a smug, self-satisfied tone. "If he tries to speak, the pain stops him before he can even make a sound. I promise he's perfectly docile now."

Nielsen's eyes light up and he rubs his hands together. "Well damn, excellent work, Miss Wintree. That will do nicely."

Azalea performs a pleased, mocking curtsey with the pleats of her tiny plaid skirt. "Are you ready for the next bit?"

"Indeed, go right ahead."

I brace myself for more pain, eyes following every move Azalea makes and my body preparing to block or dodge whatever comes flying at me. Even though I know it's unlikely I can change the outcome, my fight-or-flight response has taken over control.

Azalea is standing in front of the cell now, chanting with both her hands up, palms toward the magic field. When nothing hits me after thirty seconds, I unclench my muscles and pay closer attention. Flickers of bright white and hazy purple streak across the space between us, and in just a few more seconds, the magical wall buzzes once, then flashes out of existence.

And I understand. Her magic wall kept me from freeing myself of this prison with my magic. Now that I'm collared and magically gagged, they don't need it anymore.

Nielsen laughs with delight. "Excellent! Now we can move forward. Come on, son, let's get you out of that cell. It's served its purpose."

I glare at him warily, backing into the corner. I can't fathom a reason that removing me from this room will mean anything good.

"Now, don't be like that," Nielsen chides, as if I'm a misbehaving toddler. "I'm sorry for it, but the collar is necessary. For my protection, you understand. Until I can trust you, I can't have you working spells and turning me into a barn owl or something!" He grins widely, as if I'm in on this joke. "But come on, son. I have a better facility for you, much nicer than this one. You've got a bed, and a shower, and of course a toilet. I'm sure you'd like to clean up a bit, change clothes?"

I still don't trust it. I feel like a caged animal and the only safe place is the one I already know.

Abruptly, Nielsen sighs as if he's bored and drops the friendly act. "Fine, have it your way, then. Miss Wintree?"

A wicked grin curls Azalea's lips. "With pleasure."

A handful of spoken words accompany a flick of her fingers, and a black leather strap appears in her hand. My eyes follow the line in horror to realize it's snaking across the floor and directly up my body, where it's attached to the collar by the ring that was behind my neck a moment ago. Now it sits directly below my chin.

She hands it to Nielsen smugly. "Here you are, sir."

"Incredible." His expression is awed and yet calculating, as if he's considering how easily she could put a similar leash around *his* neck.

After a beat, he switches his focus to me. "Alright Leaf, I'm going to ask you one more time before I make you come with me. This doesn't have to be hard; in fact, I'd prefer to do it nice and easy. Wouldn't you?"

That he's got a leash and is now threatening to forcibly remove me solidifies the feeling that nothing good waits for me outside this room. I know, logically, that it won't pay me to resist; clearly he's going to get his way no matter what. However, I can't force my body to stop fighting in the face of such an imminent threat.

Nielsen shakes his head slowly, as if he's a loving but disappointed father. "How does this thing work, Miss Wintree?"

"Just give it a tug like a normal leash. You'll see."

Without missing a beat, he yanks on the leash, hard. I was expecting a powerful pull; I was not prepared for an irresistible force that throws me across the room to land sprawling at his feet. The side of my face smacks the concrete floor, causing immediate stars to dance in my vision and a throbbing pain to spread from the impact. The rest of my body feels as though I've just been hit by a car, and I can do nothing but lie there and gasp for breath once again.

"Well, I'll be," Nielsen comments, as if he just witnessed something mildly entertaining. "I guess I don't know my own strength!" He laughs at his own joke and Azalea joins in, her affected peals sounding rather forced.

Still chuckling, Nielsen crouches by my side. "Now, I'll give you another shot, son. Are you going to walk, or is this how it's going to be?"

My attempt to answer shoots immediate fire down my throat, so I nod in response, gasping for breath.

"Good, we're understanding each other. Now, why don't you hop up and we'll head to your new room."

Trying to ignore the shooting pains across my body, I force myself from the ground and bring my feet beneath me, standing shakily. My vision is blurred, my head spinning, but I stay erect and try to appear uneffected by the shocking blow.

"Good boy," Nielsen comments, as if he's training a rottweiler who just performed a trick. "Now we'll head out the door and swing a right. As long as you don't resist, I won't pull, understood?" I nod again, and follow him stiffly when he walks toward the doorway that Billy disappeared through a moment ago.

Azalea's heavy boots clomp behind me, and once we pass through the door, Nielsen says dismissively, "That's all, Miss Wintree. I'll call you when we need you."

I don't have to turn and see her face to know his abrupt dismissal pisses her off. "I think not," she replies hotly. "I have a vested interest in making sure-"

"That's all I said!" Nielsen thunders. "If I have further need of your services, I'll let you know. Now get out! Billy, will you kindly show this witch to the door?"

Eager with anticipation, I turn to watch Azalea's reaction. If she loses her shit for just a moment and strikes him, there's a chance he'll drop the leash and I can make my escape. Grannie could certainly undo the spell on this collar, and then I can go back to Smoky Falls.

But it's a vain hope. Despite her face turning red with fury, Azalea doesn't make a single move against Nielsen. Billy approaches her cautiously, gesturing her down a hallway that splits from ours, and in a huff, she turns on her heels and stomps away. "You'll hear from me soon!" she shouts back at us threateningly.

Nielsen acts as if she doesn't exist and continues down the hall. "Come along, son."

I fall into step a few paces behind him, supremely aware of his grip on the leash. This place is like a maze; I try to keep track of all the lefts, rights, and forwards we take, but my brain's too muddled and given that I arrived with a bag over my head, I don't even know how I got to my old cell from the outside.

It's obvious when we reach my new room: two guards are already waiting outside. My heart is absolutely racing in dread of what's coming, but I follow Nielsen dutifully through the door.

To my utter surprise, the room has all the things he promised. There's a comfortable-looking bed, a night-stand with a lamp that emits a warm glow, and a dresser. A stack of towels and clean clothes sits on the bed, and a doorway to the left reveals a small bathroom.

It's not until I turn to my right that the full story hits me. Where the left side is a snug little space with a decidedly cozy feel, the right is an industrial wall-to-wall metal cage like you'd expect to find in a kennel. The interior is nearly featureless except for a large, sinister looking drain in the floor.

And directly behind me, just outside the cage, hang a number of torture devices on long poles, locked in a clear plastic case. Some look like sharp stabbing or cutting instruments, and one I'm fairly certain is a cattle prod. I don't know what half of them are, which is even more disturbing.

"See?" Nielsen gestures. "Just like I promised."

The memory of the searing pain when I tried to speak is still at the forefront of my thoughts, so I keep my mouth firmly closed. My eyes dart to him in alarm, and he knows what I'm thinking without me having to say it.

"Well, son, now that you're here, we have a minor problem. I can't claim you as my heir, truly, until you shift and prove you're a wolf under that sheep's clothing. I didn't build this room for you, mind. It's common for some folks to need help connecting with their wolves. So we have a program and it's actually quite successful; often people just need the right motivation if they're struggling to shift."

Seeing my disgusted expression, he pats my shoulder in what I suppose is meant to be a reassuring way. "Don't worry, son, we don't start with the hard stuff. Tonight you'll get yourself cleaned up, have a nice meal, and a good night's rest in a cozy bed. Tomorrow we'll get to work at Level 1. And if that's all it takes, the better for everyone. But if you don't respond to the treatment, well… let's just say things get a bit more complicated. For those who struggle, we find that sharing the room with the cage, even when you're not in it, is extremely motivating. I hope you won't learn that lesson tomorrow."

And with that, he unhooks the leash from my collar, smiles benignly, and strides back through the doorway, whistling.

Chapter Eleven

LILLIANA

～

It's not until dusk two days later that Dom returns with his 'friends'. Roxanne met him at the border to our pack lands and allowed them access, with my uncle vouching for them.

Since he has no actual authority in the pack, he can't even invite anyone from Montrose in following my proclamation; it's a small thing but I draw satisfaction from reminding him of his lack of standing in *my* pack.

Along with several of our security team, Roxanne escorted them—blindfolded—to Harridan House, where my mates and I were waiting.

Four Pack Montrose members come through the door, their eyes immediately devouring the cavernous entrance. Reaching out with my senses, I can get a vague read on their emotional states, but nothing so concrete as what I draw from my pack. There's a nervous energy, which is to be expected, but nothing that leads me to believe they have evil intentions.

Nothing to tell me they'll be at all helpful, either. Dom insisted we could trust them, and without a better plan, I decided it was worth a shot.

As I scan their appearance, the only thing that strikes me is that they look... normal. Not remotely like henchmen to a supervillain who wear matching black turtlenecks and combat boots. They're all just normal guys, ranging from mid-twenties to mid-forties, if I had to guess. However, they all wear matching expressions of distrust as their eyes settle on me.

Dom steps forward to begin introductions. "Guys, this is Lilliana Harridan, and her prophesied mates Jared, Landon, and Milo." They nod stiffly in my direction. "Alpha, this is Brad, Jeff, Billy, and Matt." Dom lists their names in order of where they stand facing me, with the apparent oldest and youngest in the middle. All of them are fit, but the eldest, Jeff, is significantly muscled, and the youngest, Billy, is rather thin in comparison.

"Thank you for coming," I address them directly. "I assume Dom gave you the basics about why we've requested your help, so let's sit down to a meal and discuss what we can do for each other." I gesture toward the formal dining hall, then turn and walk in that direction with my mates, leaving the others to follow.

There's really no need for us to dine in this massive room—it's simple to add a second table to the breakfast room—but I decided a small show of authority couldn't hurt. We sit on opposite sides of the long table: Montrose with Dom on one side and Roxanne with me and my mates facing them, allowing the security team to claim seats on both ends and make the group feel even larger, and our guests less significant. Jeff is directly opposite me, and I quickly conclude that he's the de facto leader.

Mr. Carson and Mrs. Dowling have arranged an impressive dinner service, and fragrant dishes releasing curls of steam are soon moving around the table. The guests are served first, but even when they've filled their plates, their gazes remain locked on me, their expressions firm as they wait.

I'm not their alpha, but perhaps this is a sign that they're showing me deference, anyway? The only other thing I can conclude is they either have superb manners or suspect I've poisoned the food. Jeff's steely grey eyes watch me select a fork, and once I take the first bite, he picks up his own and the others quickly follow suit.

My heart has been racing since the second they stepped foot in my house, but I do my best to appear relaxed, hoping it will reassure them. Aside from the scrape of silverware on plates and the crackling fireplaces, very little sound travels through the cavernous room.

Finally, I can't take the tension anymore. Noting the hat the youngest is wearing, I ask, "Are you a UT fan,

Billy?" I state the question casually and continue eating while I wait for this response.

His eyes immediately dart to Jeff, who nods subtly, and then back to me. "Yes, ma'am. I grew up in Knoxville."

"Do you like it there? Or do you prefer Montrose? I've heard both are very scenic. Quite different in sizes, though."

This time, his answer comes slightly faster. "That's a troublesome question, ma'am. In some ways, they're both home for me."

I flash him an understanding grin. "That makes perfect sense to me. I grew up on the west coast, so I still somehow think of LA as home. But as soon as I came to Smoky Falls, it was also home. I wonder how different it would feel to have always been here."

Billy seems relieved by my reaction and smiles tentatively before turning his attention to his food. Jeff, on the other hand, is still eyeing me like a snake that could strike him at any moment.

"Did you all grow up elsewhere, or were you raised in Monrose?"

The blond man Dom identified as Brad answers first. "I grew up in Charleston. Most of my family is still there."

"Did you like it there? Do you visit often? It's only a few hours from Montrose, I believe?"

"About three, ma'am. And I visit as often as I can. I stay pretty busy with the baby and all."

A family man, then. "That's understandable. And congratulations! Is it a boy or a girl?"

His cheeks turn pink and a genuine smile cracks his stern expression. "A little girl, Olivia Jade. She just turned two months."

"That's a beautiful name. I'm sure you and your wife have your hands full. Is she your first?"

"Yes ma'am. We do, but I wouldn't have it any other way. She's perfect." Brad is now grinning so broadly I wonder if it hurts his cheeks.

"Congratulations again," I smile back. Turning my focus to the other side of their group, I ask, "And Matt, what about you?"

"I have two kids, ma'am, and I was born and raised in Montrose. It's a great town to raise a family," he adds, as if expecting my next question. "Are you looking to move?"

I laugh lightly. "Not at the moment, I'm afraid. But I haven't been able to see much of this area since I arrived. I would love to visit sometime."

Suddenly, the four of them shift uncomfortably, and the conversation dies.

Sighing, I turn my focus back to my plate. Clearly, I'd said the wrong thing.

We suffer through the rest of the meal in virtual silence, and it's not until my staff clears the dishes away and brings out desserts with a carafe of coffee that I attempt again.

"I suppose we can do away with the pleasantries at this point. You know why Dom asked you to come:

Your alpha forcibly removed Derrek from my territory and I'm concerned about his safety. I don't want to interfere with your pack business, but I need to know that he's okay, and free to leave if he wants to."

The three younger men turn to Jeff, whose jaw clenches and eyebrows lower. "You say you don't want to interfere in our pack business, but it seems to me that's exactly what you're trying to do," he retorts in a gravelly voice. "What business is it of yours if he's okay? Leaf belongs to Pack Montrose."

A surge of fury rises in my chest at the challenge, and I force it down with a few slow breaths. I can't reveal just why he's so important to me, or it'll put him in even more danger. "He and I have been friends for a very long time, dating back to my childhood in Los Angeles. He was here, teaching classes, before your alpha entered my territory, claimed he was his heir, and took him against his will. I have every reason to be concerned about his well being."

"The alpha can do whatever he likes with his pack members."

"It's my understanding that Derrek was disowned by the pack when he failed to complete a mission on behalf of the alpha."

"Once he knew *Leaf* was his son, the alpha chose to be merciful and welcome him back."

"I wouldn't consider tying *Derrek* up and dragging him away very 'welcoming.'"

"Well, like I said, it's none of your business," the older man replies stubbornly.

The fury gets the better of me. "If you're so determined to be unhelpful, why did you even come here?"

Jeff meets my energy head on, snarling right back. "I wanted to know if you're the incredible alpha Dom claims you are, or if you're just a teenage girl on a power trip. So far I haven't seen anything to impress me."

A swift wave of gratification swoops through me to hear that, despite his behavior, my uncle has been singing my praises to complete strangers.

My mates have been dutifully silent until now, but at this insult, Milo jumps to his feet, his chair tumbling backward. "You will not speak to the alpha that way in her own home," he snarls viciously. "You are a guest here, and as such, I won't dishonor her by attacking you. However, if you have no interest in helping, I'm happy to show you to the door."

When he rises, my eyes turn to him in surprise. A deep angry red creeps up his face, veins pulsing in his neck as he verbally tears into the much older man. His fingers grip the table so tightly they're turning white.

"Milo." I set a hand gently on his arm. "Thank you. I can take it from here."

My mate exhales a long, unsteady breath and reclaims the seat Mr. Carson had already replaced behind him.

I give him one more reassuring pat and turn my attention back to my apparent opponent. "I'm not here to put on a performance for you," I tell him coldly. "Dom assured me there were good people at Pack

Montrose that want us to work together. I invited you here on good faith, but if you have none for me, this conversation is over."

"He's not free to leave," Billy interjects in a rush. "He's being held against his will. And they're hurting-"

"Billy!" Jeff turns to the younger man in absolute fury. "Shut it, now!"

"What does it matter? She already knows he doesn't want to be there. It's hardly as if she doesn't suspect they're torturing him."

It's not the news I was hoping for, but his willingness to talk gives me a tiny crumb of hope.

"So what exactly do you expect of me, Jeff? What were you hoping to see that would impress you? So far, I've welcomed you into my home, served you dinner, and attempted to be civil despite your behavior."

The older man snorts, his face turning red. "More than fancy houses and tea time, that's for damn sure. All I see is a spoiled little girl who surrounds herself with weak males and differential staff that play into her every whim. You-"

"That is enough," I growl, the alpha command rumbling deep in my chest as I stand and face him. "I don't hold power over my pack because I threaten them with violence or submission. My pack is strong because we all believe in one thing, despite the curse we live under, thanks to *your* pack. So I'd say it is a sign of incredible *strength* that—despite all of that—I've reached out to you in the hopes we could work together. That members of my pack are here serving *you*

138

without complaint or animosity, knowing that you enjoy freedoms your ancestors stripped from us decades ago."

Jeff stands, leaning over the table to meet me at eye level despite being nearly a foot taller. "If you're so strong, *prove* it."

I glare at him without flinching. "And what exactly would you consider 'proving it'?"

At this, he rises to his full height. "I've only been defeated by two wolves: the alpha, and the beta. If you can best me in a fight, then perhaps I'll believe you can take on *our* alpha."

He wants me to fight him as a wolf? Doesn't he realize females are stronger?

My eyes dart to Roxanne, who clears her throat. "By Montrose tradition, wolves hold contests to determine their place in the pack. It's not similar to the fights you've had in the past," she adds, implication clear: he's unable to claim my position as alpha even if he wins.

And he will lose spectacularly.

"Fine," I agree. "We'll have your little showdown in front of my pack at midnight."

Chapter Twelve

DERREK

~

"Again."

An icy water spray, strong enough to feel like a sandblast, hits my face and naked torso. I cringe against the furthest corner of the cage, willing it to stop before it removes more skin. Nielsen holds the leash from the outside of the cage, keeping me from turning away and protecting my face.

Just when my lungs feel as though they'll burst and I'll be forced to inhale water, the spray stops.

"Come on, son, all you have to do is shift and this'll be over." He's still doing the 'patient dad' voice, but I can tell the hours spent with nothing to show are wearing on him.

I'm all out of patience. I march right up to the metal loops separating us and slam my wet palms against them, snarling. Immediately, magical bolts of pure electricity shoot down my throat, reminding me I can't use my voice at all. I've gotten somewhat used to it—it took a while to resist the urge to scream every time they hit me with something—but it still drops me to my knees, gagging.

"I'm sorry this is so hard on you, Leaf."

I draw in careful breaths, my hands shaking with fury, and glare up at him with all the hate I can muster.

Nielsen crouches down to my eye level. "I know you don't believe me, but you'll see, it's worth it in the end. The more repressed your wolf is, the harder it is to draw him out. For people who don't have the instinct to shift, it takes an extremely strong emotion to bring it about. It's not about the pain; it's about how angry it makes you, how frustrated, how humiliated to be locked in a cage and treated like a dog. We have to keep pushing until you reach your breaking point before your wolf will finally be free. And then you'll thank me, son. This is just part of the process."

Unable to vocalize what I think of that statement, I respond with a hand gesture that tells him exactly how I feel.

Nielsen tosses his head back and laughs. "Well, no one can deny that you've got spirit." Standing, he turns to the man beside him holding the hose and sprayer. "Again."

After another hour of the water, Nielsen concedes defeat and decides it's time to escalate my torture. I'm still soaking wet, shaking so hard with cold that my teeth are audibly chattering. I watch warily as the latest henchman coils the hose and tucks it away in the bottom of the case. It's a vain hope, but for a brief moment I allow myself to think we might be done for tonight, and he's going to offer me a towel and a meal with the promise to start again tomorrow.

Instead, the man pulls two items from the rack: one that looks sort of like a bowie knife strapped to a pole, and the cattle prod.

My stomach lurches.

He flicks a switch, and a bolt of blue electricity connects the two prongs, sizzling.

Nielsen accepts the cattle prod and the other man hefts the knife pole as if testing its weight.

"See, this here is a special invention of mine. We took a regular cattle prod—which hurts, don't get me wrong—but we souped it up a bit, so it's a fitting instrument for a wolf shifter. We heal so fast, you understand. A regular cattle prod is more of an annoyance than a motivator to a powerful wolf."

My eyes dart to the weapon the other man holds, then back, my question clear. "Ah, yes, that's exactly what it looks like. We find having two types of motivation at the same time to be far more effective than just one. You don't get used to the sensation as fast."

143

When they approach the cage, I scrabble back to my corner, but I know it's no use. Not only does Nielsen have the leash that can lay me out with the slightest tug, but the weapons are clearly designed to hit everywhere in the cage; there's no escape.

I wish fervently for my wolf to emerge and end this. If all he wants is for me to shift, I'd happily do it. No torture required. Unfortunately, the hairy beast hasn't shown a flick of interest in helping me out of this scenario.

If I even have one at all.

"Hey Jessup?"

"Yes alpha?"

"Let's make sure and make a note of the time. I'd like to know how long it takes a half-breed to heal compared to a full-blooded wolf."

"You got it, sir."

"You ready to get started, Leaf?"

I just glared at him from my corner, fist wrapped around the leash as if I could gain some sort of control by holding it. Just, I think bitterly, like a dog carrying his own leash in his mouth.

Nielsen raises the electrified wand and slides it through the wide mesh of the cage. "I wish I could say this won't hurt a bit, son, but that'd be a lie. It's gonna hurt, and it's gonna hurt a lot. If it makes you feel any better, I tested it on myself first. You'll survive."

And then, with no warning, he stabs the prod into the flesh of my right pectoral. I have a split second to imagine our rolls reversed some day in the future before the pain becomes so extreme I can't help crying out. In a coincidence I'm certain Nielsen didn't plan on, the searing magic combined with actual electricity is enough to knock me out completely.

Chapter Thirteen

JARED

~

"I don't like this at all." Milo's growl is deep and throaty, conveying a barely restrained fury I've never heard from him before.

"Me either, but she's gotta do what she thinks is best." I pause for just a second before I ask, "Hey, you okay, man?"

He swats angrily at a tree branch as we continue walking toward the clearing, and doesn't answer. It's cold out tonight, the moon lamp-bright in the dark, cloudless sky. Our breath forms clouds of vapor as we walk, matching the crowd surging from Harridan House as we trudge along together. Dried leaves cover the trail, making for a noisy crunch with every step. More people appear from the shadows between the

147

trees, taking the shortest distance from the parking area behind the greenhouses to the clearing.

"I'm fine," he answers finally. "I've just been… annoyed lately."

That definitely feels like an understatement.

"Did something happen? Is there something you're not telling us?" When he doesn't answer immediately, I add, "You know we're always here for you, right?"

Milo's eyes dart my way for a fraction of a second, then return to the moon-bleached path ahead. "It's no big deal. I'll get over it."

"If you say so."

In truth, I'm sort of worried about him. I don't know if it's the rescue mission getting to him, or the stress Lily's under;or that she's so insistent on getting Derrek back in the first place… or maybe it's just because he still doesn't like the way Derrek eyes our mate.

Either way, something changed drastically the day after the unfortunate homecoming dance and he's not talking. But I don't have the time to probe him for answers, because we've arrived at the clearing and it's barely five minutes till midnight.

We follow the crowd until they split, household staff joining the outer tree line and Lily, Landon, Milo and I, along with her 'guests' and security, heading straight for the center. Lily glances around at the murmuring crowd, and as if they feel her eyes, they quiet down as one.

"Good evening, Smoky Falls!" She greets them with a wide smile, and I can see the pack returning the grin as if following from cue cards. "It's my honor to spend another midnight run with you all. First, you may have noticed that we have a few guests with us tonight. These gentlemen are from Pack Montrose-"

A wave of gasps and hisses rises from the crowd, forcing Lily to wait before continuing. "They're from Pack Montrose and they're my *guests*," she emphasizes the last word forcefully to drive home the point. "They've come to potentially help us retrieve someone important to me that the Montrose alpha took, but they wish for me to prove my worth as an alpha before they take that risk."

Now the crowd is furious. An angry rumble rises as they react to this news.

Lily's voice lifts to compensate. "I am *happy* to provide them with this demonstration, and I expect that you all will serve as witnesses without interfering. Is that understood?"

The rumbles quiet down to a dissatisfied murmur, and Lily smiles in response. "Excellent. Since we're just a couple minutes out, I think it's best we prepare ourselves for the shift. After our little demonstration, we'll head directly out for our run!"

The pack begins stripping in unison, peeling off warm layers and exposing their bodies to the icy wind that's rattling branches overhead. I follow suit, unzipping my puffy vest and dumping each piece of clothing on top of a pile of leaves. My eyes stay trained on Lily. As she pulls off her own clothes, she reveals gleaming white skin that seems to be made of light itself. All of her soft curves catch and reflect the moonlight. So much skin I haven't gotten to explore yet...

Saliva gathers in my mouth and I swallow it down with difficulty; my throat seems to have closed. Lily gives the appearance of focusing solely on the task at hand, but I know the look of concentration she wears; she's reaching out with her alpha senses, keeping tabs on everyone without making it obvious.

The Montrose guys are stripping in a tight circle, the security team surrounding them still in full gear. It suddenly occurs to me that the security team is there to protect the visitors from *us*, and not the other way around. Given the way the surrounding pack is sending distrustful glares their way, I can't blame my mate for her caution.

Milo, Landon, and I form a tight semi-circle behind Lily once we're clear of our clothes. It's so cold I can see the heat rising off our bodies, and those of the crowd, like veils of steam in the moonlight.

"Are you sure about this?" Landon's voice is gentle, just asking and not questioning her.

She turns to face us, a hard smile on her lips. "I've got this. Don't worry about me."

Lord help me; my eyes dip down, just a moment, to take in her perfect breasts and the dark triangle where her legs and hips meet. I clench my hands to restrain myself from reaching out and gripping her ass to lift her to my height. My mouth floods with saliva once again, and I readjust my stance to position my hands in front of my crotch. I should not be getting myself turned on right now.

Lily's eyes drop to my hands, and her determined expression softens into a teasing grin. "Jared, is it a little cold out here for you?"

"What? I mean, yeah it's cold, but that doesn't mean… I mean, I'm fine. Are you?" My stammering is incredibly embarrassing, but apparently all the blood has left my brain. I glance sideways and see immediately that Landon is in the same boat, obvious discomfort etched across his face as he tries, and fails, to avoid ogling our mate.

I don't know what the issue is; we've been naked with Lily before the shift tons of times, and we've never had a problem. I mean, of course I *enjoy* the view every time, but it's always been easy to behave myself, filing the image away for a time I'm alone and able to enjoy it properly.

When I glance to the other side, I'm shocked to realize Milo isn't having the same issue at all. In fact, he's standing with his arms crossed, glaring at the dudes from Montrose, who are staring at Lily. Not with any sort of lustful expressions on their faces, thankfully. The spokesman for the group, Jeff, wears a battle-ready look. The rest of them just appear curious, as if they are looking forward to this little showdown.

And just like every night, a sudden riot of sound emits from every cell phone among the pack, loudly and chaotically proclaiming that it's midnight, and time to shift.

~

LILLIANA

~

I take in the hard planes of my tallest mate's body, the way the light and shadows play across those cheekbones, his lean, muscular arms and pecks, the impressively narrow waist and defined 'V' of muscle below his belly button, which is practically at my eye level. Aware that I'm ogling, I glance up and give Landon a flirty smile. He grins back widely, dimples appearing like deep shadows in the stark moonlight.

When I turn my attention back to Jared, I can appreciate the difference between Landon's milky skin and Jared's dark complexion. The moonlight drains the world of color, rendering him all shadow with gleaming silver highlights on the curve of each well-defined muscle. Where Landon is tall and lean, Jared is thick and wide, his body reminding me of a Greek statue carved from onyx with every muscle perfectly defined and polished. I long to run my hands over every smooth, hard curve, particularly his sharp hips and well-rounded butt.

My belly clenches and the awareness that I'm losing myself to incredibly inappropriate thoughts for this setting hits me full force.

Then the alarms go off.

The shift is so familiar now I don't even have to think about it. Before the last buzz sounds from a nearby phone, the clearing is now filled with every size, shape, and color of wolf I can imagine.

My mates creep closer, nuzzling me with their furry heads while I try to give each of them a comforting lick. Milo's body presses tightly to my side, a low growl rumbling deep in his chest, with his head turned to the left.

A large brown wolf is approaching the center of the clearing, his steel-grey eyes focused intently on me. I spare one more nuzzle and lick for Milo before I issue him a commanding growl of my own, warning him to knock it off. He quits immediately and steps back, leaving me to face my challenger.

We'd sorted all the details before leaving Harridan House, so there isn't much to do besides begin. I trot forward to meet him and can feel my mates retreat further, melting into the outer circle but still close enough they feel secure. When I reach the exact center of the clearing, I sit and wait for him to make his move.

With my position as alpha, I'm due a fair amount of deference even if he doesn't belong to my pack. I accepted his stupid challenge, but that was verbally. Now he has to issue me the challenge as a wolf.

When he approaches, a low growl emanates from the surrounding wolves, all of them disliking this foreigner being so close to me. I examine their color map swiftly; mostly orange for anxiety or discomfort, nothing I need to be too concerned about. A sharp bark silences them immediately, and my gaze darts to the other three visitors, where they wait patiently with their guard, who are still in human form.

Jeff is a sizeable wolf, and with his hackles up, back arched to make himself look even larger, he could be intimidating.

Except I have no reason to be intimidated by him. My wolf remains silent, simply waiting for him to make a move.

With a snarl he launches himself at me, and I spring forward with a snarl of my own, jaws snapping at his throat in a near miss when he twists away in response.

My nails dig into the ground, sending dried leaves flying behind me as I stop my momentum and turn to face my challenger again.

My wolf is furious that this unranked male would dare to challenge us. The alpha voice rumbles through my mind without conscious intent, but of course has no effect on him, since he doesn't belong to my pack.

When he charges again, I jump aside and focus on learning his tactics. He's like a freight train, barreling forward with the obvious intent of running over me. We're nearly the same size, and he seems to rely on brute strength with a goal to overpower me. Such an amateur mistake.

My wolf eyes are sharp, tracking Jeff's every move as he charges again and again. Learning his rhythm, the way he moves, the way he steps and how he leaps forward to attack.

Once I'm confident I have his number, I go on the

offensive. But for every charge I make, snapping at his throat, I make him charge me several times, using up his explosive power to tire him out. He just doesn't seem to know how to switch tactics; it's like an arcade video game where the player knows the character's special move and just keeps mashing that button despite it continuing to fail.

The crowd is restless, their concern clear in the low growls and whines they make with each of Jeff's attacks. My mates aren't concerned, although the furious snarls Milo keeps making continue to surprise me.

Abruptly, I push the attack, rearing up on my hind legs and settling my jaws on the back of his neck like a misbehaving puppy. He thrashes beneath me, trying to shake off the teeth that are deeply lodged in his flesh, hot blood trickling onto my tongue.

But it's no good; my grip on his neck is solid, and I force him down into submission. When he gets his belly on the ground, he makes one last attempt to fight back, trying to use his hind legs to spring upward and break my grip.

My force is too strong, and his lower body bucks futilely against my inescapable force. A deep warning growl rumbles in my chest, and he stops kicking. With a series of small shifts, I work my jaws slowly around his neck until my teeth are imbedded below his chin. Now I could easily rip his throat out. If I wanted to.

All it takes is one more threatening growl, and the fight drains out of Jeff. His body relaxes, laying heavily on his side as a high, clear whine emits from his throat.

I hold on for one more moment, just in case he gets any ideas, then release him.

Standing tall over his limp form, I issue a long, clear victory howl to the moon. My pack answers with joyful howls of their own. If there were any normal humans within a ten-mile radius, I'm certain they'd be calling the park rangers to report us. But as it stands, there's no one here to interrupt our celebration.

Once I've finished celebrating, I step away from Jeff's prone body casually, as if to remind him how low his desires rank compared to mine. He shakes out his fur, meets my gaze for one long moment, then dips his head in respect. The remaining three members of his group trot forward, released by the guards, and my mates join me, yipping cheerfully. Milo takes a few extra moments to inspect me for injury and pepper my face with kisses.

Something hot and bubbling grows in my belly. The power I feel surging through me, or the delicious glory of victory, perhaps.

But also an indescribable *hunger*. Milo and I sneaked off after dinner and scratched the itch that's been plaguing me since we left his house. This time I was absolutely certain the others would notice something, maybe even the smell of us all over each other. And yet no one seemed to notice a thing.

However, I caught both Landon and Jared's eyes lapping up my naked body before the shift. Whether or not they realize it, something has been set in motion and our bodies know it, even if our brains are not fully on board. The need for Derrek remains in the back of my mind like a constant ache, a sore spot that reminds me every so often that it's there.

But it's currently overridden by a deep, unabiding need to claim the mates right before me, the ones who share my bed and whose bodies clearly crave mine as much as I'm craving theirs. I don't know if it's hormones or more magical wolf stuff, but I'm determined to trust my instincts, and they're screaming for me to take these two to bed.

Soon.

I butt Milo in the chest to get him to stop, and then we trot toward the trail as one. I release a howl and the rest of the pack answers joyfully, falling in behind. The visitors from Montrose melt into the pack, and as one we run our circuit through the black and white world of the midnight trees.

Chapter Fourteen

LANDON

~

In the wake of Lily's absolute domination of the Montrose guy, our run is fast and excited. We make it back to the clearing in what I'm sure is record time, and enjoy a few moments to play as wolves before it's time to shift back.

Even though he already inspected her immediately following the fight, Milo checks Lily all over again, searching her creamy skin for any marks or abrasions with clinical focus. My eyes dart to Jared's in confusion, and he shrugs as if to say, "I don't get it either."

Once he's apparently satisfied, Milo and Lily share an uncomfortably intense kiss, his hands roving over her butt as I try not to notice and tuck my swollen self back into my suddenly tight pants. Jared catches my eye again and this time we share a knowing look; something is *definitely* up.

When we've replaced all our clothes, the clearing is nearly empty aside from us and a few stragglers. The Montrose guys, their guard, and the staff are already heading back to Harridan House, disappearing down the trail. Lily finishes zipping up her coat and we leave as one.

Milo seizes Lily's hand and tugs her forward, speaking intently into her ear. Jared and I slow our pace down, allowing them to pull ahead and have some space for their discussion. Not that I don't want to know, desperately, what the hell is going on, but I also know that being a trio of mates doesn't give us the right to insert ourselves into literally everything. We'll all have things we share with Lily alone, just as we'll have things we share with each other. As a family, that's how we'll operate.

It leaves me feeling a little left out, but at least I know Jared's in the same boat.

We watch them as they get further ahead, clutching hands and carrying on a clearly deep conversation.

"What do you think that's all about?" Jared asks, his voice low.

"No idea," I answer honestly. "But I'm sure if it's our business, they'll let us know. If it's not, well, I'd want some privacy too."

"Yeah," Jared kicks up a small pile of leaves. "I just don't like secrets."

"I'd try not to think of it as secrets, man. Sometimes it's just private. Don't you want privacy sometimes?"

"Honestly? Not really. I've never had privacy with all my sisters at home. If I'm not with them, I'm with you and Milo, or I'm at practice with like forty guys. I like being around people."

"I wish I could relate. Barrett is so much older than me, we never had many reasons to hang out; I was just his dorky little brother. I mean, we love each other and he's never been a jerk, but it's not a relationship like you have with your sisters."

"You mean how I want to string up every single one of their necks at least twice a week?"

"Oh, come on," I laugh. "You're not fooling me. Whenever we go over to your house, they're climbing on you like a jungle gym and you love every second of it. Maybe not Sasha, but she comes in and out of your room all the time like she lives there."

"She practically does, just to get away from the younger three."

"See? You can't say you love being around your sisters and then say you want to strangle them, too."

"You don't have a sibling around your age, you just don't get how it works."

"That's fair. But either way… I dunno, I enjoy being alone and then I don't, if that makes sense. Like, I can only write songs when I'm alone. It's too distracting to have someone there, and I get embarrassed working through chords and progressions when I know people can hear me.

"But on the other hand, when I'm with you, or Milo, or Lily, I feel complete in a way I don't by myself." I pause to think over what I just said. "That's really weird, isn't it?"

Jared shrugs. "I don't think so. Maybe because I've never really had the chance to get used to being alone, I just can't appreciate it? But either way, I'm happy that we're all fated to be Lily's mates. I can't think of a time I didn't want to hang out with you guys, and we're already like family." He bumps my arm with his shoulder.

"Yeah, I feel the same." My gaze drifts ahead, where Milo has his arm around Lily's shoulder now and she's leaning into his side, the pair of them walking slower than before.

"I wonder what it's going to feel like when we get closer to her, if that'll change anything."

"Closer?"

"Yeah, closer."

"What do you mean?"

Heat rises to my cheeks. "You know… like when she claims us as her mates, officially. When we… seal the bond."

"Ohhhhh," Jared tips his head back in dramatic realization. "Yeah, I dunno. I guess it's up to her, really. Whatever she wants."

"I guess." I try to keep my voice neutral and not sound too disappointed; I was hoping he imagined it how I did. Growing up, particularly when puberty hit me like a train, I'd imagined all sorts of scenarios involving our phantom mate and the three of us. Some were just me, but mostly they involved everyone. The three of us all working together, pleasuring her and being pleasured in tandem.

"I mean, from what I've heard, the four alphas are always really close," he adds. "There's a reason she's got that giant bed."

My excitement perks up. "But that's not even the alpha suite, is it? Does the alpha have an even bigger bed?"

"I don't think so. Mr. Carson said the alpha suite is whichever set of rooms she chooses to take. I guess once she officially claims us and we move in, we all pick a suite as well. We can have it renovated or leave it as is."

"We all have separate bedrooms? I don't remember hearing that."

"I think it's mainly for necessity. Like we all need our own closets. You know she's already got hers mostly filled. And have you seen room in that bathroom for all of Milo's hair products?"

That comment draws a chuckle from me. "Fair. I hadn't thought of it that way. Also separate toilets, that's definitely a must. No way in hell I'm going in there after you. Love you, man, but I know you too well."

"See? Exactly. And there's other reasons, like you already said you don't like composing music in front of a crowd."

"There's an entire music room here for me to do that."

"Yeah, well regardless, I think you're going too deep in it here."

"Fair enough."

We follow the garden trail back up to the stairs and eventually to the back door of Harridan House. Once we get inside, Mr. Carson immediately appears to take our coats, but I notice Milo's still wearing his when we enter the main hallway.

"You got somewhere to be?"

Milo plants a kiss on Lily's temple before stepping away. "I'm going home, actually. I've got a few things to work on for school that I've been ignoring. But I'll be back tomorrow sometime, okay?"

Jared and I exchange another loaded glance. "Okay, well, take it easy, man." I throw up a hand for a one-armed hug.

"Yeah, don't work too hard," Jared adds, receiving his own hug.

Milo flashes us his lazy grin. "You don't have to worry about that with me. Have a great night, you two." He turns and strides for the door, tossing his keys in the air.

"Well," Lily says brightly, drawing our attention from Milo's retreating form. Her cheeks are rosy, green eyes practically glowing in the wake of her victory. "Mr. Carson has set Jeff and the guys up in some guest rooms, and Dom and Roxanne have already called it a night. You guys ready for bed?"

Not in the least. "I'm not really tired, to be honest. I think I'm still a little wound up from the fight and everything." Not to mention whatever happened when I was drooling over her absolute nakedness. "Maybe I'll watch some tv or something if you want to sleep."

Lily's wide smile curls, turning into something incredibly seductive with one eyebrow raised. "Who said anything about sleep?"

Chapter Fifteen

LILLIANA

~

Their matching dumfounded expressions almost make me cackle.

"What do you mean, *who said anything about sleep*?" Jared asks slowly.

"I mean, I said we should go to bed, not that we should sleep."

Landon seems to search for some kind of innocuous explanation. "You want to… read?"

An amused laugh burst from my lips. I close the distance between us with a single step, and trail my fingers from their belts to their chests and back down. My eyes travel slowly between them, making sure they're absorbing my every word. In my most seductive voice, I purr, "I don't want to read. I want to do naughty things with you. *Both* of you."

It's obvious they're not sure what to think about this dramatic shift, but I have a feeling they'll get over it quickly.

Landon's head whips toward the door. "But what about Milo?"

I lift a shoulder with a devious sideways glance. "Milo and I have already done some exploring. I think it's your turn."

The two of them exchange a look.

Jared speaks with the tone of someone who just pieced together several clues. "Now *that* explains it. That explains everything."

"Explains what?" Landon clearly hasn't figured it out, and I have to admit I'm curious myself.

"Why Milo has been acting so weird the last couple of days, flying off the handle at everything."

"I don't get it," Landon replies.

He's piqued my curiosity. "Me either."

We both turn expectantly to Jared.

"My dad said sometimes guys get super protective of their mates if they seal the deal and aren't officially claimed yet."

Landon's eyes widen. "I didn't know that was a thing!"

My brain rewinds on everything that's happened since Milo and I first made love, and it all adds up. It was like his emotions were all out of whack minutes after we finished.

I decide to file that away for later, but the guys have apparently lost track of where this conversation was going before it switched to Milo.

"It's totally a thing. In fact-"

"Guys!" I grip their belt buckles and give them both a tug. "Can we focus?"

Their eyes whip back to me lightning-fast.

"Yes ma'am," Jared drawls with a smirk. "Whatever you say, gorgeous."

I give him a coy smile. "Hmm, I think I could get used to that. But first, let's move this party upstairs."

"Yes, ma'am!" They repeat in unison, and the three of us chuckle.

Taking the initiative, Jared grasps my hand and tugs me gently toward the elevator. Landon threads his long fingers through mine on my other hand and brings up the rear.

My heart beats faster as the realization that this is about to happen sets in. An excited shiver runs down my spine, that clench deep in my gut returning.

Jared mashes the elevator button, and it opens immediately. After we pile in and close the gate, Landon hits the button for the second floor and the doors slowly close.

As if they'd rehearsed it, Jared grabs my hips and pulls me against him, dipping his head to claim my lips. Landon presses up behind me, pulling my hair aside and kissing along the curve of my neck while one hand runs over the curve of my ass and squeezes. The heat of their bodies spurs my heart even faster, the thrumming energy of their touch running over my skin in waves.

When the elevator slows and dings, Jared breaks off the kiss, leaving me breathless, and allows Landon to pull me away by my hand, down the hall toward my suite.

My face is hot, body practically shaking with anticipation. I felt Landon's considerable length pressed against my butt, and somehow knowing that a similar treat waits for me in Jared's pants doubles my excitement. Even up to a few months ago, I'd never imagined myself in this kind of scenario. What teenage girl assumes she'll have multiple lovers, let alone at the same time? Now it feels as inevitable and natural as the turning of the seasons.

We make it to my suite and close the door without my panties actually starting on fire, so I figure that's a win.

Once again, they move as one and press me between them. Landon claims my mouth this time, his long fingers running delicately over my breasts and plucking at the tips through my shirt. Jared's strong hangs tighten on my hips and pull me against him, then slip under my shirt. He caresses the skin on my sides before dipping his fingertips below my belt and pressing his hardness against me. One of my arms hangs around Landon's neck and the other reaches behind me to squeeze Jared's ass in return.

My heart is absolutely racing now, my breath coming in excited pants. There's so many sensations, hard and soft, stroking and pressing, pushing and claw-ing, gentle and firm and forceful.

With a gasp, I free myself from Landon's lips and press his chest away. He immediately takes a step back, a confused look on his face as he draws in heavy breaths. "Is everything okay?"

I tug Jared's hands from my pants and step away from him, too. They both give me the saddest pair of guilty expressions I've ever seen.

"Sorry we got carried away, gorgeous," Jared apolo-gizes rapidly. He blows out a deep breath before contin-uing, "I'm not sure what just happened."

That draws a laugh from me, and my heart slows down a bit despite the desperate and growing need within me for *more*. "I'm not upset, guys. Trust me, I'm loving it. This just isn't how I want this to go right now."

"And how do you want it to go?" Landon asks care-fully, a hopeful glimmer in his eyes.

My gaze travels between the two. "I want to be in charge."

Jared smirks. "Is that so?"

"That's so. I'm not exactly an expert here, but I'm assuming neither of you has much experience either?"

They glance at each other and return their gazes to me, shaking their heads.

Another little thrill runs through my body. I assumed as much, but there was something even more exciting about the knowledge that I'd be their first for everything. Milo confessed that he'd practiced certain skills with other girls but saved the most intimate experiences to have with me. Jared, Landon and I get to have a lot of these firsts together. "Okay. Let's try where I tell you what I want and see how that goes."

Jared glances at Landon again, a hawkish grin on his face. "Our little alpha mate, suddenly so bossy. Kinda turns me on. You?"

Landon's answering seductive grin almost melts my panties on the spot. "It's pretty hot," he agrees, sidling over to stand next to Jared by the couch and turning the full force of his rockstar sex appeal on me. "Tell us where to start, alpha."

Suddenly just a teensy bit nervous, I swallow hard before approaching them both like a predator stalking my prey. I have a couple of things on my list, but not exactly the well-laid-out plan it probably sounded like to them. Taking my time, I drink in the sight of them, waiting with matching expressions of amused lust on their faces and matching bulges straining below their belts.

By the time I reach them, an idea has already formed in my mind. "First, I want to taste you both."

Reaching up, I pull Landon's head to my height, running my tongue over his lips before claiming them in a deep and aggressive kiss. His mouth is sweet, a faint trace of peppermint that I didn't notice before, and his citrusy fragrance fills my senses. My fingers slide through his silky hair while I savor him for a moment, and his arm curls around my back to support me. Heat washes through me in a wave, and my pulse picks up again.

Landon's eyes are warm pools of desire when I disengage gently with a stroke of his cleft chin. He pulls my hand to his pillow-soft lips and kisses it, and I smile lustily at him before turning my focus to Jared.

Lifting my left hand, I pull Jared's face to mine, and our tongues duel for dominance while my right hand runs lazily down Landon's body to center on his bulge. Jared's kisses taste like strawberry candy, and the knowledge that he's able to indulge in his favorite treat no matter the circumstances causes a tiny giggle to tickle my throat. The skin on his neck is silky smooth, a contrast to the neatly trimmed fade of his short, coarse hair that my fingers can't seem to stop running over.

After another moment, I pull back and allow my fingers to drop from his neck, trailing down to below his belt buckle. A low groan escapes his lips and his eyes follow my hand, where it lightly strokes him over the rough fabric of his jeans.

"What do you want next, gorgeous?" he asks, panting slightly with a teasing glint in his eyes.

I withdraw my hands from both of them, making an exaggerated show of pondering his question, then decide to tease him right back. "Hmm, I think I'm going to put my mouth… right here." I smooth my finger along his jaw. "And here."

Caressing his neck, I nibble at his jawline before dragging my tongue down to his shoulder, reveling in the salty taste of his skin. Turning to Landon, I pepper kisses along his jaw from ear to chin. True to their promise, both guys remain pliable, allowing me to move them around with the lightest touch. Slowly, I plant open-mouthed kisses down to where Landon's neck meets his shoulder, while allowing my free hand to rove over Jared's body again.

My breath whispers over his skin as I work my way back to Landon's ear. "Take off your shirt." I turn my gaze to Jared with a devious grin. "You too, handsome."

Landon immediately lifts his shirt from the hem, while Jared whips his over his head and tosses it to the floor. They wait patiently, hungry eyes watching my every move. Their naked torsos are even more delicious in the low, warm light of my suite. Such handsome, delectable mates, and I have them all to myself.

With another painful swallow, I tug off my top and expose my lacy bra with a teasing grin. "Only fair that I join you, don't you think?"

It's almost comical when they nod in unison, wearing matching wide-eyed expressions with their gazes glued to my breasts.

"Definitely agree," Landon says, gracing my jaw with kisses, one large palm sweeping over my chest. His fingers tug at the scalloped top of the lace. "This is really… really… sexy," he adds, interspersing his words with light nips of his teeth.

Jared drifts behind me and wraps his hand around the bulk of my hair, tugging lightly and drawing a low moan from my throat.

"What's next, my sexy goddess of an alpha?" His

lips tease the shell of my ear, hot breath causing shivers to run over my body. Once again he's pressed into my backside, free hand pulling my hips against him and dipping lower, cupping me through my jeans. My hips tilt backwards involuntarily, another moan ripping from my throat when his fingers press more firmly.

My breath hitches at the promise of pleasure in his touch, and a shudder ripples across my body. "This."

Chapter Sixteen

LILLIANA

~

I slide my hands up Landon's sides and lean forward, circling my tongue around his nipple before I pull it between my lips, adding a graze of my teeth for good measure. Landon rewards me with a throaty growl, tossing his head back in pleasure and sinking his fingers in my curls.

Realizing I've ended up between them again, I step out and attempt to retake control by tugging their belts in unison, positioning them both hip to hip and placing one foot between each of their legs. Jared gives me a naughty grin, and Landon's teeth pinch his plush lower lip, pupils dilated so far I can only see a thin line of his iris.

Running a hand over Jared's rich brown skin, I flick

my tongue over his nipple as well before nipping gently with my teeth. When Landon peppers fervent kisses down my throat, I curve backward to allow him more access, and Jared takes advantage by returning the favor and drawing my stiff nipple into his warm mouth, teasing over the fabric with his tongue. His hand slides between my legs again, pressing firmly and making the heat coil like a spring low in my gut. A strained gasp escapes my lips, quickly followed by another as Landon's kisses find their way to my other breast. His fingers slide under the band of my bra and draw it up, exposing my peaked nipple completely. My hands rise, caressing both of their heads and holding on for dear life.

Warm liquid pleasure flows across my skin, pooling between my thighs where Jared's fingers continue to tease. It feels as though I'm barely able to stand, with so many sensations drawing my attention and rendering me weak in the knees. Tasting and teasing each other is even more fun than I'd expected, but the need for more hasn't abated at all. If anything, it's continued to grow, almost painful in my desperation for release.

I'm breathless and quaking by the time they disengage from my breasts. With shaking hands, I unhook the bra that is now serving no purpose, and Landon's hands immediately rise to cup me, thumbs running over my peaked nipples and pinching lightly.

Their hands continue to stroke me, both observing me with adoring eyes but not pressing further. They're clearly on their best behavior, waiting for my next instruction.

I'm definitely ready to get this show on the road. I trail my fingers down Jared's abdomen, watching his muscles ripple in response, until my hands meet the top of his jeans. When I hook my fingertips in his waistband, I comment coyly, "Looks like these are in my way."

"Allow me to fix that for you, gorgeous." Needing no further encouragement, both guys step back to shed the rest of their clothes. I shimmy out of my jeans while enjoying the view of their delicious forms. So different, yet so similar in the way their skin moves over lean muscle, the power and hard-yet-soft planes of their bodies.

All that remains between us are my lacy panties, so wet with desire I'm surprised they haven't disintegrated. With hungry eyes, Landon kneels in front of me and cups my breasts, working my nipples while he plants sensual kisses from the valley of my chest to below my navel. Goosebumps erupt in his wake, and a shiver dances up my spine while that painful coil of need tightens even more.

"How's this?" he murmurs, gazing up at me with liquid eyes and flicking his tongue across my belly.

"Very good," I pant, breathless.

Abruptly, his powerful hands spin me toward Jared, who also drops to his knees and caresses my flesh with his lips.

"Lower?" Jared asks in a husky voice, nuzzling the scrap of lace.

I shake my head, trying to be coy while I tip his chin up. "Not yet."

My heart is pounding painfully as I pull gently at both their chins, signaling for them to stand.

Voice shaking, I focus on Landon, point to the couch and say, "Sit down."

He eases his long frame onto a cushion, wearing a curious but excited expression as I toss a couch pillow on the floor. When I kneel before him, a look of apprehension crosses his face, but I plant my hands on his thighs and press them apart.

Landon's throat bobs as I lean further down and swipe my tongue across the tip of his hot flesh. His hips scoot forward, granting me easier access, and he raises his hands to the back of his head with a shuddering groan.

Slowly, I ease him into my mouth, working my way further until he's stroking the back of my throat. Excitement courses through me, my hands kneading his thighs. I'm already much better than last time, and hearing the sounds he makes, knowing Jared is watching me, makes it even more exciting. After a few more minutes, I ease back, stroking him lazily with one hand while I turn my attention to my other mate.

I crook a finger at Jared, who's standing to the side, stroking himself as he watches with glazed eyes. "Get over here, handsome."

Jared wastes zero time moving to where I'm eye-level with his throbbing shaft. I wrap my fingers around his impressive girth, enjoying the hot, silky-smooth skin, before raising my gaze to his and easing him into my mouth.

His eyes close and head tips back, a hand running over his face. "Oh, fuck, gorgeous. *Fuck*."

Self-satisfied, I ease him deeper into my throat, continuing to caress Landon from root to tip. Jared's hand tangles into my hair, pulling my head toward him gently as I continue moving.

The taste of them, the scent of their desire for me and the sounds they make at my touch; it's intoxicating. I want to continue exploring this power, but my need is excruciating at this point. I ease Jared from my mouth to stroke him, but he quickly kneels beside me, his hand slipping between my legs. The first touch of his fingers on my leg sends a course of shivers through my body, and I realize my desire for them is actually running down my thighs.

Jared runs a finger along the liquid trail, then lifts it to his lips, sucking my arousal from his hand with his eyes closed in bliss. When they reopen, his gaze is hooded and intense, eyes claiming mine when he pleads, "It's your turn. Please let me taste you, gorgeous."

I slip his fingers into my mouth before kissing down his palm and murmuring, "Not right now; I can't wait anymore. I want you inside me."

His eyes widen, and I cover his mouth with mine, releasing Landon so I can move.

With shaking legs, I turn slightly, positioning myself in front of him, and Landon in front of me. I grip his hand, flipping it palm side up, and slide it down to the gap between my thighs, then leave him to figure out the rest. Refocusing my attention on Landon, I bend forward.

Jared doesn't immediately take the bait. His hands smooth over my curves, squeezing and massaging my body before finally slipping under and caressing the spot in desperate need of his attention. My legs spread to give him better access, satisfied moans pouring from my throat.

My attention now fully returned to Landon, I suck him back into my mouth with an audible sound that makes him hiss in pleasure. Losing his restraint, Landon gathers my hair in one hand and uses the other to press lightly at the back of my head, his hips lifting every time I slide my mouth down the length of him.

"God... damn... Lily I want-" He tries, but can't seem to form a coherent thought.

It's so close now, this new height of release I've been seeking. I add a hand to my efforts on Landon and buck my hips backward, hoping Jared takes the hint.

His movement changes from gentle exploration to firm strokes, two fingers sliding deeply into me. His hand pumps a few times before sliding out and dragging the wetness from between my legs up the channel between my cheeks. The unfamiliar but delicious sensation forces a moan from my throat that vibrates over Landon's shaft, and he gasps while I freeze, my muscles clenching with anticipation. Jared grips the full cheek of my ass while his other thumb continues to tease at my backside, pressing gently at the entrance and circling with the slippery coating I made. A deep growl rumbles in his throat, and I resume my ministrations to Landon, sucking and squeezing.

Abruptly, Jared's hand returns to the heat between my legs, this time dragging his palm across me before disappearing completely.

"Fuck, gorgeous, are you ready?" Jared's voice sounds almost as desperate as I feel.

The frustration peaks, and I slip Landon from my lips and continue stroking him. I answer my other mate with a snarl. "Yes, I'm fucking ready, Jared. How many times do I have to ask?"

Before I even finish getting the words out, Jared finally lines himself up and pushes into me.

We groan in unison, my entire body clenching, which causes Landon to jerk from the unexpected pressure. This position is altogether new and takes me a moment to adapt.

I rock my hips back and pull Landon back into my mouth. Jared moves inside me with slow, measured strokes.

The pair of them, both hot and firm and inside me, together, are hitting that infuriating need. Jared's hands grip my hips from the sides, squeezing almost painfully hard and spreading my cheeks. His abdomen hits the spot he was so recently teasing with each stroke and I discover a desire I didn't know I had.

I slide my lips from Landon again. "Jared, I want you to touch me like you were doing a minute ago, just... more."

For some reason, I find it incredibly difficult to verbalize what I'm asking.

Fortunately, he understands. Slipping himself free of me, he collects more of my wetness on his fingers, then resumes his strokes. When I feel his slippery fingers teasing my other entrance again, I almost cry out with the intensity of the pleasure. I renew my efforts on Landon, and Jared continues moving inside me while drawing tight, teasing circles with that slippery finger. It disappears and a wet sound reaches my ears, but I don't have time to contemplate it because his finger is back, even wetter, and now it's moving faster and pressing at my entrance.

It's a completely different pleasure, and it builds its own coil, quickly tightening and growing, increasing my need for release until my body is bucking and twitching with desperation.

My thighs shake, my entire body quivering as it reacts to so much stimuli. Jared's body slaps into mine at a quickening pace. My strokes on Landon increase, but I'm so focused on what's happening behind me he's not reaching the same depth in my mouth. Jared's slippery finger continues twirling just around my entrance, and my body pulses and shivers as I chase the pinnacle of release. The sensations grow until I'm abruptly spiraling over the edge, pleasure hitting me like a tsunami with wave after wave of earth-shattering starlight.

My body clenches rhythmically around Jared, sending him to meet me among the stars with a groaned curse on his lips. Gently, his hands disengage from my body and he kisses my shoulder, panting, his exhausted body draping over me.

I plummet back to earth, reveling in the intimacy with Jared but still eager to share with my other fated mate. Jared settles onto the floor, still panting. I release my grip on Landon and glance up at him, only to find he's gazing at me with pure adoration, not a hint of jealousy to be had. His hand reaches for his erection, probably to finish himself off.

Clearly he doesn't realize I'm not finished, either.

I lick my lips and smile up at him. "Nuh-uh, that's mine. I'm not done with you yet."

His eyes drink me in like a blind man seeing the sun for the first time. The tension in my belly quickly coils again, anticipating the feeling of my third mate nestled deep inside me. I rise on shaky legs as I climb onto the couch and straddle his thighs. Landon's hands immediately claim my hips, long fingers gripping tightly to my tingling flesh. Gradually, holding his eyes with mine, I sink down on him. I'm so slick and ready, I take him to the hilt in one fluid motion. His head tilts back and eyes close, a deep guttural groan escaping from the back of his throat.

I move slowly at first, exploring the way this new position feels and how it hits. After a moment, Landon adapts to the sensation and his hips begin to move in tandem with mine. Hungry lips cover my breast, teeth scraping over my sensitive nipple and pushing me closer to climax again.

Soon our motions are rapid and aggressive, my body bouncing on his lap as his hips thrust, hands slamming me back down on his length. He's long since abandoned my breast, an expression of fierce concentration taking over his handsome face. I spare a thought to note that of the three, I never imagined that Landon would be the aggressive one in bed.

His eyes never leave my face, watching me beneath thick lashes as we both race toward completion.

Jared, apparently recovered, returns a hot, slick finger to my back entrance and I freeze, drawing in a sharp gasp. His other hand grips one of my breasts, pinching the nipple as I arch back against him. Landon's thrusts slow and deepen, lifting me with his hips and hands then slamming me back down on him. The sharp wet smack of the tiny nub at the apex of my thighs against his belly sends pleasurable sensations coursing through my body.

Jared's teeth drag along the curve of my neck, both his hands busy.

Instinct takes over, and Landon and I find our rhythm again, moving faster as one. Sweat pours from my body, sticking my hair to my neck and trickling between my breasts. The speed and friction work, building the tension once again, and his lips find their way to my collarbone, one hand claiming my bare breast.

The collection of sensations continues to build, tightening the coils that spring me toward release. My entire body quivers and when I think I can't hold myself up any longer, pure molten pleasure has me shouting my release. The guys continue the movements that sent me over the edge, wringing every last drop of ecstasy from my body. I feel the hot pulse of Landon's completion as he shivers and jerks beneath me.

"Lily." My name falls from his lips with such reverence that my heart stutters before resuming its racing rhythm. Our lips meet in a deep, soulful exchange while he continues to throb within me.

I reach back for Jared to pull my other mate into a mind-shattering kiss. The three of us together in this moment are just… perfect.

I drink in his soulful gaze before softly pressing my mouth to his again. Jared's hands slip away, and a few moments later he returns and settles into the couch next to us. My body is practically liquid. The two of them spread me across their laps, fingertips trailing over my sweaty skin, and we cool down as one.

"Now that's the way to celebrate a victory." Jared lifts my hand to press a kiss to my palm.

"I'm not so sure," I reply in an uncertain tone.

"What's wrong, Lily?" Ever concerned for my well-being, Landon sounds upset.

"I just think we ought to keep practicing. I want to make sure we get it right."

There's a long, pregnant moment of silence.

Then Jared asks carefully. "When are you wanting to practice again?"

"Again? Who said we stopped?"

The boys shake with laughter, but after a beat they realize I'm not laughing.

"What are you saying?"

"I'm saying I have multiple fated mates. I think I should work on my stamina."

They exchange another of those glances. "And what exactly is your plan?"

I pretend to check my watch, then stretch lazily. "I'm going to get a drink of water, and then I'm going to lie naked in my bed. You two figure it out."

With that, I stand up and strut toward the bedroom without a backward glance.

Chapter Seventeen

DERREK

"Derrek." The seductive whisper curls my toes and sends blood rushing to my lower extremities. It's Lily's voice, a throaty purr promising pleasure that starts shivers coursing over my skin.

I roll over and open my eyes to find myself in a giant bed, with a nest of snow-white covers and a pale, raven-haired beauty gazing at me with lust-filled emerald eyes. Bright sunlight pours in from tall windows, and gauzy curtains drape the bed around us.

"Lilliana," I sigh, reaching for her body and pulling her close. I could cry from the joy of seeing her again, safe and lovely, wearing scraps of black lace over her luscious curves.

My hands rove over every inch of her silky skin,

mouth devouring hers. Her clever tongue teases mine, delicious moans pouring from her throat in response to the skilled touch of my fingers.

I pull away to trail kisses along her neck, and my name tumbles from her lips in ecstasy. "Derrek... Derrek!" It's the most beautiful sound I've ever heard, and it spurs my need to join our bodies, to feel her as intimately as one person can another.

I have no more patience, not even to remove her lingerie. I need to be inside her, to feel that connection.

She wants the same, rolling onto her back and spreading her legs for me to settle between. I'm rock hard, so incredibly beyond ready for this moment. I've been ready for it for months. Lily's eyes are practically glowing as she gazes up at me with adoration, chest rising and falling rapidly with desperate little pants. Her fingers trail hungrily over my chest.

Braced on one arm, I ease the thin barrier of lace aside and lovingly bury myself inside her.

I've never felt anything so incredible, like she was made for me. Lily's back arches, her chin tilting back in ecstasy as my name continues to tumble from her lips.

"Leaf!" For some reason, her switching to my given name empowers me, sending energy coursing through my veins.

We move together slowly at first, quickly increasing the pace until I'm slamming into her with powerful strokes that make her gasp, her body writhing beneath mine and encouraging me to move faster. Her arms and legs cling to me, leveraging her strength as we race toward completion.

"Leaf, Leaf!" Her voice is thick with desperation, and I'm determined to bring her to an earth-shattering completion.

"Lilliana… Lily, I love you," I groan, gazing deeply into her eyes as we reach the peak together, her body shuddering and clenching around me while I fill her with hot spurts.

My body collapses on top of hers, and her limbs wrap around me tightly, squeezing me to her and pressing our hot, sweaty skin together. An unbidden thought takes over, and I find myself hoping my seed takes root in her belly. The desire for her to carry my child catches me by surprise, but once it's there I can't get rid of it; images of her with a sweet, round belly flit through my brain, almost making me hard again.

When our breathing returns to normal, I brace myself on one arm and gaze lovingly down at her perfect face. She smiles up at me, eyes gleaming, and says, "Well, that was entertaining."

The voice that came out of her mouth was not hers, and it pulls me up short.

My face contorts in confusion, and I ask, "What did you say?"

The gruff male voice comes out of Lily's perfect lips again. "It's time to rise and shine, pup." Cold dread sweeps over my body, and as if a magical hook is buried in my stomach, I'm yanked back to reality. My eyes pop open and I sit up, body on high alert.

The bed is comfortable, but it's not the luxurious, heavenly place I was a minute ago. There's no bright sunlight, no plush comforter, and no beautiful girl in my bed. The erection that grew in response to my dream withers immediately, and I draw in a deep sigh before raising my gaze to the rest of the room.

Sure enough, just a few feet from my bed sits the torture chamber. A spike of anxiety shoots through my veins when my eyes land on it, and I realize Nielsen was right. It *is* another form of torture to sleep in the same room.

Speaking of torture, three men stand in the doorway, smirking down at catching me asleep. Nielsen, of course, Jessup, and Billy.

"What were you dreaming about, son? Sure looked like an interesting dream from the way you were moving around." The other two men snicker, but I just glare at them, knowing they can't possibly know the subject of my dream. I also know Nielsen doesn't expect an answer, given the absurd torture device he had Azalea fashion for me.

"Well, it's time for you to get up. I'll give you a few minutes to get ready, and then we'll begin."

With a menacing grin, he turns and follows the other two men from the room, and I wait until the door clicks closed before dropping my head in my hand.

Before I rise to my feet, I do a quick assessment of my pain level before pulling back my bandages and checking the cuts and scorch marks they left on my body yesterday. I feel surprisingly well-rested and am shocked to find my skin unblemished.

After I woke up from the first shock yesterday, he alternated between the prod and the knife, lancing me first with electricity, then sharp slices across my chest and rib cage. The torture went on for what seemed like hours before he finally declared I could rest. I cross check my reflection in the bathroom mirror, but it confirms there's not a single mark on my skin.

So there must be some truth to Nielsen's claims that I'm half wolf. Witches don't have the innate healing that wolves do; my mother always had to make poultices with spells worked in to heal up my childhood injuries. She could have drawn on her own life force, as I did with Lily following Azalea's attack, but there are limits to that kind of magic and besides, no reason to waste it.

A memory of her in a bright kitchen flashes into my brain. She's humming to herself, stirring a bowl filled with a thick, herbal-scented concoction. As if sensing me watching, she turns and smiles, crouching to my height. "Well now, that looks pretty clean." Her gentle fingers tilt my chin up, examining the deep scrape I got falling off my skateboard. "We'll just put some of this on there and it'll be good as new by tomorrow, okay?"

I nod, and she scoops a fingerful from the bowl, smoothing it over my tender skin. Immediately, the ache deep in my chin from the abrupt contact with pavement eases, the poultice cool and soothing on my bruised face. The scent of lemongrass is strong but comforting; I always associate it with my mother.

"There you go, all set. You run along and play, and let's hold off on the tricks for the rest of the day, alright? If you break an arm, that'll take more than a poultice to heal."

Her warm hand cups my cheek and I grin back at her, already feeling completely restored.

The memory warms me from the inside out, and I try to hold on to that feeling for as long as I can.

If mom were here, she'd have no problem getting me out of this situation. But after being banished by the pack, she's taken up residence in Charleston and there's no way for me to get ahold of her from my cell, regardless. And she's happy there, running an apothecary shop behind her main business, a luxury store selling herbal bath products. The binding spell took a while to remove, and I didn't have time to stay and chitchat, but she told me about her husband and how happy they are together.

Another memory pops into my head: mom explaining how she learned to do spells nonverbally.

"There's no trick to it," she explained, shaking her head affectionately. "It's simply a matter of will. You have to believe, with every fiber of your being, that you can do it. Once you have the spells memorized—which is the majority of how you spend your apprenticeship— it gets easier. Learn to let go of your voice as a crutch and pull the magic from within you, solely using your will."

"But then why don't you skip the part saying the spell and go straight to learning how to do it without speaking? That seems simpler to me." My eight-year-old self was quite the problem solver.

"Because you have to know *exactly* how to pronounce the spell, the pace at which to speak it, and how to blend that with the actions of your body. Otherwise, it could go terribly awry. It's sort of like a dance, and if you get one step wrong, you've ruined the entire thing."

"So that's why you practice."

"It's dangerous to get spells wrong, Leaf. Incredibly dangerous. Please promise me that once your magic begins to rise, you'll do as I say."

I release a heavy sigh. "Fine, Mama, I promise."

The memory aches, knowing if I'd been able to apprentice, I would be able to perform silent spells as easily as breathing by now.

My heart picks up speed.

Because of so many factors, the least of which was my mother binding my powers, I never got to be an apprentice.

But that doesn't mean I learned nothing. Even without my magic, mom always had me help her with spells, and I'd stand beside her and watch every step, hear each word, over and over again.

Like a lightning strike, I realize she had *always* planned to unbind me. Why else would she insist I help her for years, despite showing no magical promise at all? Why insist I read every ingredient in her grimoire, learn how to prep each specific herb, speak each spell along with her? She knew, at some point, I'd need my magic.

And the time has certainly come.

My mind skips forward about a dozen steps, and I put together a plan so easily it's like it'd been hanging over my head, just waiting for me to look up.

As quickly as I'm able, I search every inch of the tiny bathroom. I'm fairly certain there are cameras in the room, besides the obvious dome that hangs over the metal cage.

But in here I'm not so certain, and I hope I'm right.

I press my finger to the mirror and verify it's not a 2-way, then feel my way around and examine every tiny facet of each surface.

It's a spartan room, with nothing more than a shower stall, a pedestal sink, and a basic toilet. Despite my thoroughness, it only takes me a handful of minutes to confirm there are no cameras or listening devices in this tiny room.

Which gives me a tiny, glimmering shred of hope.

Just in time for the door to the hallway to open and Nielsen to call out brightly. "Ready to get started, son?"

Chapter Eighteen

MILO

~

It was surprisingly difficult to leave Harridan House knowing what was about to take place, and knowing that it wouldn't involve me. Since Lily and I forged that bond my thoughts bounced back to her constantly, with no small amount of lust attached. She described it as an itch, and that feels accurate. No matter how many times we scratch it, the relief is temporary, and the itch creeps back up quickly, demanding another scratch.

Even though we slipped a hot and heavy quicky in between dinner and the midnight run with no one the wiser, I was already aching for her by the time I came home. I lay in my bed, the scent of her clinging to my pillows, and alternated between remembering what we had done and imagining what the three of them were getting up to. Then what it would be like if I were there. It didn't take me long to relieve myself once again.

The thought of her between all three of us had always been a delicious one; we didn't discuss it much, especially after Lily arrived, but I know we were all thinking about it. Not wanting to push her any further than she wanted, but definitely looking forward to the day she claimed all of us.

Then she had to tell me that Derrek is her fourth mate.

What was I supposed to do with that? My emotions have been all over the place and even though I'm not happy with the idea, there's nothing I can say that will change what she wants.

And apparently she wants him.

No, *needs* him is how she put it.

It's a problem we'll have to face, but first we still have to figure out how to get Derrek back from Montrose. I mean, I could live without him, but if Lily needs him, then there's no more to say.

I wake up surprisingly early and get ready with an excess of nervous energy. As I drive toward Harridan House, little scenarios flit through my head. Perhaps I'll arrive and they'll all still be asleep, tangled in the sheets and the air thick with the smell of sex. Or maybe I'll walk in and they'll be in the midst of yet another round, Lily making those little breathy moans that drive me absolutely wild.

Of course, in that scenario, she'll turn to me with

pleading eyes and beg me to join them, spreading her legs for me to feast on her. She'll be so wet, probably laying in a puddle in the wake of so much sex. And so sensitive that when I run my tongue over her, she'll shudder and moan my name, her fingers clenching my hair.

Shit! The road grows bumpy and I'm drawn back to the present just in time to realize I'm veering off the side of the road and about to pass my turn. I crank the wheel hard to the left, narrowly making the turn to Harridan House. Best to not continue having filthy fantasies about my mate while operating a moving vehicle.

I need to get my shit together, for real. I've never had a difficult time controlling my hormones before. Even during my experimentation with heavy petting of other girls solely for the sake of learning how to please my mate, I never lost control and went further than I intended. My mind only turned over racy thoughts when I chose to enjoy them, typically at home, in bed, alone.

Now it seems as if all I can focus on is the taste of Lily, the scent of her, the way it feels to be inside her, the sounds she makes when I bring her to new pinnacles of pleasure…

My hands grip the steering wheel so tightly my knuckles turn white. Holy goddess, something is definitely wrong with me. There's no way this is normal.

Clenching my jaw, I force myself to review everything I ever learned in our boring Pack History class in the hopes there may be something useful buried in the back of my brain.

When I finally, mercifully, arrive at Harridan House, I suck in a deep breath before climbing out of my car. Whatever happens when I walk through the door, I have to avoid making any sort of assumptions at all. I have to keep my cool.

I affect the aloof air that's served me so well before, and let myself in the front door.

Now, I'm not under any delusion that the staff at Harridan House starts their days at a leisurely hour. In fact, I know they rise pretty early just for the sake of food prep, maintenance, and other household activities. Given that it's not quite eight in the morning, I expected people to be up but for things to just beginning to move.

Instead, I walk into a scene of organized chaos. Mrs. Dowling is directing a pair of the security team to carry some sort of picnic basket out to the garage, seeing as they're on their way to pull an SUV around. Three of the Montrose members are scattered around the open area, chatting with Roxanne, Dom, and a few other pack members. Even Amber is here for whatever reason, bouncing on the toes of her pink sneakers and listening with rapt attention to Lily.

And then, as if she feels my eyes on her, Lily turns, a wide smile spreading across her face and her eyes alight. My heart throbs in response, and she walks swiftly toward me, launching herself in my arms and claiming my mouth in a powerfully hungry kiss.

My body responds instinctually, arms snaking around her body and squeezing her tightly. The room full of people around us fades away. Sounds are muted, and all I am aware of in this moment is Lily and the deafening pounding of my heart.

I could stay here forever, but she eventually breaks off the kiss, leaving me breathless.

"Hey." She grins up at me, her arms still wrapped around my waist. "Missed you last night."

"You did, huh?" I am indescribably pleased to hear that. "Well, I'm sorry to hear my brothers weren't up for meeting your needs, but I'm sure I won't let that happen again."

Her head tips back and she laughs, swatting me on the chest. "Not what I meant. We had a… thoroughly excellent night. I just know it would have been even better with you there, too."

Some of my pride withers at her correction, but I understand what she means. I lift a hand to toy with a dark, bouncy curl near her face. "I'll always be here if you want me, Lily. Just say the word."

"Look who finally made it, the legend himself." Jared's voice is practically booming, and he's grinning from ear to ear as he approaches us, Landon at his side.

The sarcastic grin spreads easily across my face. "Hey guys, you have a good night?"

Landon's cheeks immediately color pink, but Jared has no shame. "You know it. Hey, what did the tree say when spring finally arrived?"

The three of us groan in unison, but Jared continues

grinning as if he doesn't hear. "It said, 'what a relief'! Like re-leaf! Get it?" And goddess love him, he chuckles at his own lame joke, every time. The rest of us make a collective 'ah' sound and search for a change in topic.

"Alright that's enough fun and games." Lily's voice is devoid of the playfulness of a few moments ago. "Milo, I'm going to catch you up to speed. The Montrose guys are far more helpful now that I've proven I'm not some useless little girl. One had to leave because he's on shift for—get this—guard duty over Derrek! We've *literally* got a man inside, and he gave us a lot of good intel. We know exactly where Derrek is, how many guards there are at any given time, and how the schedule works.

"However, that's the end of the good news. Billy confirmed Derrek is being... that he..." distress washes over her face, and as if her throat was closing up she seems to choke on the words she can't get out.

Landon wraps an arm around her shoulders and pulls her tightly to his side. "They're torturing him."

Indignation burns in my gut. Not necessarily for Derrek, but I'm not a huge fan of hurting other people, regardless. And that it's making Lily this upset makes me want to rip that alpha's throat out. "Why the hell are they doing that?"

Jared takes over somberly. "According to Billy, Pack Montrose has difficulty with their people actually mani-festing the shift. So they have a whole 'program' to 'encourage' the shift to take place." He lifts his hands and makes air quotes along with the heavily sarcastic tone. "Since Derrek is his son, Nielsen needs him to shift before he can claim Derrek as his heir."

"But what if he can't shift? I don't know about you, but I've never heard of a half-breed before. We don't know what they can or can't do."

"That doesn't seem to matter to Nielsen," Landon answers gravely, hand still sliding up and down Lily's arm in comfort. "According to Billy, he's intent on forcing him to shift, no matter what it takes."

"So why doesn't he do some magic mumbo-jumbo and get himself out of there?"

"That's where Azalea comes in," Lily answers in a tremulous voice. Clearing her throat, she explains, "Azalea made some sort of magical collar that she put on Derrek. It can't come off. And any time he tries to speak, or even makes a sound, it does some sort of magical shock to him."

"A collar?" Heat rises in my chest, creeping up my neck. "Like a *dog* collar?"

"Yeah, exactly," Lily answers in disgust. "Exactly like a dog collar. It even has a leash."

My stomach churns. "That's sick. I don't care who you are. That can't have been Nielsen's idea; he wants Derrek to be his heir. You can't expect a pack to follow someone you've dragged around like an abused pet in front of them."

"According to Billy, Nielsen didn't specify. He just wanted something that would keep Derrek from accessing magic to use against him. But he doesn't care, either. The pack is used to this sort of torture tactics to force the shift, and he's keeping the circle of people in the know small, too. Probably for that reason."

My lips twist in disgust. "They're fucking animals, doing that to other people."

"Yeah," Landon agrees.

"Fucking right," Jared snorts.

"It's terrible. That's why we have to help them." Lily's voice is low, but powerful.

"Wait, help them? I thought the plan was to rescue Derrek?"

"It is, but the majority of that pack are innocent victims too, Milo. We can't just take Derrek and run."

"Woah, we need to slow down here." Landon's eyes widen as he holds his hands up for emphasis. "I know Derrek is your friend, but we're not trying to burn the world down to get him back, Lily. We need to be smart about this."

My eyes dart to Lily sharply, and she gives me a very subtle head shake.

So she hasn't told Jared and Landon that Derrek is her fourth mate yet. Goddess, help me.

"Regardless, that's not what we're doing today, so we can shelve this for now," Lily states firmly. "Today we are going to visit Derrek's grandma to see if she can help us come up with a solution for the collar. Given that a spell fixed it onto him, it'll probably take a spell to remove it."

"Yeah, and something tells me Azalea won't help us out," Jared snorts.

"Agreed."

"Yup."

"So what exactly is this plan? It looks like we're going on a three-week vacation here." My timing couldn't have been better; one of the house staff looks at us apologetically, silently requesting us to step aside so she can push a large trunk on wheels out the front door.

"Well… we have a couple of things going on. We assume Montrose has spies watching our territory, so we're going to send some mixed messages in the form of decoys."

"Decoys?"

"Yeah. Maxwell is going to drive the car I normally ride in south toward Knoxville, and we're faking a meeting there with the alpha from another pack. He's gonna pull over at a gas station at some point and have a 'private' phone conversation outside the car to leak some false intel."

"Okay, that seems solid."

"And while he's doing that, a couple of other cars will go in different directions just to muddy the waters. The other Montrose guys will be slipping back over to North Carolina, and we'll be on our way to visit Shuya."

"And what, exactly, will *we* be driving for this top secret trip?"

Lily's eyes turn to Jared, who grins. "You know how I have four sisters, right?"

Chapter Nineteen

LILLIANA

Just to be extra safe, we walk through the extensively long house to reach the garage instead of cutting across the courtyard. I've never actually seen this wing, but it appears to be mostly guest rooms and otherwise unused spaces. A narrow covered walkway connects the main house to the carriage house, and once we're inside the room opens up considerably.

The first thought that hits me is that I didn't know how many cars I apparently own. There are actually *three* of the SUVs Maxwell drives me around in, all sparkling under the overhead lights. A few utility vehicles wait behind those, and then a collection of classic cars that someone clearly lovingly maintains.

My eyes must be as wide as saucers as we walk past the candy colored sports cars with gleaming chrome.

"Are these all… I mean, do these all belong to the alpha?"

The guys exchange a look.

Jared asks incredulously, "You didn't know that?"

"That explains why she's never driven one," Landon answers.

"We were wondering," Milo agrees. "We figured you just enjoyed being a passenger princess," he adds, kissing my forehead.

"I mean, I'd probably be terrified to take that out and drive it, for fear I'll get a scratch on it or something." I point to a shiny red car. The only thing I can answer confidently is that it's a Porsche, based entirely on the cursive writing displayed on the trunk.

"Nah, if that happened the staff would buff it out for you. Once we get past all this mess, you really ought to go for a spin." Milo reassures me with a wink. "You can drive stick, right?"

I lower my brows and roll my eyes. "No, I can't drive stick. So much for that idea."

"No biggie," Jared squeezes my shoulder. "We'll teach you."

I hate to walk away from the gleaming life-sized toys, but most of the activity is happening further along in the garage. We reach the crowd, and I spot several vehicles that I'm intimately familiar with.

"Ah, so this is where your cars go when you're here."

"Yup," Landon pats his Jeep. "They're safe and sound, and the garage crew take excellent care of them."

"Right?" Jared agrees. "I haven't filled my own gas tank since Lily arrived, and my truck is always spotless despite how much the two of you eat in it."

"I... nevermind." The instinct to chide them for taking advantage rises and falls like a wave in my chest. Technically, they are my fated mates, which makes them fated *alphas*, and the services here are just as much theirs as they are mine. I can hardly act like I don't enjoy never having to clean my toilet.

We walk a little way further on, and Jared announces, "There she is!"

Sure enough, a slightly battered, gold-colored minivan sits with both sliding doors open and waiting for us to clamber inside. Jared's sister Sasha waits nervously by the driver side door, twirling wavy black locks around her slim brown finger. Her eyes lift from her phone the second Jared's voice reaches her, and she slides the device into her pocket as we approach.

"About time. Of course you'd leave me here staring at all these gorgeous cars, knowing I'm driving this shitbox."

She glares at Jared, but greets the rest of us with hugs.

"Thank you for doing this," I murmur with a squeeze.

"Of course, alpha. Whatever you need, no thanks required."

"Hey, it's not my fault Dad takes better care of his vehicles than Mom does," Jared continues.

"That's not even the half of it, and you know it. You got the truck with like, a year and twenty thousand miles on it. This thing is almost as old as you are."

"Again, not my fault Mom hangs on to cars forever. You're the one who said you wanted it."

"Only because I would never dream that Dad would ditch his truck that fast. I thought you were going to be stuck with a shitty second-hand car from someone else."

"Yeah, and you were super grateful that mom gave you the van. And now *we're* all grateful that you have it, so can we get this show on the road?"

She huffs a sigh then turns resignedly toward the vehicle of contention and waves her hand forward, calling us as she walks away.

"Come on kids, climb in. Don't forget seatbelts! And no eating in my car, *Jared*."

My eyes drift to Landon who snorts.

"Makes the food in the car complaints pretty rich coming from him, doesn't it?" Milo whispers in my ear. His warm hand presses to the small of my back, guiding me into the van.

The front has bucket seats, just like the second row. The third row is a bench, so I clamber in and claim the middle.

Jared stops short, confused. "You don't have to sit in the middle, Lily. Even without the front we've got enough space for the four of us."

"I know," I smile back.

A confused expression crosses his face. Clearly he'd walked around the vehicle to enter from the opposite side door and ensure he got a bucket seat. Perhaps he assumed I'd take the other.

Now it seems I've thrown his seat calculus to the wind.

"'Scuze me." Milo squeezes past Jared in his indecision and claims the seat to my right, buckling in.

Landon's eyes dart between me and Milo, and I can read the math running through his head. If he takes the remaining back seat, Jared will be in the second row alone.

With a sigh, he settles into the bucket seat and waves his hand at Jared. "Just sit down, man."

Jared listens, buckling into the second row seat just as Sasha reaches up and presses a button above her head. The doors close automatically. "The car rules are no fighting, no switching seats while the car is in motion, and all body parts stay inside at all times. Anyone need to go potty before we leave?"

The sarcasm is thick in her voice, and Jared chuckles. I assume this is a speech their mom gave them before road trips.

"Hearing none, let's go!"

She pulls forward and the garage door opens smoothly ahead of her, letting bright morning light into the cavernous space. The windows in the back of the van are dark, almost black, blocking most of the scenery outside. To a casual observer, it probably appears Sasha is alone in her van.

When we pull out completely we join a long line of vehicles, including the three identical black SUVs I saw closest to the house. As if they received a signal, the line moves forward and we roll out in a ragtag convoy of sorts. The cars remain in order until we reach town, and then they splinter off in every direction, even some that enter neighborhoods and will eventually end up in the same places.

As we'd planned, Sasha takes a circuitous route that wanders up to her and Jared's house, pausing there for a few minutes before pulling out and heading toward Smoky Falls College. Even though Sasha graduated last year, she works part time as a teaching assistant and could theoretically be going in to work today.

She parks in the faculty lot and shuts the van off, leaving us in the vehicle to wait while she walks to the nearest building. A few moments later she returns, and we continue on our way.

All in all, it takes a good forty-five minutes before we head away from Smoky Falls toward Shuya's house. The car is silent, the air thick with tension when we cross the magical line that protects Smoky Falls.

Out here we're unprotected. Out here, we're on our own.

Well, us and the security team trailing us by about half a mile. Jared watches out the windows intently, switching between gazing ahead and behind us. He sends a few texts to the follow car and waits for a response.

When his phone vibrates a relieved expression takes up residence on his face. "Security said the only vehicle that was on the road behind us out of Smoky Falls turned off. So we're not being followed."

As if he let the air out of a balloon, the tension deflates, and the atmosphere becomes noticeably more relaxed.

Milo's arm drapes across the back of the seat, his fingers toying with my hair. I lean into his body, releasing a heavy sigh.

Even though everyone has relaxed a little, the van is still silent. Every road noise is clearly audible, even the thunk sound of the tires hitting a divot in the pavement.

Jared clears his throat, and says in a serious tone, "Hey Landon, did you hear about that guy on the track team at school who was afraid of the hurdles?"

Landon's response is hesitant, as if he's not sure where this is going. "No…?"

Jared continues seriously. "Yeah, he's a great athlete, but this was a big problem for him. No worries, though, he got over it."

There's a long, pregnant pause while we all think about it, and then Landon bursts out laughing.

"Holy shit, he actually did it," Milo comments.

"Did what? Got a new joke?" I tease, realizing a beat later that I'd sarcastically hit the nail on the head.

"No, he finally delivered a joke without ruining it before he could even deliver the punchline."

"You're right, he did. Good job, Jared!"

"It was still a lame joke," Milo adds quickly, "but your delivery is improving."

"Thank you, thank you!" Jared grins back at us, dark eyes sparkling below the bill of his SFC cap. "You know how big a zebra is?"

Milo and I exchange a concerned glance. "Not exactly," he answers. "Why?"

"It's a few sizes bigger than an 'A'!" Jared chortles at his own joke with delight. "Get it? A 'Z' bra?"

"A brief, shining moment," Milo comments sarcastically, "and then he's right back to normal."

"Wait, let me try another one." Jared shifts in his seat to launch into another joke.

"No, no, no!" Sasha calls from the driver's seat. "I can't take any more. I'm putting on some music."

She turns some dials and soon enough pop music plays over the speakers.

Jared turns back around in his seat and drops his gaze to the phone in his hand.

I settle back into the cozy crook that Milo's arm and body makes, and a yawn escapes my lips.

"What's the matter, Lily? Did you have a hard time sleeping last night?" Milo asks in a wry voice.

"As a matter of fact I slept very well, thank you," I answer curtly. "I just didn't get a *lot* of sleep. What I got was excellent, though."

"Why don't you try and nap, then? I'll wake you up before we get close." His lips press to the top of my head, and I curl into him, resting my face against his chest.

It's warm and familiar, his citrusy cedar scent in my nose, and the steady, powerful beat of his heart lulls me right to sleep.

True to his word, Milo shakes me gently awake while the van is still in motion. "Lily, we're just a few minutes from the turnoff to Shuya's house."

I straighten and stretch, yawning again. "Anything happen?"

"Not a thing. Jared just checked in with the security team and they said it's all good."

"Okay, that's good." I scrub my fists against my eyes, trying to shake off the haze of sleep.

Everyone else appears to have remained alert for the ride, and a brief pang of guilt hits my chest. I'm the alpha. I'm supposed to be protecting them. Instead, I was sleeping, and they all kept watch. I have to do better than this. It's my responsibility.

A few moments later, the van slows, and Sasha flicks her signal, easing onto the unfortunately familiar gravel drive.

Jared's sister wasn't here the last time, but the rest of us were. We watched someone die here, and for some reason, I didn't expect the sick swirl of feelings from that day to come rushing back at me.

My anxiety spikes, and I reach out to sample the feelings of my companions.

Sasha is a medium orange color, her anxiety simple.

The guys are more complex, their colors like a lamp that cycles through the rainbow.

Anger, fear, anxiety, dread, concern, and love revolve around me like some sort of psychedelic light display.

I know what they're feeling, because the same confusing mix is racing through my body, too.

Drawing a deep breath, I exhale slowly and focus on what I want to happen at the end of this driveway. Shuya will answer the door when we knock, and she'll be absolutely shocked to hear what Azalea has done, pledging immediately to help us save Derrek. She'll give us some sort of… magical *thing* we can take along to disable the collar. We'll leave swiftly and be gone before anyone could even know we'd been here.

We turn the last corner and face the well-worn cottage ahead, all the bizarre wind chimes hanging from the wrap-around porch exactly as before. Now a variety of pumpkins in every size, shape, and color line the stairs, and brown leaves have piled up around the bushes.

Jared's phone buzzes, and he reads aloud. "The security team stopped a quarter mile before the turnoff to avoid drawing suspicion. They can be here in 3 minutes if we need them. Are you guys ready?"

A shudder runs through my body, and even though

I avoid looking at it I'm keenly aware of the spot where Jeremy bled out in front of our eyes. I peer out the windows but there's no sign of Azalea's souped up sports car, so I unbuckle. "Let's go."

Sasha remains in her seat but hits the button to open the side doors. "I'll leave the doors open and turn around so we can make a fast exit if we have to," she promises, a slight tremor in her voice.

Jared claps a hand on her shoulder. "Thank you, Sash." He steps out of the van on the right side, eyes sweeping the trees that surround us on three sides.

Landon hops out behind him, and Milo nudges me ahead so he can take up the rear. We move as one up to the house, taking the porch stairs with slow, deliberate steps.

I feel like some kind of movie star, only not in a glamorous way. The guys are big and protective, surrounding me with their bodies as if I'm some kind of frail weakling that can't defend herself. And it grates at me, to know in this circumstance I actually need their protection.

Jared reaches up and knocks swiftly on the door. "Ten minutes, guys, like we planned. Last time it took Azalea over twenty to arrive once we set off her 'alarms', so we should be out of here in plenty of time. Landon?"

"Timer's already started," Landon answers grimly.

Steps approach the door, and we draw in a collective breath. It feels good to finally be doing something, moving closer to getting Derrek home and safe, with me where he belongs. Shuya can help, I know it.

The only problem is that when the door opens, it doesn't reveal the person we were expecting.

Chapter Twenty

JARED

~

"You." Lily's voice is flat and furious.

"Me!" Azalea replies in a bright yet somehow threatening tone, her purple-coated lips curving into a devious smile like that damned cat from Alice in Wonderland. She even looks the part today, her hair electric purple with dark streaks. She leans against the doorway lazily. "Why are you so surprised to see me here, princess? This is my grannie's house, after all."

Adrenaline coursing through my system, I smash the send button on the text I'd already drafted to the security team and step directly between Lily and the witch.

"Get her out of here, now!" My command is directed at Landon and Milo, even though my eyes never leave

Azalea's face. I may not be the tallest of the three of us, but I can provide our mate the most cover while she makes her escape.

Plus, I have a sneaking suspicion there isn't a spell for dodging a right hook.

"Azalea! No hurting people on my property, you agreed!" Shuya's voice calls out from somewhere in the house. "You know what happens if you break the rules." The verbal threat is surprisingly strong, and the witch visibly cringes in response, her smirk faltering slightly.

"I know, Grannie, don't worry. I haven't forgotten." Her eyes roll and she calls over her shoulder in an annoyed tone. Heaving a dramatic sigh, she refocuses on me. "Grannie made me promise not to attack anyone on her property, so you have nothing to fear from me. Witch's honor," she adds sarcastically, drawing the shape of a star in the air with one purple-tipped finger.

The others were a few steps away already, but they paused when they heard Shuya's ancient voice.

I, however, am not convinced. My feet remain planted, arms crossed, and my body physically blocking Azalea from sneaking past. "Awful nice of you, to keep promises to your granny," I reply sarcastically. "I'm sure you've never lied in your life, either."

"Ugh, wolves are so fucking dense. I *promised* her, dimwit. *Magically*. If I break that promise, there would be consequences. Dire ones. Are you following? Let me dumb it down for you: Promise, good. Break promise, bad. Got it?"

Everything about this witch sets my teeth on edge, and that's before her infuriating condescension makes my blood boil. "Got it, witch. Your granny has you on a leash. That *is* the best way to train dogs, but I've always believed feral cats belong in a cage."

"Ooh, so clever. You really hurt my feelings, mutt."

"I don't give a fuck about your feelings, witch. We're not here to talk to you, we're here to see Shuya, so if you wouldn't mind…" I gesture to the doorway she's blocking.

Just then, the security team comes tearing down the drive, gravel spraying as they hit the brakes and hop out of the SUV. In a matter of moments, they've pounded up the steps and surrounded Lily, weapons drawn.

Azalea's eyes light up with delight, and she delicately presses her fingertips to her chest. "Aww, you're not afraid of little ol' me, are you? You have an entire team of dogs to protect your little princess, that's so cute. Useless, but cute. Just so you know," she leans around me to address Lily, who pushes through the group and steps up to my side, glaring, "if I wanted to kill you, no number of trained animals will stop me."

"Good for you," Lily responds cooly. "But we're kind of on a schedule here, and as my mate said, we're not here to see you. Shuya!" She calls through the doorway.

But despite having spoken earlier, the elderly witch doesn't appear at the door and she doesn't respond.

The infuriatingly superior grin has returned to

Azalea's narrow face. "Ah, well, you see, that's going to be a problem. Because Grannie also made a promise to me, and she has to keep her bargain, too."

A growl of annoyance rumbles in my chest. "What did she promise you, exactly? And what has it got to do with us?"

"Weeeelll…" she draws out the word, examining her nails lazily. "Grannie promised that she'd allow me to protect her as I see fit. There's a lot of crime around these parts, you know. Can't be too careful. So I'm afraid I can't let you inside. Family is precious, you understand."

"We're not here to hurt your grandma, and you know it," Lily snarls. "We're here to ask for her help."

"That's the thing, princess. I'm firmly of the belief that helping you will be detrimental to Grannie's well-being, so it's gonna be a no from me, dog. You're welcome to try, of course, but I wouldn't recommend it if you want to keep breathing. I'm not allowed to attack anyone on her property, but I *am* allowed to defend her if I think she's in danger." She crosses her arms and smirks at us, the challenge we can't accept hanging in the air.

"You're despicable, you know that?" The double-timbre of the alpha voice is rumbling in Lily's chest. "All I want is to free your cousin and reunite the packs. To put an end to the curse and all the hatred between us. Can't you see how that would help you *and* your family? There's far more of the Smoky Falls Pack than Montrose, and we don't have a pack witch.

You could be so much more, but you cling to these scraps."

If Lily thought that speech was going to change Azalea's mind, she's definitely disappointed at the witch's reaction.

Azalea tips her head back and releases a deep, throaty belly-laugh that rumbles her entire body. Lily stiffens beside me, infuriated.

"Now I know you're crazy, if you think that's so hilarious."

The witch takes her time, ending her chuckles, wiping at her black-lined eyes like she was crying from laughing so hard. "You know what? I like your spirit, princess. I haven't had a laugh like that in a long time. Really, thank you."

Lily throws her hands up in frustration. "This is impossible! I don't know why I'm wasting my time. You obviously don't get it."

"No, *you* don't get it, princess," Azalea's reply is sharp as the crack of a whip. "These… *boys*…" she gestures dismissively in our direction, "are your mates, right? Your fated mates?"

I bristle at the word *boys*, and Landon and Milo shift their weight behind me.

"So?"

"And you want to reunite the packs?"

Lily just glares at her.

Abruptly Azalea's voice turns gooey sweet, like dripping honey. "Well, I'm guessing you don't know how to do that, do you?"

"We're working on figuring it out," Lily says through clenched teeth. "There has to be a way. I don't buy the whole 'it's impossible' schtick. Nothing is impossible."

"Oh no, you're absolutely right. There is a way."

My eyes dart to Lily, who glances my way briefly before refocusing on Azalea.

"And I'm guessing you know what it is?"

"You're right, I do." Azalea goes back to examining her talons. "But I don't think you're going to like it."

"We're over your little games, witch," Landon growls behind me. "Either tell us what you know or don't."

"It hurts my feelings that you think so little of me," she pouts. "I'm happy to share. I just wanted to prepare you. The solution is actually pretty simple, but I know you're not gonna want to do it."

"I'm willing to do whatever it takes." Lily's voice is firm and determined.

Azalea looks up again, and a delighted grin spreads across her face. "You are? Well, that's excellent news. Because it really is simple, you know. If you want to reunite the packs, all you have to do is truly *unite* them. The Smoky Falls and the Montrose alphas just have to take each other as mates. I dunno how that would affect the curse, but it would solve your little pack problem."

Lily sucks in an audible gasp.

"And you're in luck," Azalea continues. "Nielsen's single. His fated mate died years ago, and he's never taken another. So all you have to do is add him to your little collection and poof, problem solved!"

My heart drops like a rock in my stomach, and I glance aside at Lily again. Surely she wouldn't? Nielsen is like fifty years old, and we didn't didn't spend a lot of time in his presence, but from what I've heard, he doesn't exactly sound like a man we'd welcome to family dinner.

To my complete surprise, Lily doesn't fire back at Azalea with any of the number of expletives I wanted to launch at her. Instead, her tone is calm and polite. "Thank you, Azalea. That was actually quite helpful. Give Shuya my best, will you? Tell her I'll be in touch."

Turning on her heel, Lily commands softly, "Let's go."

LANDON

The car is silent for the ride back to Smoky Falls.

Lily doesn't say a word, and the rest of us can't find something to break the silence when she seems to be concentrating so fiercely. Sasha has the radio on, and this time Lily sat in a bucket seat where she can stare out the window. Jared took the navigator spot to keep his sister company, and sensing that Lily needs space, Milo and I share the back.

When we pull up in front of Harridan House and pile out, I realize a thick blob of apprehension has been expanding in my gut. I'm not sure why, but after wishing she'd say something for the entire ride, I suddenly dread what comes out of her mouth next.

Lily thanks Sasha and we wave her off before trudging into the house. There's a heaviness to the atmosphere I can't quite explain as we follow our mate up the long, curving stairs. Ordinarily we'd pile into the elevator, but it feels good to stretch our legs after the car ride.

Plus, it drags out the time until I find out what Lily's been silently mulling over.

When we finally reach the suite and shut the door behind us, I catch a long, pointed look between Milo and Lily. At that moment I realize he knows something, something he hasn't shared with me, and probably not Jared, either, since he's terrible at keeping secrets from us.

Nervous energy zips up my body and I can't bring myself to sit down, preferring to pace slowly around the room. Milo sits and stretches out, always the picture of ease despite the tense atmosphere in the room. Jared sits as well, but his knee bounces and he doesn't lean back into the cushions. Clearly he feels it too.

Lily sits in one chair, her back ramrod straight, and clears her throat.

Here we go.

"Landon, would you sit, please? We need to talk about something."

Nerves coil and clench in my stomach. I pass the second chair in favor of the middle seat on the couch. The second I sit, the memory of being in this very spot with her all over me flashes into my mind, making my cheeks hot, and I mentally shove it down again.

We've got something more important to deal with. I can feel it.

Lily locks her hands around her crossed knee. "So…" her voice trails off as if she doesn't know where to start. "That didn't go like we expected."

The three of us grunt in agreement.

"It wasn't what we hoped," she continued, "but it wasn't what we feared, either. And we did actually get some useful information."

"I'm not sure I'd agree with that," Jared growls. "What that witch told us was useless."

I nod; totally useless.

Lily shakes her curly head. "That's not exactly true. We found out Azalea can't attack us on Shuya's land. And that Azalea's protecting her. Which presents a problem for us, but I also took it to mean she's protecting her from Montrose, too."

I hadn't considered that. It could be useful.

Jared asks the question on my mind. "But isn't Azalea working with Montrose?"

"Sort of, but Billy, the guy who works directly for Nielsen, mentioned that his alpha kicked Azalea out of his house after she put the collar on Derrek. Said she was pretty pissed. So maybe she's not as cozy with them as we thought."

"Could be useful, but I don't see how right now," I reply, and Jared nods beside me.

Lily draws in a deep breath and releases it slowly. "That's not the part that I want to talk about. I have something to tell you, and I know I should have done this sooner, but I didn't exactly know how to. I don't want to give you guys the wrong impression or hurt you, and I definitely don't want you to think any of you are not incredibly important to me." She pauses, and as she meets the gaze of first Jared, then me, I see the gleam of tears pooling in her eyes.

My heart lurches; whatever she's about to tell us is so bad she's practically crying over it. The lead in about not wanting to hurt us makes me incredibly uneasy, combined with the obvious emotion it's creating in her.

When her gaze lands on Milo, he nods solemnly. "Just tell them, Lily. It'll be okay."

This time, the slow breath she releases shudders as it escapes her lips. "The fact that mating the Montrose alpha is the way to unify the packs... may not be a problem."

Jared immediately stiffens beside me. "Are you saying you'd *mate* that monster? Bring him *here*, just to unify the packs?"

"There's no way," I add swiftly to reassure him. "He's not her fated. Besides, she wouldn't do that, especially not after we found out what he's doing to Derrek."

The second his name leaves my lips, a heavy realization sinks like a cinderblock in my gut. My face goes slack, and I stare at Lily, willing her to correct me. "You're not talking about Nielsen, are you?" My voice is almost a whisper. "Because he's not the only option. He has an heir."

"No." Jared's voice is as deep and threatening as I've ever heard it. Fury rolls off of him, so much heat rising from his skin that I can feel it through my sweater. "Not *that* guy. I haven't liked him since the day I met him. I'm trying to accept him as your friend, since he's important to you. But he's *not* one of us! He's a witch who they sent to *kill* you, and then groomed and lied to you, Lily. Repeatedly. How could you even *consider* it?"

The tears spill over onto her cheeks, and I swallow down a thick lump that suddenly formed in my throat. Jared's too angry. He hasn't even realized the truth yet.

I break the news to him. "It's too late, Jared. She's already decided. Haven't you?"

She nods. "I'm sorry guys, I know this is a lot. I'd choose differently if I could, but it's not a choice. Derrek is my fated mate, the same as you are. I feel it-"

"Bullshit!" Jared stands, furious. "He weaseled his way into your life, took care of you when you were just a kid, and the whole time he *knew* who you were. He was *planning* this all along. Don't you see it? Then he shows up here and draws on all of those memories, how you feel you owe him, and manipulates you-"

"Jared! That's *enough*." Milo shouts to be heard over

Jared's angry rant. He's on his feet now, standing chest to chest and glaring down at him. "Look at what you're doing to her!" He points an angry finger at Lily, who's hunched over in her chair, face buried in her hands.

"How could you possibly think for *one second* this is something she chose? For what reason? I can't believe you, man. She is our *mate*, our *alpha*." An angry red flush has crept up his neck; I've never seen Milo lose his shit so hard before.

His voice is laced with disgust as he continues ripping into Jared. "Who the *fuck* are you to shout at her like that, or question her decisions? If she wanted to, she could have you on the floor, tail between your legs with *one word*. And yet there she is, silently taking it, because she feels so shitty over something she can't control. Fuck you for doing that to her."

Jared had leaned back, as surprised by Milo's attack as I was. But as the dressing down continues, Jared plants his feet, puffing his chest and crossing his arms while staring Milo down from beneath the brim of his hat. He waits until Milo pauses, then launches the venom right back, poking his finger into Milo's chest.

"Don't get me started on you, *brother*. You obviously already knew about this and left Landon and me in the dark. How are we supposed to be a team, a *family*, keeping secrets from each other like that?"

They stand directly in front of me, and framed between them, all I can see is Lily, alone, watching them fight with tears streaming down her face.

I was too stunned to speak at first, but now anger floods my body and spurs me to action. Springing to my feet, I force them apart, a hand on each of their chests. "You two need to cut this shit out right now." I turn to look at Jared first, who's glaring up at me with dark, angry eyes. "Milo's right; you've always had it in for Derrek, and it's probably because you sensed a connection from them before you even knew better. We don't *own* her, do you realize that? Just because we're her fated doesn't mean she doesn't have any others, and making her feel like shit because of it is a real dick move."

Turning the other way, I stare down at Milo, who's wearing a self-satisfied smirk. "And you, don't be too proud of yourself. You're right, but that doesn't mean you're the only one who's right. Jared has a point that keeping secrets will only drive a wedge between us, just like it's doing *right now*."

He opens his mouth to protest, but I cut him off. "I know you were keeping the secret until Lily was ready to tell us, but I'm willing to bet you didn't exactly encourage her to fill us in, either. You don't get to play Switzerland here, Milo. We're a family, just like Jared said. We have to work together or we're going to tear ourselves apart."

Drawing in a deep sigh, I remove my hands from my brothers. They're no longer pressing against me, and their expressions are more ashamed than angry. "I'm going to get Lily out of here while you two sort your shit out. When we get back, we're going to have a conversation about how we can best achieve the goals she has for our pack."

Without another glance at the two of them, I cross the sitting area to offer Lily my hand, and she stands, shakily, rubbing at her red-rimmed eyes.

Even a blind man could see she's so drained she can barely keep her feet under her.

"Come on, baby," I murmur, crouching to scoop her gently into my arms.

"I'm taking you home."

Chapter Twenty-One

DERREK

~

"Hold on there, Jessup." Nielsen's voice is bored, as if my continued torture is just not entertaining him any more.

Jessup steps back, breathing heavily, and lowers the club to his side.

Once again I'm crouched in the corner, panting, with my arms around my head for protection. After easing my arms down, I turn my head painfully, straightening my neck, and spit a bloody glob onto the concrete floor. There's already a fair amount of crimson dotting it; today they opted to go for a more basic form of torture, testing the idea that the direct physical contact from someone would spur my wolf to the surface. My entire upper body is battered, dark purple blotches already spreading on my ribs. I'm nowhere near a mirror, but judging from the way it's throbbing, I can only assume my head is just as bad, if not worse. Hot liquid trickles down the sides of my face, but I can't tell if it's blood or sweat. Or, most likely, a combination of both.

Nielsen decided to be sporting today, and have a couple of his thugs start out hitting me with fists. He even let me take a few swings, hoping that allowing me to fight back might do something for my wolf. When it didn't, they went back to the tried-and-true method of using inanimate objects designed for causing pain.

They keep saying they have a very specific, very successful program, and yet I haven't seen anything to convince me they aren't just winging it.

It *was* satisfying to land a couple of hits on Jessup, the sadistic asshole. But all it earned me was some split knuckles and an eventual yank on the leash that sent me sprawling across the floor.

One of my eyes has swollen shut, so I squint the other toward what has become my most hated voice in the world. Nielsen's standing outside the cage, examining me like a specimen in a lab. Which, I suppose, to him I am.

"What do you say, Jessup? Do you think he's done for the day, or should we push him a bit more?"

My one good eye darts to Jessup, anxiety spiking with absolute certainty he'll want to continue.

But even Jessup looks rough. He's still panting heavily, his t-shirt damp with sweat and dotted with blood. He's sporting a swiftly developing black eye, with blood still running from his eyebrow where it split on my knuckle. His dark eyes glimmer with malice, although I'm not sure what reason he could possibly hate me for. It's not as if I did this to myself.

"Eh, fuck him," Jessup spits in disgust. "We don't want to beat him so badly he's not recovered by tomorrow. As it is, his ribs may not be fully healed. I say we stop and let him heal up for Level Five in the morning."

Nielsen chuckles. "Already Level Five, huh? I suppose I shouldn't be surprised that my son has my cool head and stubborn streak. It took weeks for my father to break me and draw out my wolf. Alright, let's wrap it up. Fetch the hose."

My body had relaxed when he said they were going to wrap it up, but it tenses again immediately. The hose wasn't the worse they've done to me by a long shot, but it took me hours to warm up afterward. The shower only has room temperature water and the room itself is always cold. I'm not looking forward to hours of shivering to combat hypothermia.

The older man opens the cage from the outside, allowing Jessup to exit with the club before closing it again. He drops it below the 'tool box' and pulls the hose from a mount on the wall, turning the knob on the top.

When the hose stiffens with water, he walks back to the cage, dragging the coils behind him.

I crouch lower, tucking my head and waiting for the icy blast to hit my battered skin.

"Well, look at that, I think he's learning," Jessup

drawls, chuckling. "Don't worry, you're not getting sprayed tonight. This is for you to clean up your mess."

I risk peeking over my arm, and realize he's passing the spray nozzle through the cage.

"Now before you get any smart ideas," Nielsen warns, "if you decide to get clever and turn that water on us, you'll be spending the night in that cage just as you are, naked and soaked. So I'd suggest you do as you're told and that's it."

The thought of blasting them with the freezing water had crossed my mind, but I'd already concluded it would do me no good. Obediently, I ease myself to a standing position and shuffle to the metal barrier, grabbing the sprayer and pulling it with me.

It only takes a few minutes to rinse the spatter from the walls, rivulets of water turning pink as they race across the floor and circle the drain. When Nielsen's satisfied with my work, Jessup claims the hose and replaces it, along with the club, and locks the 'tool box' up tight.

"You get cleaned up, Leaf. One of the boys will be in with your dinner soon." Nielsen tugs on the cage door, leaving it slightly ajar. "I'm ready for the game. Do you know what time they're playing?" He and Jessup discuss some local sports team as they head for the door, as if forgetting me immediately.

That he's so blase about this entire process still strikes me as incredible. How does a person spend hours torturing someone, then act like it's just a regular day at work?

The grim realization that to him this probably *is* a regular day at work hits me like a brick to the face, and I sigh, resigned, heading for the bathroom with stiff, painful steps.

After dinner they'll leave me alone til morning, and that will give me time to experiment.

I have to get out of here. I *have* to. There's no way I can just wait this out. The only way Nielsen's letting me out is by forcing me to shift, and that's looking less and less likely.

I need to take matters into my own hands.

Over an hour goes by, and I'm still waiting in my room, restlessly, for one of the Montrose thugs to deliver my dinner.

It's depressing how quickly I've turned into a trained animal. My body is stiff, every part of me screaming in protest at the smallest movement. So I sit on my bed, with my back resting against the wall, and wait. The overhead lights are too bright; I'd turn them off if I could, but they appear to be in some kind of external control. Nielsen decides when I wake up, when I take a leak, when I eat, and when I sleep. This treatment seems eerily similar to the sort of torture covert operatives would use against terrorists they don't plan to release, ever. I can only hope he means it when he says it'll stop when I shift.

At least I'm clean and wearing clothes again. Even

cold, the shower was nice. In fact, it probably helped relieve some of the pain. I shouldn't have been so quick to gratitude for not being sprayed with the hose. My skin is roasting, and the heat seems to radiate out of me from my very core. Never having been beaten this way, I'm not sure if it's a normal response or a wolf thing. I'm certainly swollen, particularly on my face and ribs, so that could be it.

The one consolation I have with the abuse is knowing that by tomorrow, my body will more or less repair itself. I never had these abilities before, but I just assume that was because my mom bound my magic so tightly it overrode mystical wolf healing as well.

However, I wonder if it gives them free license to brutalize people even more, knowing that it won't affect their victims the next day.

Just as my stomach rumbles angrily, the door creaks open and the sound of footsteps reaches my ears. With a groan, I drag myself away from the wall and open my one functional eye.

"I have to say, I've seen you in better shape, Leaf." Azalea's tone is sarcastic as usual, but there's a flatness to it, as if her heart really isn't in it.

She sets the tray on the low table by my bed and steps back, watching me.

Given my inability to make a single sound, I choose to ignore her and focus on my food.

If I had to say one nice thing about this place, it'd be that they don't skimp on the menu. The tray is laden with a thick steak, mashed potatoes and gravy, a pile of roasted carrots, and several dinner rolls. I'm certain it ties into the healing; from the times I remember Mom treating members of the pack, she always advised them to eat well, more than they'd ordinarily consume, if they could. She told them their innate healing would take over where she left off—typically she only saw someone if they had a severe injury like a broken bone —but that it consumes a large quantity of energy to do it. If they were half starving, they wouldn't be able to heal as quickly.

Despite the similarly large breakfast this morning, I feel as though I haven't eaten for days. I lean over the tray and shovel the food into my mouth as quickly as I can swallow it.

Azalea, unfortunately, still hasn't departed. "Well, I think they're already achieving some success with this little program, don't you? You may be dressed like a man, but you're acting like a caged animal."

My hand tightens on the soft buttered roll, and I clench my teeth against the urge to reply. The collar is as sealed to my flesh as ever, and it's reminded frequently what happens if I so much as growl.

Angrily, I shove the roll into my mouth and continue eating.

My lack of response spurs her to continue. "Look at that. It seems you *can* teach an old dog new tricks. Should I say congratulations, or 'good boy'?"

I raise my head to glare at her with my one partially open eye and finally realize something's off with her. She's changed her hair from hot pink to a shocking purple color, but that's not it. Despite her smirk and wide-legged stance, something's leaking through the façade. I study her, the food before me temporarily forgotten.

What is it? What's changed? What am I picking up on?

It takes several minutes of staring at Azalea, with her gazing indifferently back at me, before I realize it. What I'm noticing has nothing to do with her appearance.

It's her scent.

The food distracted me at first, filling my senses and triggering the powerful need to fill my belly.

But as I grew accustomed to it, I started noticing other smells. I haven't left this room for days, so every fragrance here is intimately familiar and I've grown to ignore them without conscious effort.

I draw in a deep breath, closing my eye to focus on the nuances.

Of course, there's the immediate hit of the sickeningly sweet perfume she wears, and beneath that, the scent of herbs I associate with Grannie's house; she must have been there recently.

But beneath that there's something else, and with a start I realize that I'm picking up *her* scent, something unique to Azalea that identifies her alone.

And that scent is laced with anxiety, almost like fear. No idea how I know it—it has to be some sort of wolf instinct—but I know it to the very core of my being.

Azalea is super anxious right now, despite her attempts to appear otherwise.

I pull in another deep breath, trying to determine if I can read anything else in her scent.

"Why are you sniffing like that?" She asks with a snarl. "You really have turned into a dog, haven't you?"

The ribbon of fear weaving through her scent gets thicker. Interesting.

Curiosity satisfied, I return my attention to my plate and finish my meal. Azalea's eyes burn holes on the top of my head, but she she doesn't speak again.

Maybe my lack of a response is really bothering her.

Just then, the door flies open.

Nielsen storms in, his face a dark, angry red beneath his beard. "What the hell are you doing here, witch?" he growls. "I don't recall issuing you an invitation to visit."

She doesn't turn to face him. "You said you'd be in touch and I haven't heard from you in days. Figured I'd come down and follow up on my dear cousin's progress." She's giving him the same indifferent attitude she gave me, but another breath confirms she's rattled by his presence.

I can't seem to get a read on him; either I can't scent other wolves the same way, or it's more nuanced than non-shifters.

I don't need his scent to tell me his emotions, however. They're written plainly on his face.

"I don't give a flying *fuck* what you want. You don't have the right to waltz into my house and do whatever you see fit. I can banish you just as easily as I did your aunt, so don't assume you have any kind of leverage over me. Now that I have Leaf here, he's more than capable of performing any magic we might need your help with."

"Ha!" she snorts. "You seem to have forgotten one tiny, significant detail: without speaking, Leaf can't use his magic, period. So as long as he has that collar on, he's no more good to you than every dog in this mangy pack. And since I'm the only one who can remove it, you'd be wise to remember that."

"Nobody threatens me in my own home!" The alpha is well and truly pissed now, veins popping in his neck as he thunders at her. Given her natural height and the added six inches from her thigh-high platform boots, Nielsen has to look up to continue raging, and he's clearly not happy about it.

"I can find another witch to undo it if I want to. You keep your position solely because it's my choice to allow you to remain. My good will only goes so far, and you are testing my patience to the limits, witch. Get out of my house!"

Dropping her voice to a deadly whisper, Azalea is suddenly more menacing than the hulking man. "We had a deal, Nielsen, and you can't back out of a deal with a witch. There is a price to pay if you don't keep your word. A *very* steep price."

He meets her threatening tone head on, growling deep within his chest. "You can't touch me, and you know it. That's been the deal between packs and witches since the beginning. You can't use your magic against the alpha of the pack you serve. And you signed the contract, so you're beholden to it unless I *choose* to release you."

Azalea's not deterred. "That doesn't release you from fulfilling our other deal. Like it or not, you owe me, and you'll have to pay up soon."

"You'll get what I promised when *I* choose. Now get out of my house before I decide you're not worth the trouble and do something drastic."

"You can't touch me either, and *you* know it. That little bargain goes both ways, and you'd be wise to remember that, dog." Azalea sniffs, then turns to stroll casually from the room. "Our little stalemate continues, but you'd better pony up before I tire of waiting. Lovely to see you, Leaf. Let's do dinner sometime!" she calls over her shoulder and saunters through the doorway.

Nielsen roars in earnest, releasing a guttural, animal sound that belongs on a Nat Geo special.

His gaze lands on me, and I realize with a start his eyes are glowing an unnatural shade of blue. "I know that witch is your cousin, but her time's coming, son. Mark my words." And with that, he storms out the door, slamming it closed behind him.

And I'm finally alone.

Chapter Twenty-Two

MILO

~

Of course, it took us all of thirty seconds to regret our fight and apologize to each other. Jared filled me in on what his dad said about mated-but-unmated males, and it suddenly makes a load of sense. My crazy emotions started immediately following the night Lily spent at my house, and now after their night with her, we were at each other's throats.

But not being able to apologize to Lily ate an acidic hole in my stomach. I tried texting and calling, but neither she nor Landon answered. Jared and I spent the night camped out in her suite, dozing off and on, hoping to get a message or see them walking back through the door so we could make amends.

It's not until we're blearily drinking the coffee Mary

was kind enough to deliver that my phone vibrates across the table.

I snatch it up and sigh with relief to see it's Lily calling me back. The second I accept the call, the apologies pour out.

"Lily, I'm so sorry for acting like that last night. Jared is too. He's sorry about all of it. We made up right after you left and we waited here all night just so we could catch you as soon as you got back and apologize in person. We-"

"Milo!" She cuts me off. "I know. I listened to your fifteen voice messages, and all of Jared's as well. Apologies accepted, we've got a bigger issue to deal with right now. Is Jared with you?"

That pulls me up short. I tap the phone and lay it on the table. "Okay, I just put you on speaker so Jared can hear. What's going on?"

"The security team called me half an hour ago. Apparently, our upgrades to the magical barrier works, because they found Azalea sitting outside of it, waiting for someone to come around."

"*Azalea?*" Jared asks, surprised. "What is that witch doing here? She's the one who didn't want to help us, and now she turns up at our border? I doubt she was trying to sneak on our land. If she was, she would have gone when she figured out it was a no-go."

"Yeah, well, that's not the only question I have. But guys, she's not alone."

Cold dread drops in my stomach. "Who's she got with her, Montrose again?"

"No, the security team said she's got a little old lady with her. Guys, she brought Shuya to us."

LILLIANA

Milo and Jared make it to the safety office in record time, and repeat all of their apologies, laying it on rather thick, until I convince them I'm okay and ready to move on.

We have much bigger fish to fry.

As a team, we leave the safety office and drive to the section of the border the security team reported. Sure enough, just beyond the cars with flashing lights stands Azalea's shiny black muscle car, with the witch herself leaning against the chrome bumper, arms crossed. White clouds of exhaust billow from the noisy muffler, and she's wearing a long black fur coat and matching black sunglasses.

When she sees us climb out of Landon's Jeep and walk toward her, she pushes away from the car and strides in our direction with one hand up.

I'm about to question if she's planning to cast a spell when I realize she's feeling for the location of the barrier so she doesn't get too close. It's invisible, of course, and anyone I allow can pass through with no knowledge of its existence. If a car of tourists were to drive by right now, they'd probably assume Azalea had gotten pulled over by the cops and not give it a second thought.

However, we all know the difference.

"Hey there, princess," she drawls, stopping just a few feet away.

Even though I bristle at the stupid nickname, I know better than to react. "What a delightful surprise, Azalea," I reply in a heavily sarcastic tone. "To what do we owe the pleasure?"

"Well, Grannie and I had a long talk last night, and she thought I had been rude. I mean, I didn't think I was rude, did you? But Grannie's pretty tough, so she insisted we make the trip out here at the crack of dawn."

"That's pretty nice of you, considering how long of a drive it is to come all this way to apologize." Something tells me there's a lot more to this story, but it's good to know Shuya can control Azalea when she wants to.

"It's not just an apology, princess. I brought you a gift, too. I hear that's all the rage in the wealthy elite circles."

"I think I'll pass on any gift you want to give me, thanks. Something tells me it's not a gift I want."

Azalea doesn't seem to take offense. In fact, her reply is suspiciously nonchalant. "Oh, really? Because I was under the impression this is what you came to Grannie's house yesterday for. But if you don't want our help to save Leaf, then I guess we'll be on our way. It's no skin off my back."

"Wait." My body stiffens and I clench my teeth, steeling myself against the instinct telling me to let her keep walking. "How can you help free Derrek?"

"I happen to know a *lot* of helpful details, princess. I even saw him last night. Didn't look too good, I'm afraid. They worked him over rather hard."

A lump forms in my throat, and I struggle to keep it together. "Okay, you got my attention. What else can you tell me?"

Abruptly her innocently helpful demeanor changes. "You know, I'm not feeling very welcome. It's freezing out here, isn't it? I made Grannie stay in the car to keep warm. Poor dear, she's just not as tough as she used to be. We can't exactly force an old woman to stand outside in the cold for hours. Maybe you have somewhere we can go for a little chat, preferably indoors?" Azalea smiles widely, and it'd almost look friendly if I didn't know better.

She waits, inspecting her nails, while I turn to consult with my mates, then confer with the security team. Finally, I re-approach the barrier. "I'll allow you —*temporarily*—onto pack land, with a few conditions.

"One, you and Shuya ride with us but in separate cars. Two, you leave the keys to your car with me, so one of my mates can drive it somewhere for safekeeping. You'll get it back when you're ready to leave, assuming you don't pull any tricks. Three, you sign a magically binding agreement that prevents you from using magic against any member of Smoky Falls, and specifies that you'll leave this land and not return without my specific invitation before sunset tonight. Upon pain of death."

If I'd expected that she'd balk at the extreme elements of my proposal, I would have been very disappointed.

But I know better. Azalea wants something from us, badly, and in order to get it, she's decided to play ball.

Once the contract is drawn up and signed, and Shuya confirms that it's magically binding, I issue the carefully worded decree allowing them to pass through the barrier.

"Here you go, princess," Azalea tosses me the keys. "Don't get too attached. Oh, and if you don't mind, fill her up before you return her? Premium, if you please."

Jared takes the keys and Landon follows the retro sports car in his Jeep, promising they'll meet us in about half an hour.

Once the security team has Azalea tucked in the back of one vehicle, I escort Shuya to the second one and help her inside.

"It's good to see you again, Lilliana." She pats my hand and smiles.

"It's nice to see you again too, Shuya. We'll go have some coffee and something to eat, unless you'd prefer tea?"

"Tea would be lovely, dear. Dandelion, if you have it." She settles in her seat and tugs on the seatbelt.

"I'll see what I can do," I promise, then close the door.

Once Milo and I climb into the third vehicle, we make our way back to the safety office, where a room has already been prepared for us.

It's a bland, corporate-feeling space, but it holds a reasonably sized conference table and comfortable chairs. Minutes after we sit, a delivery arrives from the Painted Moose. I offer Shuya and Azalea a variety of breakfast sandwiches and treats, and once they've made their selection, I encourage the security team to help themselves. Milo snatches a few things quickly, pulling them close to his chest.

When I fix him with a raised eyebrow stare, he replies, "For Jared and Landon!" I'm not convinced the entire pile is for them, but I'm glad he's thinking of my other two mates.

The Painted Moose didn't have dandelion tea, but Shuya seems happy enough with chamomile. The security team pours steaming cups of black coffee from the paper carafe box, and once everyone's received their food and drink—including Milo with his flat white and my mocha—it's time to get down to business.

"Alright Azalea, you claim to want to help Derrek, so let's hear it."

"Listen princess, I haven't even had my coffee yet. Why don't you-"

My patience thins. "I'm not here to entertain you,

witch, and I certainly don't intend to hang around all day. You may call me alpha, Lilliana, or Lily. If you can't stick to one of those three, I'll have the security team take you back to the barrier right now."

She smirks to herself, pleased to have gotten under my skin. "Sheesh, I didn't mean anything by it. Sorry to have offended Lily. My sincerest apologies."

"Let's cut the bullshit already," Milo interjects cooly. "No one here is under the delusion that we're all friends. You're clearly here because you want something, and you've offered us something we want to get it. So let's lay it all on the table, shall we?"

Shuya continues sipping her tea, her eyes darting between her granddaughter and me and Milo.

There's a very pregnant pause, and then Azalea affects a half-hearted sob. She lifts her gaze to mine, tears welling in her eyes and a sorrowful expression on her face. "I'm sorry, alright? Sometimes I get so turned around I can't tell the enemy from a friend. I didn't exactly have a great upbringing, and I don't trust anyone.

"But Grannie likes you, and she wants to help you. And I feel terrible for helping them take Derrek. Believe me, I didn't know what I was doing. And I didn't have a choice. I'd already signed the contract with them, and I have to honor it. But I thought Nielsen just wanted to recover his missing son and make him his heir. How would I know they were going to lock him in the dungeon and torture him like that? I had to fight my way into that house yesterday because Nielsen didn't want me to see what he was doing. And then he threatened me!"

I am one-hundred percent convinced that this is all an act. "If you 'didn't know what you were doing', it's interesting that you've helped so much. I've heard some interesting things about what's happened to Derrek since he left here."

Her expression goes neutral in a nanosecond. "What have you heard?"

I fix her with an indulgent grin. "Why don't you just admit to what you've done, and assume I know everything."

Sipping my coffee, I wait patiently for her to decide what to say. I can practically see the gears turning in her head, wondering how much I could know.

Abruptly she sighs, dropping her head with apparent shame. "I made him a collar that basically prevents him from using magic against Nielsen or any of his cronies. I admit it! And I'm not proud of it, but like I said, I had no choice. As the pack witch, I'm bound to follow orders and protect Nielsen. I can't even turn my magic against him. So I had to."

"You may have been told to stop him from using magic, but somehow I don't believe you really had to be so sadistic about it," I reply in disgust. Turning my gaze to Shuya, I continue, "Do you know what she did? What she *really* did? Anytime Derrek so much as tries to clear his throat, that collar magically shocks him. He's locked up in some dungeon torture chamber with a shock collar around his throat, thanks to her."

Shuya's eyes narrow, and she turns angrily to Azalea. "You did not tell me some things, it seems. Why would you do that to Leaf? He's always been a good cousin to you!"

Azalea's voice is even more remorseful now. "I know, Grannie, I'm sorry. It seemed like the simplest solution to give Nielsen what he wanted. I wasn't trying to be sadistic."

"Save your apologies for your cousin. We're here so you can make amends and help them rescue Leaf from that horrid man. So tell them what you know."

Chapter Twenty-Three

LILLIANA

~

By the time Azalea gets through all the details—interspersed heavily with expletives and a good dose of overacted remorse, I assume for Shuya—I'm tempted to go along with it. Jared and Landon arrived during her performance and inhaled the food Milo saved for them, listening with rapt attention.

The drama might be a little—or a lot—overdone, but it's easy to see that Azalea genuinely despises the Montrose Pack, especially the alpha.. She lingers quite a while on the details of how he disrespected her and controlled her. Something tells me not to rely too heavily on the embellishment, but the key factors are the same. Derrek is being tortured in order to force him

to shift, and it gets worse every day until they break through.

Azalea mentioned people die during this process, apparently frequently. The magic of their pack lands is fading, and more children are being born without the ability to shift. People have been quietly disappearing for years in fear their child will die at the hands of their own alpha.

And Derrek, being half witch and half wolf, doesn't have nearly as good of odds as those people who are full-blooded wolf.

I catch the eyes of my mates, each one in turn, and get their silent agreement before speaking.

"Thank you for sharing all of this information, Azalea. It is helpful."

She nods magnanimously, like a queen accepting the gratitude of a peasant.

"But I'm still waiting to hear how you plan to help us get Derrek out, and why you're doing this in the first place."

Azalea actually looks affronted. "Didn't you hear me? Nielsen is a rabid beast. He's torturing Derrek and I don't know how many people in that house, trying to force them to shift. It's disgusting, and he needs to be stopped."

"So you'll help us get Derrek out, but that doesn't really stop him."

"Well…" she toys with the top of her paper cup. "It's more about getting revenge on Nielsen, okay? He tricked me into signing that contract, knowing he

could control me. I'm new to having these powers. I didn't think to suspect him of abusing the agreement. From everything Grannie has told me, there's always been a code between a witch and her pack, sort of a 'live and let live' kind of thing. I didn't know what he was like."

Azalea heaves a sigh. "And… I wanted the prestige of being a pack witch after being nothing for so long. I craved that recognition. I'm not ashamed to admit it. Even to the degree that I attacked you in L.A. Which, again, I'm really sorry for."

The sudden switch of topic surprises me, but she actually seems sincere.

"I didn't know you. I just knew that he wanted me to prove myself and earn my place. And I know that's not an excuse, and I'm not proud of it. I was so desperate to belong I would have done anything. I know now it was super shitty and I hope with helping here, you might see that I mean it.

"But anyway, he's been a complete dick, and I'm tired of it. I can't use my powers against him, full stop. But I can help *others* who aren't fans of his, and that way I get my revenge without breaking my contract."

That sounds like the closest to the truth we've gotten yet.

"So you want to help us because we can get you revenge on Nielsen, that you can't take yourself?"

Azalea smiles happily. "Exactly! I help you, you help me, it's a win-win."

"That gets Derrek out, but doesn't really resolve the

issue of Nielsen abusing his pack," Milo interjects. "What's your plan there?"

She shrugs. "Honestly, that's not really my concern. If you guys want to do something about it, that's up to you."

That sounds like the Azalea I've come to know.

"But Leaf is his only heir. Nielsen is literally the end of his family bloodline, and without him, the pack will have to reform, fight for a new alpha. If Leaf were to step in, he could take over easily. But *only* if he shifts. Either way, I don't see Nielsen being around much longer."

Jared voices the same question on my mind. "Why do you say that?"

"I dunno if you've noticed, but Nielsen's kind of an old dog. The second he shows any sign of weakness, the pack will turn on him. Given how he's treated them, very few members of the pack truly respect him. They obey because he's the alpha, but when the odds look good that someone can take him down, the challenges will start. It may be five years, or ten years, but trust me, everyone is watching for it."

The potential for Montrose to have a new alpha soon is intriguing, but I have no way of knowing if I'd be able to claim them and reunite the packs at that point. The lunar eclipse is only a few weeks away and I have no idea when the next one will be. And what if the wolf who defeats Nielsen already has a mate?

A wave of sadness washes over me at the realization I may have to give up my dream of reuniting the packs.

There's just too many barriers in the way, and the most important thing right now is saving my fourth mate.

"Well, hopefully when Montrose gets a new alpha, they'll work with us, maybe forge some kind of friendship so we can stop being at each other's throats."

"You haven't heard the best part yet," Azalea leans in, fixing me with that knowing grin. "The pack will only fight over the position of alpha if Leaf doesn't claim it. But *if* he shifts, and *if* he takes Nielsen out, you'll get everything you're after."

"I'm sorry, I'm not following."

"Look, I'm no dummy. You're not this intent on rescuing Derrek because you're just good buddies from way back. If he's not actually one of your fated, I can only assume you want him to be. And as the alpha, you *can* claim more mates than your fated ones.

"Leaf can take Nielsen out and claim his place as the alpha of Pack Montrose. That'll free me from my obligation to the pack, and I'm off the hook. You can claim his as your mate, and that will unite the packs."

Heat rises to my cheeks when I realize that she's figured out so much. "I don't know what you think you know about me, but you're better off not making assumptions. We already know that claiming the alpha of Montrose is the only way to unify the packs. But your plan also hinges on Derrek shifting, which you've already said isn't looking likely."

"Perhaps he just needs proper motivation. *If* he's actually one of your fated mates, and *if* shifts, and *if* you claim him, it not *only* unifies the packs. It breaks the curse that's held Smoky Falls for nearly a century."

My eyes immediately dart to Shuya for confirmation. "Is this true?"

The older woman nods. "It's true, child. And there's no point trying to hide it—I know you and my Leaf are fated. I felt it as soon as you walked through my door."

That takes me by surprise. "Why didn't you tell me?"

"Bah, in front of these boys? Fists would have flown the second I opened my mouth. Besides, you weren't ready for the truth, not yet. You two needed more time to simmer."

"Well, there you have it, Harridan." Azalea leans back in her chair with a self-satisfied smirk. "I help you get Leaf out, you get to figure out how to get him to shift, and then all our problems are solved in one fell swoop."

"I don't know how to provoke someone to shift. For us, it just takes the right circumstances, and it happens on its own."

"Then perhaps you need to create the right circumstances. If anyone can motivate him, it's you. Maybe you just need to shake your furry little tail at him." She waggles her eyebrows, and Jared releases a snort of disgust.

Once again, my eyes travel to each of my mates in turn, waiting for them to object or come out with another question. Instead, they each give me a slow nod, as if to say, *I trust you.*

The certainty that this is right, that we finally have all the pieces to the puzzle and are ready to move forward, fills my body with energy and buoys my confidence. Even if Derrek doesn't shift and we can't break the curse, there's hope that the next generation could do it.

"Alright," I return my attention to Azalea and fix her with a determined stare. "Tell me how you plan to help us rescue Derrek."

Chapter Twenty-Four

DERREK

~

"I've got a little surprise for you today, son."

They allowed me more time this morning than usual, including time to digest my breakfast. I used it to sneak twenty minutes in the bathroom working on my own little surprise with no disruption, and it worked all the better because I had healed and rested.

But I knew it wouldn't last.

I stand, resigned, and start stripping off my clothes before being ordered to. Nielsen's quick to attach the leash if I don't hop to, and they don't seem to replace my clothes when they get damaged. They just launder and return what's left. With no idea how long I'll be stuck here, I don't want to end up left in bloodied rags.

"Oh, hold up son, you can leave your pants on for

now. I mean, if you want to," he adds with heavy innuendo lacing tone.

I finally look up, and realize he's right: it's definitely a surprise.

Standing beside a pleased-looking Nielsen is a beautiful woman, whose eyes rove over my body like a farmer taking stock of a bull she wants to buy.

I swiftly pull my shirt back on, hiding my naked skin from her hungry gaze.

When I catch Nielsen's eye, he reads the confused expression on my face and laughs. "Since the normal techniques don't seem to have any effect, I thought we'd see if the carrot works better than the whip. The next level of the program can get a little intense and I don't like to use it, if we can avoid it. She's unmated, and I thought she looked like your type. What do you think?"

With a shock, I realize what he's done. The woman is petite, curvy, with wavy dark hair and bright blue eyes. He literally went out and found me a discount Lilliana.

But the warning is clear: if this doesn't work, things are going to get much, much worse.

My stomach flips nervously. What exactly is he expecting to happen here?

"Hi Leaf," she approaches me like a lioness stalking prey, hips swinging and a seductive smile on her glossy red lips. "I know you can't speak, but that's okay. Your father told me all about you, and I see that you're everything he promised. He thought we should spend some time and get to know each other better. That perhaps I might draw out the beast inside you," she purrs the last bit, trailing her fingernails down my chest and across my stomach.

Raising my hands, I back up until my legs hit the bed and I have nowhere else to go. She's undeterred, pressing forward. "My name is Erica. I think we're going to have a *de*lightful time."

My gaze darts from the woman already toying with my pants to Nielsen, who's watching the exchange gleefully.

Sidestepping, I slip away from her and try to find some way to escape this new, horrid reality I find myself in.

An idea strikes me, and I turn to Nielsen hopefully, trying to look interested in this offering. I make the motion of writing with my hands, then gesture to Erica, my would-be mate.

Nielsen scrubs his beard thoughtfully. "I suppose that would be alright. I'm not much of a talker myself, more of a doer, so I wouldn't waste time if it were me. But I know you're into that romantic mumbo-jumbo. I don't think it'd hurt for you to ask her some questions. Billy!"

The younger man pokes his head through the door-way. "Yes, alpha?"

"Fetch Leaf here something to write on. He wants to have a conversation with his future mate."

"Yes, alpha."

Erica slides up next to me and ducks under my arm,

pressing herself to my side and wrapping an arm around my waist. "That's so sweet. He really wants to get to know me better. Thank you, alpha. I look forward to providing you with many grandchildren."

A nervous sweat breaks out on my upper lip, my heart pounding, but I force a pleased smile and rest my arm across her shoulders.

If there's anything I know, it's that my best hope right now of avoiding intimacy with this woman is by getting her talking. Maybe I can keep her engaged and avoid the implied expectation for a couple of days.

Billy returns with a legal pad and pen, and I take them eagerly.

"Well, I suppose I'll leave you to it," Nielsen chuckles, heading for the door.

"Oh, one last thing: Leaf, I expect you to be a gentleman. Don't embarrass me, and you'd better take care of the lady. And Erica, if he doesn't mind his manners, use this."

He pulls the leash from the 'tool box' and sets it in her hand. My heart leaps to my throat.

"If you have any trouble with him at all, just call Billy. He'll help you get it on him. The witch made it so the slightest tug and he has to obey. Leaf knows that very well, don't you, son?" His gaze returns to me with a knowing smile.

Her seductive grin turns wicked when the leather touches her palm. "Thank you, alpha, I absolutely will."

Swallowing down a thick lump in my throat, I

gesture to the bed and once she takes a seat, I plop on the floor and start writing like my life depends on it.

I have to admit, spending the entire day convincing a woman I'm deeply invested in getting to know her is far better than the previous forms of torture.

However, it's a great deal of work to keep her from being overly amorous. I'm not sure what's driving her; if it's hormones or a threat from Nielsen. Either way, I spend an enormous amount of energy doing mental tango to avoid the physical version of the dance. Fortunately, she doesn't seem inclined to use the leash or any of the other tools at her disposal.

Erica doesn't seem like a bad person. She's a small-town girl who loves living in Montrose and wants to raise a family here. From the sounds of it, they've been struggling to form true mated pairs in this pack for some time, and so she jumped at the chance to be mated to me… assuming I manifest as a wolf.

I'm sure my position as potential future alpha is also an important perk. She has a good deal to say about the alpha's house and how glamorous it would be to live in this hellhole.

Well, the house *above* this hellhole, specifically.

So she's a social climber who wants more, but seems like a decent person. I'm surprised to find out she sees nothing wrong with this reform camp punishment to force people to shift. Apparently, she didn't have to go through it, but her father and three brothers all did. Which means there's no way to appeal to her humanity about my current condition.

But every time we have a decent exchange—me scribbling questions or answers and her speaking—she tries to move in physically and force things along, and I end up scooting away and saying I just want to move slowly.

By the time she leaves, I'm completely drained, almost as bad as the beatings, but at least I'm not in physical pain. I wolf down my dinner and head to the bathroom, planning to spend a few hours in the bathroom working on nonverbal spells.

I don't know how long Nielsen is willing to spend on this gambit, but the sooner I can regain control of my powers, the sooner I can take control of my own fate.

Chapter Twenty-Five

LANDON

~

"Is this everybody?" As I look around the assembled group, it feels like it isn't enough. Not nearly enough.

"Yep!" Lily answers a little too brightly. "Azalea said to keep the team small so it's easier for her to cover us. Her magic can get us through the barrier and up to the house, but we have to do it quietly. The plan is to get into the house and sneak Derrek out, not do a full-on assault Braveheart style."

"And we're sure this is the best crew for this?" Besides myself and Lily, it's Jared, Milo, and two of the security team. We all agreed Derrek might trust no one but Lily, and if she goes, the three of us go. The other two are the real muscle; we're only going for her sake.

Dom and Roxanne are here, but only because Lily wants to keep them informed.

She slips her hand into mine and tugs, tilting her chin up toward me.

I duck instinctively, accepting the quick kiss, but it doesn't do much to reassure me.

"As long as I have you guys, I'll be fine. Azalea swears it's a skeleton crew at night, because that's when they leave the people in the 'program'," she shudders, "alone to *heal*. Nielsen always attends the high school sporting events to keep up the façade of being a good mayor, and they're having an away game, so he's gone for the night. It'll go smoothly, I promise. I feel great about this plan."

I have to ask. "And you feel great about trusting Azalea?"

Her smile falters. "I'm still not sure about her. I want to believe she feels bad and is trying to make amends. I'm relying on the fact that she promised her grannie more than anything. *Shuya* I feel good about, and it's obvious Azalea keeps her word to her grandma. If nothing else, I believe she wants revenge on Nielsen for disrespecting her, and I hope that's enough."

"Fair enough," I reply. I wish I was as confident, but I still have a bad feeling about the witch.

"It'll be fine," she squeezes my hand.

"You're right, it'll be fine," I reply with a smile, just to reassure her. I don't want her worried about me on top of everything else.

One of the security team steps forward. "Alright, we should get started, if that's okay with you, alpha?"

"Sure thing, Richardson." She beams at him and he grins widely in return. It's so easy to see what a great alpha she already is.

"Okay. The plan is for us to drive around to the eastern side and meet the Montrose witch here." He pokes a finger at a map where a red 'X' has been inked. "It's longer of a drive, but it's closer to the alpha house and less time we have to be in their actual territory. There's a state park that abuts the pack line, and we'll leave the cars there. Hopefully, they won't be patrolling that side as much, and it'll be easy to slip through.

"Once we're in, we'll follow this hiking trail that leads right up to the house."

A surge of pride rises in my chest and I catch Jared's eye, who's grinning as well. Our little trip was useful, after all.

"The witch claims that there's only two guards at the back door at night, so it should be easy to take him out. They do security checks every twenty minutes; we'll wait until they check in and then our timer starts. She'll use a spell to keep our movements silent. We'll unlock the door and then take out two more guards just down the hallway at a central station of some sort. The witch'll lead us to Derrek's room, which will have two more guards in front. Once we have him, we'll return the way we came, and hopefully we'll have time to get back to our cars before they even know we were there."

"Doesn't Derrek have some sort of collar on?" Jared asks. "What if that keeps him from leaving the property somehow? Or sets off an alarm?"

Lily steps forward. "Azalea assured me that all the collar does is keep him from speaking, so he can't cast spells. He's completely free to move aside from that. Since time is tight, she's going to remove it when we get back safely to Smoky Falls."

"Somehow, I don't feel very assured," Milo grumbles quietly.

"Me either," I agree.

"Questions?" Richardson looks around expectantly. "Hearing none, let's get started. If we leave now, we'll get there before midnight, and hopefully be in and out of Montrose by one."

We divide into two cars, and distribute two-way radios. In the event we can't get a cell signal, we'll have a way to communicate.

I wish I was driving my Jeep, but I know it's smarter to take the unremarkable Harridan House SUVs. It's already dark when we leave, and even though we've brought a stock of caffeinated beverages—energy drinks for most of us, but Milo insisted on his stupid coffee—no one cracks them open for our long drive. I guess everyone, like me, is too wired with nervous energy to need a boost.

Lily hooks her phone to console and puts some benign playlist on as soon as we climb in, filling the vehicle with music. It's a smart move—none of us feel much like talking, judging by what I see in the rearview. Milo and Jared are staring out the dark windows as we depart Smoky Falls, the same as Lily in the passenger seat.

Which leaves me with my own thoughts.

If I'm honest with myself, I don't like this at all. I'm still not a fan of having our Lit professor as a brother, let alone sharing Lily with the much older man. Jared and Milo aren't excited about it either, but we all know we don't have a choice. If he's really her fated mate, she doesn't have a choice, either.

So there's no point in acting butthurt about it, since there's nothing we can do. And all it does is hurt Lily.

But it *would* be amazing if he broke the curse. We grew up resigned to the idea that once the next Harridan heir officially mated with us, we would all be tethered to Smoky Falls forever.. Not that we aren't already, but at least we can leave for things like overnight games and family vacations. After the eclipse, we'll have the 24-hour clock just like Lily.

So if we can escape that fate, end the curse for ourselves and all the alphas from now on, it's definitely worth it.

And if the curse ends, that wouldn't just affect us. With a start, I realize we hadn't discussed an important factor of the curse: that the entire pack can only shift between midnight and one am. If Lily and Derrek break the curse, that goes away too, and everyone will shift whenever they want.

The concept is almost too large to wrap my head around. We could just slip into the woods on a sunny day and run free, maybe find a river to splash in. The *freedom* that would mean!

I glance at Lily, excited to discuss it with her, but her eyes are closed. I don't know if she's asleep or not, but I can't bring myself to disturb her.

I refocus on driving, but I'm suddenly much more enthusiastic about bringing Derrek into the family.

LILLIANA

"We're here." Landon's voice is low, probably because he didn't want to scare me. Even so, it makes me jump.

Staring out the windshield, all I can see are deep shadows broken up by trees with scraggly branches. The headlights point straight ahead, following the curve of the road as the tires crunch over gravel and eventually slow at a parking area where the second SUV waits.

I face Jared and Milo, who also appear as if they've just been startled awake, and I can't help but grin.

"Thanks for driving, Landon." I place my hand on his arm and he smiles warmly, his dimple appearing.

"Of course, Lily." Then louder for the other guys, "I obviously couldn't trust those two to stay awake for it. We'd have ended up in a ditch."

"Haha," Milo groans, stretching. "It made the most sense to rest up in the car. If I'd been driving, I wouldn't have had a problem staying awake."

"Me either," Jared agrees.

Taking in Landon's tired eyes, I ask, "Do you need a minute to rest?" My gaze darts to the console. "We got here a little earlier than we planned. You could easily sneak in a power nap."

"Nah, I'm fine," he assures me, popping the top of his energy drink. "Just give me two minutes to pound this down and I'll be ready."

I clamber out of the car while zipping up my coat and realize it's even colder than I thought. Frost has formed on the fallen leaves, and our breath comes in thick clouds of vapor. My nose is instantly cold.

"Alpha," Richardson steps out of his still-running vehicle. "I received a text from the witch. She's already in place. We can move whenever you're ready."

"Okay, thank you. Let's take a few minutes to stretch and shake off the road. I'll let you know when we're ready."

"Copy that." He climbs back into his car to wait.

The guys have stepped out and are stretching their long limbs. Landon's drink can rests in the cupholder, and if I had to guess, he's already finished it.

Nervous energy zips across my skin. I have to project confidence, no matter what. The first sign of doubt from me will make them worried, and I need everyone convinced we're heading safely back to Smoky Falls with one extra passenger.

Even if I'm not so sure.

"You guys want to do some calisthenics, maybe take a few laps?" I tease them brightly. We've all dressed in dark colors. The security guys have their uniform on, complete with combat boots but with no logo. Landon, Jared and I have on hiking boots and similar cold-weather coats akin to ski gear, and Milo—of course—sports expensive-looking leather boots and a heavy pea coat.

Jared shifts his weight from one foot to the other. "To be honest, gorgeous, I just want to get this show on the road. I won't feel better until we cross back into Smoky Falls."

"Same," the other two agree in unison.

"Alright then, I guess it's time to move. Richardson?" I signal the others, and they shut off their car and join us.

"You guys have your radios in case we get separated?"

Milo and Jared hold up the devices.

"Good. If we need to, Jared will go with Lily and Landon with Milo. We should always be in pairs, and always with someone who has a radio. And set your ringers on silent, understood?"

We all nod; no need to answer. Only old people use ringers; the rest of us keep it on vibrate all the time.

"Let's go."

With the cars off, there's very little light to see by. The sky is overcast, and we quickly come under cover of the trees, anyway. This area is remote, and the closest structure is the alpha house over two miles away.

Richardson leads us in a silent, single file line for a while. He's got some sort of coated, printed map he's following, and he checks it regularly with a tiny flashlight. It's nice to be surrounded front and back with pack members, but something about this place feels really exposed and almost threatening. As if I'd called him, Jared walks up beside me, and I slide my hand into his, grateful for the company.

We continue walking in silence. I'm just wondering how much further we have to go until the barrier when Richardson stops. "We're almost there; I'm going to signal the witch, but be ready to run."

We wait while he walks forward, and my heart pounds against my chest. A dozen ways this could go wrong fly through my head, and I clench Jared's hand tightly.

Richardson stops, then lifts his flashlight and flicks it on and off three times in rapid succession. He waits a moment, then repeats it.

My nerves are on edge, ready at a moment's notice to turn and flee. Then a condescending voice calls to us from the shadows.

"Oh, for goddess's sake, this isn't mission impossible! Get over here already."

~

I'm not surprised that Azalea's decked out head-to-toe in black. She even put on a black hat to cover her electric purple hair.

Passing through the barrier is surprisingly easy. Even though the guys got on the property several days ago, Azalea didn't know if Nielsen had specifically banned me. But her family's magic created the barrier, and she's officially a member of Pack Montrose, so she has all the authority she needs to pass us through safely.

It's probably just in my head, but it feels more dangerous on this side of the magical field. Azalea leads the way, muttering to herself about the cold, but the rest of us follow in silence.

I'm still not sure that trusting the witch was the best plan, but it's our only option. At the very least, I know I can trust her to abide by her own self interest, and she seemed sincere in her professed need for revenge against Nielsen. At a certain point you have to stop questioning everything to death and just decide, so I did.

For better or for worse.

It seems to take forever, not knowing exactly where we're going in the dark, creepy forest. On the plus side, we keep a pretty good pace, so I'm warm enough despite the frosty air. I've fallen into the rhythm of following the back ahead of me, Jared in step at my side, so when we stop it feels very abrupt.

We're at an intersection of trails, and we all gather to huddle together.

Azalea speaks in a low voice. "The house is about a hundred yards further up the trail, up on a hill. It's pretty easy to get up, and no one will see us from this direction. Once we're all there, I'll cast a pass-through spell to get us through the hedge. There's no camera on the side because it's basically right next to the house. From there, we'll go around back and then it's up to you guys to get us in."

Richardson nods. "The four of you hang back until we make sure the area is secure."

We nod in confirmation, knowing this was already the plan.

With nothing left to say, we follow Azalea to the hill she mentioned and climb. True to her word, there's a hedge just like Jared and Landon described. A few mystical hand gestures along with a whispered phrase, and a magical doorway appears in the hedge, allowing us through. When we hear the guard just around the corner radio in, we hold back and wait for Richardson and Levi to slip around the corner and take care of him.

Blood rushes through my body, heart pounding, and my ears strain to pick up any clue of what's going on. The guys and I are crouched and waiting, but Azalea leans lazily against the wall with her arms crossed, looking bored.

Suddenly the guys' radios spring to life, static interspersed with two clicks—Richardson's 'all clear' signal.

I draw in a deep breath of relief and follow the guys around the corner, where the two security guys stand over a pair of bodies on the ground. I hope they're not dead.

Richardson points above our heads and we note the camera angled out toward the dark lawn. Hugging the side of the building, we creep toward the back door and stop in a huddle.

Richardson nods at Azalea, who whispers a few phrases I don't understand and swoops both hands around in a large circle.

I don't feel anything, but she finishes and looks around expectantly. "For the next half hour, your movements won't make a sound. Let's go."

Richardson slides a key into the lock and turns it slowly, then eases the door open and peers inside before waving us in. Azalea and Milo follow him, then me, Jared, Landon, and Levi.

We creep down a partially-lit, innocuous hallway. It has a sort of sterile smell to it, like a hospital, along with the unmistakable scent of human misery.

My heart's racing and I feel like I might throw up, but we keep pressing forward. Azalea's spell is working. Our shoes don't make a single squeak on the polished floor, and we continue forward silently.

When we reach a cross hallway, Richardson throws up an open palm, stopping us, and then signals Levi to come forward. Once again, they slip around the corner and leave the rest of us waiting. This time, however, we can distinctly hear the muffled movements, a person trying to speak before getting cut off, and then two distinct thuds.

The radios click twice again, and we move forward again.

Just as Azalea described, we catch up to Richardson and Levi at some sort of desk that reminds me of a nurse's station. There're a couple of computers on it, and basic office supplies like pens and clipboards.

Richardson looks at Azalea expectantly, and she takes the lead, walking stealthily down the hallway.

We pass through a set of double doors and turn left, then right, then left again. Every dark doorway we pass my heart jumps, wondering if there's someone inside being tortured, someone who needs rescuing.

But I force myself to keep going; today is not about them. Today is about Derrek, but I'll come back for them. I'll come back for all of them.

Suddenly, the sounds of several people talking, along with heavy footfalls, echo down the hallway.

Richardson immediately turns and begins pushing us back around the last corner. He leaves Azalea stranded alone. Her eyes panicked as her head turns between the approaching threat and the rest of us. I gesture for her to follow before I'm muscled around the corner, but I realize the next second that it's too late.

"What are you doing here again, witch?" A nasally male voice snarls. "Alpha warned you to stop turning up like this. He's going to be pissed you don't seem to be able to listen."

"What do you care?" She shoots back with that condescending, disinterested tone. "I'm not hurting anything, and he can't banish me from the building.

Why don't you mind your own business? I have somewhere to be," she sniffs.

"Oh, no you don't," a deeper voice growls. "Alpha said that if we catch you here again, we're to give you the same treatment as the rest of our guests. He said," the unknown male chuckles, "he said that if you want to be here so badly, that can be arranged."

"Get your hands off me! Despite her attempt to sound indignant, fear laces her voice. "You have no right-"

"I have every right, witch, and you can't use your powers against me. Alpha told us that your contract forbids it. So cut the crap already. We have a nice comfy cell for you to sleep in until Alpha gets back tomorrow." Shuffling noises of an obvious struggle ensue, then a horrifying thwack echoes down the hall, and it falls silent.

"Good job. She's such a pain in the ass!"

"She'll be out for a couple of hours at least. Come on, let's toss her in a room and report her to the commander."

We wait as the footsteps fade away, and a distant door clicks open and shut. A hand on my shoulder almost makes me jump out of my skin, but it's just Landon, pointing at his watch.

Shit, we just lost half our time until the next check in. We have got to move.

Richardson makes eye contact with Landon, who shows him the timer.

The older man nods grimly, then peeks around the

corner. He gestures us forward, and we continue on our quest. When we reach the spot we'd left Azalea, a guilty lump forms in my throat; her thick black hat is on the floor, along with a few drops of blood. Several feet ahead more blood smears the white tile, leaving a bright red streak every few feet of the long hallway.

And now we're running out of time and don't know where to go from here. We pass a cross hallway that looks exactly the same as the one we left. It's like a maze in this place, probably intentionally. The house above didn't cover nearly this much ground, so they must have expanded this massive basement out like an ant's nest to keep it hidden from prying eyes.

Richardson chooses a direction and moves, the rest of us following on silent feet. We're following Azalea's blood trail, right up to another set of double doors, this time with a window.

And there, just a few more feet down the hallway, is a doorway with two bored-looking men standing outside. One of them is Billy.

Excitement and relief and fear swirl together in my gut; we still have to get Derrek out and somehow find Azalea, since she's the one who can remove the collar. And then we all have to make it out of this maze and back to the safety of our vehicles.

Richardson and Levi are both at the double doors, communicating with a series of hand gestures, probably discussing their plan.

Then something buzzes; it's just a vibration, but in

the absolute silence of the hallway it seems almost deafeningly loud.

I turn to look at the source, along with the rest of our party.

Landon's face is bright red, but he holds up his wrist, revealing that our time has run out.

Chapter Twenty-Six

JARED

When Landon's watch buzzes, I only have one thought:

We've got to get Lily out of here, now.

I gesture back the way we came, but she shakes her head stubbornly and points at the door, mouthing, "He's right there!"

And then the Montrose guards begin their check ins.

"Team one, all clear." The guys guarding Derrek report in a bored tone.

Their radio crackles as more teams start checking in.

"Team two, all clear."

"Team three, all clear."

"Team four, we found the witch sneaking around again. She's wrapped up nice and tight in suite seventeen. Otherwise all clear."

And on it goes. If every team is two people, there are far more guards here than Azalea led us to believe.

Richardson and Levi turn and gesture forcefully for us to go back the way we came.

Lily tries silently arguing, pointing toward the door again, but Richard drags a hand across his throat and starts moving, leaving Lily zero choice but to retreat.

"Team seven and team eleven, check in."

The knowledge that they know something is up gets us moving faster. I push Lily ahead of me and we practically run down the hallway, following Levi with Richardson in the rear. The security guy must have memorized every turn, because he doesn't hesitate as if he's following neon signs to the exit.

We turn another corner and pass the desk, and a surge of relief washes through my chest.

Which is quickly squashed when we pass a hallway with two bulky guards just steps away, spotting us immediately and racing down the hallway. "Red alert red alert, this is team three. We have six intruders heading toward the back door!"

"Keep going!" Richardson shouts, all hope of sneaking out forgotten. We race up the steps, flying through the door only to realize we can't get back through the hedge without Azalea.

"We have to go to the front of the house, it's the only way!" I shout, grabbing Lily's jacket and dragging her with me. We race along the house to the side we entered, speeding down the narrow strip of dirt between the wall and the hedge.

I know what they see when we follow the corner of the hedge: the long, straight path of the driveway, hedges on either side. Nowhere to split off. Our only option is to race straight ahead.

Shouts reach my ears from multiple directions, and the feeling of a wolf pack closing in on all sides tries to choke me with panic. I keep Lily ahead of me, directly behind Levi, and focus on protecting her at all costs. Feet thunder across the wooden deck, telling me more people are pouring out of the house in pursuit of us. I don't know how many it is, but I know we are in serious trouble.

It seems to take a lifetime, but we finally reach the end of the long row of hedges. I spare a glance back and realize we're farther ahead of our pursuers than I thought. When we turn left and start racing down the hill, Richardson shouts, "Split up! Use your GPS markers and stick to your specific path. Follow the plan!"

Lily and I hit the trail and immediately branch right, and she glances at me in shock, breathing too hard to speak. I've still got a grip on her sleeve; she didn't know about the emergency plan.

Thanks to a lifetime of sports conditioning, I'm probably doing better than most. "We had a backup plan to make sure you get out safe," I shout. "This way!"

I pull her down yet another path, racing the way Landon and I came on our visit.

Further into Montrose territory.

It made the most sense; they'd be expecting us to head for the closest path out of Montrose. Milo and Landon would lead pursuers that way, and Richardson and Levi would try to thin out them before heading in a different direction.

We run at top speed all the way to the trailhead and I pull Lily to the side, ducking behind a low stone wall to catch our breath and listen.

There're shouts in the distance, footsteps crashing through dead leaves and the occasional flicker of light between tree trunks, but it's all surprisingly far away.

Lily pants heavily beside me, and her breaths sound almost painful. I'm definitely going to get her on a training program after all this.

After a few minutes our labored breathing evens out, and the sounds of pursuit have grown noticeably more distant.

"I think we're clear," I whisper to her with a small smile, then pull out my radio and click the button once, then twice, then three times, letting Richardson know we made it.

A moment later, two clicks come through, another two, then three.

"Milo and Landon are good," I reassure her, and she's visibly relieved.

The radio comes to life again, three clicks, then two, then one.

"And Richardson and Levi are good. We all made it."

"Not exactly. We're still on Montrose territory."

"It's not a problem. Milo and Landon are going to come pick us up. They should be here in about ten minutes, if google is telling the truth. We just need to hold tight until then."

"Okay," she nods again, appearing more relaxed, but shivers rack her body.

"Come here." I settle back against the stone wall and put my arm around her, pulling her close. "Are you cold?"

"Not really. I'm actually sweaty. I think the adrenaline wore off."

"Yeah, that'll do it," I agree, rubbing my hand up and down her arm. "We'll get home and have a nice hot shower, followed by a decent night's rest. And we're sleeping in tomorrow, I mean it. Your body needs sleep."

"I know, I just... it's hard to relax, knowing what's going on."

"It'll be okay, I promise. We'll figure it out. I-"

Just a deep, snarling growl cuts me off, and I turn toward the sound in horror.

It seems we didn't lose the Montrose Pack, after all.

LILLIANA

The wolf snarling at us isn't the largest I've seen, although it's got a lustrous brown coat. It snaps its jaws and snarls, then starts pacing toward us.

Jared pulls me to my feet, and we back away from the wall and out toward the open area of the parking lot. We scan the surroundings but don't see or hear another wolf. Apparently this one is more clever than the others.

I know what Jared's thinking, and my mind's in the same place: We just have to keep him at bay until the guys arrive.

Talking is worth a shot. "Look, we don't want any trouble, and we didn't come here to start a fight."

The wolf continues growling angrily, lips curled and teeth exposed, tongue lashing. It's taking slow, patient steps forward, and we continue stepping backward in sync.

"We just came to rescue our friend. I know you know what goes on in there. It's sick, wouldn't you agree? What if it was your loved one being tortured, maybe killed, in the hopes they shift?"

No response from the wolf aside from more snarling.

"It doesn't have to be that way. Whoever you are, you're not stuck with this. You'd be welcome at Smoky Falls, or almost any other pack in the country, I'm sure. I know you're compelled to follow Nielsen because he's the alpha, but you always have a choice."

No response at all.

Jared and I glance at each other. Whoever this is, they must be a loyal follower.

I decide to try a fresh track. "We came to rescue Derrek, or I suppose you call him Leaf. He's very important to me. I'm sure you can understand being willing to do anything to save the people you love?"

That was apparently the exact wrong thing to say. The wolf abruptly charges, and Jared pushes me aside as it jumps.

Leaving Jared to take the full force of the attack. He cries out in pain, and before I even know what's happening, my entire body lights up with heat as if I'm a human volcano. It only takes me a second to realize I'm shifting, my wolf clawing her way free in defense of my mate.

When I've finished, I spot the foreign wolf standing on top of Jared, snarling down at his face and forcing him to lie still. My wolf unleashes a series of savage snarls, the alpha tone rumbling in my chest.

Now that I'm in wolf form, I know the other wolf is a female.

And when she turns to me, jumping lightly off Jared's chest to stalk my way, I realize this is what she wanted all along.

Well, if she's after a fight, she's might just get it.

We circle each other, and I slowly make my way toward Jared until I'm between the two of them. A steady stream of snarls flows from both my wolf and hers.

I have no interest in attacking; I don't want this fight.

So if she really wants it, she'll have to attack me first.

"Five minutes, Lily," Jared murmurs behind me.

Okay, I just need to hold her off for another five minutes. We continue circling, but I refuse to let her get closer to Jared than I am at any point.

When she charges the first time, I sidestep the attack deftly, sending her skidding across the dirt surface with her nails. She immediately turns and charges again, and I perform the same maneuver, just clearing her path.

Then she changes tactics, charging toward Jared.

Which leaves me no choice but to jump between them and stop her from hurting him.

I spring forward, my jaws closing on her neck with an angry snarl.

My bite isn't strong enough, and she twists out of my teeth then immediately attack again.

I meet each of her attacks and keep her from seriously hurting me, but only just barely. My alpha command doesn't work on her. Despite my desperate attempts to use it, she's not my pack and I have no power.

And the panic begins to rise.

The only reason I beat Amber was finding my alpha voice and commanding her to stop. It didn't occur to me to continue training to improve my skills as a wolf. Why would I? They already accepted me as alpha. But now I realize how sadly outmatched I am in a fair fight.

And she realizes it, too.

She's faster, smarter, and stronger in every way. It was one thing to fight a male, but clearly their pack is like ours in that the females are the better fighters. They don't realize it, or maybe they don't care, because they insist on keeping males in the positions of power.

A female like this could lead their entire pack if she was just given a chance.

As soon as I thought it, I banished the idea to the back of my brain. If she were alpha, I wouldn't be able to unite the packs. For better or for worse, Pack Montrose's misogyny is actually helping me.

I'm getting tired. My wolf is getting tired. I can feel it in the slower response of my muscles to the onslaught of attacks. But my opponent doesn't seem to slow down, and I'm in actual danger of losing this fight.

Just as I think it, I move a millisecond too slowly and she sinks her teeth into my neck.

It's not a killing bite, and I'm able to slip out of it, but she's drawn blood, and I can tell she's pleased with herself. It encourages her, and she comes at me with renewed ferocity.

"Lily!" Jared shouts, and I duck under the flying wolf and steal a glance toward the road, hoping against hope that my mates have arrived and that's what he wanted me to know.

Sure enough, a pair of headlights comes barreling through the trees, and the black SUV screeches to a stop in the tiny parking area, spraying dust and gravel. I jump aside, toward Jared, and the vehicle stops between me and the other wolf.

Landon throws open his door, shouting, "Get in!" and I leap onto his lap without a second thought. I hop lightly to the passenger seat and stare out the window and the Montrose wolf, who's on her way around the back of the car.

Milo's already leapt out and helped Jared up, and as soon as they pile in the backseat he yells, "Go!"

The SUV tears out of the parking area like a bat out of hell, and we leave the wolf in our dust almost immediately.

It only takes us a handful of minutes to pass through the sleeping town, and at the border I'm forced, painfully, back to human form. Landon stares at me in horror, likely from the sounds I'm making, and Milo passes me his pea coat for cover. I huddle under it in a cold sweat, completely drained.

We hit the freeway and we don't stop until we reach the agreed-upon rally point, a 24-hour truck stop thirty miles down the road.

Jared insists he's okay, that she just knocked the wind out of him and drew a little blood. Richardson checks us all over, agrees that Jared is fine, and offers me a spare uniform he brought for some unknown reason. I pull on the black cargo pants and rough long-sleeved shirt and it's not great, but it's better than nothing.

After that, there's nothing left to do but drive home, disappointed at our spectacular failure.

We didn't rescue Derrek. We were so close, but we took too long and barely made it out alive.

And to top it off, we lost Azalea. However Nielsen punishes her, it's clear she won't be able to help us again.

So we're back to square one.

Chapter Twenty-Seven

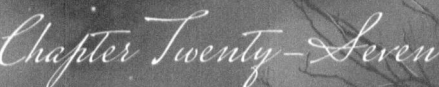

DERREK

That was a long night.

It was difficult to dredge my childhood memories for the right words to perform spells—most of what my mom did was potions, so that's what my brain knows best. Since I have no access to potion ingredients, I have to summon basic spells from the deep recesses of my mind.

And with a good deal of work and a fair amount of luck, I started a fire in my bathtub.

I put it out immediately, but the success was thrilling.

Fire won't get me out of this collar, which is the biggest problem, but it could help.

After a few hours' of rest and finishing my breakfast, I sit on my bed trying to brainstorm other spells I can work on.

The door opens and Erica strides in.

I draw in a deep breath and smile widely...showtime.

But when I wave at her in greeting, I know immediately something's off; she looks furious.

I grab my notepad and try to write out the question, but it's swiftly ripped out of my grasp.

Surprisingly powerful hands grab my shoulders and shove, sending me sprawling back onto the bed. Erica wastes no time mounting me and forcing her tongue down my throat.

I'm so shocked and confused I make the mistake of vocalising my surprise, which immediately sets off the collar and my body gets wracked by convulsions as the shockwaves go through me.

Erica sits back, still settled firmly on my hips, and waits out my magically applied punishment. By the time I'm able to breathe again and glance up at her, her expression has settled into a state of disappointment.

"Alpha's right, you just don't learn. Why don't you just accept that you're mine now?"

I shake my head at her and try to reach for the notepad.

"Look, this isn't about us being friends, or even lovers. This is about us becoming *mates*. Alpha wants it, so it's going to happen. The more you fight it the more you're going to suffer."

She switches tactics and smiles at me seductively,

sliding her hand up my chest and leaning over me again. "You might as well just relax and enjoy it." I turn my face away from her, but she's not deterred, kissing along my jawline while her hand slips under my shirt.

Everything about this feels dirty. My skin crawls where she touches me, and my heart is racing in my chest. Not out of excitement, but out of fear.

I've always done my absolute best to avoid laying hands on a woman, but now I have to draw the line.

Reaching up, I grab both of her upper arms firmly and shift her bodily to the side so I can slide off the bed. She stays there, smiling at me lazily like this is some racy game and I'm playing hard to get. I snatch up my pad and write out a quick note.

I know what he wants, but can't we just take our time? I don't see what a few days will hurt if we're going to be mates. I still have so much to learn about you!

I turn the page to her desperately, and she reads it, then laughs. "Listen Leaf, I don't know what you think is going on, but this isn't a love story and I'm no clueless farm girl. I know about you and the Harridan girl. Alpha told me he picked me because I look so much like her. He thought it might help. And I'm not in this for romance, so you shouldn't be hoping for that either, if that's even why you're doing it. I suspect you're just trying to drag it out as far as you can. Which, I'll admit, if it were me in your shoes, I might do the same.

"But the point is, you don't have much time to play with. Alpha wants results, and this is just another tactic.

If it doesn't work, he'll move on to something else, something much worse."

I can take whatever torture he has in mind.

When she reads it her eyes brighten, and a sadistic expression crosses her face. "Oh, you think so, do you? I'm not so convinced. But that's not really the point right now. I don't intend for this tactic to fail."

I don't care what you're planning, it won't work.

"So confident. It must be nice to have that conviction. But I wouldn't be so quick to make any assumptions. Alpha gave me free rein to do whatever I want in here. Are you sure there's *nothing* that would work?"

I can't help it; my eyes dart to the 'tool box' where the leash hangs.

Erica doesn't miss a thing. "Not such a big fan of all the tools, huh? Or perhaps it's that magical leash? Don't like the idea of being tied up?"

All I do is swallow; it's enough.

"Hm." She taps her lips with a glossy red nail. "You know, I've never tried S&M, but I have wondered what it'd be like. I'm no expert at knots, but I'm sure I could get your guards to help me out. What do you think would be more fun: If you act like a gentleman and treat me nicely? Or if you force me to tie you up and take what I want, anyway?"

My heart races faster; this threat is so different, so much more sinister than cattle prods and clubs. Would he really do that? Would *she* really do that? It only takes one long stare at her expression to realize, yeah, she definitely would.

My stomach twists, my undigested breakfast sloshing inside. After I determined she was a decent human, it's jarring to realize there's nothing some people won't do. It could be alpha compulsion, but I know what that feels like and she doesn't appear to be fighting it.

There's no way I can be a willing participant in this, even if it was tempting. It's too violating; I can't.

Sighing, I write out my response and hand her the pad.

I'm sorry, I can't give you what you want. Do what you must.

Chapter Twenty-Eight

MILO

It's a long, silent ride, but we eventually make it home.

We're all too exhausted for a debrief, so once Jared's given a clean bill of health by Mrs. Dowling, we trudge upstairs and pass out in a pile on the bed.

When I wake up late in the morning, I realize that I'm the only one left. Which is shocking in its own right, since we can usually count on Jared to be that guy.

Ignoring my rumbling stomach, I opt for a shower first.

Albeit, a quick one.

I make my way downstairs only to find everyone else deep in conversation at the breakfast table. Richardson and Levi are even there, along with Dom and Roxanne, Landon, Jared, and Lily.

"Thanks for letting me sleep in," I mutter, swinging by to drop a kiss on Lily's damp hair on my way to the coffee station.

"Don't worry, you haven't missed anything. We've just been filling Dom and Roxanne in on what happened," Landon explains. Jared's too busy shoving food into his mouth to say a word.

"You were out cold." Lily pats the empty seat next to her. "We actually tried to wake you. You must have needed the sleep." She doesn't look like she got much sleep herself.

"Oh," I reply, embarrassed. "Sorry."

"No worries." She takes a long sip of coffee, ignoring her full plate of breakfast.

I prepare my coffee and take that first glorious sip before I ask her, "So what's the plan now?"

"Dom heard from Billy this morning. He's going to call when he's sure it's safe; I guess he keeps a burner phone at a fishing cabin his dad left him, so he's going there to get it."

"If that's the case, how did he call Dom to tell him this?"

"Smoke signals," Jared jokes around a mouthful of bacon.

"Ha ha." I don't feel that joke merits more of a response.

Landon clarifies. "I guess they have some chat room that they both log into where you open a new room and then when you both leave it closes, like it was never there."

Sarcasm is my favorite form of communication. "I don't care what Azalea says, that sounds just like *Mission: Impossible.*"

Lily cracks a small smile. "I'm dying to find out what happened, but I'm also terrified to find out what happened, too. Does that make any sense at all?"

"It makes sense to me," I reassure her, pulling her hand up to my lips. "You really should eat, Lily. I know you're stressed, but you need energy to keep going, and coffee doesn't count."

"Says the coffee addict." She smiles again.

"Exactly. So you know if I'm saying it, it's serious."

"Fine, I'll eat if you do."

"You have a deal, my darling."

I happily fill a plate and tuck in, and Lily follows suit. The rest of the group alternate between eating and talking in low voices, and overall there's a general feeling of waiting. My eyes dart repeatedly to Dom's phone, laid out in the center of the table, screen black.

We're halfway through breakfast when it finally starts buzzing, some annoying ring tone practically echoing in the abruptly silent room.

Dom checks the number, then accepts the call and hits the speaker button. "Go ahead, you're on speaker."

Billy's voice is as cheerful as ever, despite the apparently paranoid measures he took to avoid getting caught. "Whoohee, you guys sure kicked up a hornet's nest! I must say, I'm a little hurt you didn't let me know you was comin'. I coulda helped ya'll out!"

"We didn't want to get you in trouble, Billy. I'm sure

you understand. We figured it was better to not involve you in case something went wrong. Turns out we were right."

"Yeah, sure were."

There's a long pause before Dom prompts him.

"So what happened?"

"Well, once they knew something was up, everyone came rushing and followed you out into the woods. Alpha was mighty pissed you got away with that many people out there."

"I bet."

"Yeah, the only person he had anything good to say about was Erica, since she got closer than anyone else. Even laid into *us* pretty bad, and our job was just to stand outside Leaf's door."

"Who's Erica?"

"Oh, she's the one alpha's got working with Leaf right now. He figures it's a better way to bring out his wolf than the next step of the program, which… well, it gets a lot worse."

Lily speaks up, her voice shaking slightly. "Billy, is this Erica the one who caught up to me and Jared last night?"

"Yeah, that was her. That's why he wasn't as pissed with her as everyone else. Still pissed at her, though. She hasn't done what he told her yet."

Lily holds my gaze for just a moment before she asks, "And what's that?"

"Well, she's got to get Leaf to mate her. She spent all day alone in the room with him yesterday and the job's not done."

"How long does she have to 'get the job done?'"

"Can't say. He's probably going to give it a few days at any rate. He likes Erica, would have claimed her for himself if she wasn't so much younger. She's really pretty. I can see why he had the inclination. I'm sure they don't expect to have much trouble with it. At this rate, he might just stick them both in the same room until something happens."

Lily's jaw flexes, and I can read her opinion on that information all over her face. "I see. What about Azalea?"

"The witch? What about her?"

"She was with us last night. They caught her."

"Oh yeah, I remember that now. I dunno."

"What do you mean, you don't know?"

"Aside from them reporting they put her in a room, no one brought her up again. So I don't know what happened after that." Everyone's gaze darts around the room with significance.

"Okay, thank you Billy. Is there anything else we should know?"

"Yeah, don't expect to pull another sneak attack like that again. Alpha means business; he's doubling the guards on duty and adding regular patrols in town and on the territory border. There's no way you're setting so much as a foot in Montrose territory without him knowing about it, guaranteed."

Chapter Twenty-Nine

DERREK

~

Apparently, I have more fortitude than I thought.

I let her have fun with the leash for a while, but Erica quickly grows annoyed when I remain unreactive.

I don't comply with her orders to strip, so she calls in the guards to hold me still and yanks off my shirt and pants herself. And despite a good deal of effort on her part to entice me with groping, stroking, and her own strip show, she fails to draw a reaction from me. I keep still with my head turned to the side, and refuse to let her tongue enter my mouth again.

When her frustration grows even larger, she follows through on her threat to tie me up and attempts some sort of sorry dominatrix routine.

That's never really been my kink, so naturally it was a dud.

At this point I can't tell if she's trying to get my body to react so she can have her way with me, or if she thinks this tactic will force me to shift. Either way, it's completely ineffective, and she's becoming desperate.

"Damn you!" The multi-strap whip she's been cracking against my back lashes me again. "You have to be my mate. You *have* to!"

I remain in my silent kneeling position, hands behind my back, head straight and eyes closed. Honestly, it's still better than the cattle prod.

She's panting hard, and her power is fading with each stroke. She's not cut out to be a dominatrix, clearly.

When she strikes me again, she lets out a sob, and judging from the thudding sound behind me, she collapsed on the floor.

I suck in a deep breath and remain still.

It's silent for a few moments, other than her panting, and I wonder what plan she's devising for me next.

"Why couldn't you just do it?" She whispers in an emotion-filled voice. "All you had to do was accept me and we'd both be out of here."

At that, my head whips to the side and I shift uncomfortably on my knees until I can see her.

She's laying on her back in her leggings and bra, sweat pooled on her chest and her cheeks red. When she sees my confused expression, she barks a laugh but doesn't move, gazing back at me with glassy eyes.

"Oh, you actually bought my little story, didn't you? That's kinda sweet, that you're so naïve."

I can't speak and I can't write, so I just gaze at her, waiting patiently for her to continue.

"I suppose it doesn't matter now. I've already failed. There's no point in hiding it." She sits up and scoots behind me, untying the knots that chafe my wrists and have been cutting off circulation to my hands for some time. She stands up and walks to the bathroom, filling my cup with water.

As the blood rushes back through my veins it's almost painful, and I flex my fingers repeatedly to speed up the process. My body sags to the right and I straighten my legs, relieving the pressure on my aching knees.

When she returns and holds the cup out to me, her eyes glimmer with tears. "Go ahead, I promise there's no trick."

I accept the cup, and she settles beside me.

"The truth is, I've been here for over two years, in a room exactly like this one. I lied when I said I'd never experienced this torture. Granted, I don't have a magical collar to keep me quiet; I just learned that making noise causes punishment, and that I definitely wanted to avoid punishment.

"When I finally shifted, I cried in relief—that meant I could go home! I was telling the truth about my brothers, by the way. They all came here, went through this, and once they shifted alpha released them.

"But he wouldn't let me go. I got some more privileges, and no more abuse, but I wasn't free to leave. Apparently, there's a lack of eligible females in the pack that can shift. A frightening lack, in fact. And alpha decided way back that he was going to make sure all the wolves in his control mated other wolves, so I couldn't go out and fall in love with someone else. He's kept me here waiting until he was ready to assign me a mate. I mean, I do still get out occasionally. Last night was fun, at any rate."

I snatch my pen and pad and ask the question.

"Oh, you don't know? I assumed you'd heard something. Everyone was going crazy out there. Some of those Smoky Falls people snuck in, probably trying to get to you. Obviously, they didn't succeed."

That must have happened while I was holed up in my bathroom.

My heart leaps to my throat and stays there. I scribble out another note.

"No, they all got away. You know, she seems nice, the Harridan girl. Nicer than our alpha, at any rate. I can see why you like her."

I breathe a sigh of relief, scribbling, and she glances at my latest note. "No, we didn't exactly meet, per se. I tracked her down, and we tussled a bit, as wolves. She tried to talk to me first, that's all. But they came and got her and that was it. There was no way I could keep up with a car, you know?

"But anyway, I'm a prisoner here, just like you, and this was both of our tickets out. Since I've failed, I don't know how he'll punish me. Nothing I can't take I suppose.

"But you... I'm sorry to say your punishment is gonna be worse. I wasn't lying about that, either."

I raise an eyebrow at her, and she gets the hint. "It's not more of the same, I'm afraid. If he can't get you to shift and claim a mate, he plans to kill you. He can't have a son that can't shift, and he won't let anyone leave this dungeon without a mate. Period.

"But before he does that, he's going to kill the Harridan girl, just to see if that triggers it. He figures if that's not enough to send you over the edge, nothing else will."

Chapter Thirty

LILLIANA

~

It's hopeless.

I hug my knees to my chest, squeezing tighter, and stare blankly at the crackling fire.

We tried every trick up *our sleeves* to get Derrek. We had it all planned out, and then it just... failed. Spectacularly.

Now there's no way we'll sneak in again. Even Billy said it. We gave away all our tricks in that one shot. Billy's still in place, but that doesn't help much; he's not the 'start a revolution' type. And if Nielsen can't make Derrek his heir, he plans to kill him.

A tiny voice whispers at the back of my mind, and I don't want to hear it. It's the weakest part of me, the one that likes to dwell on hurts and slights, the one that sometimes has truths to tell that I don't want to believe.

It says I can relate to my mom now more than ever. It's a horrid thought; ever since I found out what she did, understood the destruction she left in her wake and the devastation to her fated mates, how it destroyed them... I *swore* not to be like her.

Granted, she knew what was happening ahead of time and I never stood a chance, but still—she chose to leave. And that little voice reminds me I *enjoyed* hating her for it. I enjoyed resenting that she kept all of this hidden from me, deprived me of my inheritance, the life I ought to have had here in Harridan House. It was deeply satisfying to blame her for being selfish and shirking her responsibilities, and sticking all of us in a never-ending battle to survive.

But now, sitting here with three of my fated mates nearby and the genuine possibility that my fourth is lost to me forever...

I really relate to her more than I ever imagined I could.

This pain, this horrendous, festering ache that never goes away or dulls, but keeps growing and pressuring me to fix what's broken—

I don't know how she lived with it.

And she only stayed with *one* of her mates; so two of the three were lost to her forever.

And—oh my *god*, she never even got to claim the one she kept!

How could she? She left before she manifested.

My heart lurches—knowing what I know now, how much my wolf is a part of me I never knew was missing, and my mates the same—I can't imagine how she got through each day without it. But she did; she had me, she worked, together with my dad she kept a roof over my head; and I grew up safe, mostly. We weren't remotely wealthy, but I always had what I needed. I was happy.

But I realize now that even though she acted happy, she must have been miserable.

And that I can understand, too.

Tucking my face down behind my knees, I try to block out the world. Connecting with the guys helped suppress the pain, but it's like a bandaid on a missing limb. It stops the blood flow for a time, but there's too much bleeding to staunch. It oozes out and runs out the side, spreading the stain wider and wider. And you get used to the bleeding, but the fact remains that your limb is still gone.

The rescue attempt pulled that wound wide open again—I was expecting to get my limb back. What would a little more blood hurt? Only I didn't get Derrek, and I returned even more wounded than when I left.

And now I just don't see how that's going to change.

Sitting in my self-made darkness, I listen to the fire crackle and pop. It's comforting, and it's a relief to be alone and just... *not okay* for once. I love the guys, but their first instinct is to fix—patch up the wound, make me laugh, find a solution.

Sometimes I just need to *feel,* without pressure to get better. I asked them to leave me alone unless it's an emergency and claimed the library for my sanctuary. And they've done what I asked. There hasn't been a single sign of a person even passing in the hallway, let alone opening the door.

My mind drifts back to my mom, and I wonder if she ever did this. If that was the reason we had so many father-daughter outings. Because he knew she was broken in a way he couldn't fix.

In the way I'm broken, and it doesn't look like I'll be able to fix.

Because I'd rather Derrek end up with another mate than dead. No matter how much that idea hurts, imagining him dead is infinitely worse.

And I want to believe that it could get better. That somewhere within me, perhaps within my wolf, is the power to move on. The strength to overcome and be the leader my pack needs.

But right now I'm just an eighteen-year-old girl with far too much weight on her shoulders and a broken, bleeding heart.

The sky outside turned dark ages ago; the fire burned down to embers, and I haven't moved a muscle. Now that it's dark everywhere, I rest my chin on my knees and savor it. I've made no effort to stoke the fire or flip a light switch. The darkness is safe here, comforting, wrapping me in a cloak of blissful emptiness.

Suddenly, someone interrupts my solitude. The antique doorknob turns squeakily and a slender shaft of golden light shoots across the sitting area, landing on my fuzzy socks. The person hesitates in the doorway, and I have a feeling I know who it is.

"Landon, I'm sorry I'm still not ready. I won't stay here all night, I promise."

"It's not Landon, Lily." The deep voice of my uncle surprises me, but it makes sense; if anyone were to ignore my *one* request, it would be him.

Annoyance shoots through me, and I glare at the shadow in the sliver of doorway. "Do we have to do this right now? I don't have any fight left to give at the moment."

"I'm not here to give you a hard time. For better or for worse, you decided and went for it. As you should. As I would have done."

That pulls me up short. "I'm sorry. What did you say?"

"Can we talk, just for a few moments? I can leave the lights off, but I would like to throw some more wood on the fire, if that's okay. It's freezing in here."

Drawing in a deep breath, I release it noisily. "Fine, go ahead."

He presses the door open further, allowing in more light, and heads straight for the fireplace. It doesn't take him long to reanimate the blaze; flames lick hungrily up

333

the dry bark and spread quickly across the logs he adds.

Once there's enough light to see by, he closes the door and only hesitates another moment before sitting lightly on the couch beside me. My gaze remains on the fire.

And then he says nothing.

I didn't realize how cold I'd become until the heat from the fire washes over my face, and suddenly I'm racked with shivers. Dom stands and fetches a thick quilt, wrapping it around me wordlessly before reclaiming his seat.

When I finally stop shuddering, he draws in a deep breath.

"Lily, I know this is long overdue, but I came here to apologize to you. I'm sorry for several things, but most particularly for treating you like a child when you've shown everyone again and again what a fantastic adult you are."

My throat tightens, and tears collect in my eyes.

"You don't know a lot about me or your mom when she was here. I know that's mostly my fault; I should have been here telling you everything you could possibly want to know and more. But I'm here now, and I'm ready, if you're willing to listen?"

I turn my face slightly toward him and nod, then resume my previous position.

Now that he's gotten my approval to proceed, he hesitates as if unsure of what to say.

"Well… uh… I guess we should start at the beginning. Your mom was my big sister, and I worshipped her. I mean, I'm sure I was still a bratty little brother plenty of the time, but I always thought she was so smart, and so grown up, and so much cooler than I could ever be.

"And at first I thought it was unfair that she got to be the alpha and not me. What second son in history hasn't felt that kind of slight? But I soon realized that it meant I had a freedom she could never have. And since I didn't have a fated mate, I realized pretty quickly that my options were limitless. I could choose to travel, go to another pack, or even leave before I manifested and be a normal guy anywhere in the world that I felt like being. Bora Bora. Australia. Sweden. There were no expectations placed on me at all.

"And most importantly, I knew my sister was unhappy, and I gloated. Because we grew up and—I know it's stupid now, but remember I was a kid—I knew she was getting all the stuff I'd never have, you know? The house, all the fancy cars, getting to be in charge of everything. When you're a preteen boy, all that stuff sounds like everything you could want in the world.

"So even though everyone else was shocked when she ran away, I wasn't, not really. I always knew her in a way no one else did. I saw her change. Maybe she wasn't trying to fool me, but I caught the way she looked before she plastered on a smile for our parents.

"When everyone was going crazy because she left, trying to figure out where she might have gone, calling everyone, I didn't bother wondering. I just went back to my room and waited, because I already knew."

I sit up in surprise and stare at him. "What do you mean you knew? You knew where she went?"

He leans to his side and pulls out an envelope, crinkled in so many places it's practically soft. The faded script on the top reads: *Dominic*.

"Go ahead, you deserve to read it." He holds it out to me, and I realize I'm trembling. I dug through everything my parents left behind when they died and I never found a single note; not a will, not even a post-it. She left nothing for me.

Despite my shaking hand, I accept the envelope and slip out the folded pages. These too are so worn the edges feel like an old flannel shirt. My eyes dart to Dom and he nods solemnly, so I lift the papers to catch the firelight.

Dom,

I'm sorry to do this. I know the burden I'm leaving you with, and I wish there was another way.

It'll be hard, but I know our mom and dads will do their best to turn you into a great alpha. And I know you; I wouldn't leave if I didn't believe you'll be amazing.

But there's no other way. If we don't find a way to thwart the curse now, our family, our pack, will never escape it. I refuse to continue cursing my children's children with this terrible fate.

So Brandon and I are heading west - please don't follow us. And please don't tell our parents!

I know this is a big secret to keep, but I know you'll keep it for me because I'm going to make you a promise: I'm coming back.

Before you get too excited, it won't be for a <u>loooong</u> while. We've got big plans, and trust me, it's for the good of the pack. Know that always and forever, my heart is in Smoky Falls.

Elliot and Peter refused to come with us. I think they didn't really believe we'd do it. I hope they realize I'm doing this because I love them. Now that they're not going to be alphas, they can have almost normal lives… as normal as it can be in Smoky Falls, anyway.

Since I know this is a lot to take in, I'm going to tell you one part of our plan: We believe that if we have our daughter and she's raised outside of Smoky Falls, she can break the curse.

So, now you know; once we have her, and she's ready to manifest, we're coming home.

I hope the time goes faster than we expect. I hope everyone is happy and safe when we come back. We won't be wolves; I'm not sure if we'd be able to manifest so late, but you never know! Sometimes miracles can happen.

Anyway, I love you, little bro, always. You know I'd never leave you forever, but I'm asking for your patience. For me, and for the future generations of

Harridans that could live a life entirely free of this curse.

Always and forever,

Lilliana (aka the COOLEST big sister ever)

Tears are flooding down my cheeks by the time I finish reading. It's strange; it sort of sounded like my mom, but it also sort of sounded like me.

But more importantly, what she said! Her plan all along was to have me, and when I was seventeen, move back here. If they didn't have that accident when I was fourteen, we'd have all come back last year. And she believed I could break the curse... somehow she knew the connection to the Montrose pack was still there. She had to have.

My mind chugs to life, the gears turning. She realized that if I grew up here, in Smoky Falls with Milo, Jared, and Landon, I'd never consider the possibility of another mate. Why would I? I'd grow up hating the Montrose pack for the curse I was bound to inherit; I wouldn't even want to consider it.

Finally, I turn to meet Dom's gaze. "So that whole time you knew why she'd done it. And when I arrived, and you disappeared, you were trying to figure out the connection."

"Yes." He's obviously relieved to get this off his chest. "And your mom didn't exactly disappear entirely. I'd get mail from her occasionally, stuff like a blank postcard from Yosemite, but I knew it was from her. It was her way of letting me know she was still out there, and still thinking of home.

"Not long before we found you, I got a package. It had a note inside from a mail service in Boise. She'd left specific instructions that they were to mail that package on a certain date; she prepaid for the shipping and for the package to be held there. Inside were all of your birth documents. So we'd know you were coming, you see? The package arrived in July, two months before your birthday. I think she left it at that mail service because she didn't want to have all the real, legal documentation on her, just in case something happened, and she was just shipping it back to herself."

Dom smiles sadly, rubbing his hands together like he's searching for something to do. "And I was so excited, you have no idea. Your grandparents passed far too young; I think my mom just felt like she'd done something wrong, failed Lilliana somehow, and the guilt ate away at her. Once she was gone, my dads weren't long after.

"But she was finally coming home, and we would be a family again. I wouldn't be alone anymore, and I didn't dare to hope, but I thought it might be possible that she'd manifest and take over as alpha. I admit, I did my best, but I couldn't live up to her potential, or yours." Giving up, he leans back into the couch and crosses his arms. His entire mood shifts before he continues.

"And then your birthday came and went, and she

never showed. We waited—she'd never said she'd be back before your seventeenth birthday, but I just assumed. So I grew more and more concerned with each day that passed.

"Then I saw that news clip; they didn't use a photo of you in the hospital. They had your library card and said they knew it was a false name, but they were hoping someone would recognize you. I didn't have a doubt in my mind that you were my sister's daughter. I mean, it's not hard to see the family resemblance. You looked exactly how I remembered her." He trails off, apparently lost in thought a few moments.

Then, as if remembering where he is, Dom clears his throat and continues. "So, that's basically it. I went out to LA, confirmed it was you, showed them all your legal paperwork to prove I was your next of kin, and the rest you know. Once you manifested and the mantle of alpha transferred to you, I didn't even think; I went straight to Montrose to figure out how you were going to break the curse. Because I knew your mom didn't want you to live with it, and the only thing I could think to do to honor her wishes was to see if I could dig up how much they knew. I'd already exhausted every resource we had, but I wasn't buying that there was nowhere to get an answer."

My mind spins, trying to absorb everything he just told me. "So my mom must have figured out more than you did; she had to have known that I'd break the cure by mating the Montrose alpha. Otherwise, why would she insist on keeping me from growing up here?"

He nods in agreement. "Once we found all of it out, the pieces clicked together. I still can't work out how she knew, but I remember that she and Brandon used to disappear—a lot. Always said they were going hiking and planning to camp overnight, but I can't help but wonder if all that time they were going to Montrose. It's the only explanation that makes sense."

"That had to have been it," I agree in a disconnected voice; my brain rapidly spun elsewhere. It seems like the only people who know anything about the curse are the witches. Obviously, one of them helped her, but who?

"So…" Dom slaps his hands on his thighs and shifts awkwardly. "Anyway, that's what I wanted to tell you. I don't know why I didn't tell you before. I don't have a significant reason. Maybe it's because that secret's the last thing she gave me. And I couldn't bring myself to break the last promise I made to her." His voice trails off at the end, a catch alerting me to the genuine emotion behind his story.

"Here." I fold the letter gently and slip it back into the envelope to return this last gift from his sister.

"No, you keep it," he replies, shaking his head. "I know you don't have anything from her. I think, if she knew this was going to happen… she would want you to have it."

"I…" I try to protest again, but he jumps out of his seat like the couch had bitten him. "No, I want you to have it, Lily. I mean it. Anyway, I'd better get downstairs before Roxanne sends Mr. Carson after me. Would you like me to have him bring your dinner up? No one will mind if you sit this one out."

A powerful feeling grows in my toes, expanding through my legs and arms, filling me to the top of my skull. The scorching, blazing need to take action. "Wait."

I take a moment to stretch out my cramped limbs and stand. "We need to have a family meeting."

Chapter Thirty-One

LILLIANA

~

Once everyone gathers I lay out my plan, then wait for their reactions. The breakfast room falls into deathly silence, and everyone turns their faces toward me with open shock..

"I'm sorry." Milo shakes his head as if trying to clear it, then refocuses his stern blue gaze on me. "You want to *what* now?"

I had a feeling this would be a tough sell. Even though I know it's right, it's hard to explain the surety I feel in my bones.

"I want to drive right up to Montrose and challenge Nielsen." Eyes around the table glance sideways at each other.

"That's… what I thought I heard, but I'm still not following. Why? And how?"

I shrug. "I'm done working in the shadows and acting as if we're doing something wrong. That's not us, that's *them*. We're the stronger pack, and the only way to take back what's mine is to prove that I'm the stronger alpha. So, that's my plan."

Dom swallows with difficulty, looking as if he doesn't know how to say what's on his mind. "What if you're not able to get on their territory?"

"I don't think that's going to be a problem," I reply with confidence.

"Care to explain?"

"Well, first let me ask a question: Have any of you had difficulty passing their border, or heard of anyone that has?I glance around the room expectantly, but all I receive in return is confused silence. "Exactly. Because their magic isn't strong enough to keep anyone out."

"But if that's the case," Landon interrupts, "Why did Azalea have to let us through it?"

"I don't think she did. When she was here, she told us all about how their magic is fading and it's so bad more people are being born unable to manifest than those that can. I don't think she meant to reveal that much, but when I think about it—if there isn't even enough magic to keep full-blooded shifters shifting, how strong can their protections be? I think she had us meet her so she could keep up the façade of her own power. Not that she doesn't have power, but she's their pack witch, beholden by contract to protect them. If they found out that we just crossed the border with no problem at all, it would have been even worse for her. We still don't even know what they've done, or are doing to her, since she helped us."

It's quiet again while everyone mulls over that last bit.

"So..." Jared asks, "You're just going to march in and demand to throw down with their alpha, and you think no one will stop you?"

"No, in fact, I expect him to throw everything he has at me before we get to his place. I'm hoping that if I put out word requesting volunteers, we'll have a decent crowd to deflect any resistance we encounter. We just need help to clear a path to Nielsen, and then the rest is on me."

Dom clears his throat. "And let's say you defeat him; what happens then? If Derrek doesn't shift, he can't claim the position as alpha and you can't break the curse."

"*When* I defeat him, that will make me alpha of the Montrose pack. You see now? Derrek doesn't have to manifest and become the alpha for me to mate; if I claim the spot of alpha, that automatically unites the two packs, and that should end the curse. And whether or not he shifts, when I claim him under the lunar eclipse, he will become one of my mates. So either way, we reach the same result."

The deafening silence returns as Dom, Roxanne, and my three mates mull over what I said. My appetite has returned with a vengeance, so I take advantage of their stunned silence to focus on stuffing my face.

"Dom, she's right," Roxanne says slowly. "Assuming she's correct about their barrier, if she can get in and defeat Nielsen, that meets all the same requirements as if she went the other way around, plus it doesn't matter if Derrek is a wolf. So in fact, this is a more foolproof plan."

My uncle stares grimly at my beta for a long, protracted moment, then turns to me with a sigh. "So, when do you want to launch this attack?"

"Tomorrow night," I reply confidently. "Billy said Nielsen's almost had it with Derrek being unable to shift, and he won't let him live if he doesn't. We can't afford to wait any longer. My plan is for all of us to roll into Montrose about ten minutes to midnight. It's only a couple of minutes in a car to get through the town and turn on the drive to Nielsen's house; I suspect that's where we'll encounter our first resistance, and at that point, it'll be midnight and we can shift."

"That doesn't exactly give us much time to recruit volunteers. How were you planning on spreading the word?"

"Well, we're the midnight wolves of smoky falls, right? So I'm going to tell the pack at the run tonight, and let them know to spread the word."

LANDON

After how she reacted to the call from Billy, and then how she hid the rest of the day, I was honestly relieved to see my mate march down the stairs energetically and start barking orders.

But despite my confidence in her abilities as an alpha, this plan of hers scares the shit out of me.

It goes against every instinct in my body to know she's going to run straight into danger and challenge an absolute psychopath to a fight. Jared said she barely kept that low-ranking female at bay, and it's a safe assumption that Nielsen will be a good deal tougher.

If he weren't, he wouldn't still be the alpha.

And as we trudged into the trees last night and stood beside Lily while she made her announcement, I could see discomfort and concern in the way the pack moved and their eyes darted around. Lily refused to order them to do this; she wanted them to choose on their own, and she said as much. I hope with every fiber of my being that she's instilled the confidence they were missing back in this pack. It'll be a real blow if only a handful of people show up.

This morning, following the announcement, we all kick it into high gear. Dom reached out to his contacts in Montrose and let them know the plan. He says he's not sure how they took it but he hopes they'll join us when the time comes, or at the very least not stand in our way. They agreed to think about it and that's all the promise we receive.

So now it's seven pm and we're waiting outside the community center to see how many people turn up for this little road trip. It's absolutely freezing out, so we're sitting in our cars with the engines running. Maxwell volunteered to drive the four of us, since he plans to take part in the attack, anyway. Most of the household staff volunteered, including Mrs. Dowling and Mr. Carson. Thankfully, Lily found a way to ask the older staff to stay back while making it sound incredibly important—yet another example of how adept she is as an alpha.

So we have a handful of vehicles rumbling in the darkness and exhaling steady streams of ghostly exhaust in the parking lot lights. I glance aside at Lily and she's staring out her window, knee twitching while she chews her nails.

I reach a hand across the seat to save her poor fingers. "It'll be alright," I try to sound confident. "They'll come."

She squeezes my hand and smiles back at me gratefully. "I know. And even if it's not a lot, it'll work. I just can't help wondering what it means if *no one* comes."

"Nothing, because they're going to show up." Jared leans forward from the third row and rests his chin on the back of our seat. "It's barely after seven and you gave them until seven twenty. Don't work yourself up for no reason, gorgeous. If you need a distraction, I have some jokes-"

"NO!" The three of us thunder at him simultaneously, and Milo bursts out laughing. "I told you, man, you're wearing out your welcome with those jokes. Not every occasion is a laughing matter."

"Says the hyena," Jared grumbles.

"I'm just not in the mood for jokes right now, handsome. I'm sorry." Lily pats Jared's cheek with one hand, and his disgruntled expression melts immediately.

We go back to waiting in silence, and Lily checks the time on her phone every thirty seconds.

After another long stretch of nothing, she sighs. "Surely someone would be here by now, wouldn't they? I mean, it's only five minutes before we're supposed to roll out."

I'm actually getting nervous myself, but my mate doesn't need my doubts right now. "They'll show, Lily. They're your pack, and they love you."

She nods in agreement, but her lips thin as her eyes scan the side streets around the parking lot.

"There's someone!" Jared practically shouts in my ear, and we track the single vehicle as it turns into the lot and heads straight for us.

No one says anything, but we're all thinking it: Just one car?

The SUV pulls alongside Maxwell, who lowers his window while the passenger in the other vehicle does the same.

"Hey guys!" Amber's voice sings out through the car. "Everyone's already lined up and ready to go on main, just waiting for you to lead us!"

My heart jumps... how many people is 'everyone'?

"Everyone?" Lily asks, echoing my thoughts as she leans forward to talk.

"Yeah, pretty much the whole town showed, like, mega early. It was too many cars to fit the lot and more just kept coming, so we told everyone to line up or we'd never get out of here on time. I suppose we should have said something, sorry. We just wanted to be ready."

"That's... wow, Amber, that's great, thank you."

The passenger window next to me rolls down, so I lower mine as well.

Savannah beams at us from the crammed backseat. "Hey guys! She's not kidding; aside from, like, my grandma, the entire pack is waiting. We actually had to tell Mimi to stay home. She wanted to go too. Dad had to remind her about her hip, and then it became this whole thing-ouch! What was that for?" She turns angrily on the person sitting next to her.

"They don't need to hear about your Mimi's hip, Savannah. We gotta go." Brad, one of Jared's teammates from the football team, pokes his head around Savannah's bushy hair from the middle seat. "You guys ready? We'll lead you over."

"Yeah, sounds great thanks!" Lily leans across me. "Maxwell, just follow their car."

Justin's SUV pulls ahead and we fall in line with the

rest of the household vehicles behind us, windows rising to stop the flood of cold air pouring in.

"Do you think it's really the whole town?" Lily asks, her voice barely above a whisper.

"Of course we do," Jared answers for all of us. "I told you, nothing to worry about."

"We all knew people would show," Milo asserts.

There's a nervous electricity in the air as we drive through the dark, sleepy town. Not a car on the street except ours, every house and business dark as we pass.

Then, we turn onto Main.

My breath is in my throat, and I'm just praying the girls hadn't exaggerated. The major thoroughfare of Smoky Falls is well lit by golden streetlights, so of course it's the brightest spot in town. Lily and I lean in to see around the front seats and I give her hand another encouraging squeeze.

Ahead, for what seems like miles, are glowing red tail lights lining the road on either side.

Lily squeezes my hand back, nearly crushing my fingers in her excitement. My heart starts pumping with renewed energy; there must be hundreds of cars; I can't even see to the end.

As soon as we pass the first pair of cars they honk excitedly, and as we roll past, more and more vehicles join the din, until it's a deafening roar that reminds me of the cell phones at our nightly runs.

Jared crows in the back seat, and Lily's eyes dart between the three of us, an expression of utter amazement on her face.

I have no doubts now; we're going to take Montrose by storm and no one will stop us until we reach Nielsen's front door.

And then it'll be entirely up to one eighteen-year-old girl, my mate, to change the world as we know it.

Chapter Thirty-Two

DERREK

I know something's up when the radios on the guys outside my door start squawking. It's late, hours after dinner, and the sound wakes me from an uneasy nap.

After Erika left last night, I haven't seen a soul apart from my regular meal times. I scarcely slept, risking as much time practicing spells in my bathroom as I dared. If Nielsen's next plan is to kill Lilliana in front of me, I have to be able to stop him when the time comes. So long as the spell I've perfected works, it'll at least give her a fighting chance.

I've shown zero signs of manifesting, and I even tried to use the threat of him killing her to shift on my own, but it was pointless.

Of course, there's always the hope that he's not even

357

able to get to Lilliana in the first place. Knowing what I do now about magic, Smoky Falls is certainly better protected than I even realized, and she has those three boys, let alone an entire pack, between her and my supposed father.

But if there's one thing I know about him, it's that he's ruthless. If he has a plan to get to her, I have to assume it has a possibility of success.

And so I focused all of my energy for the last twenty-four hours on working up a spell to free her from whatever method he uses to restrain her. I've untied knots, and even subtly unlocked the 'tool box' in my room before swiftly locking it again. Fortunately for me, the change was so subtle it wasn't caught on the cameras.

I don't know what the sudden commotion means, but I'm certain it can't be good. I lay as still as possible, trying to understand the scratchy radio voices over the sounds of feet pounding down the hallway, but it's all a muffled, jumbled mess of noise.

Then, it goes incredibly quiet.

My heart rate ticks up. What does it all mean?

Perhaps he was able to kidnap Lilliana and they're setting up some sort of show out of it. That would make sense—he'd want the entire pack to see him take her out, I'm certain. It's a century-old rivalry, filled with bad blood and mutual hatred.

It'll be even more dramatic to have me tied up with a magical leash, forced to watch. And if that doesn't make me turn into a wolf, well, I guess they'll get a two-for-one.

It's quiet for a long time, and I'm beginning to wonder if I just imagined the flurry of activity earlier. Or maybe someone got injured, and they needed extra hands carrying them, but it wasn't the big emergency like it sounded through the door.

I roll over on my bed, determined to get a little more shut eye before I get up and work on spells again.

And that's when my door creaks open.

Instantly on alert, I sit and squint toward the shadow in the wedge of fluorescent light pouring through the doorway. The lights in my room remain off.

"Leaf, come on we've got to go!" A horrifyingly familiar voice hisses.

Azalea.

I'm instantly on my feet and heading for the bathroom. I can't let her get that leash on me.

"We don't have time to tinkle, cousin," she snarls, chasing me. "We've got to get out of here!"

I dive through the doorway, but she wedges a foot in before I can slam it shut.

"I'm not here to hurt you, moron," she grunts, pushing back against the door. "Will you just calm down? We don't have time for this shit."

Counting to three, I close my eyes and flick on the bathroom light, hoping the brightness will temporarily confuse her so I can push past.

No such luck. She's like a solid wall, and even

though I slam into her with as much force as I can muster, she doesn't budge.

"OW, dammit Leaf, chill the fuck out!"

I open my eyes to glare, and that's when I actually get a good look at her.

She's been beat to hell. One eye is as black as her furry coat and swollen shut, and the other is barely half open. Purple and green bruises line her jaw and disappear under the collar of her torn shirt, and dried blood runs from a deep gash on her forehead down the side of her face.

Her appearance pulls me up short, and she grins sarcastically at me despite a swollen split lip. "Aren't I pretty? Unfortunately, I don't have any of those magical wolf healing powers, so what they do to me sticks around for a while. I might almost envy you that, freak."

When she takes in my confused expression, she sighs heavily and tips her head back. I'm certain an eye roll would accompany the gesture if she could do one.

"Look, I tried to help your princess rescue you and I got caught, alright? Grannie made me. It's not like I did it out of the kindness of my heart. But after spending a couple days here under the excellent care of that asshole, I'm not exactly inclined to hang around any longer, contract or not. There's something going on and he's called all the minions outside, so I'm making my move, and thought I'd get you out of here, too."

My eyes narrow and I try to figure out what the catch is. There's no way she's just here to help me out.

As if reading my doubt, she groans in frustration. "Fine, I figured taking you with me would be a hell of a parting 'fuck you' to Nielsen, alright? It's no skin off my back if you stay, but I'm getting out of here and you'd better not say I didn't offer. You coming or not?"

I consider how this could be another trick of Nielsen's, but I honestly can't make it work. Why would he send her here, black and blue, to fake a rescue attempt? For what purpose?

"Any day now, cousin. I have no idea how long they'll be gone, but I guarantee it won't be all night."

Deciding, I raise my hand and point repeatedly at the collar around my neck.

"Yeah, I'll get it off you, but not right now. We have to get out of here before they come back. And then I'll get it off, scout's honor."

I fix her with my best dubious look and cross my arms.

"Motherf-… Leaf, you realize we're on a clock here, right? If we don't leave before they come back, we're both stuck here. I dunno about you, but I don't think they have a slumber party planned for later."

In response, I just lean back against the sink and glare at her.

"Argh! Fine, we'll take the collar off before we leave. But we have to go back to the cell where I put it on, okay? That's where they put my stuff, and I need the floor space for a pentagram to undo it. Yes, I need a pentagram to undo it. Don't look at me like that. You know some spells are easier to do than undo."

I consider for a few moments; I don't trust Azalea any further than I can throw her. But her current state seems to add some credence to her story, and she's here offering to get me out. The outside hallway has been silent despite the door being open this entire time, which also reinforces what she's telling me.

Finally, I release a heavy breath and throw my hands up, then gesture for her to move.

"Alright, just stick close to me," she hisses. "We'll get that collar off of you, and then we're getting out of here."

Chapter Thirty-Three

LILLIANA

~

They knew we were coming long before we arrived in Montrose.

It's easy to tell; we don't encounter a single car on our drive through town, and while it's pretty late, there are still bars with glowing neon open signs in the windows that we pass.

But no people.

I can only assume they've pulled back to protect the alpha, and are waiting for us somewhere ahead in the dark.

Our long line of vehicles trails into town like a gas-powered snake, and at the point we selected this morning, we pull off on the shoulder and park. The cars behind us split, lining the road on both sides to unload their passengers.

It's even colder now than when we left; heat rises from our bodies and my breath makes dense white clouds with each exhale. The guys gather around me and we wait for our pack to close in on foot. In the distance, cars are still parking, tiny figures running up to join the massive crowd that pushes forward.

My heart feels like a hummingbird in my throat. Even though I know this is what I need to do, it's hard to put so many of my pack in danger to achieve it.

But the alpha draws strength from her pack. And Harridans have sacrificed for Smoky Falls for generations, shouldering the brunt of the curse that was laid upon us all.

The gathered people wait, watching me expectantly, and I know I need to tell them what I'm thinking.

"Thank you all for coming with me tonight," I start tremulously, my voice fragile and weak.

Milo slips his hand around mine and squeezes in encouragement. I clear my throat and try again.

"We're here tonight to take back our freedom. Generations ago, the founders of the Montrose Pack decided they no longer wanted to be part of Smoky Falls. Instead of simply leaving, they left a curse on our entire pack. Not only did they prevent us from freely shifting as we used to, but they forced the Harridans, my predecessors, to carry a heavy burden. Upon becoming alpha, I found out that any alpha is required to return to Smoky Falls before 24 hours passes or face immediate death."

There's dead silence as the pack listens, and I draw in a deep breath. Jared wraps an arm around my shoulder and rubs my arm.

"My mother left before that became her curse, and many blamed her for it. I recently discovered she did that with intent; not to run away and save herself, but to *return* with an heir who would reunite the packs and end the curse for good. An heir who didn't grow up knowing about the curse, who could believe in the reunification with the descendants of those who'd hurt us so long ago."

A rumble of surprise runs through the crowd now, people glancing at each other and whispering in response. I forge on.

"So tonight I'm here to do exactly that. I've come to challenge the Montrose alpha, hoping we can put an end to this pain and start a new chapter for everyone. I've asked you to come because I need your help. My strength as an alpha comes from the pack. And the alpha protects the pack, but sometimes the pack protects the alpha. I need you to help me get past the Montrose pack so I can confront their alpha and issue him a challenge directly. I don't know what this fight will be like; I ask you not to use more force than you have to. Don't forget that these people are still family, removed by a few generations, but family by blood nonetheless. Defend yourselves, but don't hurt anyone if you can help it."

I falter, not sure how to end this part explanation, part motivational speech.

Milo squeezes my hand, then steps forward. "My mate didn't grow up here. She wasn't raised alongside us, calling Smoky Falls home from birth the way we did. She suffered a loss most of us will never understand when her parents died. And she came here a stranger, ignorant to the inheritance she was about to receive."

My blood races through my veins... this hardly sounds good, and I have no idea where he's trying to go with calling me an ignorant outsider.

"But she's shouldered the burden that fell on her as if she'd been *raised* to be our alpha. Despite all the trials she's faced, my mate has never backed down, never given up, and never stopped hoping that there was light at the end of this tunnel for all of us. *We have the opportunity* to walk through that tunnel, reach the light together, and restore our pack to the family it was always meant to be. We're here tonight because of my mate," he glances back and Landon and Jared, "*our* mate, Lilliana Harridan!"

The still-growing crowd is silent for half a heartbeat, and then a roar, like an ocean wave of sound, rises from them. Cheers and whistles and clapping and joyful shouts. Two separate chants begin, one group shouting 'Har-ri-dan! Har-ri-dan!' and the other calling 'Smoky Falls! Smoky Falls!'

Blood rushes in my ears, and my body relaxes even

as I realize the smile on my face is so wide my cheeks are hurting.

"You see, gorgeous?" Jared leans in and speaks loud enough for me to hear over the din. "They're all here for you."

"They love you, just like I said," Landon adds before kissing my cheek.

I can feel my pulse in every inch of my body. It's as if my heart has synced to the chanting, and I can't seem to separate myself from the crowd. We're one and the same now.

After a few more moments, I raise my arms and lower them slowly, and the pack understands, quieting their voices to hear me. "The alpha house is a straight shot up this road. I don't know how much resistance we'll meet or when, so be on your guard, and let's go!"

With another roar, they surge forward, and I turn and start walking with my mates. Quickly, many familiar faces join our line as we march up the street. Dom and Roxanne; Savannah and Brad, the boy who sat next to her in the car on the way here; Justin and Amber; more members of Jared's football team, staff from Harridan house, and lots of people—whose faces I recognize but names I don't know—crowd around us.

The energy is like a living connection to all of them. It bolsters me, filling me with power like a bright light that radiates out from me to each of them. I can't touch them with my alpha senses off of our pack land, but this is almost the same thing; I feel them, every one of them, deep in my core somehow.

Now out of the main part of town, the street grows darker, the street lamps fewer and farther in between. Our crowd has quieted somewhat, but it's not as if we're stealthy; it's still a complete ruckus.

The guys have assumed the 'flying V' position we walked in at the outset of classes, what seems like eons ago now. It was just a few weeks, but feels like an absolute lifetime since I first manifested. Back when Amber was my enemy, and I barely understood what I'd fallen into as the Harridan heir. I wish I had something to say, something special for each of them, but it's as if my words have dried up; I can't force a thought from my brain to my tongue to save my life.

We turn a slight corner, and finally I can see the alpha house ahead. It's lit up like a prison complex, floodlights glaring over every square inch of the house and property within the tall green hedges that stretch down the drive. Dozens and dozens of people stand in the drive, filling the road up to the house as far as the hedges reach.

Blocking the road between us and them stands the rest of the Montrose pack.

∼

JARED

∼

The energy rolling off the mob ahead of us is like a brick wall in front of an ocean wave. Smoky Falls is flooding down this road and Montrose is formed up, waiting to break us.

My muscles tighten and flex, adrenaline coursing through my blood as I size them up. No matter what happens, we have to get Lily through that crowd and face to face with the Montrose alpha. Milo, Landon, and I all agreed that is our *one* job—to protect her at all costs. We have the pack, but ultimately it's our responsibility to be her last line of defense.

So when we're scarcely ten yards from the front of their line, we come to a stop and size up our opponents.

Their faces are mainly in shadow; they've stopped just beyond the pale ring of light from the streetlamp, and we're on the other side.

Without a word, Lily steps forward into the pool of light, and the guys and I move forward with her.

"If you don't know already, I'm Lilliana Harridan," she begins in a clear, powerful voice. "I'm the alpha of the Smoky Falls pack, heir to a legacy I knew nothing about a few months ago. My mother left Smoky Falls and raised me in the human world, hoping when I returned I'd be able to reunite our packs and restore the unity we had before.

"I don't know what your leaders told you, but I'm not here with ill intent. Your alpha came to Smoky Falls and claimed one of my mates as his son and heir. It was through him that my mother hoped I'd join the packs. But your alpha intends to kill him if he's unable to manifest as a wolf. From what I understand, he has some pretty terrible methods for getting the results he wants."

Low murmurs rumble through the opposing pack, but no one speaks out.

Lilliana continues. "I've come to claim my mate, and challenge your alpha, if I must, in order to save us all. If you feel you have to fight for your pack, believe me, I understand. I won't hold it against you. Just know that my only fight is with Avery Nielsen. If you step aside and let us pass, we will not harm you."

The shocked whispers fly around us when Lily reveals that Derrek's her fourth mate. We've digested the idea, but it's obviously quite the surprise to everyone else.

The talking eventually quiets down, and we wait in a silence so tense it prickles on my skin.

Finally, one man steps forward from the Montrose crowd: Jeff, the guy who was a friend of Dom's that insisted Lily fight him to earn her respect.

"Our pack has been slowly dying for decades, and our alpha's methods to save it have grown detrimental to the wellbeing of our families. More people leave now than stay; we're in danger of not even existing in another decade or two." Murmurs of assent rise from the crowd behind him.

"We're not here to fight you. We aren't able to help you, but we won't stand in your way. The alpha has a couple hundred wolves who are loyal, who *will* fight you, and they're waiting for you already. We wish you strength and success in your challenge."

With an incline of his head, he steps aside, and the crowd parts down the middle as if by some invisible cue.

Fully lit thanks to the floodlights, the faces of our opponents are clearly furious at this unexpected betrayal. It's plain as day they expected the people now standing aside to take the bulk of the attack, and their emotions roll over their faces.

To my complete surprise, the waiting Montrose loyalists drop to their knees and start shifting, apparently unable to help themselves in the face of such powerful emotions.

Suddenly, we're a group of unarmed humans, facing down a pack of slavering, snarling wolves.

And then, as if it's the ringing of an angel's bell from on high, a cell phone alarm goes off.

Chapter Thirty-Four

LILLIANA

~

With everyone's emotions this high, it's no surprise that we shift the second the clock strikes midnight, shredding through our clothes without even a conscious effort to do it. We're facing down a couple hundred snarling, slavering wolves, who fill the path ahead of us completely.

So there's no time to undress; within seconds, the shift is over and I'm on all four paws, my hackles up and snarls rumbling in my throat. Before I can even take a step, the wolves around me surge forward, and the fight begins.

I don't know what I expected; I've never been claustrophobic, so perhaps I didn't even register what this would be like. However, my first sensation is that I'm

375

being crushed. Members of my pack press from behind, and the Montrose wolves are pushing downhill with the advantage of gravity on their side. My mates have formed a furry wall between me and the oncoming wolves, and it's all I can do to move forward inches at a time.

All around me wolves are snarling and snapping, trying to gain ground in a bizarre game I can't even come up with an example to compare it to. Maybe the opposite of tug of war?

Bodies press against me on all sides, hard muscle and bone covered with fur squeezing and pushing. The wolves at the front line—a few yards ahead of me now —bite and claw at each other, and it's swiftly becoming a fight for every inch.

Panic—heart-stopping, undiluted terror—seizes me in an instant. There's nowhere to go; we're pressed together so tightly it feels as if I'm about to be crushed by my own pack.

And that's when an absolutely crazy idea pops into my head.

As far ahead as I can see, it's like a literal ocean of fur; bodies pressed together so tightly they almost form a flat surface.

I have to get to Nielsen, and I have to get there before the clock strikes one.

The entire plan is going to shit; I'm not supposed to leave my mates, but I don't see how we can all get to that house through this crowd. It's an impossible choice.

Summoning my courage, I draw in a breath and leap onto Jared's broad, furry back. He yelps in surprise, but realizing it's me, stops trying to shake me off.

With my sights on the house at the top of the hill, I begin sprinting across the sea of wolves.

Picking my way across living bodies is way different from navigating solid ground. The surface constantly shifts and it's impossible to know what'll happen with each paw I place. The positive side is that I have four feet, and if I move quickly, the wolves below don't even have time to react before I'm already gone.

I cross the line to the Montrose wolves, and fortunately, the ones at the front are too busy to see me coming. However, the next row does, and now I have an additional hazard to avoid: teeth.

Treading as lightly as I can, I make my best effort to dart around the wolves that try to stop me. Some merely snap at my paws when I get near; others rise on their hind legs for better reach, and still others try to pull the same move and clamber on top of their brethren. They're so tightly packed they have no room to adjust, which is beneficial to me. My heart continues pounding in the deep chest of my wolf form, and I keep my gaze ahead. Forty yards left, thirty-five, thirty…

It's slow, but certainly faster than if I were still stuck back in the crowd of my pack. I can't risk looking back. I have to keep moving forward. My body develops a rhythm, calculating each step faster than my brain can process as I navigate to the wolves who aren't looking up, creating the safest path for me to maneuver.

Twenty-five yards, twenty, fifteen...

I'm so close now I can see clear ground at last. When I reach the end I know I have to leap and keep running, as the wolves at the back will surely turn and pursue. I scan for Nielsen in the handful of people still human by the door, preparing to run straight for him to issue the challenge.

And that's when sharp teeth close around my throat.

She pulls me into the writhing mass of wolves; a surprised whine escapes my canine muzzle, and the panic sets in again. When surrounded by enemies, not only is there a possibility of being crushed but also of being literally pulled apart. My paws scrabble for purchase and I twist, trying to free myself from iron jaws. With surprise, I note that none of the other wolves have tried to tear into me, despite clearly being aware of who I am. I take courage from that, and fight harder.

But my opponent holds on tightly. I can't see her, but my nostrils flare with desperate breaths and I recognize the scent of my opponent; it's the same female I fought the last time I was here.

Dread floods my body; she's a much better fighter than me. I barely escaped last time, and she's already got a lock on my neck. The only thing I can hope for is that Nielsen wants to take me out himself and she might just be planning to drag me up to him.

Hot liquid trickles through the fur on my neck, and I fight against the instinct to rip myself free of her jaws. That route will probably get my throat torn out before I even have a chance to face Nielsen.

If that's even her plan.

Trying to think my way through this scenario is like dragging a spoon through a jar of cold honey. I'm fighting the panic with every fiber of my being, but I just can't see a way to get myself out of this situation.

And then a familiar brown wolf leaps from the crowd and lands squarely on my opponent, snarling fiercely.

It doesn't surprise me that someone from Smoky Falls took my lead and leapfrogged across the backs of the wolves. I hated to leave them behind, but I hoped a few would follow.

But it *is* a shock that the person who came to my rescue is Amber.

She's practically feral, clawing and snapping and heaving her weight against the other female, forcing her to choose between holding my throat and defending herself.

And it works; when Amber lands a particularly savage bite on the other wolf's ear, the Montrose wolf releases me and turns to face the newest threat.

I stand on shaky legs and try to think fast; I have to move before the surrounding wolves can take her place. Even now they're turning inward, separating me from Amber and tightening the surrounding space.

And then, like my personal cavalry, my mates arrive.

Leaping off some unknown Montrose wolf backs, they wedge themselves between me and the surrounding enemies, forcing them outward while pushing forward, creating a small gap to lead me through.

We're so close to the end now, the pushing is actually working. Jared is at the front; I suppose I have his years of football experience to thank for this move. I watched him use it in last week's game: The Smoky Falls Wolves were just a few yards from the end zone, and the opposing team brought out their biggest, burliest guys to form a solid wall between us and our goal. When the play started, our line clashed against theirs like a thunderclap. Jared faked a throw to the left and passed the ball to a teammate, who ran up behind our line, curling around the football and taking a flying leap over the entire group.

I know what I'm supposed to do.

Following their lead, I back up as far as I'm able to gain a few precious steps, then charge up and across Jared's wide back and leap for the space just beyond the remaining Montrose wolves. And just like the football game, one wolf bucks up and tries to snatch me out of the air as I fly overhead, but I draw my leg in close and clear him, landing at a full-out run and racing forward to the line of Montrose members still in their human form.

I have no idea what time it is, how long it took me to get here, or how much time I have left before my window to be a wolf closes. I skid to a stop, my nails raking across the pavement, and shift immediately to my human form. There's no time to consider my extreme nakedness; honestly it doesn't even bother me that much anymore.

I glare up at the hulking figure of Avery Nielsen who smirks while he gets an eyeful of my exposed body, and snarl, "Avery Nielsen, I challenge you for the position as alpha of the Montrose Pack!"

And without waiting a second more, I shift back into my wolf and lunge for his throat.

Chapter Thirty-Five

MILO

~

By the time we shove our way through the last of Pack Montrose, Lily is already deep in her fight with Nielsen. They seem evenly matched, both attacking and neither getting the upper hand. One side of the circle is filled with Nielsen's most loyal lackeys, who have remained human, cheering for him..

"Hey!" a human voice calls from the side of the house, and I turn snarling, Jared and Landon mimicking the movement.

A tall, thin figure waves to us from the shadows, and I realize it's Billy. My gaze darts back to Lily in the midst of her fight; we can't leave her, we're her mates. In theory, no one would attack during an alpha challenge; it's not allowed. But I'm willing to bet this pack has done several things that no one else would do, and I don't trust them.

Landon releases a low whine and I look back at Billy pointedly.

It sucks not being able to speak in wolf form.

"Come on, you don't have much time!" Billy waves us toward him, his voice strained.

I hesitate, glancing again at Lily, and realize a few of our pack mates have made it across the sea of Montrose too, and they're guarding her flank.

"Come on!" Billy hisses again.

My gaze lands on first Jared, then Landon, who both appear to be waiting for me to decide.

With a huff, I creep across the lawn to see what Billy wants. He's nervous, sweating despite the chilly air.

"You're her mates, right? I recognize you from that night in Smoky Falls. If you're going to save Leaf, you've got to do it now."

A low growl rumbles in Jared's chest, and despite having no ability to enunciate, his feelings come across clearly.

"I promise there's nothing you can do for her right now. Alpha may be a dick, but he still believes in certain traditions. He'd murder anyone who interfered with a challenge, and I've seen a few of these; they can drag on for a while. But if you don't help Leaf soon, he'll be dead before they're done."

"What the hell are you talking about?" Amber's voice shocks all four of us; Billy practically jumps in response. She's obviously shifted back to human and stands there with her hands on her hips, blood smeared across her face and down her chest, glaring at Billy.

He swallows nervously, his eyes darting away to avoid getting caught ogling. "The witch has him. She's doing something. I don't know what it is, but it can't be good."

Amber snorts. "Lilliana said she's on our side, remember? She's probably just trying to help him escape."

Billy shakes his head stubbornly. "No, I'm telling you she's got him in some kind of ritual, and Leaf needs help. Come on, I'll show you where they are." Without confirming that we'd follow, he turns and slips around the side of the house, following the narrow trail between the siding and the hedges.

I'm dubious about his claims, but I trust he means well.

I *don't* trust that Azalea has good intentions.

I follow in his wake, and the others fall in behind. When we reach the back door, Amber is back in wolf form. We slip down the basement stairs, then wait for Billy to lead us to the right cell. The hallways are dark, lit occasionally by a single can light placed far enough apart to leave stretches in deep shadows.

It's still a maze, but far less daunting with a guide. Billy seems to know the place like the back of his hand, trotting down the hallways and taking lefts and rights with no discernible pattern.

We turn the last corner and a deep feeling of unease settles in my stomach.

The hallway is dark like the previous ones, but unlike the previous doors, the window on this one's not dark. A sickening green glow emanates from inside.

I now understand why Billy is worried; the air crackles with energy. It makes my fur stand on end and my stomach slosh.

Whatever it is, it feels… wrong. Very wrong.

"I have to go back outside before they miss me," Billy whispers. "I'll flick the lights on the way back to leave you a path to the door. But as soon as you stop her, get him out of here. Alpha couldn't get him to shift, so he's already planning to kill him. If he wins the alpha challenge, he's going to kill your alpha and see if that will get Leaf to shift. If he loses to your alpha, he's already got someone primed to carry it out. He'll be dead before she even finds her way down here."

I swallow hard; Lily's up there with no one to protect her if she loses. No one to warn her about what Nielsen's planning. An anxious whine escapes my throat.

We have to get Derrek and get him out of here, fast, so we can go protect our mate.

Without a second thought, I creep toward the door. I pull up short when I realize it's a knob, not a handle.

Of course.

I call on the shift, stuffing myself back into my human shape, and peek through the door.

The green light is almost blinding after the darkness of the hallways, but when my eyes adjust, my heart jumps to my throat.

Azalea's face is black and blue, and she holds a jagged knife while reading aloud from a book. She's standing over Derrek, who's tied down to the concrete floor with ropes. A wide black collar covers his throat, and his eyes are round with terror even as he struggles to free himself. Green light that has the look of sinister lightning bolts whips around them in a funnel, ripping at their clothes and making Azalea's electric purple hair flutter around her battered face.

And painted on the floor is a giant pentagram, dozens of symbols I don't recognize around the outer circle.

Derrek is smack in the middle.

I crouch down and face the others.

"She's doing some kind of ritual on him, and he's tied down in the middle of a pentagram. Jared and I will attack Azalea; Amber, Landon, you focus on getting Derrek free. You heard Billy, so don't wait for us; get him out of here first. We're going to bust through that door on the count of three. Ready?"

With a chorus of affirming growls as my only response, I stand back up and grip the doorknob.

"One…"

They've lined up, Jared in front and ready to charge through.

"Two…"

My blood races through my body, the sound of it loud in my ears.

"Three!"

I swing the door open and the wolves charge

through. Azalea has just closed her book and is kneeling over Derrek with the wicked-looking knife raised when our sudden entrance distracts her. Just as she glances up, Jared hits her full-on and sends her sprawling. The knife clangs on the concrete floor and slides into a corner.

I have no time to shift, so I throw myself at the witch, trying to grab hold of her arms and pin her.

Unfortunately, we forgot one important thing: she can work spells with words alone.

Snarling, Azalea shouts in a language I don't recognize, and Jared goes flying against the wall, hitting with a sickening crack and sliding down in a heap. He doesn't move.

The witch just laughs. "You pups should have known better than this. *Spiritus prohibere!*"

Instantly, my throat seizes and I can't breathe. My lungs try desperately to inflate, but nothing will pass either way. Panic sets in and I try to keep hold of her arms, but it's no use; dizziness swamps my head and the panic gets worse. I scrabble at my throat vainly, as if my body expects to find something blocking off my windpipe other than magic.

Azalea stands and glances down at me scornfully. "Pathetic," she spits, then fluffs her hair and turns to look for her knife.

And that's when Amber strikes.

She's shifted back to her human form, and stands directly in front of the other woman, a look of utter contempt on her face. Without hesitation, she slashes the witch's neck with her own knife, preventing her from uttering one more spell. A thick wave of blood pours from the grisly cut, and Azalea drops to her knees with her fingers at her neck as if trying to stop the flow. Within seconds she tips over, the surprised expression frozen on her face.

"That's for Jeremy," Amber spits at the lifeless body on the floor.

My vision is darkening around the edges. A warm hand covers my throat, and after what feels like an eon, air floods into my lungs again. I cough and sputter, straining to pull in more oxygen to relieve my aching lungs.

Turning to see my savior, I realize it's Derrek, who's now darting around me toward Jared. His hands run over the crumpled heap of fur, back stiff while he kneels.

Landon whines loudly, and I assume it's for Jared until a bright flash of green light almost blinds me.

Amber's standing in a strange position, her body almost bowed backwards with feet wide and arms out at her sides, the bloody knife still gripped tightly in her right hand. Her expression appears frozen in shock, and my brain finally catches up that she's not standing. She's *floating* several inches off the ground and apparently unable to move. Her hair ripples lazily above her, in a gust of green energy that's swirling up from Azalea's spilled blood and wrapping Amber in what looks like a cocoon of green magic.

I'm stuck, frozen in place, and absolutely dumbfounded. I have no idea what to do or if I could even do anything to help her. It must be some kind of curse as a last revenge for killing her. I can see Azalea casting such a spell easily.

When the last wisps of magic clear the pool of blood, the swirls around Amber thicken and close in like it's going to shrink wrap her. Amber screams, and I stumble to my feet, grasping for a way to help her.

Then, with one last flash, the green magic is gone and Amber goes completely limp. She teeters over, eyes closed, and I dart in to catch her, lowering her slowly to the ground.

Checking her vitals, she's definitely alive. Her chest rises and falls visibly, warm breath passing her lips. But she's definitely knocked out.

A hand taps my shoulder, and I look up to find Derrek behind me. My eyes dart to Jared, who's back on his feet in wolf form, and butting heads gently with Landon.

"Is he okay?" I croak, my throat still on fire.

Derrek nods. When I give him a confused look, he points to his collar before miming zipping his lips.

"Right, you can't talk. Is she going to be okay?"

Without hesitation, Derrek nods a third time.

"Okay, we have to get out of here. Billy said they'd come for you whether Nielsen wins or loses, and we've got to get back to protect Lily." With a groan, I pull Amber into my arms and stand.

Derrek presses a palm to my shoulder, stopping me

from walking to the door. His hands open in an expression of confusion.

"The alpha challenge. Lily challenged him for his position of alpha. They're fighting right now. If he wins, he plans to kill her, then you. If he loses, he's sending someone down to kill you, anyway."

Before I even finish, he's already yanking open the door and disappearing down the hallway.

"Follow the lit path!" I shout after him, and barely manage to wedge a naked heel against the door to keep it from closing. With a grunt, I heft Amber's limp body and force the door back to allow Jared and Landon to slip out. They sprint after Derrek on all four paws, and I bring up the rear as quickly as I can, cradling Amber's body with the knife still clutched tightly in her hand.

Chapter Thirty-Six

LILLIANA

~

This is how I die.

I didn't want to think about it, but I accepted on the way here that I might lose, and in doing so could sacrifice my life for the chance to free my pack from the curse.

At least I *thought* I'd accepted it.

But now with my strength rapidly waning and my wolf unable to claim an advantage, it's looking more and more hopeless.

Blood mats my fur; some his, but more mine. He's gotten in several good bites, his jaws like iron. Adrenaline pumps through my body thanks to my racing heart, but it's not enough to ignore these injuries. Everything hurts, and even though I continue fighting with everything I have, emotion thickens in my chest. *I'm losing, I'm going to lose.*

We're circling each other, members from both packs forming a wide ring around us to witness. I'm too stressed, too distracted, to see if any of them are furry faces I recognize. I'm certain my fated are here; I can sense my pack around me, but I can't pick out individuals. However, I know my mates would be the first to make it through, and they wouldn't leave me for anything.

My eyes remain sharp, watching for any sign he's about to make a move while I rely on my rapid healing to help keep me in this fight.

If I lose, I know Nielsen will kill me. I'd expect nothing less from the man who tortures his own pack, kills them even, just to get them to shift. Why should I be spared in the face of such a defeat? I imagine it'll be the frosting on the cake for him, to force me to submit then snap my neck with both packs watching.

Uncle Dom won't be a terrible alpha. He cares deeply about our pack. Even if he's not the best suited, he's all they've got, and he has Roxanne to help him. They'll make it work.

In a flash, Nielsen flies across the circle, his jaws aimed for my throat. I dodge, and his teeth sink into my shoulder instead. I release a yelp of pain, but he can't clamp down so I'm able to tear myself away and retreat to safety on the other side of the circle, now limping noticeably.

Failure. I feel like such a failure. This was all my

plan, and I'm the one letting everyone down. I assumed that being male, Nielsen wouldn't be as strong of a fighter. I beat Jeff easily, and he said only Nielsen and his beta had ever beaten him. *Stupid, stupid, stupid.* There has to be more to it than that.

I have to keep trying. The surrounding faces are a blur. I can't pick an individual out. But I know some of them are my pack, my mates. I can't let them watch me give up without a fight. If I'm going to die today, I don't want it to be while I'm running scared in a circle, trying to get away from a bully.

My tongue hangs from the side of my mouth; I haven't been able to catch my breath since we started, and my mouth is so dry my tongue is itchy. That can't be a good sign. I need to end this soon or I'll have nothing left.

Resolved, I gather up the courage to go on the offensive again. I try to assess him for weaknesses to exploit, but I've struggled to find many. He's quick and observant. Stronger than me. His sharp eyes watch every minuscule movement of my paws; it's like he knows where I'm going before even I do.

Emotion clogs my throat. It's impossible. *Impossible.* I can barely stay upright and he looks as if he can go all night.

Continuing to limp around the circle, I search my body and gather up every drop of energy I have left. Mentally suppressing the pain, I focus on making one strong, final attack.

If it's going to end, it's going to end on my terms.

Nielsen's wolf eyes bore into me, as if he can read my every thought.

I refuse to look away. Maybe, if I hold his gaze, he won't see be able to predict my next move.

So without blinking, I feint right, then charge forward, redirecting at the last moment with a hop to the left, hoping to come at him from the side and lock my jaws around his throat.

Instead, Nielsen's teeth close on my neck and he slams me hard to the ground with a vicious snarl.

My feet claw at him uselessly. I have no energy left to free myself.

Suddenly, I hear Nielsen's voice in my head, like a sharp stab to my brain. It reverberates with the double-timbre of the alpha voice and rattles around in my head like an echo.

"Give up, girl. You've lost!"

I can't reply, my brain is too busy trying to understand. So all this time, we could communicate by thoughts? No one else has mentioned it. Maybe it's an alpha thing?

"I'm going to snap your pretty neck, Harridan. If that doesn't force my son to shift, nothing will, and then he's no son of mine. But before I do, I want you to concede that I won!" His teeth dig a little deeper, a fierce snarl rumbling against my blood-matted fur.

I still don't respond. Is there a way for me to use this alpha-talk to my advantage? It feels important, but I'm swiftly running out of time to figure it out.

Nielsen shakes his head back and forth, dragging

my body across the ground and deepening the gashes in my throat.

"There's no getting out of it now, Harridan. I can do this all night, if that's what it takes. But you *will* admit defeat. And when I take over Smoky Falls, this'll all have been worth it. So, by all means, drag it out in the most painful way possible. It won't change a thing."

"You have no claim to Smoky Falls!" I don't mean to reply in the weird mind-meld we have going on, but it must have happened instinctually. "I challenged you for Montrose; my pack was *never* on the table."

Nielsen chuckles darkly in my head, the sound grating on my nerves. "On the contrary, girl. When you lose, you lose it all. So, thanks for bringing such a prize to my doorstep. The magic has been fading here for some time, despite the best efforts of our witches. Smoky Falls has a much deeper, more powerful magic. It'll be a fresh start for all of us. And with so many young females, I shouldn't have a problem claiming a new mate and siring some proper heirs."

No! That's not how this was supposed to happen. A sob rises in my throat, but my wolf form can't complete it, and I refuse to whine.

Now I know I can't give up. A sadistic prick like Nielsen can't take over Smoky Falls. It's my duty as their alpha to protect them, whatever the cost.

I *have* to keep fighting. I have to drum up some energy, some strength, from somewhere.

I have to protect my pack. I *will* protect my pack.

I'm their alpha.

As if my limp body were an empty balloon, warm, tingling power floods into me, soothing the sharp pains and aches and filling my body with renewed energy. I remain still, Nielsen's teeth clenched around my neck and his threatening growls rumbling in his chest.

I'm not sure what's happening, but my mind sharpens, my spirits lifting like a tiny boat on a tsunami, and I ride the wave to its peak.

Faint voices, almost imperceptible, whisper encouragement. They don't echo and bounce in my head like Nielsen's does, but I hear them all the same.

"Come on Alpha!"

"He's nothing compared to you."

"You can do this!"

"I believe in you!"

"Find your power, Lilliana. You just have to believe."

That last voice I know without hesitation; it's my uncle Dom.

"Dom?" I think back at him, unsure if this works both ways.

"Yes! You've got it! I knew you could do it." His voice radiates pride.

"What am I doing? I don't even understand it."

"You've finally accepted your place as alpha. It allows you to communicate with the pack, and draw on their energy when you need it."

"Are you serious right now? So all this time I *still* wasn't alpha? And that's why I couldn't fight?"

"It's more complex than that, but until you fully

embraced your duty as alpha, you couldn't draw on an alpha's most important resource: the pack."

Nielsen growls again, shaking me back and forth in his efforts to claim my submission. I force myself to remain limp, allowing him to think he's still winning while I wrap my head around this new information.

I thought the 'strength of the pack' meant just having so many people, many hands make light work. It never occurred to me drawing on the strength of the pack meant literally drawing from their energy.

My voice still reverberates with the alpha timbre when I think at him, but Dom's doesn't. "Why didn't anyone tell me about this? Shouldn't they know I'm supposed to hear them?"

"They can't speak to you; you can only hear them if you reach out to listen. I'm not speaking to you so much as thinking loudly, and hoping you'll hear me. It's another talent of the alpha's, so we can monitor the pack. They don't know you can hear them."

A sudden flicker of apprehension hits me. "Can Nielsen hear us?"

"No, not unless you're aiming your thoughts directly at him."

"Good. I don't want him to know what I'm about to do."

That distinctive note of pride is in Dom's tone again. "You can do this, Lilliana. We all believe in you."

"Thank you, uncle."

As much as their whispered words—or rather,

thought words—of encouragement are buoying me up, I mentally cut myself off in order to focus.

Right now, Nielsen believes I've all but given up and have nothing left to fight him.

Of course it makes sense, now, how he could beat me so easily. He was drawing on an endless well of energy, able to recover almost instantly from the injuries I dealt him. I only had my personal reserves, so I didn't stand a chance against that sort of power before. I conjure up a silent prayer of gratitude that something in me refused to concede in those long, dark minutes, despite my utter lack of hope.

But despite his obvious frustration, I get the sense that Nielsen isn't that upset that I've yet to whine my submission. He seems to bask in the belief that he's won, practically preening with it. He drags me around in a circle as if showing off his handiwork to all the observers.

Mentally, I check myself over carefully. Of course I can't observe them, but all the wounds I've received don't seem to hurt anymore. Whether it's some kind of mental block or the collective pack energy bolstered my recovery and I'm actually healed, I'm grateful either way.

But my body feels primed and ready to continue fighting, as if I've just woken from a long, restful night of sleep.

Even Nielsen's teeth in my throat aren't painful. I can feel the pressure, but it doesn't really hurt.

My body is bursting with vitality, but I remain limp.

I need Nielsen to be convinced I'm completely out of a fight so he'll make a fatal error for me to take advantage of.

It takes a few more minutes of his ridiculous show, but he finally does what I've been waiting for.

Previously, Nielsen was dragging me around by walking backwards and hauling my body across the pavement. Apparently tired of that maneuver, he tried strutting forward and allowing my body to drag alongside him.

But now, obviously tired of the awkward positioning and absolutely convinced he's already won, he lifts his head further and straddles my body so he can haul my limp form more easily.

With a vicious snarl, I clamp my teeth on his ear and kick my legs out, clawing at his chest and his soft underbelly. My sharp claws dig in, and hot liquid coats my paws as I keep kicking viciously.

Nielsen has no choice but to release me or lose his entrails. Even rapid healing can't prevent that with the level of injury I've dealt him.

When I pop to my feet, a chorus of howls rises all around me. My pack celebrating with me. In the distance, the wolves who're too far away to witness directly take up the howl. My eyes never leave Nielsen, but I can feel the shift in the air, the other pack suddenly uncomfortable.

I can't give my opponent time to recover, so I attack him savagely. He tries to counterattack, but he's still protecting his shredded belly and waiting for the skin to knit back together, so there's not a lot he can do.

In a matter of minutes, I've got his throat between my jaws.

How the tables have turned.

Sinking my teeth in, I order him, "Concede."

"In your dreams, Harridan."

"I can see your guts, Nielsen. One more pass with my claws and all of your insides will be outside. You've lost."

"Then I guess you'd better end it, because I will never concede."

I huff my frustration into his furry neck. "Why does it have to be like this? All I ever wanted was to lift the curse your witch put on my family ages ago. Why should I suffer because your ancestors left mine? Why should my mates share in the burden of being tied to our territory for the rest of our lives? There's no reason for us to hate each other this way. I'm trying to end that, don't you understand?"

Nielsen's coarse laugh grates at my senses. "I can't believe you idiots still believe that lie. We're not the problem, princess. You are."

A snarl rips through my chest, and I shake him, tightening my jaws.

"What do you mean 'we believe that lie'?"

"The curse that keeps you from leaving Smoky Falls. There is no curse, it's a fairy tale."

"That's a lie. The curse killed my great aunt."

"Your great aunt killed *herself*, princess. Your pack blamed it on us, and here we are."

"I don't believe you," I snarl mentally, and give him a savage shake for good measure.

"Believe what you want. It doesn't matter to me."

"Why would she do that? It doesn't make any sense."

"You're a teenage girl. It should be obvious to you. She was in love with one of the men who left Smoky Falls. She couldn't handle being rejected by one of her fated, so she took her own life. It's hardly unusual, even for normal humans."

My head spins with this take on events. "But I *know* there's a curse. I haven't been able to shift whenever I want, like you all can. That's real!"

Nielsen chuckles again. "Well, yeah, that's true. The witch who cast the spell splitting the packs was petty. In Smoky Falls, there was a curfew of sorts. No one could shift between midnight and dawn; they were a bit more superstitious back then, and believed it would turn them into feral wolves, permanently. So, as a parting gift, she made it so they could *only* shift after midnight. Not what I would have done, but it wasn't my choice. I'd never punish the pack for shitty leadership."

There's no way for me to verify his version of events, but something deep in my gut believes it. My stomach flips sickeningly as realization after realization passes through my thoughts in rapid succession.

"They knew, didn't they? My family. They knew it wasn't a curse, that she did it to herself."

"Of course they knew. She left a note! They just wanted your pack to hate us for all time, and to make sure none of their descendants ever tried to reunite the packs again."

"Of course they did," I sigh mentally, but it comes out of my wolf's snout as a huff. "Thank you for telling me the truth."

"You may not like me, or my methods, but I've never lied to you, Harridan."

"That doesn't excuse you torturing your pack to get them to shift. Whatever your intentions, you've abused their trust horribly. You have no business being alpha."

"Oh, and you do? A teenage girl who relies on her hormones more than the experience she clearly lacks?"

I snarl. "I'm not interested in trading insults with you. Concede, and I'll allow you to remain in Montrose. That's the best offer you'll receive."

"And if I refuse?"

"I will kill you. You seem to be under the delusion that I'm incapable, but I will do anything to protect my pack. Montrose is also my pack, and I will protect them from you."

"You don't have it in you, little girl. You weren't raised with our ways; your soft human heart won't be able to kill me."

Fury ripples under my skin, and I tighten my jaw, teeth scraping against the bones in his neck and cutting off his air supply.

"I don't have it in me, huh?" I think savagely. "Do you really want to test that theory?"

Nielsen's wolf body twitches, his paws kicking feebly in an instinctive fight to free himself and breathe.

He holds out longer than I expected, but he eventually emits a low whine.

I ease my clenched teeth apart a millimeter, snarling, and he understands my meaning. This time the whine is louder, audible to the surrounding wolves. Howls of joy rise from my pack, and I refocus on Nielsen.

"You have tonight to get your things and move out of this house. I will send my pack inside your little dungeon to free everyone inside, including Derrek. Don't even think about interfering or I *will* kick you out of the pack."

With that final thought I release him, lashing my tongue against my teeth to scrape off the coating of blood and fur from holding him so long.

I pause for just a moment, observing the joyful crowd of wolves and searching for my mates. As much as I want to stay and celebrate, I need to go free Derrek, *now*.

I spin in circles, uselessly, unable to find them. I know their wolf faces as well as their human ones, but I don't see them in the raucous crowd. There are people still in human form, wading among the wolves. Some stark naked and some still in clothes. It's absolute chaos, and panic rises in my chest.

Where the hell are my mates?

I should have known not to turn my back on a man like Nielsen. But some part of me believed, or at least hoped, that he had some honor, however twisted it might be.

Turns out, that mistaken belief was enough to get me killed.

Chapter Thirty-Seven

DERREK

~

Even barefoot, I burst through the door at full speed and race around the corner, barely feeling the icy gravel beneath my feet. I'm unprepared for the cold, but it doesn't matter.

He will not kill Lilliana. I won't let him.

I'm fully unprepared for the sight that greets me when I reach the front of the house. As far as the eye can see into the darkness, and in pools of streetlights far below, are wolves. Packed tightly against each other, apparently just… waiting?

The sound of snarling reaches my ears, and I turn sharply to my left. There's an open space in the massive crowd, a circle made of living fence, occupied by two wolves.

One has the other's throat clenched in its jaws, and it snarls periodically, shaking its limp opponent and attempting to secure a whine of surrender. I may not have grown up as part of the pack, but my mom taught me about their ways. I know what's happening here.

I force my way toward the fight, squeezing my legs between the tightly packed wolves. At first I can't tell who's who; I've never seen either of them in wolf form. There's no clue from the surrounding wolves, since they're all staring intently at the fight and I don't even know which side any of them are on, either.

But something, some instinct, tells me that the standing wolf, the one whose fur is so matted with blood I can't really determine its natural color, is Lilliana. When she moves her head, I glimpse her glowing green eyes, and know without a doubt that I'm right.

She has the death grip on Nielsen's throat, whose belly is a mess of red. As I get closer, I can tell she ripped into him savagely. He's barely in one piece, so injured his body is struggling to heal despite his magical wolf properties.

Like the surrounding furry crowd, I pause, waiting for something to happen.

There seems to be a battle of wills going on. Lilliana occasionally shakes Nielsen or growls, and he replies with an answering snarl, but refuses to whine. The tension is thick in the air, everyone waiting, practically breathless, to catch the high-pitched tone that will signal the end of the fight.

And it feels as though it takes years, but eventually a faint whine reaches my ears. The Lilliana-wolf growls, and the Nielsen-wolf whines louder, clearly conceding the fight loudly enough for everyone to hear.

When she drops him, I start pushing forward again. All around me wolves are howling—I've honestly never heard anything like it—but my focus is entirely on reaching Lilliana. She obviously hasn't spotted me, since she keeps turning around, searching the crowd. I assume for her other mates. Or me.

I become more forceful with my pushing, earning myself a few threatening growls from wolves who don't enjoy the feeling of my knee in their sides.

But it doesn't matter. None of it matters, aside from getting to her. I don't even care if she doesn't shift, I'm going to throw my arms around her furry neck and just breathe her in, make sure she's really real and this isn't just another twisted dream I'm about to wake up from.

No one's paying attention to Nielsen, who Lily left limp on the pavement. It seems loyalty only goes so far; as soon as he lost his position as alpha, none of his supporters gave him a second thought.

But when I see Nielsen move, my gut tightens.

With even more urgency, I force the wolves aside. I have to warn her, but I can't speak thanks to Azalea's collar. There's nothing for me to do but get to her side and stop him myself.

My heart pounds; I don't think I'm going to make it.

Slowly, he regains his feet, keeping his body low to

the ground. Lily is too busy scanning the crowd. She looks almost disoriented, confused. She's already forgotten the other alpha, intent on her search.

Nielsen bunches his legs beneath him, watching Lily's circles carefully, calculating.

I know what he's going to do. I run forward now, completely oblivious to the bodies that could trip me.

I have to get to her. I have to protect her. She's my mate, and above all else, I have one duty.

To place myself between her and harm, to sacrifice myself if needs be; to protect the alpha and ensure the safety of the pack.

Without a conscious effort to draw it up, magic ripples through my body like a wave. I don't know what's happening and I don't have time to think about it. Nielsen's preparing to attack and I'm still yards and several wolf bodies away.

When he starts to spring, I leap forward, flinging my body between them and hoping to catch the brunt of the attack.

I dive as a man. But in a blinding flash of heat, with no small amount of shocking pain, I land on all fours as a wolf.

Nielsen, it seems, hesitated when he saw me coming, stopping his attack to watch my transformation into a wolf. Now his gaze rests on me, flashing me a wolfish smile, as if proud of himself for finally forcing me to shift.

I don't hesitate; instinct takes over and my wolf's

body leaps for him, clamping my jaws shut around his neck and wrenching viciously with a savage snarl.

He doesn't have time to react before he's dead. When I release him, his body crumples to a bloody pile of fur at my feet, and I pull in a deep, satisfying breath, filling my lungs to let out a wild howl. A chorus of wolf voices rise up with me, and I hold the tone until my lungs give out and I have to draw in air.

It's only when I stop I realize I just made a sound without being magically shocked. I try to search my neck for the collar, only to remember I have paws and that will not work. My eyes dart around the circle until I spot it: the wide black collar, ripped in two, on a pile of my shredded clothing.

With renewed joy, I leap into the air and howl again, spurring another chorus from the nearby wolves. My head tips back and my eyes close, filled with the deep satisfaction of finally escaping the hell I've been surviving the past week.

A head bumps against my neck, startling me and cutting off my joyful noise. My senses fill the scent of her, and a deep feeling of peace settles over me. We're finally, *finally*, together. I can't hold her in my arms, but I nuzzle my mate right back, and then immediately start licking her to clean her bloody fur.

"I knew you could do it," Lilliana's voice brushes my mind, and I freeze. She makes the equivalent of a wolfy chuckle and does it again. "Yes, it's me. I just found out this is something I can do. I wanted to talk to you, but it's too fucking cold to shift back right now, so this is the next best thing."

I gather my thoughts and try to think back at her. "It's new, but then again, turning into a furry beast is new for me, too. And, valid point on the cold. I'm just glad you're okay."

"I'm just relieved to see you whole. I haven't even wrapped my head around you being a wolf yet," she chuckles again, her hot tongue licking along my jaw. "I heard some terrible things about Nielsen. I was really worried about you."

A hum of pleasure rumbles in my chest. "Turns out being a wolf has lots of perks. Nice winter coat, and some high-intensity healing."

The rest of the guys find us, and we surround Lily in a tight circle, all showering her with affection to show our concern. She spins slowly, doling out kisses and nuzzles to each of us.

And most surprisingly, it all feels… natural. I've never been the type to share—I've always wanted my partner as consumed by me as I am by them—but there's not a single flicker of jealously when I watch her share affection with the three younger men. Well, wolves.

It takes a while, but eventually we move inside the house and someone fetches us clothes to pull on. They're not the best fit for anyone, but at least they're warm and cover our bodies.

Because Lily's covered with gore, she darts upstairs,

and showers before getting dressed. I admire her gall; the house is nice, but it holds an aura of malice that keeps me on edge. I have no interest in staying here any longer than necessary, and fortunately, our mate cleans up quickly so we can leave. I take advantage of the relative privacy inside the house to pull her into my arms and hold her tightly, relishing the feeling of her body against mine. Before releasing her to the rest of her mates, I stroke my thumb along her throat and claim a deep, greedy kiss. She bows backward in my arms, arms rising to twine around my neck and toy with my hair, oblivious to the audience of three.

I could stay like this for hours, but Lily cups my cheeks and withdraws, pressing one more soft kiss to my lips before promising, "later," in a breathy whisper. My blood surges, but I kiss her forehead and allow her to reconnect with her other mates. Once again, the sight of her with them doesn't spur the jealousy I experienced just weeks ago. Now we're all one, and what makes her happy makes me happy. Whatever she needs.

When we've all shared a moment and finally step back outside, a lot of the crowd has dispersed. The remaining individuals are in human form, and apparently waiting to report.

"We're sweeping through the... facility underground, alpha," a man with black cargo pants and a stern expression advises. "So far, we've released a few individuals. The people who worked here volunteered to assist us, so it's going quickly. I do need to advise," his sharp gaze darts to my face before returning to Lilliana's, "we found the witch, and she's... gone."

"Oh no," Lilliana sounds genuinely upset, and turns her sad green eyes to me. "Derrek, I'm so sorry. I know we had our issues, but she was your cousin, and she did help us-"

"Don't worry about it," I squeeze her against me and reassure her. "She was trying to kill me, to take my power, when these three came in and saved me. And some girl, I think she's in one of my classes. Where is she, by the way? Is she okay?"

I redirect my gaze to Milo, who nods. "Yeah, Amber's fine. She woke up not long after we came outside. Bitched about it being cold, then said she felt weird and shifted back into a wolf."

"I should talk to her. I think I know why she feels weird."

The three guys exchange a look.

The tall blond one, Landon, speaks up. "Why do you think that is?"

"Azalea had finished the ritual. All she had left to do was kill me, and all the magic in my blood would join hers. Since your friend spilled Azalea's blood instead, I suspect she may have gained Azalea's powers."

"No way." Shock flits across Jared's dark face. "I didn't know that was even possible. Can anyone just steal a witch's powers like that, if they do the ritual?"

"Not exactly. It's... well, it's kind of complicated. But basically, Amber must have some witch blood, otherwise it wouldn't have worked. And it works on witches and warlocks."

Landon swats Jared on the arm, hard. "See? I told you they weren't all called witches. The guys are warlocks."

Jared ducks his head guiltily.

I snort. "Who told you we're called witches? That'd be like calling the three of you girls."

"I dunno. I just heard it somewhere." He shoves his hands into his pockets and kicks the pavement with his borrowed boot.

"Anyway," Lilliana draws us back to the issues at hand. "Apparently Azalea's death is not a surprise, *or* something to mourn. Is there anything else?"

The older man shakes his head. "You can head out, alpha. We'll wrap things here and get everyone on their way home if they haven't left already."

"Thank you, Richardson."

He nods, then spins on his heel and heads back toward the dungeon entrance.

Lilliana smiles widely at the four of us. "Well guys, should we head home?"

As if by some undisclosed plan, the others allow me to claim the third row seat with Lilliana, who immediately curls into my side. She falls asleep quickly, so I settle in for the long ride and close my eyes, too. With my arm wrapped tightly around her, I feel as if I can finally rest.

But sleep doesn't come. Despite spending the previous night practicing spells, my body is anything but overcome with exhaustion. In fact, I almost feel lit up with racing energy rippling over my skin.

Not to mention lust.

I know my brain should run over the multitude of revelations I've had recently, but the only thing I seem to focus on is her cherry vanilla scent and what it does to my body. Every tiny movement she makes is a tease to my newly upgraded senses, despite the completely unsexy situation we find ourselves in right now. My fingers toy with a strand of her curly hair, and I try to focus on making mental lists of things I need to take care of. There's certainly lots to deal with, after everything that's happened.

But my thoughts invariably return to the details of the dream that seems to be burned into my brain. Instead of trying to fight it, I decide to lean into this train of thought and maybe work my way through it instead.

I wonder when I might get her alone, claim a night of her time to myself. I'm sure many interesting scenarios are bound to crop up, suddenly being part of a five-some. But I want it to just be us two for the first time I'm with her. I need to lavish her with the sort of patient attention I'm fairly certain eighteen-year-old boys are unprepared to muster. I'll take all the time I need to convince myself that it's truly real, that the dungeon is a distant nightmare and this beautiful woman in my arms is the truth.

Once I let my thoughts wander, the rest of the ride goes surprisingly fast. Almost before I realize it, we're passing the wooden sign proclaiming we're now in Smoky Falls, and I draw in a deep, grateful breath, knowing that she's safe now, protected, on pack lands.

I don't plan to wake her until we reach Harridan house, but Lilliana stirs the second we cross the boundary, and after a quick glance outside, says to the driver, "Maxwell, please take us to Derrek's apartment."

Dutifully, the driver turns right instead of continuing down Main. I don't even have a moment to wonder how he knows my address before Lilliana's delicate hand settles on my thigh and squeezes.

My gaze darts to her curiously, and she lifts her lips to my ear, whispering, "I need to have you to myself tonight." Her warm breath rustles my hair, tickling my ear and sending a jolt of adrenaline through my system. I am definitely *fully* awake now.

Perhaps it wouldn't be as difficult to get time alone with her as I'd imagined.

If the others dislike the idea, they don't let it show. The car remains silent, and Lilliana's hand continues to stroke my thigh.

I clench my jaw and swallow with difficulty, then claim her hand and thread my fingers through hers, tracing tiny circles on the back with my thumb.

As tempting as it is to cop a feel, I'm determined not to act like a complete animal. She's giving me this night to make her mine, and I already have a plan. There may be several enthusiastic young men to choose from, but it'll be my pleasure to show her what a man with my experience can give her.

Time slows to a crawl as I bide my time, waiting until the moment we close the door between us and the rest of her mates, and I finally have her completely to myself.

Chapter Thirty-Eight

DERREK

~

We only make it halfway up the stairs before my resolve crumbles. I need to feel her against me, to convince myself that this is real. We're actually here and I'm not just lost in another dream. I pull Lilliana's face to me and her expression is openly lustful, lips parted to release breathy little puffs of air.

My heart beats so hard in my chest it feels as though she ought to see it. I allow my palms to skim her sides gently, brushing the sides of her breasts with my thumbs as they make their way down to her hips. My fingers sink into her soft curves, and I don't have to push hard to get her up against the wall; she melts against me, her hands reaching up to pull my face close, to claim my mouth with hers once again.

The heat between us is blazing, like we're made of living fire. And to finally be here; with nothing to keep us apart aside from sheer will and a few scraps of clothing… the pressure has built so high I don't know if I'll survive long enough to see it through.

Reluctantly I draw back, and then can't help but chuckle at the sound of irritation she makes and the way her lips chase mine.

"Come on, beautiful. I wouldn't want one of my neighbors to come down and catch their alpha making out in the stairwell."

She snorts. "Well, I doubt they'd complain to me about it if they did!"

I grasp her hand and tug gently, leading her up the remaining stairs to my apartment.

Then I remember… shit.

"Ah, slight problem," I confess, supremely embarrassed.

"What's that?"

"I don't have my keys. I left them in my car at the dance. Oh god, I hope it's still there. Is crime a problem in your city, Ms. Mayor? Should I worry about my ride being stolen?"

She rolls her eyes, but smirks. "Why don't you look under the doormat?"

I raise an eyebrow at her, but her smirk only widens. I glance down and spot a small bulge in the middle of the mat.

Wonders never cease around here. "Okay, how did this happen? And where's my car?"

"Your car is in your parking spot outside, and what did you expect, that we'd let Nielsen cart you off and just leave you illegally parked in front of the community center? We're not animals. Besides, they would have given you like a million parking tickets by now."

Sliding the key into the lock, I turn it and realize it's too late to wonder if I'd cleaned up before I left... however many weeks ago that was.

But when we walk in, the apartment is pristine. Like, *sparkling* clean. I may be neat, but I'm not *that* neat.

Lilliana looks around, then shrugs. "Mrs. Dowling wanted to make sure your plants weren't neglected. I guess she felt the need to clean while she was here."

I raise an eyebrow at her. "I don't have any plants."

"Now it all makes sense," she deadpans.

"Come here, you," I growl, kicking the door closed, tossing my keys on the table, and pulling her to me again.

She releases a surprised laugh before my mouth is on hers, and now we don't have to worry about a hapless neighbor wondering by.

We are well and truly alone.

Finally allowing my body to do as it pleases, my hands run over her form, cupping her breasts, squeezing her nipples through the fabric.

Without breaking our kiss, she moans throatily in response to my touch, and it only drives me more wild.

Lilliana's fingers tangle in my hair, tugging me to her, forcing me to bend and release her breasts. My hands instead find better purchase on her perfect ass, and I squeeze, pulling her hips toward mine.

Then she moans again, and even that contact is not nearly enough.

My hands slide between her thighs and I lift her, pulling her against my body to settle her legs around my hips. Now I'm able to kiss along her jaw and down her porcelain throat, running my tongue across her sweet and salty skin.

With her head thrown back to allow me better access, her little hands tighten on my hair, fisting and tugging it, pulling my head toward her.

I have to get control of myself, or I'm going to put in an embarrassingly short performance after all this buildup.

"Derrek…" her breathy moan is like a lit match to my parched tinder. Lilliana fills my senses to the brim - her wild and sweet fragrance, her taste on my tongue, her soft curves molding perfectly to the hard edges of my body..

I manage a few steps—just to get us into the living room—before I set her gently back on the floor, savoring every inch of her as she squeezes against me. Claiming her mouth once more, I quickly realize my mate has already taken over and I'm no longer the one in charge.

With a throaty growl, she tears at my borrowed shirt, yanking at the buttons instead of taking the time to undo them. I decide to help her out and grab the collar at the back of my neck, tugging the whole thing off in one swift move.

When I discard the piece of clothing between us, Lilliana rests her splayed hands against my chest and smooths her palms over my lean muscles. They dance and flex under her touch, reacting to the sensation of electricity shooting across my skin. My hands tremble, but I don't reach for her; I know she wants to take her time.

Just like I plan to do when it's my turn.

She holds my gaze with her gleaming emerald eyes, her hands wandering lower down my abdomen until they find the fastening on my borrowed cargo pants. The anticipation is killing me; if I thought we were a blazing fire before, this is more like a solar flare. Every inch of my body is alight with heat and practically screaming for her touch. Then, with a seductive smirk, she pops the button and slowly slides the zipper open. With no further restraint, my erection bobs between us.

Tremors run through my body, but I continue to resist the urge to throw her on the couch and pillage her in every way I know how. The tension of waiting, of willing her hands to drop lower, is an excitement I can't remember ever having for another woman. Because obviously I didn't know it before, I wasn't aware; but somehow my subconscious knew there was only this woman, this *incredible* woman, who was my mate. And no one else even came close.

My gaze is locked on her face, and I suck in a breath when Lilliana's tongue darts out, sweeping a path along her lower lip as she eyes my erection. Without a word she drops to her knees, and I draw in a shaking breath in anticipation of her next move so strong it's almost painful.

As soon as her fingertips meet the pulsing skin of my erection, it throbs noticeably in response. Evidently pleased with herself for drawing a reaction from me so easily, she grins wickedly and wraps her fingers around my girth, squeezing and stroking me in a divinely torturous way. I watch her every move, drinking in the sight of the woman I've loved for much longer than I realized.

Watching my reaction, she runs her tongue over her lower lip again and then across the tip of my head. I try to maintain eye contact, but her next move is to suck my hard length into her warm, wet mouth and my eyes roll back in my head, an appreciative groan escaping my lips. I steady myself with one hand on her shoulder and the other twisted in her soft, wild hair. This dynamic, where she does what she wants to me, is not my typical style. But there's something even more erotic knowing that I didn't even have to ask; she wanted me like this, and she made it happen. I resist the urge to rock my hips, not wanting to give her more than she can handle, letting her maintain control.

But my tenuous thread of restraint snaps when she hums, the vibration increasing the sensations by tenfold. My hips jerk forward, seeking more from her incredible mouth.

Bracing herself against my thighs, Lilliana pushes

forward and swallows me whole, sliding me down the back of her throat with ease. A curse escapes my lips as a guttural groan. Unable to hold back any longer, I tighten my fingers in her hair and hold her in place so I can slide in and out of her hot little mouth.

When I pull back slowly, I instruct, "Drag your tongue along the underside." She immediately flattens her tongue and curls the tip up, licking my shaft as it moves. "Yes, just like that," I praise in a throaty growl. "Good girl." I hold her hair back so I can watch myself slide in and out of her perfect lips.

She pulls back after a few strokes and I release her, a smile spreading across my face when she pauses to give me a devious little smirk. Her hands wrap around my shaft, squeezing and sliding, and with our gazes locked, she swirls her tongue around my bulbous head, making my entire body shudder with pleasure. I feel myself throb in her hands again, the pressure delicious but almost uncomfortable because it's not moving. From the gleam in her beautiful eyes, she clearly knows exactly the power she has over me right now. And she's eating it up.

But now it's time I turn the tables and torture *her* sinful little body with pleasure.

When I pull away, her devious expression drops to shock, then confusion. But when I kick off my shoes and step out of my pants, she's grinning again. I help her to her feet and our lips collide in a kiss filled with desperate, aching need for each other. Being more patient than my feisty little mate, I take the time to unbutton her shirt and manage it successfully with no need to break our kiss. The benefit of unexpectedly shifting into a wolf and having to borrow clothes means we don't have to deal with pesky things like underwear, so once her pants are gone, she's as naked as I am.

Knowing she's shared some entry-level intimacy with the three younger men, I decide to use a few moves I'm positive they haven't tried yet.

There are benefits to having an older man as a mate, which my little minx is about to learn.

Sinking to the floor, I brace one of her legs over my shoulder and wrap my arms around her hips. Lilliana gasps at the surprise, but it changes to a throaty moan when I run my tongue across her. She digs her hands into my hair, clutching my head and encouraging me deeper.

I happily comply, lapping at her molten center and probing every corner my tongue can reach. Holding her at the hip to steady her with one hand, I slip the other between her thighs and run my fingertips through her wetness. When they're suitably slick, I plunge them slowly into her core and circle her throbbing bud with my tongue.

Finally, I can devour her with abandon, truly live the fantasy that's plagued far too many of my nights. Everything about her is even better than I imagined, from her taste to her scent to the way she feels beneath my fingertips. I'll never be able to get enough of this woman.

Her fingers twist and tug at my hair as her breathy

moans turn deeper, filling my otherwise quiet apartment with the sounds of her pleasure. She grinds her pelvis against my face in a silent plea for more. Pressing my fingers deeper, I curl them to hit that elusive sweet spot. Her thigh trembles against my cheek, encouraging me to continue.

"Oh Derrek… more…" No longer commanding, her desperate plea is even more fuel to my fire.

I thrust my fingers into my mate with more force, and her moans rise in pitch and frequency, increasing with the movement of my hand.

With a moaned curse she shatters over me, the sounds of her release the sweetest reward for my effort. I hold her tightly to me and refuse to stop, savoring every shudder of pleasure I wring from her body.

When I can tell she's come down from her high, I slow my ministrations and press a gentle kiss to her tender lips. Then I hold her tightly, waiting for her to be strong enough to reclaim the use of her legs.

So we can move on to round two.

LILLIANA

I take a few minutes to come down from this floating bliss, and Derrek supports my body while he waits.

Every time I've shattered in pleasure with one—or more —of my mates, it feels like I've never reached such heights before. And here again, the incredible power of his touch on my body feels even stronger than the last. Quickly, I find myself both satiated and yet starving for more of my fourth and final mate.

He disentangles us and stands, and when we kiss, I taste myself on his lips. That erotic flavor reminds me viscerally of my experience just a few moments ago, and it's almost like a second rush of pleasure.

Angling for something I want to try again, I push Derrek backwards until his calves make contact with the couch, then give him a playful shove. His eyes widen as he lands on the cushion and I climb into his lap, straddling his thighs. Reaching between us, I guide his rigid length into my sensitive core and ease down on him.

I savor every inch as he fills me, stretching my insides in a way that sends butterflies into my stomach. The hum he releases encourages me to keep moving, so I ride him, slowly moving up and down.

"I feel like I've waited a lifetime for this," Derrek groans, his eyes watching me hungrily. He catches my waist between his hands, slowing my bouncing. "Roll your hips, baby."

When he's buried in me to the hilt, I try to undulate my hips instead of bouncing on my knees. A gasp slips from my lips, utter surprise at the unfamiliar sensation of my clit grinding against his hard pelvis and the soaring pleasure that tears through me.

Trying it a few more times, his hands encourage my motions and I catch a rhythm, bringing our pleasure to new heights. Instead of an athletic, breath-taking event, this kind of love-making is a slow, sensual build up of sensation. Derrek's hands rove over my body, gripping my hips before cupping my breasts, rolling my nipples between his fingers. Our lips find each other like magnets, and now our kisses are slow and sensual as well. My tongue glides against his, then I nibble at his lush bottom lip before planting kisses down his neck and shoulder.

Derrek returns one hand to my hips, coaxing my body to move the way he wants. The other slips further between us, seeking entry. I angle slightly away and the pad of his thumb presses on my clit, slippery with the evidence of our desire for each other. He rubs firm circles while still pushing and pulling my hips in the deep rolling movement that's igniting an entirely novel sensation inside me, triggering that coil of pressure deep in my belly.

My movements grow faster, more urgent, as every nerve ending feels like it's on fire. I can't tell if I need more or less of all these sensations. My thigh muscles burn from the effort.

Then he begins to move with me, his hips rising and meeting mine. Not in an impact, but more like a continuation of the movement, creating even more sensation.

One hand remains busy, but the other rises to cup my cheek.

Derrek's gaze locks on mine, a depthless sincerity traveling between us.

I can't look away; all of my focus concentrates on his beloved face. The all-consuming connection between us finally pushes me over the edge, sending me tumbling into a field of stars as my body shudders and clenches around him.

Derrek's release comes seconds after mine, and as one, our motions gradually slow until we're stopped, chests heaving and bodies slick with sweat.

He still hasn't released my face, and now pulls me closer to him.

"I love you, Lilliana Harridan." The words spill from his lips and unlock the last remaining wall between us.

A tear rolls down my cheek, and I gaze just as intently back at him when I answer, "I love you too, Derrek Garrow. I always have."

His thumb swipes my tear away, and a coy smile curls his lips. "What if I told you to call me Leaf?"

I lean in and press a gentle kiss to his lips. "I'll call you whatever you want, now that I get to call you mine."

Chapter Thirty-Nine

LILLIANA

~

I shouldn't be surprised that it's midday when I'm finally roused from the deep, peaceful slumber. We didn't get back to Smoky Falls until the time some people rise to hit the gym, and then our activities once we got here... well, we were up quite a bit longer.

I'm draped across Derrek's body, my head cradled against his shoulder. He continues to breathe deeply, obviously still asleep, and I don't want to disturb him, so I try not to move. His heart beats steadily in his chest, and I listen to it, comforted by the slow and forceful thumps in my ear.

Once we cooled down from our exertions on the couch, the celebration of our reunion continued into the bedroom. And when we finally finished making love, Derrek revealed he had another surprise in store for me.

I didn't know what to expect, but I found myself lovingly bathed and caressed, then fed and cuddled until I drifted off. The way he tended to me was almost uncomfortable in his deference, as if I were some kind of deity rather than a girl who grew up on the streets.

It brought back the memories of those years without a home, and how I always felt looked after when Derrek was around. Obviously, our relationship has changed dramatically since then, but the deep surety that I'm protected and cared for is exactly the same. Well, perhaps not exactly; there's a new richness to the feeling that's tied into our new status as mates.

Four fated mates. I thought I'd wrapped my head around three, that I was coming to terms with the idea, and now there's four. I could let myself get hung up on overthinking it, spinning scenarios in my head, but I choose not to. My *heart* knows it's right. There's no more doubt, no more confusion. It's as if I've finally clicked the last piece into the puzzle and I can see the complete picture now.

And this entire time he was the heir to Pack Montrose, and a wolf-warlock hybrid. It's a lot to wrap my head around, how this knowledge colors the way I view so many things in the past. My mind wanders over the events of last night, and suddenly I freeze, my breath stilled in my lungs.

Nielsen said there was never a curse on the Harridans preventing us from being away from Smoky Falls, that my ancestors made it up to keep us apart.

But the curse that limits us from shifting outside of the midnight hour is real, according to him.

So is that curse now broken, since I've beaten the Montrose alpha?

Or do the Montrose wolves now fall under the curse, since they're part of my pack?

How exactly are we supposed to break that curse?

"Will you stop worrying for five minutes? Your thoughts are extremely loud." Derrek's voice startles me, and I jerk upright when I realize it didn't come from his mouth.

I study his face carefully, trying to determine if I'm losing my mind. His eyes remain closed, his breaths even, but a tiny smile curls the corner of his lips.

Feeling crazy, I think at him, "You can hear me?"

Without missing a beat he replies silently, "You're practically shouting, it's impossible *not* to hear, baby."

I scrunch my brows and sit all the way up. "I don't understand. Only alphas can hear unless you speak directly at them. Or rather, *think* directly at them."

The smile widens, spreading across his face, and he answers my thoughts again. "So the logical conclusion would be…"

This time, I answer him aloud. "That you're an alpha?"

"Bingo." Derrek replies in kind, his eyes still closed.

"But how? We haven't officially mated. There's a

whole ceremony with the lunar eclipse and god only knows what else I have to do to make it official."

Apparently, that question is enough to make him sit up and look at me.

It's almost a complete distraction; his messy blond curls, his face adorably sleepy. But his emerald eyes are bright, practically glowing, as he meets my gaze. "I'm not alpha through you, Lilliana. I'm alpha of Pack Montrose."

"What? No, that's impossible. Nielsen said-"

He chokes a laugh. "After all that, you'd really believe anything he told you?"

"But he said if he defeated me, he'd become the alpha of Smoky Falls."

Derrek shrugs. "Well, that part's true."

"But me defeating *him* doesn't make me the alpha of Montrose?"

"Nope. He has something you don't, or should I say, he *had*."

"What's that?"

"An heir. It doesn't matter that you defeated him; since you weren't part of the pack, alpha status passed to me."

"But you don't have the alpha voice when you think at me. Nielsen did."

He shrugs again. "I can't answer to that part. Maybe it's just because we're mates?"

"That doesn't make any sense at all."

"Doesn't it?" He scoots over and wraps an arm around

my shoulders, providing a warm surface to lean against. "The hierarchy in wolf packs is a funny thing. Succession is only determined by a challenge when the challenger is part of the pack. If they're not, it only works if the current alpha has no heir. Otherwise, it doesn't matter if the opponent wins; the position of alpha passes to their offspring."

I can't help feeling disgruntled. "So why would they even challenge at all?"

"Well, for starters, a wolf who's not part of a pack rolling in to challenge for alpha is pretty rare. In that *extremely* unlikely event, they wouldn't challenge an older alpha who has a healthy adult heir ready to take his place. But if they challenge a younger alpha, perhaps one who has younger children, and win, their next step would be to eliminate the offspring. Then the position is free to claim."

My mind spins. Every time I think I'm getting the hang of all of this, it gets vastly more complex. I'm still trying to make sense of what Nielsen said, to determine if he was lying.

"But Dom is still alive. Wouldn't it pass to him if Nielsen beat me, then?"

"No, because Dom isn't your heir. He can never be alpha again; he's been passed over now that you've claimed it."

"So if Nielsen had lived…"

"I would have still become alpha."

"And he could never have claimed it again."

"Correct. Now there might have been issues if I

hadn't shifted, but honestly, I can't help but wonder if his defeat is what finally enabled me to shift."

I shove him playfully with my shoulder. "Are you sure it's not because you were trying to save my life?"

"That too." He presses a kiss to the side of my head, and I sigh.

This is way too much for first thing in the morning. Speaking of…

"Do you know what time it is?"

"Why?"

"It's got to be late. We should probably get back to Harridan House. I'm sure there's all sorts of stuff I should be doing."

"Mmm, I think after everything that's happened, no one would begrudge you a day off."

"Alphas don't get days off," I grumble. "There's always stuff to take care of."

"I'm sure your uncle and your beta can manage for a couple more hours. Our phones aren't buzzing, at any rate. I take that as a sign we have some time for other, more *important* things." His tone turns suggestive, and my belly flutters in response.

"Time for what?" I ask breathlessly, my heart rate rising.

"Breakfast, of course. What did you think I meant?" He chuckles, knowing full well what he did, and slides to the edge of the bed. "Do you want coffee?"

∿

Fortunately, Mrs. Dowling had stocked Derrek's cupboards and fridge with fresh supplies, so he's able to cook up a veritable feast. I didn't realize it before he set the heaping plate in front of me, but I'm absolutely starving. I devour every bite of eggs, bacon, and toast, and even put away three cups of coffee.

Naturally, I checked in with Roxanne and the guys, and they all assured me everything was fine and to take my time.

When Derrek offers to tumble me back into bed, I'm sorely tempted. But the energy zipping through my veins won't let me tune out again, so I insist it's time to get dressed and head home. I can tap into the color map of the pack and see that there're no points of concern, and yet an instinct stemming from the core of my being insists I get back to Harridan House and just verify for myself.

In yet another surprise that shouldn't be a surprise, Mrs. Dowling cleared space in Derrek's closet and left me a mini wardrobe, anticipating my needs well before I thought about it. We tug on clothes and steal a few more kisses before clambering into his car and heading up the hill.

The atmosphere in Harridan House is calm, and I'm not surprised at all when Milo, Jared, and Landon greet Derrek with handshakes and half hugs like a brother. Whatever their differences in the past, we're all family now. I'm just relieved to know there isn't any lingering resentment.

Roxanne greets me just as warmly, wearing a thick

sweater over her khakis with a pair of UGG boots instead of the ubiquitous flats. When I raise an eyebrow at her, she tosses her braids and laughs. "What? A girl can't wear the same thing all the time."

We settle in the library with a tray of refreshments, where it's more comfortable to chat. I relay what Nielsen revealed to me regarding the curse, and I'm pleased to see that they're all as shocked as I am. This, at least, isn't a secret that was kept specifically from me.

"I should have known there was something strange, though," I add, sipping my tea. "The diaries of past alphas go back to the founding of Smoky Falls—literally hundreds of years ago—but the *only* one missing is the last two years of the alpha who died from the 'curse'."

"That's wild, though," Jared shakes his head. "That they would make up that story and lie to everyone for this long? All those alphas who never left the territory, and then your mom who ran away…"

"Yeah, I wonder if she would have run away if she knew the curse wasn't real. That part of it, at least. If she felt she had more time to solve the problems between the two packs." I've accepted that she left to raise a daughter untainted by the biases of this pack, but it still hurts to think of what I grew up without. How different would my life have been here? If Mom became alpha, and I had three dads to protect me? If she never suffered the pain of rejecting two of her mates, and never ended up in a car wreck that left me an orphan?

As if he could read my uneasy thoughts on my face,

Landon reaches over and threads his fingers through mine. "You'll drive yourself crazy doing that, Lily. We can't change the past."

"I know." Heaving a sigh, I squeeze his hand gently and refocus. "So, now that Derrek is the alpha of Montrose *and* my mate, does that present any additional problems?"

Roxanne shakes her head. "No, according to Mr. Carson, it should do as we hope and allow us to unite the packs during the lunar eclipse. There's no way to be sure, though."

"Do we have anything to worry about with members of Montrose? There were a lot of self-proclaimed Nielsen loyalists there last night. I refuse to believe all those people worked in that dungeon purely because of compulsion."

Milo clears his throat. "Actually, you'd be surprised at how many were grateful you defeated him. Apparently, while we were inside the house getting changed, dozens of them took it upon themselves to ask when they could move to Smoky Falls. They wrote up a list."

"We have a different list from Billy. He wrote down the worst offenders, people who seemed to enjoy doling out Nielsen's punishments, for us to monitor."

Derrek's been quiet, but he agrees in a low voice, "There were some obvious ones. I'll go over that list, if you like. Make sure Erica is on it."

Tension thickens in the air while we all grapple with the meaning behind his words. I don't know if asking him about it is the right thing to do, or if waiting until he brings it up would be better. Or maybe he never wants to talk about it.

"Okay, thank you," Roxanne replies softly, saving the rest of us from the indecision. "At any rate, no one is moving anytime soon. Of course, anyone from Montrose is welcome to leave if they want, but they aren't part of Smoky Falls yet. We'll have to find some way to vet them before the eclipse, so we have a plan."

"I trust you to handle it, but let me know if you need my help," I offer. "For now, I feel like we're all on hold until the ceremony, so let's try to get things back to normal and prepare for the last step of my ascension."

It doesn't seem possible, but things actually go back to normal pretty quickly. The boys and I return to classes, and find ourselves loaded down with make-up work for the week we missed.

Derrek resumes teaching, but they move Jared and me to a different Lit professor to prevent any perception of favoritism.

It's not a problem, though. Derrek and I find plenty of time to hook up in his office.

Roxanne is planning to get a suite renovated for each of the guys, including Derrek. He'll keep his apartment until his room is ready, and the rest of the guys plan to move into Harridan House immediately following the ceremony regardless of the status of their rooms. They practically live here anyway, so it makes no difference. At this point, they've yet to sleep anywhere but in bed with me, anyway.

And for a few weeks, everything is quiet. Derrek checks in with Montrose; he's made Billy his beta to keep an eye on things while we're sorting out logistics. In the end, most of Pack Montrose don't actually want to move. Several who'd written their names on the list rescinded their requests, realizing that life was very different with Nielsen gone. Anyone on the 'willing sadist' list—as Billy put it—was immediately banished from Montrose and Smoky Falls, and the weeks pass quietly in both towns.

As the day of the eclipse approaches, I'm once again shocked to find out the ceremony for claiming my mates is hardly anything special.

"So I literally just have to stand under the eclipse and claim them?" I scrunch my brows at Roxanne, who smiles placidly back at me from behind her desk.

"That's correct. You claim your position as alpha, and then you claim your mates, listing off their names. It's done with the entire pack to witness, and that completes the ritual. Then we all go for a run like any other night."

"And that'll break the midnight curse?"

"We can only guess at that, Lily. But if the original curse was part of the spell splitting the packs, reuniting them should lift it. We won't know until we try."

We sit in silence for a moment, pondering.

"I wonder what it'll be like if it works. You know what I mean? If everyone can just… shift whenever they want? Or when they get super upset and lose control?"

Roxanne grins back at me. "I'm sure there'll be a learning curve. Folks will have to manage their own reactions, learn how to stop their wolf from clawing its way out without their permission. I, however, am looking forward to the challenge. The big question is: will you still do midnight runs?"

"I hadn't thought about it," I admit. "If everyone has the freedom to shift whenever they want, there's no need to meet up every night for it. It'll be a relief to go to bed at a decent hour. But those runs are also my favorite part of being a wolf. It's almost as if that curse forces us to be closer as a pack. You see what's happened at Montrose? they're barely a pack at all."

"True, but I'm not entirely sure that has to do with their habits as much as their leadership."

"That's fair," I agree, but a melancholy feeling blossoms in my chest. "I know it'll be good, but I can't help feeling like it'll hurt our closeness somehow."

There's a long pause while Roxanne considers. "I'm sure we'll come up with a solution to ensure we don't lose it. Our pack is closer than ever since your return, Lily. You being here, just being the person you are, is what the pack needs above everything else. We can face anything else as it comes."

"You're right," I agree. "What matters most is that we're finally all together."

∾

I stand in the dark clearing with all four of my mates around me. The air is unseasonably warm tonight, compared to the last several weeks. Almost as if mother nature knows.

The pack encircles us, murmuring and watching the sky, waiting.

It's only eight thirty, but it might as well be midnight. The moon will be fully eclipsed in just a few minutes, and we're all watching the circular shadow creep across its surface. As more of the glowing moon is gobbled up by shadow, it's turned orange instead of stark white. With each passing second, the color deepens, and I squeeze Landon's and Jared's hands while we wait.

I had no idea lunar eclipses took so long. Solar eclipses are over in like twenty minutes, and we've been out here almost an hour already.

Roxanne told me I have to make the announcement when the eclipse is at its peak. Tonight is a total eclipse, so we'll wait until the moon is completely blacked out.

Then it's game on.

Of course we're hoping the curse will lift so we can go for our pack run immediately. It'd be pretty shitty if everyone has to leave and come back in a few hours.

Roxanne arranged for Harridan House to host a celebration in honor of completing this process and truly becoming alpha of Smoky Falls, so our worst-case scenario is that we'll have the party before the run instead of after.

I didn't sleep a wink last night, so I'm really hoping

this'll all wrap up neatly and I'll be in bed well before midnight.

My eyes remain locked on the creeping shadow, so close to the other side there's just a thin fingernail of red light remaining. Breath stills in my lungs and my muscles freeze. I'm afraid to blink, as if I'll miss my chance in the millisecond it takes my lids to close and reopen.

When the last sliver of light disappears, I can practically hear the pack suck in a collective breath and wait, their eyes dropping to me.

It's incredibly dark now. The sky is clear, so the stars are out, but without the moon, it's virtually pitch black in every direction.

Jared and Landon squeeze my hands, and I feel two more warm, solid hands land on my shoulders. I know it's Derrek and Milo without question. Something about having all four of my mates touching me at the same time sends a flood of security and strength washing through me as if we truly become one.

Not being able to see anyone almost makes what I have to do easier.

Delving into my power as alpha, I pull up the color map and feel my pack instead of meeting their eyes. When I speak, my body settles into the double-timbre of the alpha command without conscious effort.

"I am Lilliana Harridan, direct descendant of the first Harridan alpha who gave her blood to create the Smoky Falls pack. Tonight, before all of those in attendance, I claim my position as true alpha, a responsibility I will bear until I am gone from this earth." I pause to breathe, and my voice seems to echo in the absolute stillness of the clearing.

"Tonight, I claim my fated mates for all time. From now until our death, we will be alphas of Smoky Falls, equally responsible for the safety and well-being of every member of this pack."

I have no way to see them, but in my mind I picture each of their faces as I list them.

"Milo Vernice, I claim you as my mate. Landon Crews, I claim you as my mate. Jared Miller, I claim you as my mate." I mentally stumble over the next part, but manage to get it out the way he asked. "Leaf Derrek Garrow, I claim you as my mate. As you are the alpha of Pack Montrose, your pack has become part of the Smoky Falls pack, and due our protection and loyalty."

Just as I finish the last words of my speech, a bubbly sensation runs over my skin, as if I'd jumped in a glass of alka-seltzer. At first I think my eyes are playing tricks on me, but it only takes a few seconds to realize what I'm seeing is true: a glowing vapor rises from our bodies, pale blue and wispy. And not just me and my mates, but every member of the surrounding pack. The collective glow is so bright I can make out the faces of people in the crowd, and every single one of them is beaming in my direction.

The fizzy sensation dissipates, and I know instinctually that it was the curse dissolving into the ether. Heart leaping with joy, I'm about to announce the run when a familiar voice interrupts.

"If I may," Dom starts, "I would like to share my own joyful news with the pack."

I smile widely, even though I know he can't see it. "Of course, uncle."

He clears his throat. "I, Dominic Harridan, have asked Roxanne Penhart to be my mate, and she has accepted."

Before he even gets the last few words out, a raucous cheer rises from the crowd. Even though he struggled to keep up with his alpha duties, the pack still cares deeply about him.

A sudden red glow appears overhead, making the clearing appear like a giant darkroom for developing film. I watch the red sliver of moon slowly grow while I wait for the whoops of celebration to quiet down. I have no desire to cut them off; we're long overdue for celebration.

When it's finally quiet enough for them to hear me, I raise my voice once more and shout, "Now who's ready to run?"

∼

Derrek

∼

Naturally, Lilliana was right: the joining of our two packs indeed ended the curse that prevented them from shifting at any hour of the day. The subsequent run is absolute mayhem. Of course, the pack remains behind Lilliana and her four newly claimed mates, but the joyful yipping is a constant chorus for the entire circuit.

And then, as soon as we return to the clearing, the howls begin. I admit we probably started it, but in my mind it would be one celebratory howl and then we'd wait for the rest of the pack.

However, the pack clearly has other plans. As they reach the clearing, every wolf howls, and doesn't stop as more arrive. Eventually, we catch on that the plan is to keep howling until every wolf has made it back. The din is wild, but somehow not annoying. It's just pure happiness, and it radiates through my body, filling me up with so much enthusiasm I have to join in. We howl to the slowly returning moon, celebrating many things, but most of all, being alive.

Finally, when the stragglers have all made it back, there's a beat of silence as the pack seems to pull in one giant breath together, waiting. Lilliana tips her head back and howls, and the boys and I join in, followed a beat later by the pack as if they have one voice.

We're a team, the five of us the burning core of the pack. But Lilliana is like the beating heart, her light connecting to us and refracting out to the thousands that are now ours to protect.

Suddenly, I feel it. Or rather, I feel *them*. The pack, the people all around us, like a living, glowing organism that pours its hope and belief into us, buoying our sense of purpose to a height I've never experienced before. They need me, and I live for them. If I concentrate hard enough, I can isolate each individual, but the true glory is in the pack as a whole, their collective energy an incredible, almost overwhelming joy.

And in that moment, I know I've finally made it home.

Epilogue

LILLIANA

~

Surprisingly, the pleasant weather holds, and for a few days it's almost like a second summer. Through an email from the president of Smoky Falls College, my mates and I were all granted a few days reprieve from classes in the wake of our union, so we've taken advantage of the nice weather by exploring the grounds and running as wolves in the middle of the day.

Dom and Roxanne conspired to treat the household staff for their loyalty—and for their work on the massive party the night of the eclipse—and they've set up a giant projector to play a movie on the sprawling lawn outside the greenhouses. The guys and I actually have the house entirely to ourselves for a few hours, and my stomach has been fluttering with anticipation all day about what we might get into.

There's still one thing we haven't done all together yet, and while it's not required by pack traditions, it feels odd that all five of us haven't shared a night. Granted, there are limitations to the bed situation—Mrs. Dowling custom-ordered me a bed big enough to fit all of us, and I swear the poor woman was blushing when I asked for it—because five is just too many for a king bed. To be honest, it was tight with the three guys and me, but we made it work. The last few nights I've been spending alone time with each of them instead.

It's always delicious—my mates are quite insistent on making sure they tend to my needs—but when it comes to my sexual appetite, it feels like we've opened a floodgate that can't be closed again.

A very uncomfortable Mr. Carson explained the reason for this to me, gruffly advising that following the claiming, I'd experience 'a period of intense desire to bond with my mates' and that it was perfectly normal and I shouldn't be embarrassed to ask the household staff for whatever I needed, they were prepared for it. The look on his face said he'd prefer for me to make such requests to anyone but him, but I thanked him anyway. Jared immediately started thinking up crazy sexual things to ask him for just to watch him sweat, but I ruined his day by forbidding him to mistreat Mr. Carson that way.

You'd think I took away his Christmas.

So tonight it's just me and my four mates, and we

decide once more to enjoy the unseasonably warm weather by heading outside for a private nighttime run.

As we wander outside onto the lawn, the moon rises through the trees and beams down on us like a spotlight. Since the eclipse, that glowing orb brings back the memory of the moment following our run when the special traits I have as an alpha spread out and engulfed my mates, making them my equals in the eyes of the pack. It was impossible to describe, but instead of feeling like my powers were watered down and divided, claiming my mates expanded the power, multiplied it, and has made me even closer to every pack member. As if I only had limited capacity before, but now I'm capable of so much more.

We're planning to run on a different trail tonight, one that won't take us near the greenhouses, and I'm already imagining us shifting after our run, racing into the house butt naked and choosing some insane place to consummate this union fully. My stomach wobbles again, with anticipation and no small amount of nerves. I think I managed pretty well with two of them, but I'm not really certain how it works with four men at once.

I'm definitely looking forward to finding out.

We don't make it far out of the house before I realize a large part of the lawn has been transformed. Soft glowing lights hang in thin strands, dangling from the beams of a wide, square structure with no walls. Instead of grass, the space below is covered with thick layers of blankets, and tossed with colorful pillows.

Confused, I turn to my mates. "What—?"

That devious grin spreads across Milo's handsome face. "I was thinking about how much you enjoyed the evening we had after the fall festival, and I thought we could…" His eyes flash, the smirk widening. "Recreate that, but with all of us."

It's not what I had been imagining at all.

It's better. This night with my mates, under the full moon, is exactly what I want right now.

My gaze travels around at my grinning mates, realizing they were all in on this little surprise. Four pairs of hungry eyes watch me expectantly, waiting for my response.

Heat rises immediately in my chest, my belly clenching. I lick my lips. "Quite the little ambush you have here, boys. What would you do if I said no?" I struggle to keep my tone lightly disapproving, enjoying the sudden flash of uncertainty in the wake of their smugness from a moment ago.

Not wanting to torture them for too long, I grin devilishly before looping my arms around Milo's neck and pulling him in for a kiss. His lips part against mine and I plunder his mouth hungrily. My senses fill with the taste of his mouth and his woodsy cedar scent.

Following our run in the woods this afternoon, we donned casual lounge wear; even Milo is in sweatpants, albeit fancy ones. Playfully, I run my fingers under his waistband, then up under his soft cotton shirt, exploring the hot skin of his firm stomach and up to the planes of muscle on his chest. One of his hands tangles in my hair, tugging gently while the other pulls me against his body. I bow backward, the pressure on my scalp ripping a moan from my lips.

Before I get too caught up in just one mate, I slip away and into the arms of my stockier mate, Jared. Hands roving over his muscular arms and across his wide shoulders, I lean in and claim a kiss. The telltale flavor of strawberry candy coats his tongue, and my blood begins to race in earnest. His palms skim over my thin tank and drawstring shorts to caress my curves, leaving a trail of heat in their wake. I need to take my time, ensure each of my delicious mates gets their share of attention, so I ease back and settle my gaze on Derrek.

As soon as I catch his eye, Derrek grabs my bottom and scoops me up. My legs wrap around his waist as our mouths collide, his kiss deep and claiming. There's no denying his growing hardness as he holds me against him, and I press myself against it, anticipation coiling in my belly. A groan vibrates in his chest and I smile to myself around our kisses.

Pulling back, I gaze into his determined emerald eyes and slide a finger across his lips; a promise. Obediently, Derrek lowers my feet to the ground and spins me toward my fourth mate. Landon's dimples briefly appear when he bends down to cradle my face and claim my eyes with his deep, soulful gaze. When our lips meet, it's a gentle kiss that drives me absolutely wild. His citrusy scent sets my heart pounding, and I want to tear his clothes off and claim his body with mine.

Panting, I pull away and take a step toward the love nest to address the four delicious men who are now staring at me like a pack of hungry wolves. I adopt the best sarcastic tone I can muster when my knees are practically shaking with desire for them. "So, are we gonna do this or not?"

A chorus of deep growls are my only response. As one, they step forward and I instinctively stumble back a step, but I'm not fast enough. Landon's long arms reach out and he picks me up, tossing me over his shoulder like a caveman. I let out a shriek of surprise before bursting into laughter.

That was apparently the wrong thing to do, because a firm hand swats me on the butt, and I bite my lip to keep from moaning. I wouldn't have guessed I'd enjoy that, but it makes me squirm in a delicious way.

The anticipation is building rapidly now, and it sends a shiver down my spine. I press my thighs together and try to peek around Landon's side to gauge how far we are from our destination.

Before I can really tell, Landon tugs me from his shoulder and sets me down on the soft blanket floor. In a flash, he turns me roughly away from him and then curls around my body, rubbing himself against me while his lips seek the curve of my neck.

Milo appears and drops to his knees, smirking up at me as his hands skim up my bare thighs and across my hips, tugging the drawstring bow loose. Landon's arms hold me firmly, his teeth gently scraping my earlobe while Milo slides my shorts down and leaves me bare to him. With one touch of his finger, my thighs part auto-matically, and he tugs one leg over his shoulder, then ducks his head to taste me. The air is cool on my exposed skin, but my body feels like an inferno that's only getting hotter. When Milo's tongue lazily sweeps across my sensitive flesh, I draw in a sharp gasp and try to chase the sensation with my hips.

Derrek finds my mouth and kisses me tenderly, before trailing down my chest to draw in one pebbled nipple through the thin fabric of my tank. The myriad of sensations their three hot mouths create are intense, and a desperate, pleading moan escapes me. My hands reach up to lock around Landon's neck just as Jared leans in to tease my mouth with his pillow-soft lips. There's so much to explore, but I have no purchase, no way to chase after the feelings I want. I'm entirely at their mercy.

I turn my head to plead with my tallest mate. "Lift me up. Lift me so that Milo can—"

Landon's large, deft hands drop from my waist and wrap around the backs of my thighs. He lifts me with ease, settling my back is against his chest and leaving my legs dangling off the ground. Milo hums in appreci-ation and buries his face deeper in my core. He makes good use of the improved access, and I nearly jump out of my body when his tongue and fingers go back to work. My legs tremble, and I bury my fingers in his silky hair, pulling him even closer.

Jared reclaims my mouth and Derrek's lips find my other nipple, his fingers working the first with firm twists and tugs. I slide one hand behind my back to find Landon's rock hard length and stroke him, desperate to give back to my mates. He continues nibbling on my neck and shoulder, his breath coming in heavy pants.

Pressure builds low and fast in my stomach, escaping my body in increasingly high-pitched whines that Jared swallows with deepening kisses. The cascade of pleasure erupts so suddenly that I arch back against Landon and cry out my release. My body pulses in the wake, clenching around Milo's fingers while he continues to lap up the rewards of his effort.

Before I even catch my breath, Milo stands and Jared's hand slips between my thighs. Shudders rack my body as he teases me, the sensitivity fading and the desire for more coiling rapidly.

Landon whispers in my ear, his tone gruffer than usual. "Are you doing okay?"

I nod, words momentarily failing me. Jared steps away, his gaze holding mine while he slips his coated fingers into his mouth.

Derrek drops to his knees and starts trailing kisses up my thigh. "Are you ready for more, baby?" he asks me in a throaty growl, his nose moving upward, inhaling my scent. "If you need a break-"

I cut him off, twisting my fingers in his hair. "I'm rea-"

I don't even get the word out before Derrek buries his face between my legs. I gasp with surprise and find the desperate whimpers pouring from my lips again. Milo silences them with his lips, and Jared grabs my free hand, sucking two of my fingers into his mouth with a moan. I gently pull my hand free and slide it down his body, slipping my fingers under the waistband of his pants to wrap around his erection. He's impossibly hard, pure steel cloaked in velvety silk. He groans and I squeeze harder, pumping him to draw more of those delicious sounds from his lips.

My tongue dances with Milo's, our kiss growing deeper. I grow closer to the edge of oblivion again, and I have to rip my head away to unleash the moans of pleasure that pour from deep within my body. Suddenly Landon bites down on my neck with a growl, and I'm sent directly into the stratosphere. Stars burst across my vision. The sound that leaves my throat is utterly inhuman.

I'm so sated that my body's completely limp in Landon's arms, my legs resting on Derek's shoulders. For a moment no one moves. We all simply take a breath together.

Milo's thumb strokes my cheek, his eyes gleaming with adoration. "How do you feel, Lily?"

"Ready to be on the ground," I admit with a laugh. Then more seriously, "ready for more."

"We can wait if you need more time to recover," Jared assures me. "I think Milo has some water and snacks around here somewhere-"

"I said I'm ready for more," I snap, then more gently, "Landon, will you put me down, please?"

"If I let you go, can you stand on your own?" he asks, concern coloring his tone.

That draws a chuckle from me. "Probably not."

"We've got her." Milo and Jared lift me from either side, and Derrek braces my legs while they set my feet gently on the blankets. When I'm sturdy, Derrek steps in and restarts my engine with a toe-curling kiss.

Landon stretches out shirtless on the blankets and props his head on a pillow, dark eyes devouring me from below.

On wobbly knees, I lower myself and nearly collapse beside him. My hungry fingers wander over his lean build, teasing him through his pants then tugging at the waistband. Taking the hint, Landon lifts his hips and tugs them off, his soulful eyes locked on me.

Wrapping my fingers around his length, I lick my lips then pull him into my mouth until I can't take any more. Landon groans his enjoyment and I find my own pleasure building within me, my body tightening and coiling from the joy of pleasuring my mate. I feel the eyes of the others on me, watching, and I look up to catch Derrek's gaze while my mouth slides up and down Landon. He's already nude, his eyes half-closed while he strokes himself, enjoying the slow.

I'm definitely ready for more.

I sit up and drag the tank top over my head and toss it away. The thin garment flutters to the ground, but before it lands, I'm already straddling Landon. I slide myself along his length before I position him at my entrance and sink onto him.

"Oh, god, Lily..." Landon moans, his hands

sweeping over my breasts before dropping to my hips. Instead of riding him, I undulate my hips like Derrek taught me, eliciting a chorus of increasingly explicit praises from my mate.

He feels incredible, but it's not enough.

Glancing around, I realize my other three mates have shed their clothes and are pleasuring themselves lazily, enjoying me enjoying myself.

I set my sights on Derrek, then crook a finger at him, beckoning him closer.

His lower lip disappears between his teeth and he approaches from the side, already anticipating what I want. Easing my movements on Landon to slow, deliberate thrusts of my hips, I wrap a hand around Derrek and slide him into my mouth. His hand grips my hair and tightens, holding my head steady while he slides in and out.

"That's my good girl," he groans, his eyes never leaving mine while I swallow him.

Landon takes over moving my hips, and for a few moments I explore this new combination of pleasure.

But it's still not enough.

I pull my head back and Derrek releases my hair but still holds my gaze.

"I want you inside me now," I growl. "I want both of you inside me."

Derrek's hand caresses my cheek. "Are you sure, baby? I don't want you to feel pressured. We all know you're one woman to the four of us. So you decide what you want, always."

The others murmur their assent.

"It's what I want," I answer simply.

Needing no more encouragement, Derrek settles behind me. His hands grip my hips and lift me up from Landon, so I'm on all fours. I didn't realize it before, but I've literally created a puddle from my pleasure; Landon's hips are slick with it, and the blankets are soaked. At this point, I'm wondering if I should be concerned about dehydration.

Derrek drags his hand through the slippery mess between my legs and starts working my other sensitive entrance with his fingers. A shudder of pleasure rips through me, and I lower my body onto Landon's chest, opening myself more for Derrek. He coats his fingers one more time, then slides his hard length between my legs while his fingers continue to work behind me, now slipping inside and circling gently. Landon strokes my head and Derrek moves within me, his fingers easing deeper and moving wider, tightening another coil I didn't know existed.

Apparently satisfied, he slows, leaving me edged and desperate for release. Withdrawing from between my legs, he slides himself through the wetness between my folds then helps me back onto Landon, who thrusts and seats me firmly back in place.

Derrek's fingers resume working, and that tension builds again. "Are you ready, baby?" He asks, his voice strained.

"Yes!" I whine, leaning hard against Landon and attempting to open myself wider for him.

His fingers withdraw, and the hard tip of his erection presses against my backside. I freeze with a gasp, and he slowly begins moving, sliding in and out, a little deeper each time. I lie still on Landon, feeling him throb within me while Derrek slowly works his way entirely inside me.

The sensation of having them both is out of this world. I'm deliciously stretched, every nerve ending buzzing with pleasure, and desperate for the release I feel building within.

After a moment to adjust, we move together, in tandem. I rock forward and they both withdraw, then I rock backward and they both thrust into me. Jared and Milo are nearby, drinking in the scene with glossy eyes. I motion them closer, and they take positions kneeling on either side of me. First, I take Jared into my mouth, tasting him, allowing the motion with the other two to dictate the speed he slides in and out of my lips. Then I switch to Milo, enjoying the differences in their shapes and the way they taste on my tongue.

Landon takes control of my hips, setting a rhythm for all of us while he groans and curses with determination. Derrek teases my curves, his fingers gripping my hips and pulling himself to meet me with a wet smack against my ass every time I rock back. Sweat trickles down my spine and between my breasts, and I'm too busy to care. My animal instinct has completely taken over, ridding my mind of thought as the way our bodies move together takes over every ounce of my consciousness.

Landon's tempo speeds up until I'm bouncing on top of him, desperate high-pitched moans pouring from my lips. I'm forced to focus on the two of my mates who are deeply inside me now. Derrek grunts behind me, moving his hips in a slight circle and magnifying the sensation once again. His fingers circle the button between my thighs and I ride right over the edge again.

My body tightens and convulses, squeezing around both of them, and I shout my release in unison with Landon. He pulses within me, and I lean forward to kiss him and open myself more for my other mate. Instead of continuing, Derrek stills inside me, and wraps his arms tightly around body.

Without warning, he rolls us over so that he's on his back, still buried deep within me, and I'm sprawled against his chest. He skims his palms up the inside of my thighs, then strokes my clit, immediately preparing my body for more. I open my legs wider, the cold air delicious on my damp skin, and crook a finger at Jared.

Jared greets me with deep, claiming kisses before he slides into my core with a grunt. He spreads my legs wider, then sets a new pace that's swiftly matched by Derrek. Derrek's hands toy with my nipples while he thrusts up from beneath me and I just hang on for dear life. I'm lost in a new kind of euphoria, drunk on the feeling that I could go all night. It never has to end. Whatever doubts I had before are gone—*I was made for this*.

Soon I'm panting, then shattering into a million pieces beneath the full moon. Derrek loses it completely this time as I clench and tighten around him while he groans his release into my hair. Jared's hips jerk and a flood of liquid heat courses through me. It's only then that I realize we aren't just playfully making love this time; this is for real. This is mating. The pack's heir could come from our union tonight. I make a mental note to talk with my mates tomorrow about whether I should visit the pack seer for a potion to prevent it, or allow nature to take its course.

Jared drapes his feverish body over mine. Even though I'm sweating, I love the sensation of being pressed between my mates. Instead of feeling hot and overwhelmed, it's warm and comforting. Our breaths mingle as we all come down from this high. They pepper my skin with kisses and I wrap myself around Jared like he's an anchor in a stormy sea. His mouth finds mine and we share a few delicious, tender kisses.

Gradually, we untangle our bodies and separate, but not before I claim a few sated kisses from Derrek, too.

The night air has grown chilly, and my skin cools even as the desire builds in me again. There's one of my mates whose pleasure I have yet to achieve, and for the moment I need nothing more than him.

My gaze roves over my resting mates, and lands on Milo, who's seated and watching me with that tempting half smile. Like the animal I am, I prowl in his direction on all fours and fix him with a teasing grin of my own. When I clamber onto his lap, Milo welcomes me with patient, deep kisses, his hands caressing my back and tangling in my hair. After a few moments, I reach between us and settle myself on him, and we make slow, deliberate love in the gleaming moonlight, string lights twinkling over us like so many stars.

In this moment I'm not desperately seeking the more, more, more of having so many mates around me. In this moment I'm wholly focused, body, mind, and soul, on the man who was so many firsts for me.

The first mate I met in Smoky Falls.

My first kiss.

My first sexual encounter, not to mention my first of such things under a ceiling of stars.

The first of my mates to consummate our bond.

And most importantly, always the first to accept my needs and desires, and advocate for them with the others.

Relationships are never perfect. Everyone knows that. Having four partners is incredible, but it'll always be possible for us to have five differing opinions. My mates support me but I know we won't always agree, and sometimes we'll have to work hard to reach a consensus.

Derrek may be the oldest, but Milo has a way of bringing people together and finding common ground. I didn't realize how much I depended on that until tonight, when he was obviously the ringleader in creating this incredibly special night for me. Obviously, the others didn't object, but I'm fairly certain they didn't propose it, either.

So I revel in the deep, beautiful connection we share as we make love. Our lips break apart and my body moves at a leisurely pace while my eyes claim his. In the moonlight, they appear almost silver instead of the ocean blue I'm familiar with. But they're the same, currently sparkling with pure adoration instead of sardonic humor. My breaths grow shallow, lost in the intensity of his gaze, and my pace quickens. Pleasure grows slowly within me, tingling across my skin and coiling in my stomach. Our patient love-making becomes more driven as we chase that pinnacle of joy together.

Milo's hands grip my hips and drive me, his own rising slightly with each thrust. And still he holds my gaze; I can't look away. I caress his cheek then rest my hands on his shoulders, pushing for more leverage.

When I think I can't keep this pace another moment, the glimmering release washes over me once more. It seizes Milo as well, who refuses to relinquish my gaze even in the face of such an intense feeling. His hands rise to cup my face, and he pulls my forehead to his while we catch our breath together.

My body slowly goes limp—the consequence of so much activity with very little rest.

But instead of enjoying their reprieve, Derrek, Landon, and Jared have been busy.

As soon as my eyes lift from Milo and seek the status of my other mates, they appear and slip a warm, heavy robe onto me, then ease me up from Milo's lap.

My legs are weak and unsteady. Landon and Jared each have one of my hands, but Landon decides to scoop my legs out from under me and just carry me instead.

I'm a little disoriented, but after a moment, I realize he's planning to carry me all the way back into the house. Landon steers toward the elevator, refusing to set me down while the others pile in and close the gate. We ride in silence up to the second floor, but instead of steering toward my bedroom, he turns the opposite direction and takes me to the library. There, a fire's roaring and a second love nest is spread out before it, the furniture already pushed back to create an open space large enough for all of us. Landon continues to hold me, pressing kisses to my damp forehead, while the others arrange several trays of drinks and snacks before gesturing in our direction. He gently sets me in the middle and my mates, similarly clad in robes, settle around me.

I turn a questioning eye to Milo, who I'm certain is the one with answers.

He flashes me that signature crooked smile, and shrugs demurely. "We thought we should spend the entire night together, but the temperature's about to drop so outside will get too cold, and your bed isn't big enough. So camping out in the library it is."

I swallow thickly, trying to hold back the sudden emotion threatening to spill from my eyes. "Thank you," I choke out, then allow my gaze to travel across all of their faces. "Thank all of you. This night is just... perfect."

And I mean it; there's nothing left to hope for right now, no wishes to be made on stars.

My mates humbly ignore my thanks and start insisting on feeding and hydrating me. Once our bellies are sated, we slip into the nest of covers, the warm, solid comfort of my mates surrounding me on all sides.

A yawn stretches my lips, and I snuggle against Jared's chest while Derrek curls around my body from behind, his arm tight around my waist.

This is perfection.

I hope dawn never comes.

THE END

***

Not quite ready to quit Smoky Falls?

I'm going to have some extra scenes and an additional epilogue that I'll send out to my newsletter soon, so if you'd like to see those make sure to join my newsletter http://www.laurelnight.com/newsletter

Want a sneak preview of Laurel's best-selling RH wolf shifter series? Read on!

Wolf Shunned – Chapter 1

KALIYA

A single droplet of sweat trailed down the side of my face, working its way from my pale blonde hairline to my clenched jaw. Hands flexed on the hilts of my blunted practice swords, fingers stretching to relieve the pressure and adjust my sweaty grip. Heart pounding, breath slow and even. Across the fighting ring, four male opponents were just collecting themselves from the heap I'd left in my wake.

Their combined scent drifted across the ring, sour with frustration. My eyes narrowed in the mid-morning sun, waiting for the last one to regain his feet. They all watched me with trepidation, perhaps hoping I was done with training for the day and they could go home to lick their wounds in peace.

No such luck.

"Again," I growled.

Emory spoke up behind me, where he remained safely outside the training area. "Kaliya, don't you think they've had enough?" His voice was gentle; suggesting, not commanding. He knew better than to challenge me.

I ignored him. Raising my swords over my head, I clanged them together and shouted, "AGAIN!"

A collective sigh rose from the males as they girded themselves for another attack. I brandished my swords at my sides, a feral grin curling my lips as I waited for them to approach. This time they rushed me as one, maybe hoping they would land a blow with so many swords flying at me simultaneously. I swirled through them like a hurricane, striking and dodging, stabbing and weaving. I struck several blows that would have killed the recipient if I wielded my lightning swords. According to the rules of engagement in the training ring, they should have stayed down, but I didn't mind if they hopped back in the fray; I'd just knock them down again.

One of the males apparently had enough of this humiliation. With a savage growl he burst from his training clothes, unleashing his wolf in an embarrassing lack of control. At over twice his human size, the mass of mottled brown fur and pearly white teeth was impressive. His ears lay flat on his head and he snarled at me, slaver dribbling from his jaw as we circled each other, my other opponents ignored.

The rest of the males immediately retreated to safety outside the training ring. They probably assumed I'd shift in response; it wasn't an unreasonable expectation, given that's what most wolves would do when faced with such a direct challenge.

However, I wasn't in the mood to kill anyone today. My wolf remained firmly in my control.

She growled in frustration, the sound vibrating in my chest. She rarely got to come out and play, and my refusal to respond to a direct challenge tortured her wild soul. Especially since she'd have this pup bent and submitted—if not broken—in seconds.

The wolf feinted left, tongue curling and jaws snapping as he tested my reactions. His dark eyes watched me; mine never strayed, steadily holding his gaze as we circled.

When he realized I would not shift, the wolf grew cocky, charging straight at me. I vaguely heard Emory's sharp intake of breath as I crouched, leaping and twisting mid-air to land on the massive wolf's back just behind his head. Flinging my useless weapons to the ground, I wrapped my right arm tightly around his furry throat, using my left to tighten the grip and hold myself in position while he writhed beneath me.

The wolf was stuck; my legs wrapped around the barrel of his body, and my arm was cutting off his air supply. He attempted to shake me off, bucking and snarling as he ran out of oxygen. A sudden whimper escaped his throat and he collapsed on the ground, struggling to breathe. He whined loudly in surrender, but I held on until I was certain he passed out. When I felt the fur recede signaling his return to human form, I released him and stepped off his naked body. He was small and pathetic once more.

But luckily for him, still alive.

I walked away without a backward glance as the rest of the team hopped the wooden fence to check on their fallen comrade. Once they confirmed he was still breathing, the biggest one shouted angrily, "You psycho bitch! You could have killed him!"

I stooped to grab one of my practice swords, calmly wiping the flat of the blade on my leather pant leg. "He should have thought of that before he shifted during a training session and challenged a stronger wolf. He's lucky I didn't kill him."

"You're full of shit," he snorted. "I bet any of us could take you; you just don't want anyone to see your freak of a wolf. No wonder you spent so much time learning sword fighting; your wolf just isn't up for the challenge of a real male. Frigid *bitch*."

I finished collecting and cleaning my second sword, ignoring the angry snarl of my wolf. *It wouldn't help anyone to give in to his goading*, I reminded myself. Focusing on my control, I breathed in deeply and resolved to ignore the taunting.

However, I forgot that we had an audience.

A pale streak crossed my vision in the taunter's direction. *Shit*.

The sound of fist meeting face seemed to echo in the suddenly silent training arena. "You fucking apologize, pup!" Emory shouted.

Sighing, I turned just in time to see the much stronger man hit Emory with an uppercut so hard his head snapped backward, lean frame flying several feet until his unconscious body landed in the dirt.

My wolf strained at my control, and I narrowly kept her within the reins as I charged the taunter, spinning behind him and knocking the bully to his knees with a swift kick. Placing one knee on his back, I scissored his neck between my swords. "There is no honor in beating a weaker foe," I hissed. "But for you, I may make an exception. It seems you have not yet learned your lesson."

"He attacked me first!" He choked out. The training swords were blunted, so they didn't slice his flesh to ribbons. But the pressure of the steel on his neck was still uncomfortable enough to make him rethink his position. He held perfectly still, his scent tainted with the bitter tang of fear.

"He's not a challenge to you," I growled, "As you are well aware. You beat him because you *could*. That is a sign of weakness and cowardice, not strength. You're a pathetic excuse for a warrior." I withdrew my swords and the knee from his back, then gave him a sharp kick that sent him sprawling in the dirt. "Don't ask for my help again until you know your place."

Emory was just stirring when I reached him, shaking dirt and bits of straw from his wavy brown hair. He grinned when I offered him a hand up, then winced. "Ow. He didn't break my face, did he?" He rose and stretched, his lean frame half a foot taller than my five-foot-seven, before ducking his face closer to mine for inspection. The sweet, untainted scent of chocolate and cinnamon filled my senses, and I breathed him in with relief.

I lightly ran my fingers along his narrow jaw, pressing gently as I traced the sharp curve below his ear down to his adorably cleft chin and up the other side. "Nope, you're not broken. It'll swell up but you'll be fine in a few hours, thank the Ancients." I brushed my hands over his wide shoulders, helping to remove the dirt from his fall. "That was stupid, by the way," I commented mildly. "You know he's much more dominant than you, even as a pup."

Emory shrugged, unapologetically re-rolling his sleeves. "He shouldn't have spoken to you like that. You're doing him and his pathetic friends a favor; they're lucky you didn't kill them all. If you would not defend yourself, someone had to." His warm brown eyes met mine with a glint of mischief. "If your wolf wants to teach them a lesson, I could leave for a few minutes. By the time I get the healers and return, she should be about finished."

I chuckled. "As tempting as that is, it wouldn't please Alpha for me to be teaching *that* kind of lesson to his newest warriors. They're just young; they'll learn."

Emory wrapped a lean, muscular arm around my shoulders, squeezing lightly. "You're too kind, Kaliya. If it were me, I'd unleash the beast and give them all an epic beat-down. You'd only have to do it once."

"As a male, I'm sure that would work well for you. As a female, I shouldn't be able to. It's bad enough that I've defeated nearly every male our age and up; flexing on younger wolves is just cruel."

Emory was thoughtful as we followed the wooded path back toward the village. "A younger wolf may be your only chance, Kali," he reminded me softly. He didn't finish the phrase, but we were both thinking it as we continued in silence.

A younger wolf may be my only chance to avoid expulsion from the pack. At nineteen, I only had a few more months to find a mate. Wolves had to contribute to the replenishment of society, and our prime pup-bearing years were the younger ones. We didn't live long happy lives, thanks to the beasts that stalked us at night. Something else we had to thank the Ancients for. Whether we called them night stalkers, wraiths, or just 'creatures', they were adept at keeping us constantly on the edge of extinction.

It was an unfair rule, but a rule nonetheless: if a wolf wasn't mated by their twentieth birthday, they had no place in the pack. It mostly ensured we didn't waste time finding a mate, and I only knew of one time they actually enforced it.

From the way things were going, I might be the second.

Of course, Emory had the same issue. We were born mere minutes apart, and neither of us had mates. Not that Emory was unattractive, or weak. He was tall, lean yet muscular, and objectively handsome with his sharply angled jaw, warm eyes, and lips made for kissing. He was also incredibly intelligent, if a little awkward at times. His brilliant mind was one of his finer attributes, and that was saying something. If people could choose their own mates, Emory would have been happily settled years ago.

But humans didn't choose mates; their wolves did.

Emory's issue was that his wolf struggled to find a female submissive enough for him to mate, while mine was the opposite: I had yet to find a male who could force my wolf to submit.

Mates were chosen when a male issued a mate challenge to a female and submitted her. The stronger the pairing, the stronger and more dominate the pups would be. Therefor every male tried to mate the most dominant female he could handle.

Fortunately, there was one small nod to the female in this archaic process. The male could force the Mate Challenge, but he couldn't force the mating. The female had to accept him and seal the pairing. In theory, it could be years before he earned her respect enough to mate, and he just had to wait for it.

For me, the issue was bigger. I'd already been mate challenged by most of the eligible males in the pack, and my wolf defeated them all. Since I reached mating age, the only eligible male who had yet to challenge me was the pack's despicable Beta, and I destroyed him thoroughly a few weeks before I turned fifteen. He'd spent the last five years ignoring me completely, clearly bitter about the ass-kicking he'd received as a pup. Since he was younger than me, he still had over a year to find a mate.

Whereas I was swiftly running out of time.

My thoughts turned to the upcoming Clan Gathering at the Blackwood Fortress. All five packs in our territory would come together, as they did every five years. It was a festival of sorts, but it served multiple purposes: One was to have a variety of games and tests of battle prowess. Another was to exchange information with all the other packs, find out what the wraiths in their territories had been up to, and discuss any recent issues the rest of the clan should know.

But the purpose that mattered the most to me was the chance to find a mate outside my pack. The Clan Gathering encouraged the intermingling of pack members to make stronger wolves. There was an entire arena dedicated to official challenges, and they started on the Summer Solstice, longest day of the year. Many held out hope of finding their mate at the event, if for no other reason than the chance to leave their own pack and live somewhere new.

I suspected Emory was hoping he'd find a submissive female at the Clan Gathering who was closer to his own age. Fifteen was technically mating age, and many females were more submissive when they were young. Less dominant males tended to prey on them to secure a place in the pack, which was partially why Emory was still unmated.

But they were little more than pups at that age. I couldn't imagine finding a fifteen-year-old attractive enough to mate, no matter how dominant his wolf could be. Emory felt the same way.

I was just hoping that there was one wolf among the thousands across our territory that was dominant enough to mate me.

Surely, there had to be one.

***

Want to keep reading? Get the entire Alpha Queen Legacy series by Laurel Night in ebook or paperback on Amazon.

THE WARRIOR QUEEN LEGACY - COMPLETE SERIES

A SLOW-BURN REVERSE harem romance featuring a fantasy dystopian setting that has been compared to 'I Am Legend' crossed with 'The Shanarra Chronicles' and wolf shifters. Named one of Book Authority's Top Fantasy Books of 2021, and Red Feather Romance's 10 Top Adult Fantasy Romances. Available on Amazon and Kindle Unlimited.

SCENT OF DECEPTION - A STANDALONE IN THE BONDS OF STEELE OMEGAVERSE

Raised to be a pampered omega, Sapphire Steele never manifested. Desperate, she accepted a lucrative proposal: Pretend to be the omega for a wealthy pack until one of the alphas receives his inheritance, then disappear with her share of the money.... But someone knows her secret... Available on Amazon and Kindle Unlimited

GLAM - A STANDALONE MAFIA-LITE REVERSE HAREM ROMANCE

The hardworking daughter of two cops finally lands her dream job, only to be interrupted on her first day by three devastatingly handsome mafia brothers she recognized from college. Always out of her reach before, they're suddenly obsessed with her, and insist she become a part of their glittering world. Then, one night she witnesses first hand what happens in the back room of those shimmering parties, and how the Vargas family have ruled over Miami for decades.

Terrified, she knows with certainty that one of two things will happen: Either she becomes theirs, beholden to them and immersed in their world of wealth and privilege for the rest of her life.

Or no one will ever hear from her again. Available on Amazon and Kindle Unlimited

About the Author

LAUREL NIGHT IS a long-time fan of romance and adventure. She's traveled the world, and currently resides in the shadow of the Great Smoky Mountains with her daughter Tessa.

For more about Laurel, her books, and future projects, you can find her at www.laurelnight.com, or hanging around in Laurel's Night Queens, her group on Facebook.

If you'd like to stay up to date on Laurel's work, you can join Laurel's newsletter.

www.ingramcontent.com/pod-product-compliance
Lightning Source LLC
Chambersburg PA
CBHW030846030726
47495CB00005B/1392